The Basker Twins in the 31st Century

The Mystery of the Pendant

by

Kristi Wright

Happy Reading :)

Kristi Wright

The Basker Twins in the 31st Century series
(in reading order):
Danger at the Clone Academy
The Mystery of the Pendant

"The Basker Twins in the 31st Century: The Mystery of the Pendant," by Kristi Wright. ISBN 978-1-60264-790-9.

Library of Control Number on file with publisher.

Published 2011 by Virtualbookworm.com Publishing Inc., P.O. Box 9949, College Station, TX 77842, US. ©2011, Kristi Wright. All rights reserved. No part of this publication may be reproduced, stored in a retrieval system, or transmitted in any form or by any means, electronic, mechanical, recording or otherwise, without the prior written permission of Kristi Wright.

Manufactured in the United States of America.

To my loving husband, Dan (you are first and foremost), my amazing daughter, Sarah, my incredible mom, Liz (better known as Lizzy Appleseed for populating much of Silicon Valley with the first Basker Twins book), and my wonderful dad, Cliff. Thank you for always being proud and supportive of my work—you all are the best!

CHAPTER 1
Winners and Losers, or Not

Every B12 student at the Academy of Superior Learning, otherwise known as the Clone Academy, wanted to witness the fight between the 12-year-old clones, Vlas and Dar, and the ute-baby—uterus born—twins, Elsie and Everest Basker. Well before the 13:00 fight time, the spectator area in the B12 fight room was jammed with kids, all jostling for a better view. Plenty of the twelve-year-olds were forced to wait in the recreation room outside, hoping to hear reports on the action. Students from other age groups were denied admittance due to space limitations, but they still participated in the betting. Virtual currency had been placed on various outcomes, despite such activities being expressly forbidden on campus.

It was exactly a month to the day since Elsie and Everest had come to stay at their uncle's boarding school for clones; one month since they had beaten the reigning 12-year-old champions in an impromptu fight match. Despite the recent adventures that had united the clones with Everest and Elsie against a dangerous smuggler, Dar and Vlas still waited impatiently for a chance to kick the twins' keisters all the way to Glagcha (that irritating world that consistently beat Earth as best planet for raising a family in the Milky Way galaxy.)

Whoever lost the fight was honor bound to treat the winner with respect for a full month, which meant no insults or aggressive behavior. In addition, the loser was expected to protect the winner from other challenges.

Because it was a half-day for students, they were able to hold the fight early. Elsie was nervous about the competition. For no apparent reason, her jellach bodysuit felt unusually snug and

1

hotter than a Krustak volcano. Tugging at her outfit, she glanced over at her brother. Quiet as usual, he took in the room with a serious expression. Elsie would have bet zetta virtual currency that he was as nervous as she was. But he would never show it.

She was a big fan of the school's zeller B12 fight space. A ten-meter ceiling left plenty of room for jumping. Strong ropes hung from the ceiling and hooks climbed the walls. A thick pad covered the floor. Her only complaint was the room's disgusting odor. While pico-brownies kept the room immaculate via their nighttime cleaning, there still were years of accumulated adolescent sweat that no quantity of pico-brownies could erase.

Would life at the clone academy be better or worse if they won? A couple of weeks ago, Elsie had confessed to Dar that she had spied on her and learned her secret: every night the tough-as-a-cyborg girl cared for the babies and toddlers who lived at the academy. Dar had been furious when she'd found out that Elsie knew, and she'd promised payback. Maybe if they lost, the girl would finally get off her back. But it was much more likely that Dar would decide she had license to torture her for the entire month.

Besides, Baskers didn't throw competitions.

"Hey, ute-twins, time to blast-off," Dar called from across the room. Her thick golden hair was pulled back into a tight pony-tail with her trademark cap neatly settled on top. Even after a month of rooming with Dar at clone-ville, Elsie still couldn't get over how weird it was to be confronted with a Shadara copy. Shadara had been the most beautiful woman in the universe before her tragic and mysterious death at a young age. And Dar was equally as beautiful though she did everything she could to hide that inescapable fact.

"What are you staring at?" Dar called out, a frown creasing, but not marring, her perfect features.

Elsie glared back. "Nothing!"

"Hey is this a fight or a tea party?" Larry Knight asked from behind the see-through pad that protected spectators from the action. "Are you aliens ever getting this freak show on the road?"

He was the twenty-first-century boy who they had smuggled to the thirty-first century, and then, against all school and galactic rules, had kept. His skin was a rich shade of chocolate, and he had shiny, curly black hair. Through some zetta fancy holoputer work and a little help from Dar's sponsor, Adriatic Mink, they had convinced everyone that he was a clone who had been living off-world until coming to their boarding school.

Vlas snickered. "Yeah, we're going to get started—and finished—at light speed."

"Don't be so down on yourself," Elsie said cheerfully. "I'm sure you'll last at least a couple of minutes before we flaser you."

She couldn't believe it when Everest scowled at her like she'd said something wrong. Just because he wasn't going to stick up for them didn't mean she wouldn't. She made a face back.

Dar ignored the verbal jab and strode barefoot to the middle of the padded room. Like their first fight, they had agreed to no skyboots since the clones owned older models, and therefore, might be at a disadvantage.

"Referee," Dar called then groaned when the same Clegl humanoid who had officiated at their last match appeared. "What are you doing here?"

The short, bald, black and white, striped holographic creature blinked the eyes in both the front and the back of his head. "You called me."

His voice was high-pitched and whiny.

"Aren't we supposed to get a random referee? You officiated last time."

"Look missy, I didn't write the program, I just show where I'm programmed to show." The man visibly bristled.

"And we appreciate the excellent job that you do." Wiry, ridiculously clever, and often charming, Vlas stepped forward so that he flanked Dar who grimaced at his obvious brown-nosing. She looked as if she'd swallowed a limonino fruit from Bandogiar, the sourest fruit in the universe.

"Don't think I didn't see your expression, missy," the Clegl referee screeched at Dar. He waved irritably at Elsie and Everest who quickly joined them in the middle of the floor.

The Clegl referee moved between the two sides. Using both sets of eyes, he stared fiercely and simultaneously at both teams. "This time, no funny business."

Dar was the picture of innocence. "Of course not."

The referee had not been happy with Dar's behavior at the beginning of their last fight. Exactly one month ago, Elsie's inadvertent use of Dar's full name had caused the girl to break the rules and start the match without the required pomp and circumstance.

"Humph." He blinked again as he planted his feet apart, fisted his hands on his hips, and stuck his chin in the air. "Today, May 12, 3002, it brings me great pleasure to announce and officiate this match that pits the honorable clones, *Shadara* and Vlas, against the equally honorable twins, Elsie and Everest Basker."

His high-pitched screeching reverberated in Elsie's ears, making them ache. The avatar had to know exactly how much Dar hated to be called Shadara. Was he testing her?

Elsie always found it a bit disturbing to be subjected to a Clegl's eyes on the back of his head since both nose and mouth were missing. But there was no arguing that Clegls were zeller referees.

"Can't we get on with this?" Dar muttered.

It became apparent that Clegls also had excellent hearing because he flasered Dar with another furious look.

"This competition," he continued, "will adhere strictly to the rules set forth by the United Nations of Earth in the year 2800, most prominent of which is the rule prohibiting any attack to the face. Do you agree to abide by this and all other rules detailed by this noble group?"

"Yes, yes, of course we do," said Dar impatiently as the others murmured their assent more politely.

The Clegl bristled. "I can and will disqualify fight contestants for rude behavior, *Shadara*. After your disgraceful performance last time, I won't need much provocation."

Though her expression tightened, Dar managed to refrain from comment, nodding her understanding instead.

The Clegl cleared his throat, and continued to screech. "Do you agree to abide by the rules set forth by the United Nations of Earth?"

"We do," they all chorused.

"Excellent." He pivoted around on his short legs so that Elsie and Everest were now treated to eyes, nose and mouth as well as a particularly stubby chin.

"And do you agree to the rules that govern the behavior of the winners and the losers of the competition?"

"We do."

He stared for several moments then turned and with the back of his head stared again. "Very well, you may bow to your opponents."

Dar's bow was curt whereas Vlas added a flourish. He grinned as if he were having the time of his life. With years of practice, Elsie and Everest bowed in precise unison.

The Clegl referee stepped back a few paces to give the fighters room, then declared in his screeching voice, "Match begin."

Dar and Vlas jumped simultaneously, grabbed ropes and twirled around, kicking out so they each made contact—Dar with Everest's solar plexus and Vlas with Elsie's. Their speed was unsettling, but both Elsie and Everest managed to go with the blows into back flips so they barely felt the strikes. In unison, they popped out of the series of moves and leapt onto the ropes. Since Vlas and Dar were swinging toward them, the twins kicked off of each other and swung their ropes in a wide arc, capturing the cord of their competitors and whipping around in circles, entangling Dar and Vlas and forcing them to drop to the ground. Elsie jumped and landed on Vlas's back, making him twirl and buck crazily in an attempt to unbalance her. The B12s shouted and booed as she refused to be bucked off. One lone clapper had to be Larry, the only other non-clone in the bunch. She barely registered that Everest had landed a few feet away from Dar and now fought against her in earnest.

Elsie was hard-pressed to hang on to Vlas. The boy was as fast as a flaser beam and as slippery as a Nurubian fire eel. Sliding off as he went into a somersault, Elsie sensed someone behind her and whirled. Dar flew at her with a double kick and landed Elsie on her back. She rolled just in time as Dar leapt to pin her. Scrambling to her feet and beating a fast retreat, Elsie now found Everest in combat with Vlas. She groaned when Vlas sent Everest to the ground with a low reverse roundhouse kick.

But Everest immediately rolled sideways and found his feet again. Elsie was too busy evading Dar to be sure that her brother was okay. She hoped for the best.

Only minutes had passed, but it already felt like hours. The Clegl referee kept up a steady stream of screeched commentary while she and Dar exchanged a series of blows, both on the ground and in mid-air, with Elsie mostly blocking Dar's assault. The girl was a demon on the fight mat. Both were breathing hard, and Elsie was sweating like a rabid cooligrar. She didn't think Dar was as winded as she was. If they didn't somehow shut down this fight early, Dar inevitably would wear them out.

"Basker Bling!" Elsie yelled and shot into a series of handsprings. Within a heartbeat, Everest followed suit. They moved toward each other so that by the time they reached the end of the room, they were side by side. Everest gave her a look as if to say that he was going to kick her keister if this didn't work. Then, yelling at the top of their lungs, they charged Vlas who stared as if they were lunatics from the asylum planet of Dementurnum.

"Deng, stop spinning into space," Vlas yelled.

At the last minute he tried to evade them, but they double-teamed him, using every two-person move they knew. Like a fury, Dar joined the mix: kicking, striking, blocking and parrying. Since she reached Everest first, he took the brunt of her attack.

He fought well, but Elsie could sense he was tiring. Who knew how much longer she could keep up the pace? Her legs and arms were the consistency of jellach. She'd hoped their choreographed attack would shake up their opponents enough to reverse the tide, but it didn't seem to have done the trick.

Then a voice rose above all the yelling and stomping.

"END MATCH!" it said with amplification.

Elsie, Everest, Vlas and Dar swung around as one and shouted, "What?"

The speaker was one of their uncle's holograms, an enhanced copy of the director with excessive height and hunched shoulders, pinched nose, sunken cheeks and dirty brown eyes. Director Lester-Hauffer ran the clone academy, but his two holograms did most of the work. While their parents were off-world, he was also Elsie and Everest's guardian, one of the main reasons their fellow students had automatically mistrusted and disliked them.

Dar strode up to the hologram, her fists clenched. "No way."

The hologram flinched. "Director Lester-Hauffer requires Elsie and Everest's presence immediately." He pivoted to the Clegl referee. "Is there a clear winner?"

"No, sir," the Clegl replied.

"Then I suggest we call it a draw."

There was a collective gasp, then pandemonium, a cacophony of jeering and yelling.

Dar lunged for the hologram, and it was all Vlas could do to pull her back. She strained against him and broke free, but by then she seemed to have remembered that there wasn't anything physical she could do to a hologram.

Sniffing his disapproval, the hologram maneuvered his way around so that he was behind Elsie and Everest. Now they could smell the slight odor of rotting vegetables that was the director's signature scent. It was zetta alien that a hologram could exude the same disgusting odor.

"Come along, no dawdling. Your uncle expects you immediately."

Elsie wished she could crawl into a dark cave and never come out. Even Larry looked angry, as if somehow she and Everest were responsible for this outcome.

"Hey," she said, "we forfeit; we lose; we don't agree to a draw."

The look on Dar's face would have terrified a Vlemutz. She crowded Elsie and poked her in the chest with her forefinger. "We beat you fair and square or you beat us, but we will never accept a forfeit." She turned her back on Elsie and strode off to pick up her gray vlatex towel. The fight room roared with silence.

The Clegl referee blinked all four eyes. "This is highly irregular—"

The hologram straightened so that he was slightly less stooped. "This is highly necessary and not open to debate. Baskers, with me." He executed a brisk turn and marched out of the room.

The Clegl referee began to screech in several languages that the match was officially a draw.

Elsie glanced at her twin. His jaw was rigid, and he seemed ready to do someone damage. She raced to keep up with the hologram, snatching up her skyboots along the way. There wasn't much they could do about the protective jellach gear. They would have to change out of it later.

All the B12s booed and hissed as they passed as if it was Elsie and Everest's fault that the director had shut down the match.

"Coming through, move aside, make way." The director's hologram parted the B12s just enough for Elsie to feel as if they were in ancient times, running the gauntlet. It was all she could do to ignore the glares and hostile language.

As they rushed to the nanovator to rocket down to the second floor, Elsie asked, "What's going on?"

The hologram sniffed. "Your uncle requires your presence in his office immediately. He has a very important guest waiting for you there."

Elsie couldn't imagine who would want to see them. Could it have something to do with their parents? Could there be news? Their parents were on a secret mission in another galaxy, and there had been no communication from them for two full weeks. That was longer than expected. It would be so zeller if there was news.

She leaned over to her brother and whispered, "Maybe it's about Mom and Dad?"

CHAPTER 2
Mysterious Visitors

Everest hoped Elsie was wrong. If this was about their parents, then it couldn't be good news. Only one month had gone by since their parents had left on their "secret mission," and they were supposed to be gone for many months. Why would anyone be contacting them now unless something bad had happened? A panicky feeling churned up his stomach as if it had been swirled into a black hole. He told himself to keep his aura on until they knew more.

When Elsie grabbed the sleeve of his jellach gear, he knew she was starting to imagine the worst too. He wanted to shake her off, but he forced himself not to. Right now, they only had each other.

The trip from the twelfth floor to the second seemed to take forever, despite the speedy and noisy old nanovator. Lester-Hauffer's hologram jabbered nervously about Italian music, gardens, and the cost of tea, but his voice shook so much from the nanovator's vibration that it was hard to understand him. Everest treated it all as background noise—the high-pitched squeal of the nanovator, the hologram's vibrating voice, his pounding heart.

Despite the worry and fear mixing up his insides, he was still furious about the outcome of the fight contest. Dar would never let them forget that their uncle had called off the match. Even if there *was* bad news about their parents, that wouldn't matter to the clones. The whole concept of family was alien to the dupes.

The nanovator came to an abrupt halt and the hologram exited at a fast clip. Elsie and Everest paused just long enough to slip on their skyboots before rushing after him.

9

"Ah, there you are, Elsinor and Everest," their uncle said as they walked into his office. "Please take a seat." He ushered them in and settled them on the nanofiber couch. "This is Dr. Jensa, an associate of your parents."

Not good, was all Everest could think. Elsie's fingers tightened on his sleeve.

The man somberly nodded his head. "Hello Elsinor and Everest." He was the epitome of a studious and dedicated scientist, with his silver hair and unusually pale skin. He looked as if he could have a brown complexion if he ever went outside, but it was doubtful he ever left the lab. His eyes squinted as if even the light in their uncle's office was more than he was used to, like a Dangor genetically-altered miner mole. He had high cheekbones, a pointy chin, a long, thin body, and narrow hands.

"It's an honor to meet you," Dr. Jensa said.

An honor? Flasers, why?

The man sat down across from them and leaned forward just slightly, resting the palms of his hands on his knees. He stared for a very long time.

Everest glanced at their uncle but wasn't reassured since his nose and mouth were even more pinched than usual.

"What is it?" Elsie asked, her voice high and strained.

"I'm sorry, Elsie," Dr. Jensa said. "I don't quite know how to tell you this." He shook his head. "There's no good way. Your parents are missing."

Elsie leapt to her feet. Everest jumped up as well not knowing what she might do. *Their parents missing?* He swallowed hard.

"What do you mean, they're missing?" Elsie asked.

"A little over two weeks ago, we stopped receiving transmissions from them. We sent someone to their location, but there was no sign of them. No notes, nothing. I'm sorry; they seem to have vanished into thin air."

"Maybe they're in a different time," Elsie said.

Dr. Jensa dipped his head. "That's certainly a possibility. Of course, we haven't given up hope. We will leave no stone unturned. But we thought you ought to be informed. We also believe you might be able to help."

"Help?" Everest asked, for once beating Elsie to the obvious question. "How?"

"You and Elsie have knowledge that we desperately need." the man responded. "It's critical that you give us what your parents gave you before they left. It may very well be the one thing that could save their lives."

"How is that possible?" Elsie asked.

"My dear girl, this is no time to be asking questions. We need action. Cooperation. Please, for your parents' sake, give us what they gave you."

Everest grabbed Elsie's hand and squeezed hard. This was serious. They had to get moving. The man was talking about the strange pendants that their mom had given them the day they had come to the academy.

"Okay, we'll go get them," he said. "Now. It won't take long. Come on, Elsie." He started to drag her to the door.

She stared at him as if he was a Zylorg who had just grown his second head. He willed her to stay shut down for once.

"I can come with you," Dr. Jensa said.

"It will be faster if we just go to our respective rooms and come back. We'll be quick—only a few minutes." Everest spoke fast, making it impossible for Elsie to say anything. If she started asking the wrong questions or making the wrong statements, who knew what the consequences might be?

If looks could kill, hers would have sent him straight to that sorry state. He ignored her glare and dragged her out of the office.

"Deng, Everest," she said when they were far enough away not to be heard.

"Shut down," he said through gritted teeth. "Just shut down."

"What kind of yocto-brain do you think I am?"

"I mean it, Elsie, not another word."

She yanked herself free. "What is your problem? If anyone should shut down, it's you!"

"I don't trust him," Everest whispered harshly. Why did she always make everything so difficult?

"Of course you don't. Who would? Mom and Dad said to give our necklaces to Dr. Yee and Dr. Yee only."

"They aren't necklaces," he said irritably, despite his relief that Elsie wasn't the yocto-brain he'd thought.

"Flasers, Everest, I wanted to catch him out in a lie, to expose him in front of Uncle Fredrick, but you dragged me out of there before I had a chance."

Everest stared. "Are you out of your mind? Haven't you learned anything from the clones? We have no proof Dr. Jensa is a villain. Why would Uncle Fredrick believe us? If Mom and Dad have disappeared, who knows what happened? There could have been foul play. Dr. Jensa, or whoever he is, could be zetta dangerous." Again, he started to drag her down the corridor.

"If you thought that, why did you agree to give him the necklaces? Why not just deny we have them?"

"He already knows we have them, yocto-brain. If we deny it, he'll just get suspicious."

"So what's your brilliant plan?"

"We're getting out of here—now."

Elsie stumbled, but Everest kept dragging her.

"Getting out of here?" she asked. "You mean, like, running away? You know perfectly well that we can't escape. He'll catch us, and then he'll know that we know he's not who he says he is."

They reached the nanovator and jumped in seconds before the doors rematerialized. The nanovator jerked to full speed as it shot straight up, shaking their cheeks and chattering their teeth with its force.

When they arrived at the twelfth floor and their cheeks no longer shook, Everest said, "He'll know anyway as soon as we don't give him the disks."

Elsie sighed. "I wish you had let me take the lead. Running is a bad idea, but it's too late now. We'll ask Dar for help. At least she can transport us onto the grounds. I have no idea what we'll do then."

"Yeah, I'm sure Dar will be happy to help us right now—after she kicks us to Xlexuri. Deng, Elsie, Dar's not feeling too kindly toward us after that fight match."

"It doesn't matter. She'll still help us. I know she will."

Elsie was probably right. Dar had helped them before without liking them.

"We'll need to steal a hover vehicle," he said. "I guess we'd better try to find Dr. Yee."

Elsie stopped again. "What if Mom and Dad are dead?" Her voice shook.

Everest turned to face her, grabbing her shoulders and looking her in the eye. "They aren't dead. We would know if they were. We just need to find someone we can trust. Dr. Yee will know where Mom and Dad are."

Everest talked reassuringly, but he wasn't feeling very reassured at the moment. It was unthinkable that anything had happened to their parents, but it also was very unlike them to have been out of communication for so long. The fact that they had vanished completely was a zetta bad sign. Whoever this Dr. Jensa was and however many lies he was telling, he also was telling one truth.

Something had gone horribly wrong for their mom and dad.

CHAPTER 3
Escape

Elsie rushed to her dorm room with Everest close behind. "Dar," she called as the door disappeared with a slight hiss. "We need your help. It's an emergency."

Elsie came to an abrupt halt. It wasn't just Dar in the room; Vlas, Lelita, Borneo and Larry were all there too. Dar had just swooshed her skyball through its hoop to the screech of whistles and a burst of lights. Lelita and Larry were eating Blackholes—no-cal chocolate that exploded in the mouth—and Vlas and Borneo hovered over PicoBoy, a zetta-clever picobot that Vlas had designed and built.

They all glared at Elsie and Everest. Even soft-hearted Lelita frowned.

Everest groaned, but Elsie was glad they were all here. No matter how much the B12s might despise them right now, Elsie and Everest desperately needed their help, and they didn't have time to track down everyone.

"Everest and I have to escape," she said. "Now."

Dar stilled, her expression shifting from a dark glare to a complete blank. "Deng, Elsie, keep your aura on."

"I can't, he's lying, and we have to get away. We have to find our parents."

"You're not making sense. Everest's lying? And why do you have to find your parents? For that matter, how are you going to find your parents? Aren't they off on some super secret mission?"

"They've disappeared," Everest said quietly. "Elsie isn't talking about me lying. She's talking about someone else."

Elsie's chest was going to explode, just disintegrate into a million pieces as if someone had pointed a flaser at her and pulled the trigger. "We don't have time; we have to leave now."

"No," Dar said, "what you have to do is calm down and tell us exactly what is going on. You need to be much clearer."

Elsie swallowed a scream.

"There's a Dr. Jensa in our uncle's office," she responded.

"He's the one who told us our parents have disappeared," Everest added.

"He wants us to give him our necklaces."

"They aren't necklaces!" Everest yelled.

Elsie shoved her brother hard. "Mom and Dad told us to give the disks to Dr. Yee. He was the only one. When Jensa asked for them, we told him we had to retrieve them. He's expecting us back right away. We have to get out of here before he realizes we've run."

Dar exchanged looks with Vlas as she rose from her bed. "Okay."

"Okay?" Elsie asked.

"We'll help you."

She sighed with relief and scrubbed at her cheeks. "Thanks."

"We're going with you," Dar said.

"No," said Everest. "This is our problem."

Everest was right. It wasn't fair to bring Dar and the rest of them into this. They could get into zetta trouble. But Elsie was afraid, and Dar always knew what to do. Already the girl was in her closet thrusting items into her Vlatex II pack, while Elsie stood there, perilously close to tears.

"Everest, you wouldn't last five minutes without us," Dar said without pausing her packing.

"You underestimate us."

Dar glanced over her shoulder, a hint of a smile on her lips. "No, I don't."

Everest stood straighter. "We don't need—"

"Please," Elsie begged, tugging on Everest's sleeve. "We do."

"Gosh," Dar said, wiping away an imaginary tear. "I'm all choked up. Come on utes." She slung the pack over her shoulder.

"We're wasting precious time. By the way, you might want to get out of that jellach gear. It's not exactly street wear, though I guess it could provide added protection."

Elsie had forgotten she still wore the fight gear. Her cheeks heated up as she and Everest quickly stripped off the jellach bodysuits. Underneath they wore their gray vlatex exercise clothes. Dar wore hers as well, but the rest of the B12s had on more brightly-colored exercise gear. Larry's was red and black, and Vlas's was purple with a white stripe.

Dar directed her attention to Vlas. "We don't have time to gather equipment from your room. We'll have to make do with my toys."

The boy shrugged. "Your toys are pretty zeller. I have PicoBoy and a few odds and ends like my scrambler in my pocket. It's enough."

"What about us?" Lelita asked, motioning to Borneo and Larry.

"You stay. We might need to be in touch. Borneo, boot up your IH. We'll do our best to get word to you."

"IH?" Larry asked. "You sure do speak a foreign language."

"Illegal holoputer. He'll need to do some fancy cloaking because the school checks regularly during the day for illegal access. But Borneo's up for the job. Right?" She patted him on the shoulder.

"Sh—sure," he said, stumbling over the word.

"Okay, let's get moving." Larry rubbed his hands together.

"Larry," Dar said, "you are definitely staying here. You have no experience in the thirty-first century."

"Girl, I don't need experience in your time. I got more street smarts in my little pinky than all of you got mashed together."

Dar rolled her eyes. "We don't have time for this." She looked to the ceiling. "Melista?"

The beautiful room avatar shimmered into existence, her golden horn sparkling and her dress diaphanous with blue and gold diamantes. As always, the sweet scent of liligilds permeated the room. "Yes, dear?"

"Cover for us?"

She dipped her horn. "Of course."

Dar shoved Elsie toward the mini transporter they had installed a month previously so they could sneak up Elsie's pet bobcat at night. "Everest, go with your sister."

He shrugged but did as he was told.

Elsie could tell he was furious with her; he wouldn't look at her, and he was zetta stiff.

She closed her eyes against the weird state of being transported, like being in the midst of a black void, with zero sensation and an absolute sense of nothingness. She couldn't smell or hear, but somehow her nose and ears felt as if they were in sensory overload. Was she in a million little pieces right now? Just when she felt as if she were truly disintegrating, they landed with a thunk under the small shelter in Pooker's prison. Immediately, her nose picked up the scent of the nearby rosewillow tree—it was as if she could smell the bark, the flowers, even the leaves. Further out, she smelled the tang of the limonino tree. She tasted last night's rain on her lips and heard Pooker's claws scratch loudly against the dirt. She never knew whether to be glad or sad that the phenom of heightened sensations after a transport only lasted a split second.

By the time she and Everest scrambled away from the transporter to make room for Dar and Vlas her senses were back to normal.

Beyond the canopy, Pooker stared unblinkingly, her bobcat hair standing on end. On the large size for a bobcat, she was nearly fifty-four centimeters in height, and she probably weighed fourteen kilograms. The unmistakable odor of damp cat still clung, a holdover from last night's rainfall.

"Deng, Larry!" Dar yelled from behind, and both Elsie and Everest swung around. Dar, Vlas and Larry shoved out of the shelter. Dar was furious. "Don't you get it? We all could have exploded into millions of atoms. This is a *portable* transporter, yocto-brain. You don't just jump on for the ride."

"Chill, babe."

Dar shoved Larry hard. "Don't—call—me—babe."

Vlas watched the altercation with a grin on his face.

Elsie wasn't sure what to do. "Uh, Dar."

She swung around. "*What?*"

"We sort of need to leave," Elsie said.

"*I know that!*" Dar paced back and forth in the pen. "Mr. Brilliant over here nearly got us obliterated."

"Girl, I told you I was coming. If you'd just listen—"

Dar threw her hands up in the air. "If *I'd* just listen? You— you suzo-shrimp—you're the one who doesn't listen—ever!"

Everest cleared his throat. "Elsie and I are leaving now; you decide if you want to join us." He grabbed Elsie by the arm and started tugging her to the edge of the pen.

"I'm coming." Dar pointed at Larry. "You stay."

"Man, you still aren't listening, are you?"

"Shut down, both of you!" Elsie yelled. She'd had enough. She yanked out of Everest's grip and crossed her arms. "I don't care who comes, but we have to leave now! And Pooker's coming too."

"No way!" Dar and Larry yelled in unison. Vlas chuckled.

Everest shook his head. "That's not a good idea."

Elsie stomped her foot. "I don't care; I'm not leaving her." She pressed the button to deactivate a portion of the dancing lights that kept Pooker penned in. "Come, Pooker," she said, and stormed down the jewel-toned gravel path.

She couldn't care less if any of them followed. Okay, who was she kidding? She desperately wanted them all to follow. She didn't want to do this alone. She wasn't even sure how to steal a hover vehicle. Still, she marched toward the History Center, hoping that one of those vehicles would do.

"Uh, Elsie?" Dar said from behind.

"What?" She kept on marching.

"We're already at the garage."

Elsie stopped and swung around. She'd forgotten there was a garage on the property too. After all, she'd only been here for a month. In all that time, she'd never left campus except via time travel. And they'd used the History Center vehicles for those trips.

"Come on." Dar quickly led them over to the massive garage doors. Crossing her arms, she studied the building. "Vlas, should we just break in?"

Larry responded instead. "Girlfriend, we better do something 'cause we've got company."

They all swung around to find Larry looking over his shoulder. Beyond him, Director Lester-Hauffer and Dr. Jensa crossed the grounds at an accelerated clip.

"Galaxies!" Elsie whispered, clutching Pooker's scruff.

Dr. Jensa broke into a run. They could hear him shouting though they couldn't make out his exact words. Two very tall, wide and intimidating humanoids stepped out of a hover vehicle sitting in the visitor parking lot. One may have been female and the other male. Their skin carried a green hue. Their shoulders were broad, their feet huge, their muscles gargantuan, and on their face, in addition to a very intense and angry expression, instead of a human nose, there was a cluster of three ugly lumps.

"What's he doing with Panktars?" Vlas asked.

"What's a Panktar?" Elsie asked.

"A mercenary," said Vlas, "from Xlexuri."

"But—"

Dar grabbed Elsie by the shoulders and shook her. "This is no time for yocto-brained questions."

Elsie wanted to object to Dar's rough handling, but the girl was right. Those Panktars looked zetta dangerous. Typical that these clones knew all about them when she and Everest had never heard about the aliens.

"Man, those are some scary-looking dudes," Larry said. "Vlas, you better put some pedal to the metal and get us inside ASAP."

"Yeah, yeah. Whatever gibberish you're spewing, I'm going as fast as I can."

Dar released Elsie and rifled through her backpack. The Panktars were running across the property now, and Elsie could have sworn she heard their heavy feet moving the ground with each step. Sparkling gravel spit up like a fountain gone awry.

"Vlas, get the garage door open, now." Dar pulled out a couple of stunners and shoved one at Everest. "You've had experience; get ready," she told him.

19

Despite their dire situation, Elsie almost smiled. Dar was never going to let Everest forget that he had stunned Larry at their first encounter.

The girl pulled out foggers and handed one each to Larry and Elsie. "Don't use these unless you have to. We may want them later."

She looked over her shoulder at Vlas who was working on the door with his scrambler, a flat, black triangle that sent out pico frequencies to jumble the security current. Carrying a strong chemical smell, it changed from blue to purple to red to pink and then finally became a pearly fluorescent-white when security had been breached.

"Is it white yet?" Dar yelled.

The Panktars were now within twenty-five meters and moving surprisingly fast given that they looked more like ugly boulders than humans.

Vlas nodded. "Yeah." He requested entry, and the door dissolved.

Dar pushed past him and ran to the nearest hover vehicle. Elsie kept pace with Pooker at her side, and the rest quickly followed.

"Deng, it's secured," Dar exclaimed. "Vlas, can you open it too?"

Vlas requested that the garage door rematerialize and secure itself. Then he turned back. "That won't hold them for long, but it might slow them down till the director gets here." He crossed over to the vehicle and stared at the door. "I think the scrambler will work."

Panktars, whether male or female, appeared to have deep, resonant voices, and the two outside were using them to demand that the kids come out immediately.

Instead, Vlas quickly breached the vehicle's security, and they all piled inside. Made out of a see-through version of jellach, the HV instantly expanded to accommodate the six passengers, counting Pooker.

Dar sat in the driver's seat and stared intently at the controls. She touched the sunergy symbol on the dash, and an almost imperceptible sigh told them the hover vehicle had sprung to life.

"Thank the Light," she breathed. "It doesn't look as if the director has any additional security beyond the vehicle's door."

"How will we leave the garage?" Elsie asked.

As if in answer to Elsie's question, the building sensed that the vehicle was now in motion, and the majority of the front wall evaporated to reveal two very nasty Panktars wielding wicked-looking stunners. Their mouths moved as if they were yelling, but the jellach muffled their words. At least they weren't waving flasers. Jellach, like so many substances, didn't stand a chance against being melted into nothingness. Hopefully, the Panktars had orders not to actually kill anyone.

Dr. Jensa was shouting too, but at the Panktars. Elsie couldn't understand him either.

Larry said something Elsie hadn't heard him say in a long time. She had no idea what it meant, but she knew it was one of those illegal words from the twenty-first century that he wasn't supposed to use in their time period.

"Those are some nasty dudes," he added.

Elsie swallowed. "Dar, I think we should go."

"No kidding, but I have to get a handle on the HV. I've never operated one before."

"What?" Elsie and Everest both yelled.

"Well, it's not as if I'm ever let out of this clone prison, you know," she said defensively.

"Flasers, Dar," Elsie said, scrambling to the front. "Switch places." She clambered over Dar, and the girl reluctantly shifted to the back. Pooker stared suspiciously at Dar, but didn't protest the change in seating.

Elsie searched for the label that would indicate the hover vehicle's identifier. Some people were too cautious to document it, but others were afraid they would forget. Luckily, her uncle fell into the latter camp. The label was discretely placed below the dash. She wrinkled her nose. It wasn't at all what she would have guessed, but she didn't waste time in speaking firmly, just the way her parents always did. "FREDCR999, take flight." The jellach hover vehicle slowly rose into the air.

Vlas snorted. "FRED?"

"His first name's Fredrick," Everest said, 'but I've never heard him called Fred."

"Jeez, Elsie, you could have just said that from the back," Dar grumped.

"Well, I had to find it first," Elsie shot back. "Besides, the vehicle only takes commands from the driver's seat and sometimes the front passenger seat if that option has been enabled."

The Panktars were now shooting at the jellach vehicle with a funny-looking tube. What came out was a steady stream of blue light.

Vlas spoke, "Uh, I'm pretty sure that's a jell-off pipe which means this vehicle could start to dissolve at any second."

"They can't have enough jell-off to destroy the car," Dar said.

Vlas shrugged. "They just have to damage it."

Elsie's heartbeat raced, and her palms were wet. "FREDCR999," she said in a louder and higher pitch, "full speed forward."

The vehicle lurched then punched, slamming all the kids into their jellach seats as it exploded out of the garage. Dr. Jensa and the Panktars dived out of the way.

CHAPTER 4
A Wild Ride

Pooker slid onto Dar's lap. The growl in the back of her throat had Dar unmolding herself from the seat and scrambling sideways right onto Everest. He immediately shoved her off. *Bleck!* She shot him a dirty look and quickly sat up again, pushing the bobcat away at the same time.

"Flasers," she said, her expression giving the impression she'd just been dipped in a stinky Sleztar bog.

They were moving so fast that the buildings blurred as they zipped past. Even the lines of yellow glow that delineated the road were fuzzy.

"Deng, Elsie, slow down," Everest yelled. In his opinion, Elsie behind the wheel was a pretty yocto-brained choice.

As they left the property and joined the regular traffic, they banged into another jellach HV. Both vehicles spun out in opposite directions, but, as usual, neither had any damage. Pooker wound up back in Dar's lap. The passengers of the other HV did not look happy. This time, Everest sort of got a kick out of Dar's disgusted expression.

Elsie grabbed the joystick to try to straighten out the vehicle.

Everest had rarely seen his parents use manual steering. Usually, their vehicles were pre-programmed for a particular destination, or they used verbal commands, or they jacked into the HV itself and directed the flight with their minds. He was pretty sure Elsie had no clue what she was doing.

Because she was going faster than the rest of the crowd she immediately bumped into the vehicle in front, shoving it forward a good ten meters so that it punched into the next HV which likewise hit the next.

"Oops," Elsie said as she righted the vehicle.

"FREDCR999, slow down," she yelled, and the HV slowed in a flash to a crawl. The vehicle behind slammed into them causing Dar to smash into the back of the jellach driver seat.

"Flasers, Elsie, a suzo-shrimp could do better than this." Dar's voice was muffled because she was still stuck to the jellach. She pulled her face out with a sucking pop.

"Deng, Elsie," Everest said, "stop screeching at the HV. You're making it crazy."

Elsie took a shaky breath then tried out a couple of deep breaths. "Okay, I'm sorry. FREDCR999, continue at the speed of traffic." The HV picked up its pace so that it was nicely spaced between the vehicles in front and behind.

Vlas and Larry, who were staring out the back of the clear vehicle, exchanged looks.

"Dudes," Larry said, "the bad guys are on us like peanut butter on jelly."

Everest swiveled around with everyone else. Sure enough the jellach vehicle was gaining on them, and inside, two hideous Panktars wore zetta determined expressions.

"Elsie," Vlas said, "how 'bout I take a whirl at the driver's seat?"

Everest breathed a sigh of relief when Elsie reluctantly clambered out of the front and gave Vlas room to replace her. Vlas was a wizard with mechanical objects. It wouldn't surprise Everest if he were a natural at flying. At least, he wouldn't be yelling at the HV. Nothing fazed Vlas. Even now, with dangerous Panktars chasing them, he had a big grin on his face.

"You need to tell it where you want to go," Elsie said as she moved to the back of the vehicle.

"Yeah, I got that."

"You can put it on autopilot once you've given it coordinates."

"We'll hold off on autopilot till we lose those green ogres." He settled into the driver's seat while Elsie took her original seat next to Pooker. Dar moved further back to be with Larry.

"Everyone, strap down," Vlas said. "This could get wild."

Strap down? No one ever strapped down.

Everest didn't like the sound of that, but he requested a restraint along with the rest. They all exchanged grimaces.

Thin jellach and vlatex straps suddenly appeared and slithered down their bodies crossways from shoulder to hip. Each of the B12s had two straps that formed a restrictive X across their bodies. Everest fidgeted. He didn't like the restraint. Though it was physically comfortable, it still felt alien. And he thought Pooker might do some serious damage. Her ears were back, her eyes crazed, and she emitted a low, constant growl in the back of her throat. Elsie quickly pressed the manual override button on Pooker's restraint and released her.

"I don't think it's such a good idea to strap down Pooker," she mumbled to no one in particular.

Just as Elsie released Pooker, they got slammed again from behind, but this time from the Panktars' vehicle. The bobcat shot into Elsie's arms, and her low growl got louder. Everest wished they could have convinced Elsie to leave Pooker at the academy.

"That's not nice." Vlas looked over his shoulder and grinned maniacally. "FREDCR999, full speed backward."

The vehicle stopped, reversed, and slammed back into the pursuing vehicle which likewise smashed into the HV behind it.

"FREDCR999, rise twenty meters." The HV rose, still moving at full speed backward.

"FREDCR999, full speed forward." It shot forward at the commuter height. They were bearing down on another vehicle.

"FREDCR999, rise twenty meters."

"I must inform you," the vehicle said in Director Lester-Hauffer's nasal voice, "that it is illegal to fly at that height."

"FREDCR999, just do it," Vlas commanded. The vehicle obeyed. It continued to eat up the sky, making the vehicles below turn into one long blur.

"Bleck," Elsie said. "He programmed in his own voice?"

Dar shrugged. "He's *your* uncle."

"Don't remind me."

"What's the situation behind us?" Vlas asked.

"They're still following," Larry said, maneuvering the restraints so he could swivel around, "But you gave us some room. Man, those green buggers are nasty looking."

"Do we have any idea where we're going?" Everest asked, his voice shaking slightly due to the extreme speed that was causing the vehicle to vibrate.

"We need to find Dr. Yee," Elsie said.

"Yeah, I got that," Everest responded, his patience wearing thin. "Tell me something I don't know. Like where we should go now so we can figure out how to find the doctor?"

She shoved his shoulder. "If you're so smart what's your super brilliant idea?"

'I didn't say I had one. That's why I asked the question."

"*Children!*" Dar interrupted. "Everest is right. We need to regroup. We'd better go to my sponsor's house."

Vlas whistled. "Zeller! What are the coordinates?"

"Not while those Panktars are on us like slime on a bogdog from Sleztar. Ideas, anyone? How do we get rid of them?"

"Well, we ain't getting rid of them driving in a straight line, that's for sure," said Larry.

"Okay, Master-of-the-Obvious, what do you suggest?"

"Well, your Darship—" He grinned as she punched him in the shoulder. "I say we take this baby four-wheeling."

"Excuse me?"

"Take it off-road where there are buildings or trees— someplace we can maneuver till we lose the nasties."

"That's really illegal," Elsie said. "We could get in a lot of trouble."

"Girl, we're on the run. Trouble's our middle name till we find your parents."

"I'm with Larry," Everest said. "We'll have a better chance of losing them where there are a few more non-HV obstacles around. Since we're already traveling at an illegal height, an illegal speed, and in a stolen vehicle, one more broken law isn't going to make much difference."

"My man!" Larry pumped his fist in the air.

"Okay!" Vlas said. "Let's kick some Panktar keister!" With those words and another maniacal grin, Vlas jerked the steering to the left and zipped off the hover highway.

CHAPTER 5
A Dangerous Game of Hide and Seek

Of course the Panktars followed.

Vlas flew the vehicle like Elsie had never seen one flown before. Not even a virtual entertainment device could have duplicated this wild ride. Travelling twenty meters above any other hover vehicle—except the Panktars'—he tore up the sky with a brilliant display of speed and agility, staying away from the actual moss hoverways, instead crossing neighborhoods and parks and commercial properties. While other vehicles traveled below him as a steady stream of orchestrated lines, he made his own path—a zigzag of chaos.

The Panktars stuck like spider boots.

After maybe five minutes with the Panktars following their every move, Larry shouted from the back, "You gotta find some buildings, man."

"Yeah, yeah, I'm trying. But everything's too low to the ground. I need tall buildings, a downtown. I'm shooting for Googleopolis—the skyline to the right."

Since Elsie was on the left, she had to crane her neck to see the buildings. She and Everest rarely went to Googleopolis. When they'd been living at home with their parents, they had lived closer to San Francisco, and their uncle's academy was in Santa Clara, closer to downtown San Jose. Googleopolis was much further south.

Despite her heart beating double-time and her palms going clammy, Elsie couldn't help but be impressed by the beauty of the city. It was zetta modern since the area had been flattened during the Vlemutz invasion. The Googleopolis of today had been built during the flourishing Golden Age that started at the beginning of the thirtieth century. Many of the zetta tall skyscrapers were made out of colorized steelorq—metallic blue, various shades of red, gold, silver, purple. They were outrageous shapes. One was modeled after a long slim fish, its tail the base of the tower, its mouth a skylight at the top. The gills were unusual window slits covering most of the building.

She had read somewhere that the people of the Golden Age had been obsessed with animals in art. Maybe because many animals had nearly gone extinct during the Age of Darkness and Despair that had preceded it, when there had been so little food that people had resorted to eating pets, rodents, insects—any animal they could capture. Animals had gone underground. When the economy had finally recovered and people had more disposable virtual currency, pets and animal items had enjoyed a revival in popularity.

Vlas veered wildly again, and Pooker plowed into Elsie. Though she murmured words of reassurance, the bobcat's hair raised, and she continued to make funny noises in her throat.

As they neared Googleopolis, Elsie saw that not only were there tall buildings, but there were HVs galore, going in all directions. Since here in the city, different directions traveled at different heights, from a distance, it looked like a very complex puzzle. The main hoverways ran alongside the cluster of skyscrapers but not into them. And where there were skyscrapers, there were also tall trees. Dwarf trees weren't required because hover vehicles either were restricted or they flew at a higher altitude.

Elsie rubbed one side of her face. "Uh, the whole city will be monitored for inappropriate driving. The cyborg police will find us as soon as we hit the city limits. I'm surprised we haven't been caught yet."

"I have no doubt our erratic driving already has been logged in the Galactic Knowledge Bank," Vlas said, grinning. "Fortunately, it's Director Lester-Hauffer who's going to have some explaining to do since he owns the HV. But in Googleopolis, odds are good a cyborg officer will take a more personal interest." He shrugged. "We have to lose the Panktars right away so we can melt back into normal traffic. It's not as if anyone's going to get hurt, but cyborg officers of law are pretty focused on rules and regulations."

"Maybe they'll go after the Panktars instead," Larry suggested.

"In our dreams," said Dar.

While cyborg police terrified Elsie because they were so much stronger than most humanoids, they still were the good guys. And she had to believe that Panktars couldn't match cyborgs for sheer strength. "Maybe we should let the cyborg police catch us," she suggested.

Four sets of eyes stared at her as if she were completely insane.

"They could help us with the Panktars," she insisted.

"We stole Director Lester-Hauffer's HV," Dar said. "And for all we know Dr. Jensa has such solid credentials that no one will believe us when we accuse him of being a bad guy. Why is it you ute-babies are always willing to let adults solve your problems?" Her words were scathing. "You might as well just hand over those necklaces. How many times do we have to tell you that adults can't be trusted?"

"They are not necklaces," Everest said. "And some adults can be trusted. But in this case, you're right. We can't just hand ourselves over to the authorities. Not if we want to find our parents. We can only trust ourselves."

"Wow, ute-boy is starting to see the light," Dar said, raising her hands high in the air and wiggling her fingers.

"Knock off the 'ute-boy,' *Shadara*."

Dead silence greeted his use of Dar's original's name. Everyone knew not to use 'Shadara' in her presence. Elsie wouldn't have been surprised to see smoke coming out of her nose.

"Point taken, *Everest*," she said instead, surprising everyone.

"Okay, we're heading in," Vlas said. "I'm taking bets on how long it takes me to lose these green monsters. I say two minutes."

"I'll take three," Dar said.

Larry called out, "Four."

"Everest? Elsie?" Vlas asked.

Elsie shook her head. "Sorry, no bets on my end." She couldn't play games right now, not with the likelihood that her parents were dead. Not surprisingly, Everest let his silence speak for himself.

"Whoever wins gets a constant supply of Blackholes from the losers for one full week," Dar said. "That is, assuming we survive this adventure."

With that, Vlas told the HV to rise another twenty meters; simultaneously, he shot over a steady stream of traffic and into a mass of impressively tall and fiendishly arranged architectural wonders.

Somewhere Elsie had read that besides steelorq, the other common building material in Googleopolis was a substance made out of similar ingredients to jellach called J28. This substance, manufactured on the planet Bafsta in Xlexuri, was outrageously expensive but perfect for a skyscraper since it was extremely lightweight, could be dyed literally thousands of colors and was virtually indestructible. It didn't expand and contract the way jellach did—which was a good thing for a building material. It was much more dense and magnitudes stronger. J28 skyscrapers easily could be identified since they were mostly translucent and their colors came off as tints, delicate shades of pink, yellow, blue, green and purple.

"You can't fly here," Elsie yelled. "It's a no-fly zone."

Vlas whipped around a translucent red building shaped like a dog standing on its two hind legs. "You know me," he said, grinning, "a rule breaker."

"Whoa, these are wicked zeller buildings," Larry said, swiveling around in his seat to see everything. "We got nothing like this in the twenty-first century."

"Focus on the Panktars, Larry," Vlas said sternly. "I can see the buildings myself. At the speed I'm going, I have to concentrate on not hitting anything. You have to tell me what's going on with our tail." He maneuvered the HV behind a triangular skyscraper and then told it to drop thirty-five meters. They plummeted, but even as they dropped he moved them behind a long-columned tower.

"Uh, it's hard to tell. They aren't behind us right now."

"Wait," Dar said, "There they are. They're still sticking."

Vlas spun them around and behind another building but bounced into it as he maneuvered so that they ping-ponged back and forth between two silvery-purple twin buildings. He swung them behind another building and then another and then another.

"FREDCR999, drop to the ground," he said.

As the vehicle dropped, he steered it to squeeze between two HVs sitting on a patch of street moss to the right of florescent white lines. It was such a tight fit that the jellach touched on both sides. They had reached a small rectangular park that boasted plenty of stubby trees and a little fountain in the middle. It also had a play structure with a series of jellach tubes in a variety of bright colors.

"Everyone out and into the tubes," Vlas said. "Now!"

They released their straps and threw themselves out of the vehicle which immediately shrunk to its normal size as they raced across to the tubes. Elsie didn't look back as she dragged Pooker by the scruff of her neck, but she saw Dar looking over her shoulder.

"Nothing yet," the girl yelled.

They dived into the tubes, crawling as fast as they could and spreading out as far as possible so they didn't look as if they were together. The tubes' bright colors masked the features of the kids inside, but they could still see out, though everything took on the color of the tube. Elsie covered Pooker with her body. If the Panktars saw the bobcat, it would be a dead give-away. The cat growled her displeasure at being squashed by Elsie but didn't immediately try to get away. The Panktars exploded around the building, and they all held their breath. If they chose to look, the mercenaries would see them in the tubes. Though the jellach hover vehicle hid in plain sight, Elsie was hopeful that the smaller size, and the fact that they weren't in it, would keep the green monsters from noticing. It wasn't the only parked HV, and they weren't the only kids in the park or in the tubes.

They all let out a collective breath of relief when the Panktar vehicle zoomed across the park and into the next set of buildings. Elsie rolled off of Pooker and onto her back and stared out of the purple jellach tube at the now purple-tinted sky. It was the most beautiful sight she had seen in a long while.

They were steaming up the tubes with all their heavy breathing, a combination of their exertion and worry.

The Panktar vehicle was still out of sight.

"Now what?" she asked, thinking about her parents. She wasn't sure if anyone else even heard her.

"Everyone back to the vehicle," Dar called, "and light speed in case they circle back. This time I'll steer. We need to get to Mink's." She shot a wicked grin at Vlas. "Oh, and it took you three minutes, so those Blackholes are mine."

CHAPTER 6
Adriatic Mink's Abode

Because she was a light-speed learner, this time when Dar took over the jellach vehicle, she was much more competent. Everest leaned back and closed his eyes. Thank the Light, they had lost the Panktars. As Dar softly spoke to the HV, offering up coordinates for Adriatic Mink's home, Everest tried to make sense out of everything that had happened so far.

Why did Dr. Jensa want their disks? He pulled his out from under his shirt and stared at the strange design. The object was a couple of centimeters wide, made of a unique and rare alloy called 1010511 that was purplish-silver and warm to the touch. In the center, there was something that looked like an ancient keyhole and etched along the outer rim of the disk was an intricate pattern of interweaving lines. His parents had been adamant that they keep the pendants a secret. *Not that Elsie had been able to*, he thought grumpily. She was such a big mouth. She could talk faster and louder than a Clegl.

Why hadn't their parents given them more information about the disks? Why all the secrecy? Now their parents were missing. What if they were dead? He shook his head. He refused to get sucked into that black hole. No way were their parents dead.

Out of the corner of his eye, he saw Elsie clutching Pooker as if the cat were some sort of lifeline. Her head was buried in the bobcat's neck. He worried about his sister. She liked a simple life with lots of friends and shopping and fun activities. Having their parents go off-world and leave them behind had been like being thrown into the middle of a Vlemutz battle. Then a criminal had infiltrated the academy, but they'd dealt. Now their parents had disappeared. Of course, Elsie would be zetta messed up. Who was he kidding? He was just as scrambled.

No one spoke while they traveled to Mink's abode. The chase had drained them all. Everest felt as if he'd run ten Mormor miles.

They were going along at a fast clip when suddenly the jellach vehicle slowed to a crawl. Everest looked around. The area was zetta old and elegant. The trees were above standard height and instead of traditional neon yellow lines this neighborhood used glittery yellow gravel to mark the moss lanes.

Dar brought the HV to a gentle halt in front of a sparkling white, majestic gate. Up close, Everest figured out that the wall was made out of crushed white rocks that were so shiny it hurt to look at them.

"Whoa," Larry exclaimed. "That's crazy bright. What is it?"

"Xlexuri whitestone," Dar said.

"No kidding? It's sort of like diamonds or snow in bright sunlight."

"Xlexuri whitestone's incredibly strong, bright, and out-of-this-world expensive. Only someone like Mink could afford to build his place out of this stuff. You can't imagine how much VC it takes to import whitestone from the Xlexuri galaxy."

The whole place was made out of the same crushed white rocks. In the distance, the gigantic mansion threw off electric sparks. A large, central rectangular block with wings on both sides and a dome in the middle, it was more palace than mansion.

Larry whistled. "He's one zetta rich dude. No wonder everyone treats him like he's some sort of god."

Dar shrugged. "Anyone who treats him that way just because he has money is a total suzo-shrimp. But he's also got more brains than all of us put together, and that plus all his freaking currency makes him pretty denged powerful." She touched the door to her left and requested that it erase. "I'll be right back."

She strode over to the gate where a guard stood in a uniform of midnight blue with white trim. The man carried himself with immaculate precision. Amazingly, he was a cyborg, half machine, half human, all intimidating. Normally, only officers of law were cyborgs. It was nearly unheard of to get permission to hire a cyborg out of the law enforcement industry into private practice. Was there anything Mink couldn't do?

Dar seemed more like an adult than a twelve-year-old as she engaged the weapon-wielding, outrageously strong guard in conversation. He had two flasers strapped to a belt that hung low on his hips, and he held a powerful stunner at the ready.

Everest exchanged looks with Elsie, whose eyes were wide as she checked out the intimidating cyborg at the gate. And he wasn't the only cyborg. Every ten meters another machine-enhanced guard stood at military attention. The next one over was a female, reminding Everest of the cyborg officer of law they had met a month ago—Cyborg Officer Lilituck.

After a few minutes, Dar returned. As she slid into the HV, she said, "Okay, we're clear." She told FREDCR999 to rise, and they flew slowly over the gate.

"It seems as if anyone could get in, despite the guards," Elsie said. "What's to prevent bad guys from flying over the gate too?"

"A force field activates if someone tries to intrude. We have permission to fly over, but others would be taught a dangerous and possibly fatal lesson."

"Whoa, your Mink is one bad dude," Larry said.

"He's not my Mink." Dar rolled her eyes. "Anyone as powerful as he is has just as many enemies as friends."

"How come they let you in?"

"They did an aurascan, and once they knew my identity they gave me permission to enter. Guess since he's my sponsor, he's given them standing orders to let me in. I had no idea it would be that easy. I was hoping he'd be here. Unfortunately, he's off-world."

"Don't you think it's weird that they didn't aurascan us?" Elsie asked. "What if we had kidnapped you?"

"Actually, I was warned that everyone would be scanned, searched and questioned once we land."

"Still seems a little unsafe," Elsie said. "We could run amuck before anyone is able to stop us."

"Mink has safeguards within safeguards within safeguards. You worry way too much. He's got it covered."

They arrived at the front entrance, and Dar eased the vehicle down to sit on a moss parking area. A dozen cyborg guards stood at attention, ready to circle their HV. Dar stepped out and motioned for the rest of them to follow.

Everest slowly moved toward the guards. He almost wished they were still being chased by the Panktars. These cyborg guards could give those green monsters a run for their VC. They towered over the B12s which was no mean feat since Dar, Everest and Elsie were tall for their age.

Each kid endured an aurascan and a search. Vlas's took the longest because he had so much junk in his pockets. The cyborg guards spent a lot of time poking, prodding, scanning and admiring PicoBoy.

As they were finishing up, an unusual alien glided toward them. Glide was the only word Everest could think of for how this guy walked. It was a smooth gait, serene, quiet and fluid. Everest immediately recognized him as a Tenorian since he sported an outrageously large nose and he lacked ears. Since he also lacked hair, it was easy to spot the missing body parts. He paused in his smooth glide and sneezed—once, twice, and then three times. Tenorians had highly sensitized noses.

This particular Tenorian wore a flamboyant outfit that consisted of a silver jumpsuit, and a long, dark purple cape. On his shoulder sat a Tenorian mouse, its fur a distinctive dark red. Every time the alien sneezed, the mouse flinched and scurried about to maintain its balance.

Everest grabbed Elsie's arm. "Watch Pooker."

She yanked away. "Wha—"

She sucked in her breath, finally seeing the mouse.

"Pooker," she warned, but the cat had seen the mouse too, and was growling so ferociously that most of the B12s hastily moved away. Even the cyborg guards flinched. "Pooker stop," Elsie said firmly, and the bobcat resentfully halted her threatening noise.

Thank the Light, the cat was fitted out with the most up-to-date pico-trainer available. Otherwise, that mouse would have poofed like a dying star. And the Tenorian would have earned some battle scars in the process.

The unusual humanoid paused in front of them and started a flowery speech with his hands, both of which sported five long, graceful fingers and one long thumb—the better to sign with.

"I'm delighted to meet you," he signed. "Adriatic Mink will be disappointed to have missed you." That comment he signed especially to Dar. "Please let me welcome you all to our humble abode." He bowed low and added the proverb, "*The ornaments of this house are the guests who frequent it.*"

Everest had a pretty decent knowledge of American Sign Language, but he couldn't think in sign. He still had to translate to English and vice versa. He thought he was keeping the meaning, but he had to convert the Tenorian's signing to grammar that made sense to him. Fortunately, the man was using ASL. He'd heard once that there were over two hundred different sign languages on Tenor and that most of the Tenorians spoke at least half of those.

Dar signed back. "We are pleased to be here. Thank you for your gracious hospitality. This is Elsie, Everest, Vlas and Larry."

"Lovely," the Tenorian signed. "I am Luca, Adriatic Mink's major domo. And this," he pointed to his little mouse, "is Memu." The creature remained quite still, its small, beady eyes trained on Pooker, who stared unblinkingly back.

Larry leaned over to Everest. "Uh, dude, I can't speak finger-talk. What's he saying?"

"He said hello and that his mouse's name is Memu."

Larry slugged Everest in the shoulder as if he didn't believe he was translating accurately. "You're a big help."

Luca ushered them toward the impressive entrance and into the zetta elegant abode. Close up, the white stones nearly blinded, but they also took on patterns so that Everest could make out imbedded spirals and animals, stars and moons, and other fantastical designs.

As he climbed the stairs and then crossed the threshold into an impressive and very gold entry hall, he noticed the same scent that always lingered around Melista—liligilds. The perfume seemed to emanate from Luca. Periodically, the Tenorian waved his left hand, and each time a translucent mist sprayed into the air.

Dar leaned over as they walked and whispered, "Bad smells literally can make Tenorians collapse. Rumor has it, some have even died. They have to keep their environment stink-free."

Had his thoughts been that transparent? Sometimes he wondered if the girl read minds.

Just then Luca waved his left hand directly at Pooker, and the fine mist of liligild landed on her fur. Elsie gasped as the bobcat growled deep in her throat.

Luca signed, "Deep apologies my dear, but one must have a fragrant atmosphere. *Oil and perfume make the heart glad, so a man's counsel is sweet to his friend.*"

Elsie gave Everest a startled look. He shrugged. What could he say? He would fill her in later. He vaguely remembered reading that Tenorians had a thing about signing in proverbs.

Luca turned to face all of the kids. "Now my dears," he signed, "one must not forget the health and well-being of one's body. You are in dire need of an infusion of liligilds, lavender, and citrus. *He who has health has hope; and he who has hope, has everything.*"

Everest struggled to identify the words and translate the grammar. Despite the stories he'd heard about Tenorians, nothing could have prepared him for the way they signed at light speed and used their extra finger to add a little flourish. He hoped he wasn't misinterpreting anything.

He tried to tell Larry the gist of what was being said, but he had the feeling that the boy still thought he was withholding information. It just seemed silly to translate all the proverbs, especially since he wasn't always sure he was translating accurately.

They were ushered into a smaller sitting room. Everest wasn't really into room décor, but he had to admit the chamber was pretty; everything—walls, tables and chairs—was a sky blue that hinted a storm was coming. The room welcomed them with the cool and delicate blended scent of citrus and mint.

Soon they were settled in chairs that massaged and warmed them as they sipped from long, thin vials of violet liquid. The drink tasted good to Everest, and strangely, it made him feel better too. Or maybe it was being in this fortress. Surely no one could harm them here? But then he thought about his parents. They couldn't just hide out from the bad guys forever. His mother and father were in danger.

Elsie leaned forward. "Luca," she signed, "we need your help."

"Of course, you do," he said with his long and graceful fingers. "*A pain shared is a pain diminished.* Tell me what troubles you."

They told him. About their parents, the pendants, the Panktars—everything. When one of the B12s wanted to add something, he or she stood up and took over the signing. Luca watched, his expression grave and his body still.

To keep Larry in the loop, they spoke at the same time that they signed.

"We need to find our parents," Elsie ended the sorry tale.

Luca did not respond at once, but Everest had no doubt that he was intensely focused on everything they had just revealed. His eyes centered on a white floral display that sat on one of the blue tables in the middle of the room. His breathing slowed, and even his mouse stayed motionless, not an easy feat for a rodent.

Having given up on the creature, Pooker now ignored everyone while she washed herself meticulously with her scratchy tongue.

After nearly five minutes when even Dar showed signs of wanting to fidget, Luca came back to the present.

He signed, "*Vision without action is a daydream. Action without vision is a nightmare.* We must act with vision and with knowledge. It is unfortunate that you missed Adriatic Mink. Only two days ago you would have seen him. However, though we are forced to act without his guidance, we can still act with his knowledge. I will take you to his private study." Luca stood and motioned for them to follow. With a sweep of his purple cape, he glided forward.

Dar's eyes had grown to about double their normal size. As she walked past him, Everest grabbed her by the arm, but she shook him off with light speed.

"What do you think you're doing?" she asked.

"Nothing." He held up his hands. "I just wanted to know why the wide-eyes?"

At first, she didn't answer. Then she leaned forward and whispered, "No one is allowed to enter Mink's private study."

"That's it? Probably he just never allowed you in."

Dar glared. "No one is ever allowed in his study. Everyone knows that. It's his one supreme rule. I'm surprised Luca even knows how to get into his private lair."

"Well, clearly you don't know everything," Everest said. He wasn't trying to be mean, but the words didn't come out right.

She sniffed and rocketed past him.

He had a feeling she was wishing she could flatten him like one of those pancakes from the twenty-first century.

CHAPTER 7
An Unpleasant Surprise for Dar

It took them at least seven minutes to walk to Mink's private study on the third floor which was as far removed as possible from the more public portion of the house.

Despite her extreme worry, Elsie still felt her head spin as she took in the mansion's opulence. Everywhere were priceless works of art—paintings, statues, light murals, even jewels as big as her thumb embedded into the walls. It seemed as if every era since the dawn of man was represented in this amazing palace. She tripped three times, walked into Everest twice, stumbled into Dar, and nearly fell over Pooker multiple times as she tried to navigate the route to the study without missing anything.

The liligild scent clouding the air made her sneeze repeatedly.

She'd overheard Everest's exchange with Dar so she knew their destination was zetta private. Would Adriatic Mink be furious when he found out they'd been there? What would he do?

She straightened her shoulders. It didn't matter what he did. Her parents were missing. That made any measure worth it, regardless of the consequence.

Mink's major domo came to an abrupt stop in front of a simple wooden door. Hardly simple, since wood was priceless in their time period. This particular door looked ancient. It seemed zetta out of place in a sea of Xlexuri whitestone. The Tenorian flattened his hand to the smooth surface, and the wood melted away, leaving behind a cold gray metal door. That, too, rearranged itself to nothing once Luca touched it. A third door stood in its place, this one pure, warm gold. Again, Luca placed his hand flat against the surface.

Nothing happened. His rather large nose twitched. He tried again. Still nothing.

He swiveled around and signed, "I don't normally go into this room without Adriatic Mink's prior knowledge. Perhaps he sets up different security for those instances. Let me think." He steepled his hands in front of him and pondered the golden door. The only noise they heard was the deep, slow breathing he did via his nose and the small clicking sound the mouse made with its sharp little teeth.

Elsie saw Vlas lean over to Dar. "Should I try my scrambler?"

She had to suppress a giggle when Dar gave Vlas a look like he was a complete yocto-brain.

"On Mink's set up?" Dar snorted then looked around guiltily as if she'd yelled in some ancient place of worship.

It was funny how they all felt as if they had to speak quietly around Luca. Elsie couldn't quite figure out why. He couldn't hear after all, and mostly they were just saying what they were signing so that Larry could understand.

Luca made a funny little sound in the back of his throat, a cross between a gurgle and a grunt. Whatever the sound, clearly he was excited. It was as if he executed a smooth dance move as he pivoted around.

"Please, Dar, come here," he requested via his hands, and then he motioned her forward too. When she didn't move fast enough, he reached for her with his long arms and literally dragged her to the door.

He pointed to her, and then pointed to the door. "You," he signed. "You touch." He placed his palm on the door to show her what he meant.

She stared at him as if he was crazy, and she resisted putting her hand on the door.

"Please," he signed again.

"Dar," Elsie said, "just touch the deng door."

With a sigh, Dar did, and all the B12s gasped as the door dissolved under the palm of her hand.

Luca clapped with pleasure.

Vlas earned himself a fiendish, "I'll get you later," look when he whispered, "Shadara," under his breath, but he just grinned.

"But—" Elsie hesitated. She was confused but she didn't want to be laughed at. She hesitated again before finally signing her question. "Surely Dar doesn't have the same handprint as Shadara?"

Luca smiled. He signed back. "No, you are right. Their handprints are unique. Mink must be using either genetic scanning technology or auralizer technology so that the door allows either Shadara herself or any of her clones to open it."

"Why?" Why would Adriatic Mink plan ahead for the possibility that Dar might need to open one of his rooms while he wasn't there. It didn't make any sense at all.

Dar's irritation was palpable.

"Understanding the mind of a great man is like seeking the bottom of the ocean," Luca signed with a shrug.

Larry stepped over the threshold first, being least in tune with Dar's dislike of any reminder of her original. He stopped suddenly. "Man, what kind of joke is this?"

Next, Vlas stepped past Dar. He whistled. "A Slarmi one, I suppose," he answered.

"Huh?" Larry looked at him as if he were a Meldoon cat with two heads.

"Forget it," Vlas said with a grin.

Elsie was dying to know what they were talking about. She and Pooker slid past Dar who still blocked the threshold.

The room was empty!

Just four walls made out of a steel-colored substance that was very smooth, and when she touched it, very cold. She turned back to Luca who had gently pushed Dar into the room. Everest followed Luca in.

"Where is everything?" Elsie signed.

"Ask and ye shall receive," he responded gracefully with his fingers.

"Who do we ask?" Elsie signed back.

"The room," he answered with a flourish and a smile.

Dar sighed grumpily then signed, "What does Mink call the room?"

"Shadara," Luca responded.

"Great, just great," she muttered.

Elsie had a feeling that Dar might have used some of the bad words that Larry was fond of if she hadn't been so well-trained not to. What was it with Adriatic Mink and Shadara? What was their past? He obviously had loved her. Had she loved him in return? It was weird thinking about it. Mink seemed awfully old now. He had to be at least forty or even fifty! She had to remind herself he would have been a young man when Shadara died.

"Shadara," Dar said, her voice dripping with icicles, "please create an atmosphere for study—tables, chairs."

A woman shimmered to life, not just any woman, but *the* woman: Shadara, the most beautiful woman in seven galaxies, golden-skinned, golden-haired, an older, even more dazzling copy of the girl who shared her name.

It had been a long time since Elsie had actually seen an image of Shadara, and she gasped at the avatar who stood before her. It was as if she shimmered with beauty, as if a halo surrounded her. She wore a gorgeous dress of spun gold that clung to her curves like a second skin, but it was almost impossible to even notice what she wore. She was so amazingly exquisite.

Elsie reminded herself that she wasn't real. She was only a room avatar—another reason for the shimmery quality—but still the impact was immense.

The boys couldn't stop staring, their jaws hanging down.

It was embarrassing.

Dar looked ready to explode. She swiveled around to Luca. "Must she be here?" she signed furiously.

Luca's eyes were compassionate. "I'm very sorry," he signed back. "And now I'll leave you in Shadara's capable hands. If you need me, she knows how to find me." He glided serenely out of the chamber.

Dar's hands clenched, unclenched, then clenched again. Elsie was very much afraid that the girl might do damage to something or someone.

"Hey, Dar, she looks just like you!" Larry said. "Only, like, eons older!"

Elsie lunged just in time to keep Dar from tackling the boy. "It's not his fault; he doesn't know."

Dar wrenched out of Elsie's grip but kept her distance from Larry. After a few deep breaths, she said bitterly, "I was cloned from a woman named Shadara, and this avatar appears to have been designed as a copy of her as well."

"Yeah, I heard something about that," Larry said. "Weird stuff being a clone." Then he grinned. "I bet Shadara doesn't kick keister like you do."

"Didn't," Dar corrected, looking as if she wanted to kick someone's keister this very second. "Shadara died before I was created."

While they spoke, the avatar of Shadara pointed to various parts of the room, causing elegant tables and comfortable chairs to spring to life.

Larry gaped then managed to pull himself together. "Nice trick, lady. Makes for some *am-bi-ance*. But I'd prefer something more solid. Something I can actually use."

Vlas draped his arm good-naturedly around Larry's shoulders. "My friend, you need to bone up on your quantum mechanics. If we can change the solid state of a door, why can't we change the room to have solid state in the form of furniture?"

"These are for real?" Larry breathed. "Wicked." He slowly eased back onto the closest couch. "Man, this is the most comfortable fake couch I've ever seen."

"It's as real as anything else in this world," Vlas said.

Larry snorted. "If it's so real, how come we don't always use couches like this?"

Elsie had to chime in. "It's awfully expensive technology. Only the richest of the rich can afford it. The room has to be stuffed full of inert sunergy that can be converted safely into matter like that couch. It has got to be costing a fortune." She felt like a yocto-brain for not having realized what sort of technology was in the room. But then it was hard to think in terms of the zetta-rich. She couldn't even comprehend how much currency someone would need to make a chamber like this happen. What other tricks did the room have up its sleeve?

"Shadara," she said, "do you know where my parents are?" It was a stretch, but who knew what resources were at Mink's disposal?

The woman nibbled on her lower lip, looking unbearably beautiful as she did so. "No, I'm afraid I do not."

Now that was creepy. She had the same voice as Dar, only throatier and a little deeper. It was an older voice, but it was hard for Elsie to distinguish why it sounded older.

"I do know where they were," Shadara added, blinking her wide, emerald eyes.

Everest stepped forward, losing the glazed look on his face. "Where?"

She smiled, and immediately Everest looked as if he'd been zapped by a bolt of lightning. Elsie shoved him hard in the shoulder.

"Wha—?" he started to ask.

She shoved him again. At least, he was looking at her, now, instead of the Shadara hologram.

"Knock it off," he said.

"No, you knock it off. Stop being such a yocto-brained, jerk-faced idiot."

"What are you talking about?" he asked furiously.

"Stop staring at beauty queen over there. She's just an avatar. Stop it. I mean it."

Dar sighed. "Elsie, give it up. Males are hopeless around Shadara whether real or a copy. There's nothing anyone can do." She jammed her baseball cap further down on her head so that her face was even more shadowed than normal.

No wonder Dar always hid behind that cap. Talk about eww.

Elsie turned back to Shadara. "I'm sorry. Where *were* our parents?"

"They were on a planet that we call Mestor. It's in the next spiral galaxy over from ours—the Andromeda Galaxy. They were there, and then they just disappeared with no clue to their whereabouts."

"I've never heard of Mestor," Elsie said.

Shadara shifted a bit, looking uncomfortable. Worse, her eyes filled with pity. "In theory, it is a habitable planet, but just barely. It can support liquid water but fifty percent of it is generally too cold for most known life forms, and the other fifty percent is pretty much a desert wasteland. Though it's just barely in the habitable zone of the star it orbits, there's not much there except for some very simple life forms. Let's just say your parents wouldn't have a lot of opportunity for socializing with the natives. "

"Why were they there?"

"I don't know," Shadara said, a vertical line creasing her perfect forehead. "Strange really, I always can find these things out, but there's no record anywhere of why they went there. The only reason I know where they were is because they had to log their intra-galactic space travel with the proper authorities. Otherwise, I don't think I would have found that piece of information either. Quite puzzling, really. It's not like the government to keep anything from Adriatic Mink."

Larry rose from the couch and Pooker took his place, curling into the warmth he left behind. The boy sauntered up to the Shadara avatar. "You seem like a smart lady. What about giving us your best guess? What do you *think* they were doing?"

She smiled again, and this time, Elsie was reminded of the famous Mona Lisa painting. Shadara's smile was distinctly mysterious. While the original Mona Lisa masterpiece had been destroyed by the Vlemutz, it had been duplicated so many times they still could study its timeless beauty.

"The infamous Lawrence Tobias Knight." She waggled her finger at him. "I had to do quite a bit of cleanup to deal with your sudden appearance in this time period."

Dar looked ready to explode. "I was the one who set up everything."

"Well, dear," said Shadara. "You left a few loose ends. Don't get me wrong, my darling girl. It was brilliant work, but there were still some things for me to do. We should find time for a few tutorial sessions."

"A few tutorial sessions?" Dar's fists clenched.

Elsie was surprised Dar managed to ignore Shadara calling her "my darling girl."

Shadara's smile broadened. "Yes, wouldn't it be fun?"

Dar's poisonous glare reminded Elsie that at least the girl's personality was not a clone of Shadara's.

"Uh, can we get back to our parents?" Elsie asked.

"Of course. With regards to Larry's question, your parents are pico-biologists of some note. They are funded through the Pico-Biology Institute of San Francisco. Previous work they've published has been centered on strengthening the body's natural immune system."

"But haven't we gotten rid of disease?" Elsie asked.

"Yes, for the most part, but that's because of constant vigilance by scientists such as your parents. Virus strains exist, and they are more virulent than ever, but current scientific research is staying ahead of the viral mutations. The same applies to bacterial infections. As long as scientists stay two steps ahead of the mutations the world remains disease-free."

"So," Larry said, "what do you think their super secret research is on?"

Shadara worried her lower lip again. "It's puzzling. I would expect the Baskers to be working on something that would boost humans' natural immune system just as they've always done. But I'm not sure how that translates to their visit to Mestor. If I had to guess, I'd say that they saw that planet as a good location to test some of their recent hypotheses around the immune system and its ability to withstand harsh environments." She shook her head. "Elsie, Everest: did they ever tell you anything?"

Elsie's hand automatically rose to where her pendant was hidden, warm against her chest, now seeping heat into the palm of her hand. She looked at Everest. Should they tell this Shadara avatar everything?

Dar said coldly, "They don't know anything."

CHAPTER 8
Of Parents and Pendants

Dar's lie surprised Everest. Why didn't she want them to tell the avatar about the pendants? The girl's glare let him know without words that he better not contradict her.

Not that they knew much anyway. What did they know besides the fact that their parents gave them disks to hold onto? If asked, Everest would have said that his parents were fundamentally opposed to pico-technology. They'd always been adamantly against the overuse of pico-pills.

The Shadara avatar made very deliberate eye contact with Dar. For several minutes it seemed as if they were involved in some sort of telepathic communication, a struggle even. Dar's green eyes grew deep and moist like a rainforest, but her lips firmed and her golden hands, which were already clenched, turned white from the mounting pressure. Everest saw a pulse beat at the girl's neck.

He looked at his sister and then at Larry and Vlas. Should they break up whatever silent communication was going on between the two? Or should they let them mentally duke it out?

Just when Everest felt he should step forward and try to somehow stop the weird communication, Dar gasped and lunged backward, shutting down the link herself.

"Don't—ever—do—that—again," she said furiously.

"Don't ever make me," Shadara said calmly, shrugging her sculpted left shoulder.

Elsie rushed to Dar, touching her arm protectively. "What did she do?" She glared at the avatar.

Dar shook off Elsie's hand.

Everest rolled his eyes. When was Elsie ever going to learn? What had made her think that Dar would appreciate being mothered?

"Nothing," Dar said, casting a look of distaste at the avatar. "She just showed me her research to prove she wasn't hiding anything. But I didn't need proof. She's Mink's avatar. Of course, we can trust her."

"Then why the secrets?" Shadara asked. "Why aren't you letting them tell me everything?"

"Why should they? You have nothing more to say. You've given us everything you've got."

"Yes, for now, but only because I need more data. I'm capable of analyzing new information at speeds you can't begin to imagine. If you withhold something important, that could be the difference between me finding something valuable and me finding nothing at all."

"Jeez," Dar said. "You're a bigger pain than I am."

Shadara grinned. "Tell me about it."

Elsie spoke uncertainly. "We have disks that our parents gave us." Slowly she lifted hers and held it forward for Shadara's inspection.

"1010511!" the avatar gasped, a nearly identical response to Dar's the first time she saw the pendants.

Dar's frown grew even more pronounced.

Shadara moved closer. "It's exquisite."

"I think there's something inside," Everest said, holding out his copy as well. He didn't care that Dar had a personal aversion to everything Shadara. He would do anything it took to find answers about his parents.

"You do?" asked Elsie. She looked a bit irritated. "Nice of you to tell me."

"Well, it looks as if there could be a key of some sort," he said defensively. Jeez, just because she was a flaser-mouth didn't mean he had to be too.

"Hmm," Shadara said, "I think you may be right. Perhaps a prototype of whatever your parents are working on. But it would be dangerous to try to open it without knowing more. You could destroy whatever is inside. The 1010511 warmth could be incubating it."

She grew silent and took on the appearance of one who meditated. After a minute or so, she came back to them. "Eight months ago, the Pico-Biology Institute of San Francisco made a formal request to the United Nations of Earth to purchase a kilogram of 1010511. The request was approved, and subsequently, the actual transaction took place. However, the purpose of the usage has been classified as Top Secret by the United Nations and therefore is not accessible."

"Is there a name on the request?" asked Dar.

"Yes," Shadara answered. "Dr. Stephen Yee."

Elsie and Everest gasped in unison.

"All roads point to Dr. Yee," Dar said. "So is he at the institute?"

Shadara's eyes grew thoughtful. "As far as I can tell, he is. There is no record of him having left the area via any public transportation—either on Earth or off-planet."

"Then I guess that's our next stop," Vlas said.

Larry stepped forward, his arms crossed. "What about this Jensa dude? Do you have any knowledge of him?"

"There was a Dr. Jensa related to the Pico-Biology Institute, but he left the institute about a year ago and hasn't attached himself to another scientific organization in the time in between."

"Aha!" Larry said. "He must be working for the bad guys."

"The bad guys?" Elsie asked.

"Elsie, get a clue!" Larry said. "The bad guys who want to twist the technology your parents are developing for evil. Don't you watch any movies? This is classic James Bond: *You Only Live Twice, From Russia with Love, The Spy Who Loved Me*. There's a villain out there, and Dr. Jensa is his minion."

Vlas good-naturedly punched Larry in the shoulder. "I have absolutely no idea what you are rambling on about regarding James Bond, but you may actually be on to something."

"Of course I am." His lower lip jutted out stubbornly. "Now we gotta find the villain's lair. Any ideas?" he asked the avatar.

"No, I'm afraid you've gone far beyond my measly knowledge," she said with an almost affectionate smile.

"We'll have to hope we can find Dr. Yee and that he has some good ideas for where to search next," Dar said. "Can you show us the Pico-Biology Institute compound and its security layout?"

"Now that I can do," Shadara said. On all four walls images popped up—aerials of the grounds, layouts of multiple buildings. Shadara walked the B12s through each image. "The institute is well secured. Fortunately, Adriatic Mink is a major patron."

"That would be fortunate if Mink were with us," Dar said. "I'm afraid I don't see how that helps us now."

"I can send a note from him to the Institute, letting them know that his major domo is escorting very important guests to the institute today who should be given all due respect and attention."

Larry collapsed onto one of the couches. "Sweet."

"Everyone knows that Mink is my sponsor. Someone could easily connect the dots and assume that I'm one of those important guests."

"Perhaps, but I'll wait to send the message till you are on the verge of arriving. You should have time to get to Dr. Yee before the bad guys—as Larry puts it—arrive. We are making the assumption that the people at the institute are innocent of wrong doing. If they are villains then I'm afraid we'll be sending you into a dangerous situation."

Dar waved that warning away.

Elsie swallowed hard and tried not to think about the many things that could go wrong. Right now, all they had to do was get inside. "Will the institute buy into five kids being important guests, even five kids who are escorted by a Tenorian?"

"You'd be surprised what people believe when Mink's involved," said Shadara. "Just act with confidence."

Dar paced across the room, deep in thought. "Okay, I think that's the best we can do, but no Luca; we'll go it alone. I don't want to put him at unnecessary risk. And we need to split up. If the institute is already infiltrated with Larry's bad guys then we don't want all of us taken down. Everest, Vlas and I will track down Dr. Yee. Elsie, you and Larry stay here."

Larry jumped up off the couch. "No way, uh-uh, nada! I am sick and tired of everyone trying to leave me behind. I got skills, you know. I can deal with gangstas better than anyone else in this room. I got street cred."

"I don't like the idea of being left behind either," Elsie said. "What if something does happen to you? How will we know? What are we supposed to do if the worst happens? We have a better chance if we stick together."

"My head tells me you're right, Dar," Everest said, "but my gut says we need to stay together, especially Elsie and me."

Dar sighed. "When we're all captured and locked up, or worse, shipped off to the Vlemutz era, don't come to me looking for a plan B. But hey, we'll have your gut to advise us."

"Jeez, Dar," Vlas said, his grin wide, "what's happened to you? It's like you've gotten a bad case of ute-baby. Where's your sense of adventure?"

She gave him a dirty look and a shove. "Wow, you sure are funny—a real allen. Okay, the five of us."

Vlas rubbed his hands with glee. "We're going to have one zeller time."

CHAPTER 9
Weapons and Intrigue

Dar handed her jellach diary to the avatar. "Please download the specs for the institute, also any information you have on Dr. Yee."

"Of course," Shadara said. In a heartbeat she handed back the JED. "If you contact Luca when you are fifteen minutes away from the institute, he'll ensure that you have clearance to enter."

"We need access to Mink's treasure trove of weapons and devices."

"Luca will take you there," Shadara replied with a hint of a smile. "Unfortunately, my world ends with these four walls."

Elsie thought Dar looked relieved. Who could blame her? It had to be so alien to be working with a Shadara avatar. She stepped forward and executed a small but sincere bow. "Thank you, Shadara, we are grateful for your help. We hope to have good news soon about our parents."

"*May angels dance on your shoulders*," Shadara said softly, an ancient sentiment for good luck. "I can offer you hope. I've done an extensive search, and neither your mother's nor your father's auras have been listed as terminated; that doesn't mean they aren't dead, but at least you know they could be alive."

"Thank you." Elsie backed up toward the door that had originally let them in. She called out to Pooker to come, and looking irritable, the bobcat eased off the couch to follow them out of the room.

Fortunately for Dar's peace of mind, there didn't appear to be any security layers for exiting the chamber. Larry was able to erase the many doors via one simple request. Luca stood serenely on the other side, the red-furred Memu equally serene on his shoulder. Luca carried a Vlatex II backpack.

After spraying them all with eau de liligild, giving Elsie the desire to sneeze, he signed, "This way please."

Elsie looked over her shoulder and saw the furniture shimmer and disappear along with the exquisite Shadara avatar seconds before the door became solid again. As far as she could tell, Dar never looked back. Elsie ran to catch up to the Tenorian. After half a minute, she tugged gently on his sleeve.

Once she had his attention, she signed, "How'd you know we were ready to leave?"

"Shadara alerted me via my JED. She said you wanted to visit Adriatic Mink's arsenal." He paused then added, *"Not the glittering weapon fights the fight, but rather the hero's heart."*

She contemplated Luca's words. To Elsie, Mink was a man of mystery. Why did he have an arsenal of weapons and other spy gear? Given the gifts he had bestowed upon Dar, Elsie had a feeling that his collection was quite extensive and might give them a distinct advantage—at least over their current situation. Not that she wanted to use weapons at all, or fight for that matter. But it was likely they would have to if they wanted to save their parents. She wished Mink were here. He was one of the only adults they could trust, and he was extremely powerful. At least, she hoped he was trustworthy; she *knew* he was powerful.

There was a part of her that was just a bit weirded out by the fact that Mink kept a Shadara avatar and had cloned her too. Her nose wrinkled. Was Mink a creeper?

Luca must have caught her expression because he suddenly signed very discretely, "Adriatic Mink loved Shadara very much. However, that's not why his avatar is Shadara, nor is it why Dar was cloned. In fact, neither was his idea."

"Whose idea were they?" Elsie asked with her hands.

"I'm afraid I'm not at liberty to say, but not Mink's. All he did—very reluctantly I might add—was to provide the funding for both." Worry lines showed on Luca's forehead and his lips turned down as he signed. "I'm quite sure I'll lose my job if anyone ever finds out that I told you this much."

Elsie glanced quickly at Dar, but she was a few meters back and deep in conversation with Vlas so she had missed Luca's communication. Dar had no idea someone else was behind the cloning of Shadara. Would it matter? Dar resented Mink's fascination with Shadara and the fact that he had cloned her as a result. But it could hurt even more to find out that Mink hadn't necessarily wanted her to be cloned either. No matter what Dar said, he was the closest thing she had to a father figure. Who had been behind the decision? Was it someone Dar knew? Why had Mink agreed? Why was it such a big mystery?

She brought her thoughts back to Luca. "I'll never tell," she signed. Smiling slightly, Luca touched his right hand to his mouth to express his thanks.

The chamber that housed all of Mink's weaponry and devices of intrigue was one floor up from his private study and a long way down a thin, ultra-white, sparkly corridor. A clean citrus scent wafted along with them, as if it was being pumped into the hallway. She was surprised that Luca had switched the scent away from liligilds, but it was a refreshing perfume, and it didn't make her sneeze.

They arrived at the door—another plain wooden one—and with the touch of Luca's hand, it and the two doors behind it erased.

Dar stared in disgust and said under her breath, "Sure, now he's allowed admittance."

Luca looked over his shoulder and signed, "Mink requires me to supervise the dusting of his weaponry on a twice-weekly basis. He prefers hand dusting over pico-brownies for this particular chamber."

Elsie felt her jaw drop with an imaginary thud. She quickly signed. "How did you know what Dar said?"

Luca's expression grew quizzical. "What did Dar say?" he signed.

Now Elsie felt like a suzo-shrimp and yocto-brain all rolled into one. Because she didn't know what to sign, she just shrugged her shoulders. Luca turned back and glided into the room. She had forgotten that Tenorians were known for being highly intuitive and even clairvoyant. No wonder Luca seemed to be able to read her thoughts.

"Jeez, Elsie," Dar grumbled as she pushed her way past and into the chamber.

Vlas looked as if he was about to explode with laughter, and Everest fought back a smile. Larry took in their amusement with confusion and asked Everest to explain, but Elsie's glare stopped her brother. Instead, he just shook his head. If he'd said even one word, she would have been forced to hurt him.

They all sobered up when they walked into the weapon room. A twenty-meter-high ceiling provided ample space for walls to be covered with a formidable collection of deadly weapons. One whole wall was devoted to flasers and stunners, another held knives and archaic swords, and still another was a hodge-podge of unusual weapons throughout the ages. On the wall where the door was located, they found shelves of devices suited to intrigue—earpatches, foggers, smellers, bolts of Vlatex II, and other bizarre objects that Elsie couldn't begin to identify.

But most amazing of all, were the rows upon rows of wood cabinets lined up in perfect precision, with a never-ending display of shelves and drawers that held even more weapons and devices. It was all too much to take in. How had Mink gathered up so much priceless wood? And why in all the galaxies did Mink own such an extensive collection of weapons?

As if he once again read her mind, Luca signed, "Adriatic Mink owns a tree farm on Bandogiar in the Xlexuri galaxy. He brings in his own wood for projects. It's quite outrageously expensive, but he likes the warmth of wood in his surroundings, and he likes to work with his hands. He's made many of these cabinets himself."

He imported trees from Xlexuri? Jeez, that was beyond zetta expensive.

"We need flasers," Dar signed, jolting Elsie back to the task at hand. "We'll take the 990s. They're light and easy to maneuver."

"Flasers?" Elsie cried. "We'll kill someone. Worse, we'll turn them into dust particles."

Dar contemplated her for a long moment before answering. "Hate to tell you this, but dead is dead. That's why a flaser was invented."

"But killing someone would be wrong."

"Elsie," Dar said, "your parents have either been killed or kidnapped. It's highly likely that whoever took them did so by force, and probably had flasers themselves. This is no time to be squeamish."

Elsie looked for help from her brother, but his determined expression seemed to show agreement with Dar. "Everest, you were upset when you *stunned* Larry. Just imagine how you'll feel if you flaser someone."

His eyes were as serious as she'd ever seen them. "Yeah, I get that, but Dar is right. We're trying to save our parents. We can't afford to be choosy about which tactics we use in the process. The people who took our parents are sure to have flasers, and stunners are no match for that."

"But what if we flaser one of us by accident?" Elsie asked. "Or some innocent bystander? I couldn't bear it."

"Girl," Larry said, "now you got me worried. If you think for one minute that you might aim one of those bad boys at me, then there ain't no way you should be packing a flaser."

Elsie made a sound deep in her throat. "I'm not going to flaser you; I just don't like the idea of all of us having them in our pockets. What if one accidentally goes off?"

Vlas shrugged. "It's more likely that we'll be flasered by somebody else, and I'd rather even out the odds."

A sharp whistle interrupted them, and they all swung around to find Luca fluttering his long fingers in the air in an attempt to gain their attention.

He signed, "You might consider an excellent alternative to flasers." He motioned for them to follow him to a tall cabinet in the far corner of the room.

As Elsie crossed the chamber she marveled over his startling ability to understand their conversation without being able to hear. Was he reading their lips? Or was it just his innate clairvoyance?

Pooker had attached herself to Elsie's side. Like Luca, the bobcat was intuitive, but in her case she read feelings. She didn't like it when Elsie was upset.

When they reached the cabinet, Luca pulled out a drawer and withdrew the sleekest flaser Elsie had ever seen.

He signed, "This is a zunner."

Dar's nose wrinkled. "Never heard of it," she said with her hands.

"It shoots faster than the fastest flaser, but it stuns rather than kills its victims. And it stuns for longer than your average stunner. The top setting takes its victim out for over an hour."

"If I've never heard of it, it's brand new," Dar signed and spoke. "How much can we trust it?"

Luca responded, "It's new but well tested. Cyborg officers of law are planning to adopt it as their standard in just a few years. Since it's faster than a flaser with the added bonus of not being lethal, even criminals are starting to get interested. The penalty for carrying an unregistered one of these is a lot lower than for carrying a flaser."

Vlas stepped forward, speaking and signing at the same time, "Would you trust it if your life depended on it?"

"Yes," signed Luca. "Adriatic Mink only carries zunners now on his travels."

Had he carried flasers in the past? Elsie wondered.

"Has he used one?" Dar asked, again signing and speaking simultaneously.

Luca's lips twitched into a very slight grin. "As a matter of fact, he has," the Tenorian replied via sign, "with quite adequate results."

Dar sighed. "Okay, zunners for all of us. At least using them should keep ute-baby," she pointed at Elsie, "from blubbering the entire time."

After that, Dar strode up and down the aisles, barking out requirements, and signing them to Luca so he could unlock cabinets. "Vlatex II backpacks all around, zunners, foggers, smellers, earpatches." She paused, drumming her fingers on the side of one of the cabinets. "I've already brought my portable matter-mover; Vlas has PicoBoy. What else do we need?"

Luca drew near, his arms full of various paraphernalia. He adjusted his pile so the goodies rested on one arm and used his freed up hand to sign. "We have some lovely Vlatex II cloaks. Also, a new form of spider gear that only needs to attach to your shoes and hands, very lightweight, very portable. *When spiders unite, they can tie down a lion.*"

Vlas signed, "What about a universal unlocker?"

"Yes," Luca responded. "Over near the door."

"A portable auralizer?" asked Dar.

Elsie had been about to ask for the same thing. It would be handy to have a device that would let them know who was trying to deceive them. Flasers, how were they supposed to trust anyone?

"Yes," Luca signed, "two models. I would recommend the nano design. Fits like a ring on one finger. The only down side to the smaller model is that it requires the person being scanned to remain still for at least five seconds."

"We'll take it," Dar replied.

"What we need is some killer truth serum," Larry said.

"Not a bad idea, Larry," Dar said as she signed the request to Luca.

Luca responded enthusiastically. "Clever boy. *One brilliant sun is worth a thousand that are done.* I believe we have something that will do the trick over here." He glided over to a cabinet then reached inside a small drawer to pull out a vial of tiny yellow pills. He signed, "One of these pills loosens the tongue so that it soars free as a swallow." He handed the container to Larry.

Elsie wished *she* had thought of the truth serum. Someone out there knew what had happened to their parents, but that didn't mean they would willingly tell.

Dar threw Vlatex II backpacks to each of them and started loading hers. "Come on B12s, we don't have all day. Larry, give me the truth serum. I'll keep it with the portable auralizer."

Larry dropped the container in her hand, and she shoved it and the auralizer ring into her pant pocket. The pocket immediately sealed itself shut.

Elsie stuffed as much paraphernalia as she possibly could into her bag. Her palms were damp and her heart raced. They were really doing this, going to find their parents. Part of her wished she could just stay in this zetta safe compound forever and that Adriatic Mink could be the one to find and save their parents. But he wasn't here and every minute they waited could be the difference between whether their parents lived or died.

What if they ran into the Panktars again? Or worse? She straightened up and slung the backpack over her shoulder. It didn't matter if they ran into an entire army of Vlemutz. They would go head to head with any number of villains in order to save their parents.

CHAPTER 10
On a Mission

Luca led them back toward the front of the compound. As he glided along, he signed, "*He is most free from danger who, even when safe, is upon his guard.* It appears we have some unwelcome and rather green visitors at our gate.

"Panktars," Dar hissed.

"Oh, no," Elsie cried.

"My dears, do not be alarmed," he signed. "*Better a thousand times careful than once dead.* My first inclination was to invite them in for an extended stay until Adriatic Mink might be available for a few words. However, on second thought, I feel that it would be best to allow them to continue to watch the estate while you slip out the back door. Long ago, Adriatic Mink built a secret passageway for just such a need. There is a jellach vehicle on the far end. The Panktars will have no idea that you have left. *He who waits for roast duck to fly into mouth must wait a very long time.* They should be well distracted while you search for your parents."

To Everest's disgust, Elsie flung her arms around Luca, causing Memu to scurry about to regain his balance. "Thank you," she said in a muffled voice, clearly forgetting that he didn't hear and couldn't see her lips to read them. "Thank you for everything."

She was such a suzo-shrimp, Everest thought. But Luca seemed pleased by her outburst. His large nose and the top of his head turned bright red. He sneezed twice.

When Luca made eye-contact, Everest used both hands to sign their many thanks, which Luca dismissed with a graceful wave. "*It is an honor to help the baby dove to fly.*"

When they reached the massive golden entry hall, instead of leaving by the front entrance, they turned to the right and walked down a long corridor of iridescent lavender. As far as Everest could tell the walls and ceiling were still built out of the whitestone but color had been glazed on top. The ceiling dripped with icicle sunergy lights. The strong scent of lilacs wafted along with them as they walked. Everest frowned and wrinkled his nose. He didn't care for all these floral scents.

At the end of the very long passage, Luca made a slight bow of respect, then ushered them into a chamber. It was an unusual room, a grotto really, with stalactites dripping from the ceiling, statues of fanciful creatures lining the rough-hewn walls, and an intricate fountain in the middle. The steady drip of water harmonized with the gushing and splashing of the fountain. Stone benches scattered throughout the room offered visitors the opportunity to sit and meditate. But the chamber was so cold that Everest had a hard time imagining anyone taking advantage of the benches.

At the far wall, he was surprised to see a statue of a female creature who looked just like Melista. She wore flowing robes, her hair streamed down below her waist, and her horn spiraled with gold. Dar seemed caught off-guard too, though she quickly erased any expression from her face.

Luca glided over to the Melista statue and tugged on her ear whereupon a loud crack filled the air. Stone rubbed against stone as a portion of the wall loudly swung inward. He motioned the kids to the opening.

Because Everest was so used to doors that erased, he almost jumped backward when the wall actually moved. He walked directly behind Dar who led the party. Larry came next, then Elsie and Pooker, with Vlas taking the rear.

Luca signed, "You'll find the HV at the end of the passageway, and when you start it, it will trigger an opening. Be quick about leaving. The opening will close within twenty seconds of the vehicle having started up. SHADARA is the HV's identifier."

Dar groaned. "You are killing me," she signed.

"I'm very sorry," Luca signed back. "*A trial overcome is a happy remembrance.*"

She grimaced, and Everest could almost hear her snarling, "I don't think so," in her head, but she managed to restrain herself from signing or speaking.

Luca proffered the backpack he'd been carrying and signed that it was filled with food. He added, "Be vigilant; be careful. *Good fortune quickly slips from such as heed it not.* You will find danger; let not danger find you." With that, he waved gracefully and stepped back into the grotto. Soon the stone door noisily crunched shut, and they were alone in the poorly lit corridor.

It was even more fiendishly cold in the passageway, and water dripped incessantly from the ceiling. Though numerous pico-brownies scrubbed and buffed every surface, the dank and dark odor of wet dirt replaced Luca's constant perfume. Were these the type of brownies that did surveillance as much as cleaning?

For a little while in the mansion, Everest had felt safe again, his worry melting away. He had almost forgotten that his parents were in jeopardy. Okay, not really, but the feeling of being safe had been a good one.

"Hey, Basker, I've been thinking," Larry said from behind.

"Yeah? About what?"

"Those bad guys are looking for those necklaces."

"Pendants," Everest said through gritted teeth.

"Yeah, yeah, whatever," Larry responded. "They're going to be expecting them to be on you. I don't think it's such a great idea for you and Elsie to be the keepers. Maybe you should give yours to me, or Elsie should give hers to Dar. Or maybe Vlas should wear one."

"Mom and Dad told us never to remove them. All sorts of bad things happened the last time Elsie took hers off."

"Hey, something good came of that. You got me, man!" Larry grinned. "Besides, I don't think your parents had these bad dudes in mind. They're righteous parents, right? Not creepers like some are. They wouldn't put you in danger—not on purpose. That means they weren't worried about Panktars or evil scientists. Otherwise, they wouldn't have given the pendants to you in the first place."

"He's right," Elsie said. 'Mom and Dad couldn't possibly have thought that people like Dr. Jensa or those green monsters would go after us."

"Even if he *is* right, now that we're all together, won't the bad guys assume that the pendants could be on any one of us?"

"Maybe," Vlas said, "but switching them up could slow the bad guys down. It's a good idea."

"I don't like the idea of both of us giving our pendants away."

"It doesn't have to be both," said Larry. "One would do."

"They'll go after Elsie first," Dar said. "They always go after girls first."

"I'm just as good a fighter as Everest," Elsie said, irritated.

"Yeah," Dar said, "we know that, but they don't."

Elsie reluctantly handed her pendant over to Dar. If Everest hadn't been so worried about his parents, he might have grinned at his sister's expression. She looked like she'd just eaten a limonino.

"You're a girl too," Larry said to Dar. "How come you get to carry the pendant?"

"Because I'm meaner than everyone else."

"Ain't that the truth," Larry grumbled.

Dar punched him in the shoulder.

They navigated the rest of the secret passage in silence.

When they arrived at the end of the tunnel, Vlas came to an abrupt stop and whistled long and low. "Now there's a hover vehicle."

"Sweet," added Larry.

If jellach could shine, this one shone. It was still clear, still capable of stretching and shrinking to match the number of occupants, but it was sleek and it screamed light speed. Vlas rubbed his hands, a maniacal gleam in his eye.

"Maybe I'd better drive," Everest said. He wasn't happy with the way Vlas eyed the vehicle.

"I don't think so," the boy said.

Before anyone could protest, the driver's seat was his. Everest rolled his eyes and climbed into the seat behind. Pooker and his sister came next with Larry piling in practically on top of her. Dar took the seat next to Vlas. The vehicle spread out just enough to give them all leg room.

"Okay, SHADARA, let's rocket," Vlas said causing Dar to flinch at the use of her original's name. The jellach vehicle hummed to sunergy life. In front of them, atoms silently rearranged themselves into a large opening in the tunnel wall.

"SHADARA, take the fastest route to the Pico-Biology Institute of San Francisco. Light speed, now."

The vehicle took Vlas's request seriously. In a blink of the eye, it went from zero to a speed Everest had never experienced in an HV before.

"Deng," Elsie whispered and grabbed Everest's hand. His knee-jerk reaction was to shake her loose, but a small part of him wasn't opposed to holding on for dear life.

"Cowabunga!" yelled Larry at the top of his lungs. "Man oh man, wicked zeller."

It never ceased to strike Everest that Larry was some sort of spiritual clone of Vlas's.

As Luca had promised, they left Adriatic Mink's compound behind without a single Panktar in pursuit. The tunnel dumped them out on the back side of the mansion which was so palatial that it blocked them from view. By the time the Panktars in the front of the mansion would be able to see their jellach vehicle, they would be just another HV in a sea of HVs. Except their vehicle was going four times faster than anything else.

"Uh, Vlas," Everest said, "maybe we should drop to the speed limit so we don't draw attention to ourselves."

"Yeah," Dar said. "Knock off the hotrod moves."

"What a bunch of fun-suckers!" Vlas rolled his shoulders. "SHADARA, please drop down to the boring speed limit."

Immediately, the vehicle did so, jolting them all out of their seats with the dramatic shift in speed. The change coincided with them merging into the steady traffic of a hover highway.

And Everest breathed a deep sigh of relief at their sudden anonymity.

CHAPTER 11
Finding Dr. Yee

The Pico-Biology Institute was drab gray steelorq. Low to the ground, it gave the distinct impression that most of it resided under the surface. Following the Shadara avatar's directions, they had contacted Luca fifteen minutes before their arrival. As promised, the guards had been primed to expect them and ushered them inside the compound with minimal delay and a great deal of respect.

Vlas parked the hover vehicle in the visitors' parking lot and they all tumbled out. The vehicle quickly shrank to normal size.

Dar said, "I don't think we should bring our backpacks in. If they search them, they won't be too pleased by our cache of weapons and stink bombs."

"I'll bring PicoBoy," Vlas said.

"What if we run into bad guys?" Elsie asked.

Dar shrugged. "We'll just have to hope that for once our luck holds. I'll sneak in a few things just in case." She stuffed a couple of small devices into her pocket.

"Should Pooker stay in the vehicle?" Elsie asked.

"Yeah," Dar responded. "No one's going to let a bobcat wander around the labs."

Elsie thought about requesting that the HV door be erased so Pooker could get fresh air, but it made more sense to leave everything as is. The parked jellach vehicle would sense the big cat's presence and automatically pump in and circulate fresh air. Elsie just hoped Pooker wouldn't be horribly claustrophobic. With luck, the cat would sleep.

She didn't think much of the grounds. They were pristine, but not decorative. The trees were little soldiers lined up in perfect rows. None were the flowering type. Much of the area was covered by perfectly-groomed grass. Symmetrical hedges lined the plain gray gravel walkways. The grounds smelled green but not floral or even herbal—just a sort of clean scent.

The inside was even more pristine than the outside. Pico-brownies appeared to work twenty-four-seven. The almost invisible miniscule specks floated along the walls in large quantities, disinfecting, cleaning, and possibly monitoring. There was a harsh odor to the disinfectant which was odd really because cleaning products didn't generally smell nasty, though Elsie had heard that in the far distant past they had.

A sleek, gray table sat in the middle of the lobby, and a woman of indeterminate age, wearing a white lab coat and white slacks, sat at the table with her hands folded. Her sensibly-shod feet were firmly planted on the gray tiled floor, and her light gray hair was captured into a very tight bun. Only when they stood at the table, did they realize she was a hologram. It was almost impossible to detect her shimmery edges. She was definitely the latest and greatest in holographic technology.

With a tight smile she asked, "What is your business?"

"We wish to speak with Dr. Yee," Dar said.

"Do you have an appointment?" the hologram asked.

"Adriatic Mink has arranged an appointment for us."

The hologram sucked in her breath at the mention of Dar's sponsor and made a slight gurgling noise in the back of her throat. "I see," she said crisply as she looked down at her JED. "We are very short staffed today. I'll have to escort you to his office. We close at 17:00—please, be prompt." After signing them in, she stood up primly. "This way, please." She spoke in a low tone to a guard as they passed, and he took her place at the front desk.

Elsie tried to memorize the path they took to Dr. Yee's office, but it was complicated, almost as if their escort had taken them the most roundabout way. Despite the images the Shadara avatar had provided earlier, she felt turned around. Fortunately, Vlas appeared to be giving PicoBoy a chance to learn the route, and she had much more faith that the little creature would remember the way out of the maze.

She stuck close to her brother. He was acting all stiff and irritable. He probably didn't like her shadowing him, but her heart pounded like an ancient drum and her palms were clammy. She couldn't get rid of the zetta terror swirling in the pit of her stomach. What if this whole institute was behind their parents' disappearance?

Someone jostled Elsie from behind, and she swiveled her head to find all the B12s jumbled together.

"Jeez, Larry," Dar said crossly. "Watch where you're going." He had walked right into her, knocking her into Vlas who had then bumped into Elsie.

"Oops, sorry," Larry said, his face contorted to look zetta sad. He spoiled the effect by grinning as soon as Dar pivoted around to continue her march down the corridor.

Elsie stared thoughtfully. What was Larry up to? Could he have rammed into Dar on purpose? But why?

After at least fifteen minutes and too many stairs, mostly going down, they reached a simple steelorq door. The hologram requested entry, and the door disappeared. The room was in shadows with only minimal light.

"Dr. Yee?" the hologram asked.

"Yes?" said a tenor voice in the gloom.

"Adriatic Mink's party is here to see you."

"Excellent," Dr. Yee responded. "Thank you."

Elsie saw him across the room, but his features were impossible to distinguish. He was working on a holoputer.

Their escort sniffed audibly. "I'm quite busy today. May I leave these young people in your capable hands?"

"Of course," said Dr. Yee. "I'll escort them back when we are done."

"Thank you." The drab but pristine woman turned on her heel and exited, her firm footsteps programmed to echo realistically in the hallway as she strode rapidly away.

Dr. Yee walked out of the gloom, his expression serious. "Light, please," he said, and the room illuminated his features.

He was not a tall man. Dar, Everest and Elsie all topped him in that department. He was trim and tidy. His eyes were nearly black and slanted slightly. He had black hair, a strong jaw, and high cheekbones. For a scientist, he was surprisingly young and handsome.

"Elsie, Everest, thank the Light," he said. He clasped his hands so tightly that his knuckles went white.

"How do you know who we are?" Elsie asked, immediately suspicious.

"Your parents have photos in their office. I've been so worried ever since I heard that Dr. Jensa visited your school."

"We didn't trust him," Everest said.

"We had to run," Elsie added.

"You did exactly right. Your parents would have been very proud."

"Would have been?" Elsie's heart was in her throat.

"I—that is—" Dr. Yee cleared his throat. "Shall we sit down? I'll tell you everything I know. But first, who are your companions?"

Elsie was afraid she would be physically ill. With her eyes, she begged Everest to answer. He grabbed her arm and dragged her over to the couch, sitting quickly and taking her with him.

Everest leaned forward. "These are our friends: Dar, Vlas, and Larry."

"Do Dar, Vlas and Larry have last names?" Dr. Yee gave them a kindly smile.

"No," Dar said shortly.

"Ah, clones." He turned back to Elsie and Everest. "Given that you've been staying at the academy, I should have been able to guess that." He sat down in a chair across from the couch. "Sit, sit." He motioned to the other chairs, and the B12s followed his command.

He turned back to Elsie and Everest. "I am so relieved you came to me. Your parents have been on a secret mission for the past month. We shouldn't talk about that in any detail, but I can say that before they left on that trip, your parents made a startling discovery, one that could well change the universe. They are brilliant, truly brilliant. However, two weeks ago, they stopped all communication. Only two cycles into their research, they stopped sending us their daily reports. Needless to say, we've been zetta concerned."

"Why didn't you let us know?" Elsie asked.

"We didn't want to alarm you till we knew for certain what had happened to them. Unfortunately, in hindsight, that backfired on us, because it gave Dr. Jensa the opportunity to try to insinuate himself." He leaned forward. "You didn't give anything to him, did you?"

"No, of course not," Everest replied.

"Excellent, excellent. Brave of you to run; brave of your friends to come with you."

"We had no choice," Elsie said.

Dr. Yee shook his head. "When I think of what could have happened if those pendants had fallen into the wrong hands. Your parents did tell you to give them to me if something went wrong, correct?"

"Yes," Elsie replied. "But what has happened to our parents?"

He shook his head again, this time his eyes were deep pools of sorrow. "We sent a ship to the planet they were on, to see what had happened to them."

"Mestor?" Elsie asked.

Dr. Yee flinched. "You know that much? How?"

"We know how to research," Dar said.

"You certainly do. That's classified information. We could use a few of you on our team. Yes, Mestor. But when the ship arrived, no trace could be found of your parents. Their ship was still there. Their supplies also. But they had vanished. Mestor's a harsh world. We can only assume that it took your parents' lives."

Elsie doubled over, her body shaking uncontrollably. Tears tumbled onto her cheeks, dribbled down her chin. She couldn't stop them.

"There, there." Dr. Yee reached across and patted Elsie on her head.

Larry interrupted. "I don't buy it."

Startled, Elsie looked up and saw the doctor staring intently at Larry.

"Excuse me?" Dr. Yee said.

"I don't buy it. Why would Dr. Jensa be after Elsie and Everest if their parents died of natural causes?"

"He used to work here. He knew that Justine and George had chosen to leave key research with their children in the form of pendants. When he heard that the two were missing, he saw an opportunity and took it."

"Ha!" Larry said, crossing his arms. "I think someone kidnapped them, has them in a secret lair, and now is forcing them to continue their research for the bad guys."

Everest turned to him, "Jeez, Larry, can't you see how ridiculous that sounds?"

Larry's lower lip curled. "Which would you rather believe? Your parents are dead, or your parents have been kidnapped? They've disappeared, man."

Dr. Yee's initial surprise over Larry's theory turned to thoughtfulness. "Clearly, Dr. Jensa wants to abuse Justine and George's research, but I don't think he had anything to do with their disappearance. He's been here in California the past two weeks. Larry, I appreciate your concern, but I think in this case, we just have a very sad circumstance with an opportunist taking advantage of the situation."

"How come Dr. Jensa's got Panktars after us?" Dar asked.

Dr. Yee's expression grew puzzled. "Panktars? I don't understand."

"Panktars chased us."

"You mean those green mercenaries?" Dr. Yee asked. "I'm beginning to think I don't know Dr. Jensa at all. Thank the Light, you got here safe and sound. You can give me the pendants, and your involvement will be over. We'll take steps to guard them from Dr. Jensa and his cohorts."

"You tell us our parents are most likely dead, and you say our involvement is over?" Elsie wanted to hit him.

He looked horrified. "My dear, of course, I don't mean to minimize your loss. George and Justine were my good friends. This is a nightmare, a tragedy, for everyone their lives touched, but most of all for you. I'm so very sorry."

Everest stood, his face white, his eyes brimming with unshed tears. "As long as our parents' remains haven't been found shouldn't we hold out hope? What do we do now? Can we search for them?"

"For now, you should return to the academy. Your uncle is your next of kin. He may know what your parents' wishes were. Meanwhile, you can give me the pendants, and at least, you won't have to worry about Dr. Jensa anymore. I'll inform your uncle that he is not to be trusted. Don't worry, I'll ensure that none of you get in trouble for running away. I'll do anything and everything I possibly can to help you through this horrific time."

Elsie swiped at her cheeks and eyes. She was not a crybaby. *She was not.* With her sleeve she rubbed at the last vestige of tears. She swallowed hard and stood, her fists clenched. She avoided looking at the rest of the B12s. She had the sensation that Dar was close, and seeing movement from the corner of her eye, she thought Larry was sort of skirting around the room, maybe avoiding being involved in all this heavy emotion. Even though he knew what it was like to have parents and even to lose them, he didn't seem to have had the same emotional attachment to his parents.

She realized that none of them had responded to Dr. Yee. He now stood as well, his expression patient and kind.

She glanced quickly at Everest then cleared her throat. "Thank you, Dr. Yee. We appreciate the help."

Her brother reached inside his shirt and pulled the pendant up and over his head. He held it out. "Here."

Dr. Yee accepted it with a little bow. "Thank you. I'll take very good care of it. I can promise you that your parents' work will not be in vain. I will nurture and carry forth their research. Someday, they will be famous."

Everest nodded quickly. "Okay." He stepped back, moving closer to the door.

"But there's another pendant," Dr. Yee said. He looked at Elsie expectantly. She darted a glance at Dar.

"I don't have it. I gave it to—" Instead of finishing her sentence, she motioned to Dar.

The girl seemed more reluctant, but still she reached under her shirt for the pendant. Then she frowned, her expression puzzled. She did a funny search around her neck and even down her back. She stared at the floor, turning around slowly. Finally, she looked up.

"It's gone," she said.

"What do you mean, 'it's gone?'" asked Dr. Yee sharply.

He'd been so warm and sensitive, his change in tone caught Elsie by surprise. Of course, he would be anxious about the pendants. They were top secret, an important element of the research that he intended to move forward.

Dar looked at him with bewilderment, an expression Elsie had never imagined she would see on her face. "I don't know. It was there a few minutes ago. It must have slipped off in the corridor." She turned on her heel, intent on finding the pendant.

Elsie rushed after her.

Dr. Yee called out, "Wait! When was the last time you remember seeing it, or feeling it on."

Dar shrugged. "I felt the 1010511 warmth when we were at the main desk. I don't get it. It's not the type of necklace that would just fall off."

"Are you sure you clasped it properly?" asked Everest.

She glared. "Yeah, I'm sure."

Dr. Yee shook his head. "This is quite disturbing. Come along now. We need to retrace your steps."

Motioning for them to follow, he pushed past the B12s, his eyes glued to the floor. They all fell in line.

Elsie swiveled her head back and forth, desperate to find the pendant. Panic caused a crazy churning in her belly. *Darn Dar.* How could she have lost the necklace? Of course, Elsie had too, but that was different. She hadn't been wearing it at the time.

They searched the floor frantically.

At one point, a woman in a white lab coat ran into them. She looked a bit bewildered. "Hello, James," she said.

Dr. Yee lifted his head and absently responded, then returned to staring at the ground. The woman looked as if she might want to chat, but after a few seconds, she continued down the hallway.

Elsie had a strange, niggling sensation. She felt a bit out of body, as if all of this, their parents' disappearance, their escape from the academy, their meeting right now with Dr. Yee, was happening to someone else. It was as if she had forgotten something important, something that would help them, if only she could remember.

Half way down the next corridor, Dr. Yee stopped abruptly, his arms crossed. Indistinct voices could be heard in the distance. "I wonder if we could have missed it in my office. Maybe I should return and do a more thorough search there. Why don't you all finish up from here to the lobby and return with your results. Do you know how to get back to my office?" He seemed to sense that Dar was their leader because he addressed the last question to her.

Dar nodded.

Now that they had done such a thorough search in the corridors, Elsie was pretty sure any one of them could find their way back.

"Excellent. Please hurry. That pendant should not be left lying around. It was exceedingly careless to drop it."

Dar's lips thinned. Elsie knew from experience that she didn't like to be criticized.

They all turned with Dr. Yee to watch him stride back to his office. At the same time, Larry whipped around the corner and practically flew down the hallway toward them. The moment he saw them, he slowed down, but it took him a few seconds to come to a complete stop.

"Uh," he said, "I thought I saw something glinting, but it wasn't anything. Figured I'd better catch up."

"It's not a good idea for you to separate from the group," Dr. Yee admonished.

"Couldn't agree more!" Larry said.

"Dr. Yee is going to go back to his office to search there," Dar said, "and we're going to search from here to the main lobby and then report back. Okay?"

"Sounds like a plan to me." Larry offered up his most agreeable smile.

That look of innocence usually meant he was up to something. Who knew? Who cared? Elsie didn't. Nothing mattered anymore. Her parents were dead. She felt empty inside.

As soon as Dr. Yee disappeared from view, Larry grabbed Dar. She automatically shook him off, glaring.

"Listen," he hissed, "this is important. We have to get out of here, *now*."

Elsie couldn't bring herself to ask the obvious question, "Why?"

But Dar engaged immediately. "What's up?"

"I don't know what Dr. Yee is up to, but I do know he's a murderer."

CHAPTER 12
The Imposter

There was a collective gasp.

Though Everest had remained silent, his heart pounded so loudly he figured it could be heard in the next galaxy. Wasn't there anyone they could trust?

"Yeah," Larry shook his head, "this dude is bad news. I had a creepy feeling about him, so I stayed behind in his office for a closer look. There's a very dead body in his closet."

"Was it—was it one of our parents?" Elsie asked before Everest could find his voice.

"I don't think so. From what I could tell, he didn't look much like you. I'm guessing it was the real Dr. Yee."

"But who were we talking to?"

"Didn't that lady call him James when she walked by?" Everest asked. Deng, what a yocto-brain he'd been.

"Yes—" Elsie stopped suddenly. "Wait a sec, Mom and Dad said his name was Dr. Stephen Yee. James must be someone else at the institute pretending to be Dr. Yee."

"Okay, brainiac, we get it that he's not Dr. Yee," Dar said. "Now it's time for light speed. Just play it cool in the lobby."

Half running, half walking they moved quickly but also cautiously toward the exit.

"Deng," Everest said, "I gave him my pendant."

How could he have been such a fool? But even the hologram had acted as if it was Dr. Yee. No wonder the man had remained in the shadows till she had left.

"And the other one's lost," Elsie moaned.

"Not exactly lost," Larry said. "Just relocated."

Elsie whipped around. "What?"

Dar grabbed Elsie by the arm and started dragging her down the corridor. "I think Larry's telling us he's been up to his old tricks. We'll thank him later, but for now, let's get out of here. And get rid of the crybaby eyes. Someone will notice."

"Leave her alone," Everest said. Flasers, Dar had no heart. They'd just been told their parents were dead.

"I'd be glad to," Dar said bitingly, "but you both obviously need a keeper."

They all shut down when they hit the lobby. The hologram motioned for them to sign out at the desk, but they pretended not to see and instead rushed out of the building. As soon as they were outside, they raced to the hover vehicle.

As they scrambled in, Pooker made a funny noise in greeting.

"Vlas, get us out now," Dar said urgently.

"Where do we go?"

"Anywhere," Dar said. "Not Mink's compound. It's being watched."

"It'll be dark in a couple of hours," Larry said. "That'll make it easier to hide."

Vlas told the HV to leave the compound. "I guess anywhere is better than here. We can figure out a destination later."

"For now, head back toward the academy," Dar said. "I've got the beginnings of an idea."

Vlas gave the guards a happy wave as they exited the facility. A moment later sirens rang out.

"Jeez," he muttered. "SHADARA, ten meters up and maximum speed south."

The HV popped above the other vehicles and jammed away from the institute.

This time no one followed. When they were a couple of kilometers away from the institute, Vlas slowed the HV down and dropped it back into the steady stream of traffic.

Pink and orange streaked the sky, the beginnings of a sunset.

"Does anyone remember if there's going to be planned rainfall tonight?" Dar asked.

"SHADARA, is rain scheduled for tonight?" Vlas asked.

"No," the vehicle replied in Shadara's and Dar's all too familiar voice.

Everest wondered why Dar had asked, but he didn't have the energy to question her. There were no words to describe how he felt. Empty? That was close. Like a black hole? Closer. Were his parents dead? Or did the fact that Dr. Yee was not really Dr. Yee mean that they should have renewed hope? Someone *was* dead so that made it likely that others were too. What a horrible mess.

"Spill, Lawrence," Dar said. "I take it you picked the pendant off of me when you bumped into me in the corridor?"

"Yeah, pretty zeller, eh?"

"Yeah," she grinned, "not bad for a thousand-year-old ute-baby. Now give the pretty pendant back to Elsie."

"I got no problem with giving it back, but it'd be safer with me. No one'll think to go after me for the pendant, but all the bad guys'll be going after Elsie."

"You're right," Elsie said though Everest sensed she wasn't thrilled to be agreeing with the boy.

Everest wasn't happy about Larry keeping the pendant, but he could see that it might be safer.

"I wish we could figure out why everyone's after the necklaces," said Dar. "With Dr. Yee dead, it's a bit more complicated finding answers."

"A bit?" Elsie asked wearily.

"Yeah, but not impossible." Dar swiveled her chair around so that she faced them. Everest was surprised by the gleam in her eye.

"What are you thinking?" he asked.

"I'm thinking we need to find someone who can give us answers."

"Brilliant," he responded sarcastically. So far they'd had just a ton of luck finding someone they could trust who knew what was going on.

She grinned. "The answer's simple."

"The suspense is killing me," Everest said coolly.

"Larry, any ideas?" she asked.

"Hmm." His brow wrinkled in concentration. Then he broke into a grin. "This is the thirty-first century. You can time travel. We just go back in time to someone who knows the 4-1-1."

Everest didn't have the energy to find out what Larry meant by the 4-1-1.

"So who do we ask?" Dar prodded Larry with a grin.

"Good question," Larry said. "There're all those dumb time travel rules about changing the future…yada, yada, yada…blah, blah, blah."

"I don't think we can ask our parents," Everest said.

"They would totally alien," Elsie said. "But we could warn them that someone is after them. We could save their lives."

"Elsie, you know we can't do that," Dar said softly, touching her hand. "Listen, just because that fake Dr. Yee said they were dead, doesn't mean they are. He was lying to us the whole time; he could be lying about that too. You mustn't give up hope."

Elsie was fighting tears again. "Do you really think so?"

"Yes, I do."

After a few seconds, Elsie straightened her shoulders, took a shaky breath, and then swallowed hard. She seemed to have a grip on her tears.

Everest was not inspired by Dar's little pep talk. Anyone who thought this was going to end happily had to be the biggest yocto-brain in the Milky Way.

"You guys aren't listening," Larry said. "I told you. Your parents have got to be kidnapped. This proves it."

"Not really," Everest responded. "It could be that they died on Mestor, and everyone just wants to steal whatever they can of their research." He wanted to believe his parents were still alive, but there was no proof that Larry's outlandish theory was true.

Pooker bumped her head against Elsie, running her sandpaper tongue over her ear.

"Ow!" Elsie rubbed her ear then hugged Pooker hard. She looked like she might cry again.

"Jeez, Elsie, could you power down all the water works?" Everest asked. They needed to keep their auras on in front of the clones.

Elsie scrubbed at her face, managing to give him an evil look at the same time.

"Give her a break, tough guy," Dar said. "Just because we don't have family doesn't mean we can't imagine what you're going through. Maybe you should let go yourself."

"I don't think so," he said.

She shrugged then turned to Vlas. "Ideas?"

"How 'bout we return to the institute but earlier in time," Vlas suggested.

"Yeah," Larry said, "we could see if your parents have any records. Maybe they kept one of them scientific journals."

"Maybe we could find the real Dr. Yee," Elsie said.

"Well," Larry looked thoughtful, "that might be a problem. We can't tell him he's about to be offed. I'm pretty sure that breaks at least one of your time travel rules."

"What if we go back in time to Adriatic Mink? Maybe he could find out something." Everest looked to Dar for her reaction.

"Hmm, maybe. But he would have to be willing to still go away in this time so that we don't screw up the future."

"What if he can't get the answers?" Larry asked. "I know he's a zetta cool dude and everything and richer than everyone else in the world put together, but what if he doesn't have access to the information?"

Dar shrugged. "Once we're back in time, we could always break into the institute as a backup plan. And we have this HV. Unfortunately, we didn't think to ask Luca for a time travel device. That means we have to steal one from the clone academy and install it on this vehicle. We know the HV has been sitting in Mink's secret lair, so it can easily go back there. If Mink can't get the answers himself, he might be able to hook us up with someone who can."

"Okay, I guess that's the way to go," Everest said.

"Now we just have to break into the academy," said Dar.

"And steal the time travel mechanism," said Vlas.

"And get out of there with light speed," said Elsie.

Larry grinned. "Piece of cake."

CHAPTER 13

Breaking into the Clone Academy

They waited till dark. And then they waited till after curfew so that no one would be wandering around outside. While they waited, they ate some of the snacks that Luca had provided. At least, Elsie tried to eat, but her appetite was gone. Everest wasn't jamming food down either. Larry on the other hand seemed to have an expanding universe for a stomach. If Dar hadn't done some quick rationing, he would have eaten every last bite. He proclaimed Tenorian food to be a lot like Indian food—wicked awesome.

All was quiet when they arrived at the academy. The glass-like tevta gate with its engraving of galloping wild horses provided an eerie sensation of light. And even from this distance, the limonino tree wafted its very strong and achingly familiar citrus scent. Already, the place felt strangely like home, but it also caused Elsie's heart to pound. It was a threatening place too.

Would Pooker remain calm in the vehicle while they were gone? The poor bobcat didn't like confined spaces, and they'd been cooping her up a lot in the HV. On the plus side, darkness was her friend. She felt safer when she was cloaked in shadow.

If only they could go to their uncle for help. But that was out of the question since he'd been completely taken in by Dr. Jensa.

"Nighteyes, everyone," Dar said, holding out a small dropper bottle.

Elsie applied two drops into both eyes, grimacing at the metal aftertaste. She caught Larry making a face too, after he applied the drops.

Up above, the stars and HVs were bright balls of light, but they did not provide much in the way of illumination. Jellach hover vehicles had been designed to minimize light pollution in the cities. It was one of the reasons that stars remained such beautiful additions to the night sky.

"Let's jam, B12s." Dar shrugged off her Vlatex II pack and rifled through it till she found the matter-mover.

In less than a minute, there was a square hole in the gate big enough for them to enter the academy's gardens.

Once inside, Elsie ran to catch up with Dar who moved rapidly along the jewel-toned gravel walkway.

"Uh, Dar, aren't you going to rearrange it back to solid?" She motioned to the gate.

"We may need a quick get-away," Dar said, not slowing down. "Come on, B12s, light speed. And be prepared. If you have room in your pockets stash some foggers and smellers."

Elsie promptly followed her direction.

After that, they remained quiet until they got to the History Center. Only the sound of their boots crunching the gravel disturbed the otherwise normal sounds of the night. When they reached the building, Dar stepped aside to make room for Vlas.

"Okay, do your magic," she said.

Vlas cracked his knuckles then pulled out his triangular scrambler and placed it against the tevta wall. The device glowed bright blue.

"Whoa, dude," Larry said at the strong chemical odor that filled the air, "I forgot how much that thing stank." He tilted his head. "How come the scrambler changes all those colors?"

"When it's white, we know that the security currents are jumbled so we can enter," Elsie said.

"You'll have to ask Vlas how it works, and why he gave it such an interesting smell," Everest added, almost grinning.

"I told you I could fix that if I had a real lab available," Vlas said irritably.

"How come we're not using the universal unlocker that Luca gave us?" asked Elsie.

"We know this device," Dar said. "There's no benefit to introducing another gadget."

Vlas cleared his throat, looking sheepish. "Actually, I forgot we had the unlocker." When the scrambler had shifted to fluorescent white, Vlas removed it and shoved it back into his pocket. "Okay, after you, Dar."

She requested entry and the door dissolved. She moved determinedly into the cavernous room.

The lights immediately went on, and someone asked in a very deep voice, "Who goes there?"

Mid step across the threshold, Elsie froze.

They all froze.

A dragon blocked their path, standing fifteen meters high with a wing span of at least thirty meters. Each claw, sharpened to stiletto dagger point, had to be nearly as long as Pooker. The dragon stank to the next galaxy as if he had been dunked in the worst of Sleztar's bogs and then been dunked again. The long whiskers around his snout seemed to be stuck together with some sort of gummy substance. He was either bronze in color or a drab brown. There were so many layers of dirt it was hard to tell. His scales looked like shields after a long and brutal war—gloss under mud.

"Who goes there?" the dragon bellowed again.

Dar tried to step backward, but there was nowhere else to go unless she wanted to knock down Elsie. They awkwardly bumped into each other before freezing again. Elsie could hear everyone, including herself, breathing hard, gasping really.

"It's a room avatar," Dar whispered, "but I'm not sure why he has come to life. Have all the avatars been reprogrammed to wake up on room entry?"

The room shook as the dragon lumbered forward, making it hard to remember that the creature wasn't real.

"There's nothing he can do to us," Dar said.

"You have got to be kidding me," Larry said. "It looks like he can do plenty. The frigging place is earthquake-ville when he walks."

"What about the people he can call?" Elsie asked. "They can do plenty to us."

"It's the middle of the night," Vlas said in a low voice. "There are only two adults on site. He's not going to sound the alarm unless he has to."

"The Panktars could be here waiting for us to return," Everest said.

Dar suddenly switched to signing. "We just need to stall him till we've got one of the time-travel devices and can make a run for it. So, you all keep him occupied until I get back."

It was clever of Dar to start signing so the dragon wouldn't hear. Unfortunately, Larry wouldn't understand either. The air felt hot and heavy as if a nearby fire was on slow burn. It was almost impossible to remember that this was just a room avatar. How were they supposed to stall a dragon?

Elsie sighed. Deng, they had to do this—for their parents. She took two steps forward so that all she could see, smell or hear was the zetta large monster, with its whirling eyes, its putrid odor, and its hot and heavy breath.

"Uh," she said, "my name's Elsie, and this is my brother, Everest. Our uncle, Director Lester-Hauffer, runs this academy."

"You are not currently on academy grounds," the dragon said in a voice as deep as an underground cave.

Elsie exchanged looks with Everest. Was this avatar a yocto-brain?

"Yes, we are," she said slowly, "This building is part of the academy. It's called the Lester-Hauffer History Center."

"I know what this building is called. My records show that you are not on academy grounds today. You left at 13:46 this afternoon in a stolen vehicle. I have no record of you returning."

"We didn't steal the HV," Elsie said quickly.

"We borrowed it," Everest added.

"The director was adamant that the vehicle had been stolen by you," the dragon said. "At 13:48 his hologram informed all the avatars. We've been ordered to contact him if there is a sighting, and I've done so."

Oh no, Elsie thought. How long did they have before someone in authority showed up?

The dragon cocked his head. "Why are you here?"

"School project," Larry said quickly. The rest of the B12s avidly nodded their heads.

His answer made no sense, but Elsie hoped the dragon was simple-minded enough to keep chatting despite the ridiculous response.

Dar had disappeared. Elsie was glad the girl was good at being stealthy. She hoped she would find the device at light speed.

"Why are you here?" Elsie asked the dragon. "I didn't know there was a dragon avatar in the History Center."

"The director was worried about unauthorized visitors. He created me as an added precaution." The dragon sniffed loudly, and a spurt of red flame sizzled out of his nose. "Your visit proves he was right to worry. Please sit on those benches until the proper authorities arrive." He waved a claw in the general direction of the seating area.

Elsie looked around nervously and saw Dar charging toward them, sweeping her arm to indicate that they should get moving.

"Uh, we're awfully sorry, Mr. Dragon, sir, but we really have to leave. We'd like to help you out by staying but—"

Dar gripped her arm and jerked her backward, dragging her toward the door.

Elsie wrenched free and swiveled around to look over her shoulder. "We really are sorry."

"You cannot leave," the dragon responded haughtily.

Dar whispered the request to exit, but the door refused to erase. The academy must have instituted a lock-down. "Deng," she muttered. She pulled something out of her pocket—the universal unlocker—and placed it on the door. After a slight snick the door erased. "Well, at least we know it works," she mumbled. The universal unlocker had fallen to the ground. She picked it up.

"What are you doing?" bellowed the dragon. "You cannot leave. Stop this instant."

He blew a red fire at them, and it actually felt hot and fiery, but not hot and fiery enough to burn them. Just enough to make them flinch and rocket even faster than they already were rocketing.

They all scrambled through the opening and ran at light speed, crunching and splattering the jewel-toned gravel as they went. Elsie pumped her arms and legs, keeping pace with her brother, right behind Dar.

Larry and Vlas brought up the rear.

Just as they reached the gate, lights blazed on across the grounds and within the buildings. A siren pierced the sky. Dar dived through the hole they had made and somersaulted, ending up on her feet. Elsie followed. After her, the rest tumbled through. They piled into the vehicle, and Vlas had them up and away in a pico-second.

"Please tell me you got the device," Elsie said.

"Yeah, I got it," Dar replied. "Now we just need to find a quiet place to touch down so we can take a little trip back in time."

CHAPTER 14
A Trip in Time

It was Larry who suggested they put a few cities between them and the academy. Despite being anxious for news about his parents, Everest agreed wholeheartedly. They had to avoid being caught. Vlas drove sedately by his standards, keeping within the speed limit, hovering at the correct height, only bouncing into a few vehicles, well below the legal number of HV bumps. He grinned, as always, as if he was having the time of his life. Everest tried not to hold that against him. After all, the boy didn't know their parents. This was just another adventure.

Normally, Everest liked hovering at night, with the soft globes of light on all sides and the bright stars above. Even an occasionally planned rainfall was zeller seen through the clear walls of a jellach vehicle. But now all he could think about was whether their parents were alive. Who cared about stinking lights?

Elsie sat with Pooker in her lap, her hands clenching the bobcat's scruff, her knuckles white. There was probably something Everest should be doing to try to comfort his sister, but, flasers, even the thought made his stomach heave.

Dar was deep in concentration, staring out at the nighttime sky. With her hat shoved down as far as it could go, Everest could only see half of her face. Mostly, he saw her tightly-pursed lips. A thick strand of golden hair had come loose and fell down in a long coil. She was so strange. Different from anyone else he had ever seen, except Shadara herself. Even her skin color was different. It was as if she was lit from within, not just golden, but exuding a warm, metallic hue. He quickly averted his eyes. Looking at her made him feel funny.

Larry was eating up the view and sort of muttering to himself as they zipped along the hover highway. Everest wasn't sure if he was singing or just muttering. He was another one who could have cared less about the fate of their parents. He was just in it for the adventure, the fun.

Everest had the sudden and zetta strong impulse to shove both Larry and Vlas out of the HV. Instead, he forced himself to look out into the night and count hover vehicles in the sky. He tried to think more positively. After all, the other B12s were risking their lives for people they had never met. It wasn't fair for him to hold it against them that they were having fun along the way. It was just their nature to be thrilled by danger.

"Dar," Vlas said, "we're in Palo Alto. Do you think it's safe?"

"Yeah, let's find someplace quiet. Too bad it's not raining tonight. More people would be inside."

"I'm going to find an office building of some sort. I think there are still a few in the area. Parking lots should be pretty quiet this time of night."

"If this is Palo Alto," Larry said, "aren't there offices all over?"

"Nah, most people work from home nowadays. Only research institutions still have central offices. But I think there are a few near Page Mill Hill. If I'm really lucky, I'll find a vacant one."

Vlas negotiated the HV through traffic till he found exactly what he was looking for: a vacant gray building with an empty parking lot. A brightly-lit sign advertised its availability for lease or purchase. He gently glided the HV down and landed it with the smallest of jolts in a dark corner. The entire lot was a sea of street moss with florescent pink lines delineating parking slots for vehicles.

"Okay, Vlas," Dar said, "let's switch places." She held a small black device in her hand. She and Vlas clambered over and on top of the rest of the B12s until they had swapped seats, causing groans and shouts in the process. Dar attached the black device to the dashboard then programmed in a series of numbers.

Feeling like a total suzo-shrimp, Everest stared intently, unable to stop watching the girl, despite the fact that there was really nothing interesting to see. "When are we going back to?" he finally asked.

She bit her lip. "Luca said that two days ago Adriatic Mink was on-planet, in-residence. We'll try three days ago and see if we can catch him at home. Not in the evening. He's usually at some social function." She grimaced. "Let's try morning. He's typically an early riser."

"Plan it for breakfast time," Larry said. "If I don't get more food soon, I'm liable to use my zunner on someone. And it may not be on a bad guy."

"You ate plenty not even an hour ago," Dar responded as she worked on the device without pause. "I can give you a pill to curb your appetite."

"No thank you!" Larry responded.

After another minute, she was ready. No longer plugging in numbers, she held out a little bottle of purple pills. "Vlas, pass out motion sickness pills."

Vlas, Elsie and Everest were quick to swallow. Larry, on the other hand, stared hard at the pill as if it were a dangerous alien. "Hey guys, I seen what funny-colored pills do to people, and you keep shoving them at me. I'll pass." He made to hand the pill back to Dar.

"This is one pill you'll regret not taking," Dar responded. "But it's your call."

"My ma died taking too many purple pills."

Everest had a hard time understanding how Larry's mother could die of too many pills. It was regulated, wasn't it? Some of his confusion must have shown on his face.

"She was a drug addict," Larry said slowly, as if he spoke to someone who had trouble hearing. "She overdosed."

"A drug addict?" Everest asked, still puzzled.

Dar swung around and glared meaningfully at Everest as if willing him to shut down. "I'm sorry Larry, that's rough, but this isn't one of those kinds of pills. It's just supposed to help you avoid feeling sick from the time-travel. If you'd rather we can stun you like last time."

90

With a grimace, Larry took the purple pill.

"Alright, B12s, let's blast off," Dar said.

Everest didn't think he'd ever get used to the spinning and mounting pressure of time travel. He hated the way his cheeks rippled and his teeth chattered. However, this time, the motion stopped before he could actually feel as if he was about to explode. Maybe the purple pill *had* been unnecessary. They had only gone back a couple of days.

"Cool," Larry said, shaking his head as if to clear it.

"Nah, that was disappointing," Vlas said. "You should see what it feels like to go back one hundred years. Now that's a ride."

"Did it work?" asked Elsie.

Dar skewered her with a look, but didn't answer.

Jeez, Everest thought. Didn't Elsie know by now that you didn't question Dar's actions? Not unless you wanted your keister kicked to Xlexuri. Since it was the same tunnel where they had originally found the hover vehicle, it was a safe bet they were back in Adriatic Mink's lair in the anticipated time.

Dar didn't seem to be in any hurry to get out of the HV. Instead she stared at the tunnel walls where pico-brownies industriously scrubbed.

"Uh, Dar," he said, "shouldn't we be trying to find Mink?"

"That won't be necessary," she said, never taking her eyes off the walls. "He'll have been alerted by now. I'm just trying to figure out if there's a way we can ensure that not too many people know about our visit. I hope he's already thought about that."

"You make him sound like a mind reader," Elsie said.

"We're talking about Adriatic Mink," Vlas said. "He's more than just a mind reader."

"Yeah, he's a frigging superhero," said Larry.

"Dar and friends," SHADARA, the HV, said, "Mr. Mink requests the pleasure of your company in the grotto."

Dar sighed as she exited the jellach vehicle, motioning to the rest of the B12s to follow. "Come on; let's hope he's in a good mood."

Everest followed Elsie and Pooker. Larry and Vlas took up the rear. Dar, of course, led. When they reached the grotto, they found the stone door ajar. They filed in one by one.

Inside the cold, damp room, Adriatic Mink lounged elegantly on the bench nearest the Melista-like statue. He wore perfectly tailored black: a long Vlatex jacket, simple slacks, and a Vlatex shirt that boasted sparkly diamond buttons. While his skin was darker than Everest's, his hair was pure white. He had extraordinary blue eyes that missed nothing. Everest was grateful those eyes focused on Dar.

"Hello, my dear," he said. "To what do I owe this unexpected but delightful visit?" His voice was low, silky, and a little scary. He wore a pleasant but firm smile.

Dar straightened and her expression was just a little scary too. "We need your help."

Adriatic Mink drummed the fingers of his left hand on his left knee. "Do you, indeed?" He rose slowly, unfolding his tall, lean body to its full, intimidating height. "You must be in need of quite a lot of help in order to risk time travel to obtain it."

CHAPTER 15
A Chat with Adriatic Mink

Mink's words startled Elsie, but then again, she wasn't all that surprised that Mink knew about their time travel. Did anything get past him? Dar didn't react to Mink's statement, but Elsie wondered if she was also surprised that the man knew they had actually traveled backward in time.

"We'd like to tell you everything," Dar said, "but we need reassurance that what we tell you will be for your ears alone."

Mink motioned around him. "These walls do not have ears. You are safe to confide in me here."

"There were surveillance pico-brownies in the tunnel," Dar said.

Mink raised an eyebrow to extraordinary heights. "Are you seriously questioning my understanding of the inner workings of my compound?"

Dar sighed. "No, of course not."

"Thank the Light," he said. "That would be most distressing." He crossed his arms. "Now, what is going on?" His voice went from silk to stone in a heartbeat.

"Who else knows we are here?" asked Dar.

"Please, I'm nothing if not discrete. At this moment, I'm the only one aware of this delightful, if mysterious, visit."

Elsie shivered. The room was freezing, but Adriatic Mink also made her nervous. The combination gave her the shakes. She wished she could pick up Pooker and hold her for warmth and comfort.

Everest stepped forward. "Sir, is there another room where we could hold this discussion? This one is zetta cold."

Elsie looked at Everest in surprise. It wasn't like him to speak up.

"Hmm." Adriatic Mink stared.

After a moment, Everest broke eye contact and looked down at his skyboots. "I'm sorry if my request was inappropriate," he managed to mumble. "We are in desperate need, and we would be very grateful for your help."

Dar made a noise in the back of her throat. "Flasers, Mink, shut down the intimidation tactics. You know perfectly well you're dying to hear what's going on. Move us to a more comfortable room so we can get on with it."

Only Dar would have the guts to speak like that to Adriatic Mink.

After a tense moment, he chuckled. "As usual, Dar, you are impossible to intimidate." He rose fluidly and motioned to them. "Follow me."

He led them out of the grotto and down a series of elegant corridors until they arrived at a wooden door, not unlike the two they had seen on their last visit. When he placed his hand on the door, it disintegrated at his touch, as did the two gray metal ones that came next.

Inside, they found a sitting room where all of the furniture was made of real, not simulated, dark wood. The upholstery was a rich material woven in many shades of brown and gold with a fleck of purple. Comfortable, color-coordinated pillows dotted the couches and loveseats. The furniture was an interesting combination of both ancient and modern design. Lining the walls, floor to ceiling, were wooden cases of ancient paper books.

Mesmerized by the packed bookcases, Vlas let out a long, low whistle. "Zeller!"

Elsie had never seen so many antique paper books in one place before. Her parents were proud owners of two paper books that they treated as prized possessions. And here there had to be thousands.

Mink sat in a rich dark brown, high-backed chair that reminded Elsie of a throne from an ancient fairytale. He motioned the B12s to the other couches and chairs and they quickly made themselves comfortable. Elsie dropped to a loveseat with Pooker at her feet. The chair immediately contoured itself to her body and began a gentle massage, but she was too nervous to relax.

Mink leaned back and raised an eyebrow. "I do hope this suits you? Warm enough? Comfortable enough?"

"Yes, sir," Everest said.

Elsie was pretty sure her vocal chords weren't working properly. Mink had to know that this room was attuned to each one of them and had immediately accommodated their body temperature needs.

"Then would someone please fill me in on why you've gifted me with the pleasure of your company?"

Dar popped up from where she had momentarily sat on a brown and gold couch. She stood, as if at attention, with her hands clasped behind her back. Taking a deep breath, she began to recount their adventures. Mink listened attentively, inserting a question or two along the way. At the end of Dar's explanation, Mink studied Elsie and Everest.

"May I see the pendant you still have in your possession?"

Larry jumped to his feet, and Elsie did too, tripping over Pooker in her haste. She grabbed Larry by the arm. What if they couldn't trust Adriatic Mink either? What did they really know about him? Dar trusted him, and she didn't trust most adults, but still, they had no proof that he was any better than anyone else. For all they knew, he could have smuggled in these paper books. He could be just as bad a criminal as Instructor Gerard...as Dr. Jensa.

Mink tilted his head, a smile hinting. "You're not sure you can trust me."

Deng, she wished he wouldn't read her mind. He was as bad as Luca. She shrugged one shoulder.

"I don't blame you for wondering," he added, "but as far as I can tell, you've got no one else to turn to."

"We've got each other," Dar said. "Elsie, if you don't want to show Mink the pendant, you don't have to. But for what it's worth, I wouldn't have brought you here if I hadn't thought he could be trusted."

Elsie contemplated Dar then Mink then Larry. She nodded her head slowly. "This is crazy. In one month I've gone from trusting pretty much everyone, to trusting almost no one." She turned back to Larry and motioned him to join her. "Show him the pendant."

Mink stood up to study the item that Larry held out. "Hmm. 1010511." He took the pendant and turned it over, inspecting the engravings and rubbing the warmth. After staring at it for another minute, he handed it back to Larry before turning to Elsie and Everest. "I've heard rumors that may shine light on your parents' research and possibly even their disappearance."

Moving to stand next to Elsie and Larry, Dar crossed her arms, and raised her eyebrows. "And these rumors would be?"

"A few months back I heard that there may have been a breakthrough in femto-technology."

"Say, what?" Larry asked.

"Femto-technology is on the scale of femtometers—smaller than picos, infinitely smaller than nanos."

"Like, microscopic stuff?" Larry asked.

"You could say that," Adriatic Mink's lips twisted wryly, "only inconceivably smaller. A source told me that scientists were about to beta test femto-boosters designed to enable humans, any humanoid actually, to survive under the harshest of conditions. To be warm in freezing temperatures, to be cool when it's burning hot, to boost their strength, sight, hearing, who knows what else? I think it's likely that your parents were involved in the recent femto developments. Perhaps this pendant holds the key to that research."

"Zeller," breathed Vlas again.

"Sweet," Larry said, his eyes narrowing as he studied the pendant in his hands. "One boost and you're Superman? Where do I sign up?"

"Exactly," Mink said. "One can only imagine how this technology could be abused in the wrong hands."

"Okay, that's one possibility," Dar said. "Any others?"

Adriatic Mink raised his eyebrows. "Sorry, that's the only theory I have at the moment."

"Do you really think my parents are involved in this femto-booster project?" Elsie asked.

"I think it is likely."

"Have they been murdered for their research?"

"I think not." Mink's expression was zetta serious. "It's more likely that someone has abducted them. If they were murdered then their research would be jeopardized. Your parents have brilliant reputations. You must keep your hopes up."

"I knew it!" Larry exclaimed.

"We're actually supposed to be hoping they've been kidnapped?" Elsie asked in a high-pitched voice, ignoring Larry's outburst. "Could the world be any more alien?"

Mink's eyes softened though he remained serious. "Wishing for an abduction does seem pretty alien."

"Sir," said Everest, "What should we do now?"

Adriatic Mink stood up. "I have a new device that might help."

"Zeller," said Vlas. "What is it?" His eyes were bright. Gadgets were near and dear to his heart.

"An aura-positioning unit."

"An APU?" Dar asked. "That's handy."

"What's an aura-positioning unit?" Elsie asked.

"We can pinpoint the location of your parents' auras. At least, we can do so if they've returned to Earth."

"What if they're dead?" she asked hesitantly.

Mink pursed his lips, his expression grave. "The APU needs an active aura to pinpoint a location." He reached into an inner pocket and pulled out a slim device that looked a lot like a jellach journal. He handed it to Dar who contemplated it a few minutes then slipped it into her Vlatex II backpack.

"Uh, Dar, don't you need to find out how to use it?" Everest asked.

Dar rolled her eyes. "I think I can figure it out."

"It's a simple device," Mink said. "Self-explanatory."

Elsie grimaced at her brother. The fate of their parents' lives could very well rest on Dar being able to use this tool, and she didn't want instructions on how to make it work? What was the matter with these people? Everest was acting zetta serious. She wished they could talk privately, so she could get a fix on his thoughts.

"What else can you do for us?" Dar asked Adriatic Mink.

"It sounds as if Luca will be extremely helpful when you show up at my compound in a couple of days. I'm rather surprised at how accommodating he was. I don't believe I've ever given him instructions where you are concerned. Why should I with you safely tucked away at the academy? Just to be safe, I'll tell him that if Dar ever arrives at the estate, she should be given access to anything and everything in my domain—that my home is her home." He stood up with purpose. "In addition, I can offer VC."

"Virtual currency." Larry rubbed his hands together. "You are the man."

"That would be helpful," Dar said stiffly. "We'll pay you back as soon as we can."

Larry and Vlas exchanged grins. Elsie frowned at them sternly. She could almost hear what they were thinking, and it had nothing to do with returning the money.

Mink dipped his head. "As you wish. I'll transfer some to your account, Larry's, and Vlas's. I don't think the Baskers should be drawing attention to themselves. However, just in case, I'll transfer some there too. If you get separated, you won't be completely without resources."

Elsie rose as well. "Thank you, sir. We greatly appreciate your kindness."

"I am not generally considered a kind man," he said as he rose.

She crossed the distance that separated them and touched his hand. "Then generally people are foolish."

Her warmth seemed to surprise him, and for a second she thought he would back away, but he stayed still. After a long moment of silence, he moved his hand slightly so that they no longer touched. He clapped briskly. "Well, B12s, it is time for you to leave. I'm not sure that I can keep your presence secret much longer. Luca typically meets with me at this hour."

"Can't we get some food before we go?" Larry asked, his face scrunched up into a cross between a frown and a pout.

Mink chuckled. "Hungry, are we?"

"Luca gave us food already," Dar said with a shrug. "But Larry, here, seems to have replaced his stomach with a bottomless pit."

"Ha!" Larry responded.

Vlas smirked.

Mink crossed the room, looking impossibly elegant. He touched a spot on the wall, and it erased to reveal a storage unit behind, filled with a variety of snacks. He waved at the closet, beckoning the kids. "Grab as much as you like. Stuff your backpacks full."

Larry whistled. "Wicked zeller." He managed to elbow his way to the front. "Thanks, Mr. Mink," he said as he shoved protein bars, Blackholes, dried fruits, nuts and other snacks into his bag. "I could really use a cheeseburger right now, but I'm still grateful that I don't have to do anything unnatural to get rid of these hunger pains."

"You're welcome," Mink said with a dip of his head. "You know the way back to the HV, correct?"

"Yeah," Vlas said, "I've got it."

"I would suggest some light speed," Mink added.

Dar slid a handful of protein bars into her bag before nodding her head, "Yes, sir. Come on, B12s, time to jam."

Elsie grabbed another container of nuts and one of protein chips. She hoped she had enough food in her bag to feed Pooker too. Sighing, she quickly followed Dar. There was no safe haven for them anymore. As much as she would like their adventure to be over, it was barely begun.

Mink cleared his throat. "Dar, a moment, please."

The girl paused and looked over her shoulder, a combination of irritation and confusion on her face. "What?"

"This will only take a second. The rest of you make all due speed for the hover vehicle. I assure you, Dar will be right behind you."

With an irritated shrug, Dar crossed back over to Mink.

What was that all about? Elsie wondered as she left the room.

CHAPTER 16
An Unforeseen Betrayal

Dar caught up to them just as they arrived at the hover vehicle. Everest thought she looked even more rigid than usual—as if she were made out of a piece of marblon.

"What did Mink want?" Elsie asked, as usual unable to bite her tongue.

Dar looked as if she would have liked to bite it for her. "Nothing," she said furiously. "He wanted nothing."

Jeez, Everest thought. Even for Dar her reaction was extreme. Had Mink yelled at her? Was she in trouble for bringing them here? Whatever Mink had said had really made Dar go supernova.

Elsie still couldn't keep her mouth shut. "If Mink is mad at you because of us—"

"Shut down, ute-girl, the world doesn't revolve around you." Dar stumped over to the jellach vehicle, erased the door and slammed into the driver's seat. "Jeez, are you all moving in slo-mo? What a bunch of yocto-brained suzo-shrimp." She growled her words, not at any one of them, but at all of them.

Everest quickly jumped into the back of the HV and the others piled in after him. Elsie had to drag her bobcat back into the vehicle. In the past, they'd been very careful never to confine Pooker in tight places for long spaces of time, and now the cat was stuck twenty-four-seven in one tiny compartment after another. The cat growled, circled twice and settled tensely, her fur bristling on end.

After Dar fiddled with the time-travel gadget, she shoved her hat lower on her head and took a deep breath. "Everyone ready?"

"Yeah," Everest mumbled with the rest of the kids.

"Okay, back to the present."

Everest swallowed as he dived into the spinning, pressure-filled world of time travel. But just as quickly, he exploded back into normalcy, though it took a few seconds for his teeth to stop chattering.

They were back in the large, empty parking lot of street moss and iridescent pink lines. The evening was still young, the sky still chock-full of luminous hover vehicles.

"We need to plan our next move," Dar said.

"We've got to figure out how to get those femto-boosters out of Elsie's necklace," Larry said, studying it.

It seemed to Everest that Larry hadn't stopped studying the pendant since Adriatic Mink had speculated about what was inside. The way Larry pushed and prodded it caused Everest unease even though it was sturdily made. He didn't say anything, though. After all, he was the loser who had given his pendant to the enemy. What right did he have to complain about Larry's behavior?

"We need to find our parents, first," he said curtly, though he desperately wanted to figure out the secret of the pendant too. How did it work? Could they find a way to open it and use whatever was inside?

"Can we try the APU now?" Elsie asked. "Please."

"Soon," Dar said. "But first, we need a safe base where we can plan. Any ideas?"

"Mink's place seems awfully safe in comparison to all of our other choices." Elsie said in a quiet voice.

"That is no longer an option." Dar said firmly.

Everest wished he could have been a pico-brownie on the wall during that last conversation between Dar and Mink. What in galaxies had happened? Whatever it was had really caused Dar to go off like a rocket.

Navigating around that black hole, Everest suggested, "What about our home?"

"They'll have it monitored twenty-four-seven."

Larry straightened up, momentarily swinging his focus away from the pendant. "What about this place?"

Dar swiveled around, raising one eyebrow.

"It's vacant, right?" Larry continued. "And it's big. Even if a cleaning service shows up, we should be able to make ourselves scarce."

"Yeah, that could work," she said. "Good idea."

Everest figured he should be used to Dar preferring Larry's ideas to his, but somehow it still irritated him. Which was totally alien since Larry's idea was better.

Vlas rubbed his hands together. "Another building to break into. This is my lucky day." He chuckled.

Flasers, their parents might be dead—at best they were kidnapped—and Vlas thought it was his lucky day?

Everest took a deep breath and forced himself to stay shut down. Elsie's hands clenched and she worried her lower lip. He hoped she would keep her aura on too. The clones weren't trying to make them feel bad. There just was no way in this millennium that they could comprehend what family meant.

"Okay," Dar said, "let's do this."

"Cool," Larry said, the first to scramble out of the car and into the brisk night air.

Contemplating the low gray building, Everest slowly followed. So far, breaking into places hadn't worked in their favor, but they needed to hole up somewhere, and at least this site was vacant.

The sooner they got inside, the better. He was as anxious as Elsie to try the APU. Maybe a miracle would happen and they'd find out their parents were alive.

As a group, they walked silently across the street moss parking lot, Pooker padding along at Elsie's side. Then the bobcat came to a complete stop, bristling and making an eerie noise in the back of her throat. Everest tried to make out what was bothering Pooker, but his nighteyes had dissipated during the travel back in time. His eyes wouldn't adjust to the dark.

He grabbed Elsie's arm. She was searching just as intently. All he could make out in front of them was the plain gray building with its over-large, flashing neon vacancy sign. While the bright neon illuminated the area a little bit, it also made it harder for him to adjust his eyes to the shadows.

Noises were amplified. Every funny snap had them swiveling around. They formed a tight circle of back-to-back bodies and faced outward, all of them anxiously straining to determine why Pooker was so spooked.

"Stay calm," Dar whispered. "Weapons ready."

Everest eased his zunner out of the backpack he carried, as did the rest of the B12s.

"Those won't be necessary," a voice said.

Everest's stomach flipped in recognition. When Elsie sucked in her breath, he knew that she'd recognized the speaker as well.

"Lester-Hauffer," Dar spit out.

Their uncle.

"My dear, Shadara, I'm exceedingly grateful that you are safe and sound." Director Lester-Hauffer emerged from behind the large sign. As he neared, he made a sweeping gesture. "I've been worried sick about all of you." He shook his head, tsking with his tongue. "Elsinor, Everest, running away like that. Can you imagine my concern? I am your guardian while your parents are off-world. It is my sacred trust to keep you safe."

He had gone through a lot to track them down. Everest jolted when Elsie clutched his arm. Jeez, she looked terrified. Surely there was no reason to be afraid? The man was their uncle, after all. But it was a little creepy that he had found them. How had he managed that?

Everest cleared his throat. "Uncle Fredrick, we apologize for worrying you." It felt strange to use the term 'uncle.' He'd gotten used to thinking of him as Director Lester-Hauffer. Using "uncle" would irritate the clones, but he thought he should try to be friendly.

The director had continued to approach and was now within a few feet, so close that Everest could smell his distinctive odor of rotting vegetables. Even without his nighteyes, he could see deep lines etching the man's normally smooth face. Lines of worry? Concern?

"Why are you still pointing a flaser at me?" Lester-Hauffer asked, shock harshening his features. "What would your parents think?"

Everest was almost surprised to see the zunner in his hand. Jeez, he was only twelve years old, not someone who should be carrying around a dangerous weapon. His parents would freak if they knew the risks he and Elsie had been taking. Of course they wouldn't be taking these risks if their parents' hadn't disappeared.

"I'm sorry, sir," he tried again.

He was on the verge of telling him that it wasn't a flaser, only a zunner, when the director sternly stretched out his hand, a look of acute distaste on his face. "Give that to me now."

Everest's hand lifted of its own volition to comply with his uncle's demand.

"How did you find us?" Elsie asked their uncle.

Yeah, Everest thought, *that had been his question.* He paused, waiting for his uncle's answer.

The man harrumphed. "Our time-travel equipment is quite expensive. As part of our security measures, we have tracking engaged so that we know if someone uses it. The instructor in charge is immediately alerted in that event. We tracked you to this deserted parking lot."

That made sense.

"But—" Elsie started then stopped just as suddenly. She looked at Everest, and even in the dark, he could see that her expression was intent as if she wanted him to read her thoughts.

"What?" he whispered.

She pinched his thumb hard.

"Ow." He wrenched his hand back.

Then he remembered something that Elsie must have been hoping he would remember. He looked up sharply.

Uncle Fredrick had his arms crossed, his lips tight.

"That must be awfully expensive," Everest said. "Have you always taken such measures?"

"Of course. Security is of primary importance."

Liar, Everest thought. The academy hadn't had this level of security a month ago when they had gone back in time to find Elsie's pendant and had returned with Larry in tow. Otherwise, their uncle would have caught them then. Why was he lying? They were so conditioned to think everything was a conspiracy.

Maybe he just wasn't telling them it was new security because he wanted his academy to seem perfect. Who knew what motivated him? Did it have to be dark and dangerous?

"Everest, I'm trying to be reasonable, but you and Elsie need to hand over those lethal devices immediately. The rest of you, as well. I'm horrified that you have these flasers. You are breaking any number of laws. I realize that the news about your parents was devastating, and I will take that into consideration when determining any disciplinarian action, but you must give me your flasers, now. You could kill someone." He spread his arms. "Look at me—unarmed and acting in good faith. Show some good faith in return."

Everest's feeling of horror over the zunner he held intensified. It might not be the flaser his uncle thought it was, but it was still zetta dangerous. His arm fell to his side, and his mouth opened to explain what he held and why. Then Dar stepped out of the circle. She raised her arm and aimed her zunner directly at the director's chest.

"Everest is not going to give you his weapon and neither are we," she said.

"Dar!" Elsie cried.

"You can't trust him, Elsie. He's one of the bad guys."

Everest didn't know what to do or who to believe. In Dar's mind all utes were bad guys. Then again, Dar would be the most severely punished if they dropped their weapons and returned to the academy. Didn't they owe her for all she had already done for them?

But she was letting the director believe they held flasers—the deadliest of weapons. Wouldn't that make things so much worse? They'd be in trouble for the next millennium.

"We're going to leave, now," Dar told the director. "As long as you don't try to follow us, we'll let you be. But you must step back slowly—back at least twenty paces." Dar motioned violently with her zunner.

Their uncle sniffed and it sounded amazingly loud in the dark. "I knew you would be trouble. You have been a thorn in my side since the day you were cloned."

105

"You must be zetta relieved to be getting rid of me," she said sweetly.

"Believe me, I'll be more than relieved when I get rid of you," he said in a tone that made Everest think he had something more permanent in mind.

"Back up, director," Dar said sharply. "Back up, now."

He took three slow steps backward. "Everest, Elsie, you need to seriously consider where your loyalties lie. Dar will lead you down a path from which there is no recovery—a world where you will be outlaws, with cyborg officers of law nipping at your heels. Look at you with your killing weapons. By the Light, you are twelve-year-olds—my wards. Do you truly want to destroy your lives? What would your parents say?"

"Our parents are gone," Elsie said, tears clogging her throat so that Everest almost didn't recognize her voice.

"And this is how you wish to honor their memories? With rebellion, violence, and lawbreaking? You should be ashamed of yourselves," he hissed. "Your parents would be heartbroken."

Elsie was openly crying now, sobbing and clenching her stomach with her arms. Her zunner slipped from her fingers to the ground.

Everest didn't know what to think. Their parents would be shocked by their exploits, but what choice did they have? They were trying to protect their parents' research, and even now still hoping to save their parents' lives.

"Elsie, shut the water works down," Everest said harshly as he bent and snatched up her zunner. "I'm sorry, Uncle. Until we're sure that our parents can't be saved, we have to keep trying to find them. If that means becoming outlaws, then so be it."

"Save them? Don't be ridiculous. What can you children possibly do to save your parents?" Their uncle's face contorted in fury. "I had hoped I would find reason from my sister's offspring; instead, I find madness. This is behavior I would expect from Shadara and her reject gang." He paused, his breathing harsh. Slowly he regained his composure. He straightened a bit.

"But, Shadara, you seem to be missing a few members of your gang." He laughed now. "Oh, wait, I know why. You are missing them because *I* have them. Dr. Jensa? Would you be so kind as to request that your associates bring out Shadara's little buddies?"

Two gigantic, green monsters pounded out from behind the large sign, their heavy steps flattening the moss. Under each of their left arms were bundles. Behind them, Dr. Jensa followed, holding a weapon in his hand, most likely a flaser. As they neared, Everest recognized those bundles as Lelita and Borneo. Blood rushed from his face, making him lightheaded.

"Perhaps, Shadara, you and your compatriots can be persuaded to be more reasonable?"

CHAPTER 17

The Stakes are Raised

Elsie's heart stopped—just for a second, but it was a second she would never forget. Their uncle was holding Lelita and Borneo hostage? He was in league with Dr. Jensa? And the Panktars? How could this be true? She looked to her brother for reassurance, but it was as if he'd been turned into a marblon statue, only now he held two zunners—one in each hand. One was aimed at their uncle and the other at the Panktars and Dr. Jensa.

Clearly, his thinking mirrored Elsie's worst nightmare.

How had their world spun so far off its axis?

"I'm sure you realize," the director said, "that Panktars are quite capable of squeezing the life out of these pitifully small clone rejects."

Dar made a noise that mimicked a bobcat's snarl. "Don't—call—them—that."

"You are in no position to make demands," he responded, brushing off an invisible piece of lint. "You are only in a position to accept defeat. Whether you do so with grace or not is hardly significant."

"Uncle Fredrick," Elsie said, purposefully using the family name instead of director, hoping to appeal to any tenderness he might have for his family. "Dr. Jensa and his friends are responsible for our parents' disappearance—your own sister's disappearance. You must believe us; we have proof. We beg you to help us—to help your sister."

He shook his head, a small smile playing at his lips. "Oh my poor, delusional niece. You are quite wrong. I pity you, I really do."

"No, sir," Everest responded urgently. "They are criminals. Earlier today we visited Mom and Dad's research compound and discovered that their associate, Dr. Yee, had been murdered. Someone was masquerading as Dr. Yee. We can only imagine what has happened to our parents. You must believe us. You must!" His voice had risen with passion.

Another form stepped out from behind the vacancy sign. With disbelief and horror, Elsie watched the man approach. It was none other than the fake Dr. Yee. He also held a flaser in his hand.

"When you left my company so abruptly, I did suspect you had figured out I was an imposter. I did not, however, anticipate that you had become aware of the real Dr. Yee's current state—or lack thereof." The fake Dr. Yee chuckled as if he'd made a witty joke.

Elsie lunged, but Everest managed to unfreeze enough to grab her. She sagged against her brother. "How dare you?" she screamed at the imposter. "You killed him—an innocent, brilliant man. You killed him, and now you are making jokes about it?"

"Elsie," Dar said, "shut down."

Elsie struggled out of Everest's arms and turned on Dar. "You shut down! Dr. Yee was a friend of our parents. Now he's dead." She gasped for breath then rounded on Lester-Hauffer. "You can't possibly be working with these monsters."

Dar remained focused on the group of villains, her zunner hand steady. Everest trained his zunners on them as well. As did Vlas and Larry. Elsie wiped at the tears that flowed down her face. It was embarrassing to be the only person unable to control herself, but how was she supposed to be emotionless when confronted with so much evil?

Director Lester-Hauffer cleared his throat. "As I was trying to explain, Elsinor, you and Everest are under the mistaken impression that I have some sort of affection for my half-sister; perhaps you even believe that I hold some affection for you. Please, let me disabuse you of this notion. My only motive in allowing you to stay at my academy was because it offered me the opportunity to keep a close eye on you. I was able to intercept your messages from your parents and to ascertain what you were hiding—the pendants that your parents had given you. You cannot appeal to my finer instincts my dear, because I have none."

Nothing the director could have revealed would have shocked Elsie more. All this time they had been living at his academy, believing that at the very least, he saw it as his duty to protect and take care of them. But that was a lie. He was a villain. Even worse than Mr. Kisses. At least Mr. Kisses hadn't betrayed family.

"You Vlemutz," she said with every gram of hatred she could muster.

The director dipped his head. "Your histrionics are wasting time, my dear." His smile was a lightning bolt of cruelty. He clapped his hands. "Now, what are we to do about the little clones currently being comforted by our Panktar friends? Shall we have the Panktars give them one final hug?"

"There's no reason to bother with them," Dar said. "They have nothing to do with all of this. They haven't even been with us."

"Borneo, here, was caught with an illegal holoputer," Lester-Hauffer said. "Besides, I've been observing you, Shadara, and I know your sad little secret."

She sniffed. "I don't have sad little secrets."

"As a matter of fact, you do," he responded with a grin. "And your secret is a doozy. Shall I tell you?"

"I couldn't care less one way or another." Her chin jutted into the air.

"You, Shadara, feel tenderness. For those snotty toddlers and babies you take care of each evening, and for a handful of snotty twelve-year-old clones." He tsked. "You can't help it. And worse, once your affection is given, it appears to be impossible for you to take it back. In addition, you are very protective of your loved ones. You care about Lelita and Borneo, and I'm quite sure you'll do anything to keep them from being squeezed to death by my fine green associates."

Not by a blink of an eye did Dar react to Lester-Hauffer's words, but Elsie could tell there was something inside her that had coiled itself into a tight ball. Thank the Light, she wasn't the one who had revealed so much about Dar. Whether Lester-Hauffer was right or not really didn't matter. All that mattered was that the girl would get even someday, whether now or twenty years from now. Lester-Hauffer was history. And Elsie was glad. He was a horrible man. Much worse than any vlem.

Of course, for Dar to get even, she still had to be alive, and the odds were not looking good on that front.

Lester-Hauffer briskly clapped his hands again. "To business. You'll give us the second pendant; we'll give you Lelita and Borneo. Easy as a trip to the moon."

"How can we trust that you'll give us our friends in exchange for the pendant?" asked Everest. "And that you won't try to kill us afterward?"

"And what about our parents?" Elsie asked. "Where are they?"

"I'm afraid you are in no position to negotiate with us. As you see," he waved at the Panktars and the struggling bundles they held. "We hold all the clones." He chuckled. "Or perhaps I should say the clones are stacked in our favor."

The fake Dr. Yee joined the laughter.

"You are an evil man," Elsie said.

"If you say so." Lester-Hauffer smiled.

"What is it with the clone academy? First, Mr. Kisses, now you. Is anyone who works there actually good?"

"Ah, yes, Mr. Kisses—Instructor Gerard. He showed much promise as my assistant, but in the end, he failed to deliver."

It was as if Elsie was shot with sunergy. "*You* are Mr. Snickers!"

Lester-Hauffer's mouth twisted. "Mr. Snickers, indeed. You may call me Captain Reeses."

Elsie fought hard to regain her composure. If her uncle's code-name was Captain Reeses then Mr. Snickers was still at large. Could Dr. Jensa be Mr. Snickers? Or the fake Dr. Yee? Not that it mattered. The only thing that mattered was that their uncle was still lying. He had no intention of letting them go free. No way, no how. He'd revealed way too much about himself and his criminal activities. Did everyone else understand that they were already as dead as a black hole?

"Is he Mr. Snickers?" she pointed to the fake Dr. Yee, stalling for time, trying to think of a way to save them all.

"No, he is not Mr. Snickers," Lester-Hauffer said. "Now stop wasting time. The pendant, please."

Elsie felt like the most ridiculous suzo-shrimp for having dropped her weapon. What a yocto-brain! She had to do something. The others still had their zunners aimed at the vlems, but both Dr. Jensa and the fake Dr. Yee held flasers. And it would only take a heartbeat for the Panktars to crush Borneo and Lelita. She did have foggers and smellers in her pockets. Also, Pooker stood next to her, her fur still bristling. Elsie sensed that the bobcat's focus was Lester-Hauffer, and as far as she could tell, the vlem didn't have a weapon of his own.

Somehow they had to orchestrate an attack. Would the Panktars immediately try to kill Lelita and Borneo or would they wait till they had no other options? Lelita and Borneo had to be terrified. And it was all her fault. If she hadn't asked Dar for help, Lelita and Borneo wouldn't be hostages now.

She caught Dar's eye and stared, trying through sheer will to convey her intent. They had to do something. None of them would survive if they let Lester-Hauffer and his associates take the lead.

She took one step forward so that she was directly in front of the rest of the B12s. "Okay, I'll give you the pendant." She wasn't quite sure what she would do next since she didn't actually have the denged necklace.

She looked back at Larry and said distinctly, "It's the only way. We have to save Lelita and Borneo. That's all that matters." Then she mouthed, "Foggers…smellers." She hoped they saw her lips move despite the dark.

She pivoted back to Lester-Hauffer. "It's in my pocket." Slowly she reached inside, her hand closing around a fogger. She turned back one more time to her friends. "I'm sorry, but this is the only way." She mouthed: one, two—and on the three she whipped back to the villains.

With one swift move, she yanked out the fogger and threw it at her uncle. Then she dived into a somersault to give room for the rest of the B12s to attack.

CHAPTER 18
The Pendant's Powerful Secret

Zunners flashed, and everyone dove helter-skelter as the Panktars dropped their bundles and charged. Director Lester-Hauffer yelled for the Panktars not to lose their hostages, but it was already too late. Since the foggers turned the world into a thick white haze, Everest wasn't sure exactly who he was aiming his zunner at, but judging from the massive thud, it appeared that at least one Panktar was down. Since the Panktar had not disintegrated into a pool of ash, the director was bound to figure out that they weren't using flasers.

How was it possible that they had missed the director? He'd been at point-blank range, and Everest had aimed at him. He must have dived out of the way when the fogger exploded.

Larry yelled, "Dar, your object cloner, now!"

She hesitated for a nano-second before tossing it. Larry grabbed it just as he was enveloped by fog. What in the galaxies was he doing? He should be running away from the bad guys. Everest thought he heard Larry's voice, but he couldn't make out the words.

Lelita screamed for them, but he couldn't find her in the dense fog. A monstrous form barreled at him, and he shot his zunner over and over again. Sure enough, it was a Panktar running straight for him. Everest kept his zunner shooting. Just as they were about to collide, the green monster wavered then toppled. He smashed into Everest and took him down. Everest tried to twirl as he fell, but he still landed hard with the Panktar covering a good portion of his body. The air swooshed out of his lungs. Was he going to be crushed to death?

The smellers had done their job, and it stunk like the slime off a Sleztar bog.

When he called for help, it came out as a deflated squeak rather than a yell. It hurt to breathe. Lelita and Borneo ran out of the fog and fell over him or rather over the Panktar on top of him. They scrambled to their feet and tried to push the Panktar off Everest, but the creature wouldn't budge.

"Try lifting him," he managed to gasp.

Grabbing the Panktar's arms, they pulled up, grunting with the effort. Everest managed to wiggle backward just slightly.

"A little more," he said.

Lelita sobbed with the exertion, and Borneo grunted as if he was in acute pain, but they managed to lift the dead weight just a little higher. Everest wiggled again and fought his way out. He hurt all over. He slowly stood up.

"Well, aren't the little children showing some spunk?" Director Lester-Hauffer called out, still lost in the fog. "Perhaps, it's time you learned about our secret weapon."

"We're shaking in our skyboots," Vlas returned.

The director laughed. "My dear children, you knew him as Dr. Yee, now meet James Powers—if you dare." Cloaked in white, his voice was eerie and disembodied.

A gale wind threw Everest back a good ten meters. He landed forcefully on his spine. The fog lifted, and Everest saw the man now referred to as James Powers blowing so hard that they were all now flattened to the ground and very much exposed.

Only Larry had escaped this new onslaught because he was behind James and their uncle. Everest didn't think the bad guys knew he was there.

James laughed harshly. "Would you like another demonstration?"

Everest shook his head, a resounding "no." Not that James had seriously been asking the question. Everest and the other B12s dragged themselves to their feet.

Without warning, James sprung into the air and landed behind them. Everest whipped around.

"Vlas," Dar yelled, "watch the director."

Everest felt like a fool for having turned his back on his uncle. By the time he managed to face him again, the man had a flaser targeting him. If the director shot him, he would be a mound of dust. Fortunately, he seemed reluctant to shoot. Probably because he was afraid he might destroy the pendant.

With James behind him, Everest felt zetta vulnerable. Dar and Vlas had had the presence of mind to go back to back, each holding a zunner on one of the villains. When James leapt again and landed to their side, Everest tracked him with one of his zunners. This time he stood sideways and pointed the other zunner at the director.

"You think you can stop me with a puny weapon?" James said, laughing. "Go ahead and try. My body can absorb anything you shoot at me quicker than you can say 'Xlexuri.'"

"Stop playing with them," Director Lester-Hauffer screamed. "Get the pendant now."

This time when James leapt, he landed in front of Elsie. Everest lunged for him, but once again found himself flying through the air as if he were a skyball. Again he landed at least ten meters away.

Meanwhile, James picked up Elsie and shook her. "Give me the pendant!"

Adrenalin pushed Everest back to his feet, and he rushed James who, without even a glance, brushed him off with another backhand that sent him soaring. He fell hard, and this time he wasn't sure he could get up. Every muscle, bone and centimeter of skin ached. As far as he could tell, nothing was broken, but everything seriously hurt. How could he save Elsie? James now had his hands around her throat and he was choking her. Everest desperately tried to move, but all he could do was lie there in excruciating pain.

Out of nowhere, "Cowabunga!" boomed across the sky. To Everest's amazement, Larry shot over James, legs and arms flapping wildly.

He twirled in the air and landed facing the vlem, his hands clenched into fists, his thin body in a fighting stance. "You'll never get that pendant."

"Oh really? It's Larry—Larry with no last name—isn't it? And you think you can stop me?" The man laughed and the noise seemed to consume the sky. "A scrawny little twelve-year-old clone. What fun!"

"You'll find out just how much fun it is when I kick your keister to Xlexuri Galaxy. And I'm Larry Knight, as in your worst 'Knight-mare.'"

Everest slowly dragged himself to his elbows for a better view. Larry must have somehow opened the pendant and popped a femto-booster.

James smiled broadly. "You wish."

"Get him, now," the director screeched.

"My pleasure." James tossed Elsie aside, and she landed on her rump on the parking lot moss, gasping and rubbing her neck where he had choked her. Relief washed through Everest. She was moving—that had to be a good sign.

James leapt high in the air toward Larry who jumped simultaneously. They met in the sky, and the force of their clash shot them both back twenty meters. Everest gasped as he watched them fly. HVs tried to evade them, but a number crashed into them and spun out of control. And then there were the HVs that crashed into each other. The sky was a chaos of spinning lights.

Larry somersaulted mid-air and then slammed into James, grappling with the older man fifteen meters above ground. Everest had a feeling his jaw was somewhere around his knees right now. His parents had invented something that could do that? *Zetta zeller.* Were there any femto-boosters left?

Remembering his uncle and the flaser he held, Everest pushed himself to his feet, fighting through the pain. He found the director staring at the battle in the sky. Everyone was mesmerized by the fight. Each clash was enormous, impossible to survive, yet both Larry and James bounced off each other without injury. Despite his inhuman strength, Larry was more awkward, his legs pumping as if he were treading water.

Everest told himself to ignore the display. This was his best opportunity to stop his uncle. He fought to lift his bruised arm so he could zunner him, but the director seemed to wake up and pivoted quickly to point his flaser at Dar.

"Noooo!" Everest dived, the pain in his body so intense he nearly screamed. He took Dar down to the moss. He rolled off her immediately—bleck—and shot both zunners at the director, but the man swiveled sideways, and the zunner stream went wild. Less than a meter to his left, Everest saw a gaping, steaming hole in the ground where the flaser had left its mark.

Elsie and Vlas both threw foggers at the director, obscuring his view. They ran to Everest and Dar. Each grabbed one of them by their shirts to make them move toward the HV. Everest gasped in agony with each jarring step. Dar fought out of Vlas's grip and swiveled around.

"Lelita? Borneo?" Dar yelled.

Everest saw them running ahead to Mink's jellach vehicle. Good for them.

"Dar," he yelled and motioned to the two clones.

She nodded then quickly returned her concentration toward the spot where they had last seen the director. It was now obscured by foggers. She blasted her zunner in the general vicinity of the man as she ran backward toward the HV. It was impossible to tell if any of her shots met their mark. They didn't hear a tell-tale thud, but there was so much noise going on in the sky there was a chance they might not hear their uncle drop to the ground.

Everest decided it was time to run in earnest—especially since his current run felt more like a crawl. Before he did, he glanced up. Larry grappled with James in a strange wrestling match.

How were they going to get Larry's attention? He seemed to be rising farther and farther away. By now, the traffic was giving them a wide berth. Why hadn't cybercops arrived? Surely someone had alerted them? He realized that what seemed like eons of time was probably just a minute or two.

"Larry, I sure wish you could hear me," Everest whispered.

"I can," boomed a voice from the sky.

Everest's jaw dropped. "Wha—?"

"I can hear you, man," Larry interrupted in a resonate voice that seemed to blanket the entire sky. In fact, many of the nearby hover vehicles literally jumped when he spoke, as if the drivers were spooked by the unexpected noise. Some of the closer ones slowed down out of curiosity.

"As can I," boomed James. Suddenly, he jackknifed and dove toward Everest. "I can see you too." He laughed, a booming, irritating noise. Larry followed James in a dangerous freefall.

This time adrenalin got Everest moving at almost full speed toward the HV. He felt a huge force against his right hand and one of his zunners flung itself so far away that he couldn't see it land. Heat grew on his back. Not a flame but something more like a shower that in one instant went from warm to hot to very hot to scalding. Somehow James was causing the heat, but Everest didn't waste time by looking around. Instead, he started to serpentine, but there was no way he could outmaneuver James. He bit the inside of his mouth to keep from yelling at each new pain the vlem inflicted. Wasn't it enough that his entire body already felt like one monstrous bruise?

"Everest," Elsie yelled.

From the corner of his eye he saw his sister running at his side holding out her hand. Pooker loped beside her. He knew intuitively that she wanted him to throw her the zunner, but he was down to one now, and without it, he would be defenseless. On the other hand, with James' attention trained on him, Elsie had a bit more leeway. Hoping he wouldn't regret it, he tossed her his last defense. She caught it and stopped mid-run. She trained the zunner on the fast plummeting James and hit him with multiple streams of ultra-powerful stun. But it was as if she were a tiny gnat and he a colossal elephant. There was no effect except that now his attention switched to Elsie.

Everest knew immediately when James switched gears to target his sister. The burning sensation on his back disappeared, but he suspected Elsie's back was heating up. He looked over his left shoulder and saw that James had his hands out and was exuding a stream of heat from his palms. Tears of pain streamed down Elsie's face, but she wore her most determined expression. She didn't falter as she ran.

Shooting through the air with his hands out as if he dove into a deep lake, Larry finally caught James. He lunged and grabbed him around the neck, choking him with all his might. James bucked to dislodge Larry, but the kid from the twenty-first century refused to let go. They jolted and grappled and wrestled through the sky.

The B12s were distracted by Larry's scrappy fight, but Everest knew they had to focus on escape. Up to this point, the director had avoided destroying them because he had been afraid of destroying the pendant. Now he had to know that Larry had it. That made the rest of them expendable. The bad guys had flasers, and the B12s only had zunners. The vlems had the upper hand. Everest grabbed Elsie by the arm and got her moving again.

Vlas and Dar made it to the HV a little ahead of Everest and Elsie. Lelita and Borneo stood shakily, their expressions dazed. Dar erased the door and shoed everyone in. As soon as they were, Dar quickly made the door solid.

"What do we do about Larry?" asked Vlas.

"We wait as long as we can," Dar said.

"I can still hear you," Larry said, just slightly out of breath from the epic battle that tore up the sky.

"So can I," James said, laughing evilly. "You better get while the getting's good. We'll take fine care of this one." Having wrestled himself free from Larry's grasp, he aimed an upper cut at Larry's solar plexus, popping him into multiple backward somersaults. Then he added, "Not that we're going to let you get too far. But I'll deal with you after I rid myself of this pesky fly."

Larry swept back and managed to choke James so that he couldn't speak, but Everest couldn't really imagine Larry besting James in the long run. Despite his amazing powers, the twenty-first-century boy still was just a kid, and James was a man, one who had killed before and had no qualms about killing again.

The two continued their lethal dance in the sky.

Everest looked around for Director Lester-Hauffer and found him emerging from the fog with a flaser in his hand. The Panktars were passed out on the ground, but one showed serious signs of waking up. His leg twitched.

Elsie must have seen the same thing because she tugged on Dar's shirtsleeve and pointed at the green monster.

"The director has to know we don't have flasers," Elsie signed since James could hear every word they said.

Dar started to detach the time travel device. "Come on, Larry," she whispered as she popped the box off and shoved it into her pocket.

"SHADARA, rise," she said. The hover vehicle came to life and rose until Dar whispered, "Okay, SHADARA, that's good." The HV hovered quietly, awaiting her next command. Dar took a deep breath, and glanced over at Vlas, who gave her a 'thumbs up.'

Everest hated when they did that mind-meld, silent communication thing, but he supposed that was what he and Elsie did too. What would Dar do next? Wait for Larry to decide to join them?

Manipulating the joystick, Dar maneuvered the HV so that it faced Larry and James who were still locked in a deadly, spinning embrace.

"Larry, disengage," she commanded in a loud voice despite the fact that the boy probably could hear the merest whisper.

Larry struggled free of James' grasp, and making himself a human bullet, shot up twenty meters.

Simultaneously, Dar yelled, "SHADARA, full speed now." The vehicle exploded forward. Fortunately, Everest remembered the first time they gave the vehicle its head, and he grabbed his chair to keep from shooting out of it. The HV rammed toward James. Everest heard Elsie gasp, or maybe that was him. Lelita let out a small, strangled scream.

The vlem remained unconcerned. Smiling evilly, he let the vehicle come toward him. At the last second, he raised his arms as if he meant to stop the HV with just his bare hands. They soon found out that instead of stopping the vehicle, he meant to do much more. He pushed as they connected, and the HV shot out of control, spinning wildly, high into the sky. Everest landed heavily on Lelita, rolled and ended up on Pooker. Elsie tumbled onto him. They were all screaming, even Pooker in her bobcat way. Only Vlas laughed hysterically. The HV spun out of control, bouncing off other hover vehicles and causing a chain reaction of spinning and bouncing.

Vlas continued to laugh, Lelita cried, and Pooker's screech turned into a menacing growl. If it weren't for the pico-trainer, he had a feeling the bobcat would have bitten one of them.

He'd always heard that it was best to let a hover vehicle come out of a spin naturally. He wasn't sure if that was true, but it seemed as if that was what Dar was doing. She had her hands on the joystick, but she wasn't maneuvering it.

She yelled, "Larry, get your keister over here."

"Yes, your Darship," he boomed.

Dar didn't look amused.

Everest thought Larry's humor was out of place. Jeez, their lives were at stake. Just because the boy had superpowers didn't mean they were saved. When the hover vehicle righted itself, Everest looked out. Larry blasted toward them as if he'd been shot out of an ancient cannon. At first, Everest couldn't see James, but then he realized that the man was in hot pursuit.

"Everyone, strap in," Dar said.

They quickly complied.

Dar requested that SHADARA erase a portion of the door. When the opening didn't seem big enough, she demanded that the entire door be erased. "Larry, you better come to a complete stop before you jump in so no one gets hurt." They hovered in the sky, waiting for him to arrive.

"You bet," he said happily. At the very last nano-second, he slid to a halt, grabbed the edge of the opening with his hands and hopped in.

"SHADARA, go solid," Dar yelled. The HV was quick to comply. "SHADARA, full speed."

The sleek vehicle went from zero to three hundred kilometers an hour in less time than it took to draw a breath. Everest's face tightened and shook in reaction to the speed. Either James had given up, or he was no match for the vehicle's power. The vlem quickly receded from view.

"Deng, Larry, you rocked!" Vlas said. "Any chance I can get my hands on one of those femto-boosters?"

The boy from the twenty-first century couldn't contain his massive grin. "Sweet, huh?"

"How'd you get one out? Are there any others left? Do you still have the pendant?" Elsie's questions rushed out like water gushing from a tap.

Everest could hear a rasp in her voice from James' attempt to choke her. It had to hurt. He felt like one giant bruise, but he wasn't going to say anything. Dar would just think he was a zetta ute-baby. Thank the Light, there didn't appear to be any serious damage.

"Chill, girl," Larry responded to Elsie's string of questions. "I've got the pendant. I've got the object cloner too." He dug into his pocket and pulled both of them out. "I used Dar's magic gray glob to unlock the pendant—figured it couldn't hurt to try. And, hey, it opened. There were these itsy-bitsy pink pills. Since we had nothing to lose, I swallowed one and jumped down the rabbit hole. Man, what a dive." He ran his hands through his shiny black curls. "All of a sudden, I'm a freaking superhero," he said, shaking his head. He said one of the bad words from the twenty-first century, but no one could bring themselves to correct him. "What a rush."

There was a moment of silence as Dar navigated the HV at high speed between vehicles and other obstacles.

Larry looked around grinning. Then he frowned. "Hey Lelita, don't cry. We're all okay."

"No we're not," she said through a sob. She sniffed loudly. "We're fugitives. No one's going to believe our side of the story. We'll end up in prison or worse, dead."

Elsie swiveled her chair so she could grasp Lelita's hand. "No one's going to hurt you."

"Yes, they are. We're all going to die."

"Lelita," Dar said sharply, "pull yourself together."

Everest was about to come to Lelita's defense—jeez, Dar was harsh—but then Lelita sat up straighter and swallowed hard. She wiped her eyes. He had to give Dar credit for handling the girl better than he would have done.

He looked out the window. "Uh, Dar, you might want to dial back the speed so we don't get pulled over by a cybercop."

She might as well put a neon sign on their jellach vehicle to let cyborg officers know they were criminals on the run. They had so many enemies right now. It wasn't just about Panktars and lunatics with retro candy names.

"Any sight of our friend, James Powers?" Dar asked, ignoring Everest, though she did slow down.

"Nah, you lost him," Vlas said, "but we're still carrying a tracking device."

"Larry, do you think he can hear us?"

The boy listened intently. "I can hear a lot of people talking, but I can't hear him. I think we've put enough distance between us."

"We've got to get rid of that tracking device," Elsie exclaimed.

Dar pulled the compact time-travel machine out of her pocket and held it out. "Vlas, figure out where it is and how to detach it. There's a good chance we'll need to time-travel later."

He took the little black box and turned it over this way and that, trying to identify the tracking mechanism. "Hmm. Wonder if it's inside or attached to the outside. If it's outside, it blends pretty well."

"Rub your finger over it. Maybe you'll find a different texture," Dar suggested.

He pulled PicoBoy out of his pocket. "PicoBoy, find the tracking device on this box." He placed the time-travel machine on his knees, and PicoBoy slowly crawled across it, stopping periodically for analysis. When the man-made creature was done with one side, Vlas flipped the box over. Almost at once PicoBoy began to squeal with excitement. Vlas investigated the spot that excited the little man-made creature. "Good job, PicoBoy," he said. "Yup, there's a very thin and zetta small disk attached." He stroked PicoBoy. "Can you remove it?"

The little picobot chirped. From his robot mouth a zetta sharp implement descended. With precision, PicoBoy pried the tracking mechanism off the time-travel device. When he was done, he flew up to face level with Vlas and offered him the miniscule disk.

Vlas smiled. "Well done!" He accepted the tracker. "Now what? Should I just dump it out the window?"

Dar pursed her lips. "Hmm. Let's land for a few seconds and attach it to something."

"Okay," Vlas said with a shrug, "but you better be quick. We should assume that the bad guys are on our tail."

Dar rolled her eyes. "You're turning into a regular Basker, stating the obvious like that."

"Ha, ha, ha," Vlas said. "Aren't you the allen?"

Everest grimaced. Despite everything they'd gone through together, the clones were still joking about them.

"SHADARA, ground level," Dar said. They were heading south, quickly closing in on Santa Clara. "We need to keep our distance from the clone academy. After we drop off the tracker, we'll shoot to become invisible again in Googleopolis. That worked for us last time. Vlas, when we touch down, hop out and attach the device to the closest object you can find."

"Sure thing."

They landed in a charming suburban neighborhood that consisted of rows of small houses made from Zentor vood in the 2950s. Vlas followed Dar's instructions, attaching the tracker to a dwarf pine tree. All of the homes on this street sported dwarf pine trees on their lawns.

Once Vlas returned, Dar quickly commanded the vehicle back to commuter height. "Okay, Googleopolis, here we come."

Everest watched for signs of the bad guys and sure enough, he saw an HV in the far distance with two ridiculously oversized green Panktars in the back seat. "There they are," he said, pointing. "But I don't see James."

"Jeez, Everest, put your finger away. If they see somebody pointing they might actually figure out that it's us. Do you think they've spotted us?"

"I don't think so. We're at least fifteen cars away. I'm pretty sure they're just tracking the device at this point."

"Good. Okay, now we need to figure out how to hide the bobcat."

"Most HVs can go opaque if you ask them to," Elsie said. "A lot of people prefer a little privacy in their vehicles."

"SHADARA, please go opaque." With Dar's words, the see-through vehicle went a solid white except for a large front window, a matching back one and smaller windows on each side. The bottom remained clear.

"Keep the bobcat lying down," Dar said. "Also, all of you except Vlas duck down under window height. When we've lost them completely, you can sit back up. Vlas, you watch to make sure they don't spot us. I'll take a detour soon—a more circuitous route to Googleopolis."

Everest slid off his chair to cram himself into the small space behind the driver's seat. As soon as he did so, the vehicle stretched out a little to give him room. The rest of the B12s followed suit. Now just Dar and Vlas were visible. He hoped that most of Dar's striking looks were dimmed by her cap and the night sky.

And he prayed they wouldn't meet up with the director, Dr. Jensa, James Powers or the Panktars anytime soon.

CHAPTER 19
Researching Femto-Boosters

Elsie couldn't get comfortable sitting on the floor of the HV with Pooker on her lap. The jellach vehicle had expanded a little, but not enough. Her legs were going numb from being cramped. And her whole body felt bruised, battered and burned because of James Powers.

Lelita was crying softly again, and Borneo was scary-white. He hadn't said one word since he'd escaped the Panktars' clutches. She wished there was something she could do to help him get over his shock, but she felt pretty messed up herself. First her parents had disappeared and now her uncle had betrayed them. Plus there was the horrible Dr. Jensa, the zetta scary Panktars, and finally the murderous James Powers. It was all too much.

Instructor Gerard was starting to feel like their best friend compared to all the new vlems in their lives.

Why were people willing to kill for those femto-boosters? Sure, Larry and James' exhibition had been zetta amazing, but who needed powers like that? What would they use them for? She rested her head against the seat cushion. "Larry, do you have a sense for the range of your powers?"

"We-ell, hard to say what else I could have done, but I know what I did. I flew, or at least I managed to rise up into the sky."

"Was it like a balloon or a bird?" Dar asked.

"Well, I ain't got wings... so I guess it was more like being shot into the air, maybe like a really fast hot-air balloon or a cannon ball." He closed his eyes as if that might help him remember better. "I'm not sure what the femto-booster did to make that possible. I think it just helped me to jump really high. I

126

sort of ran in place in the sky. And I could tread air with my arms. The booster gave me hecka more strength too."

"Maybe you are emitting high velocity streams of air or gas." Vlas suggested. "James seemed to be able to blast air at will. He blew people over. Maybe the femto-booster somehow augments the air you can emit either via your mouth or through other parts of your body."

Surprisingly, Lelita giggled. "Vlas, are you saying that Larry's farts propelled him into the sky?" She turned pink when she realized what she'd said.

Larry snorted.

"Not exactly," Vlas grinned, "but close! There has to be a scientific explanation. At first, he looked as if he was jumping, except when he managed to stay in the air and fight."

"Okay," Dar said, "more powerful legs for extreme jumping combined with a healthy boost for generating gas out the back door and air from the front. Obviously you get a major lung boost. What else?"

"Well," Larry added. "The extreme power was a big part of it."

"Yeah, what would cause such awesome strength?"

Vlas scratched his head. "Hmm. That's tricky. What if the booster mutated his muscles to be super dense so they packed a stronger punch? What I can't figure out is why James and Larry didn't get injured. They punched each other out pretty well, but without a scratch or a bruise."

Elsie raised her hand. "Maybe when the muscles become denser they also become springier—like jellach—creating a fast-acting, healing mechanism."

"Yeah," Larry said. "I do sort of feel more solid but also a bit more rubbery."

"James was able to generate heat," Dar said. "He nearly torched Everest."

"Yeah," Larry said. "I'm pretty sure if I think hot and then blow, the air that comes out will be hot, and if I think cold and blow, the air that comes out will be frigid cold. But I haven't tried it yet."

""You can start our campfire tonight," Dar said.

"Sweet." Larry grinned.

"The two big questions," Dar added, "are what other superpowers do you have? And, when will these powers disappear? Also, Larry, have you counted how many femto-boosters are in the pendant? We need to do that as soon as possible. We need to know how many of us can take on these powers, if necessary. And right now, we really could use a holoputer. I'd like to try to jack into the classified information on femto-technology."

"Uh," Borneo said weakly, his face still a shade of white that was inhuman, even for an albino, "I still have a holoputer."

"No way," Dar said, her eyes wide.

Borneo scrunched his shoulders. "They confiscated my full-size when they kidnapped us, but I built a hand-held illegal awhile back and that one's still in my pocket."

"You are the rocket-man," Larry said, pumping his fist into the air.

Borneo looked both embarrassed and pleased.

"That's good," Dar said, "zetta good. As soon as we find a safe spot, we'll be able to do some serious research."

Elsie curled her hands into Pooker's fur, thinking hard. "We should have Larry demonstrate some form of power every ten minutes so we know when his powers go away."

Dar nodded. "Yeah, Larry, can you do something now? I realize you don't have much room to maneuver."

"Guess I could heat this jellach baby up a bit," he said.

"Okay, but don't fry us or it," Dar replied sternly.

His face took on a look of deep concentration. After ten seconds or so, he opened his mouth and breathed softly. What came out was a stream of warm air, like that on a balmy summer day.

Lelita giggled nervously when the air touched her skin.

"Also," Larry said, "when I peek out the window I can see cars and their drivers for at least a kilometer back, and I can hear a ton of conversations right now. They're all going on at once, though, so it's one big jumble."

"That's not good," Everest said. "That means James has super-vision too. We don't know where he is, but if he's figured out this is our vehicle then they can follow us from a healthy distance. It's too bad you're crouched down. Maybe you could figure out where James and the Panktars are."

Dar made a noise in the back of her throat. "I guess I should have had you stay upright instead of Vlas."

"Hey," Vlas said, "I may not have superpowers, but I still have eyes, and I saw the director's vehicle dive down toward the tracking device. I didn't see them rise back up again, though, because we were already long gone. You turned off the hover highway a few minutes ago, and they haven't reappeared behind us. I think we've lost them."

"Larry," Dar said, "have you heard them at all?"

"Jeez, it's just a jumble of words from at least hundreds, if not thousands, of folks. I can't distinguish any actual conversations."

"You're Superman, dude," Vlas said. "You can do anything."

Larry snorted. "Ha!" He concentrated again, his brows scrunched together, his fists clenched.

"Uh, Larry," Elsie said slowly, "your hands are about to explode." They were swelling and turning a dark purple. It was scary and fascinating at the same time. Her parents had invented these femto-boosters? Jeez, she never would have imagined this was what they did at work. "I wonder how much these pills have been tested. Probably, not much. I think Mom and Dad were going to be their own guinea pigs off-world. Who knows what kinds of side effects there could be?"

Larry tried to relax his hands. When he shook them to release the tension, they blurred from the force. He stopped shaking them. "Guess I don't know my own strength."

"Did you hear anything important?" Dar asked.

"Nah, I couldn't make out anything that sounded like Panktars or evil scientists or evil uncles. Just a jumble of chit-chat."

"Okay," Dar said. "We'll take that as a good sign. Maybe for now, at least, we've lost them."

Their ride to Googleopolis went smoothly, with no sign of the director and his gang.

As they approached, Elsie had a decent view from the floor of their HV which remained clear despite the opaque walls. Since it was dark, all of the colorful skyscrapers were now brightly lit making them even more vibrant. Some of the buildings had lights that changed color every few seconds turning the skyline into a light show. They passed a multi-storied superstructure that replicated the shape of a bright orange grizzly bear. Random white lights blinked on and off from hind claw to fore claw.

As with most of California, the ground was covered with street moss, but in this city, the lines delineating the hoverways and the parking spots were a florescent white instead of the more traditional florescent yellows and pinks. Because it was nighttime it was easier to see the white lines than the street moss.

Googleopolis was known for its wide open advertising policy. Almost any surface was up for grabs. Even on the street moss there were signs advertising just about everything under the sun—insurance, travel, virtual currency lenders, clothing, perfume, plumbers, virtual entertainment games and other activities. The roofs of skyscrapers, the walls of skyscrapers, the street moss, they all offered the "best deal" to the consumer. And since it was nighttime, the advertisements were brightly lit up too. The city was a chaos of blinking and rotating lights. Under normal circumstances it would have been fun and exciting.

Lelita sighed. "I wish we could go shopping."

Elsie didn't know how to respond.

Before she could come up with an answer, Lelita gasped. "I didn't mean that I wanted to go shopping now. Not with your parents missing." She grabbed Elsie's hand. "I just meant that I wished they were safe so that we could be having fun right now. Or I even wish we could be back at the academy. I never thought I'd miss it, but now I'd give anything to be able to go home."

Dar cleared her throat. "Uh, in case you've forgotten, the academy is run by a bunch of criminals."

Lelita frowned in a way that Elsie would have thought was physically impossible for such a sweet girl. "I know." She crossed her arms angrily. "I'm talking about going back to an academy without bad guys."

"I get it, Lelita," Elsie said. "It's almost impossible to believe everything that's happened." A wave of sorrow washed over her. "We're supposed to be living on one of the safest planets in the galaxy. Things like parents getting kidnapped or murdered shouldn't be possible."

Lelita squeezed her hand again. "They're alive. I just know it."

Elsie didn't know any such thing, but she appreciated Lelita trying to make her feel better, especially since the girl still had to be reeling from her own kidnapping.

"Can we use the aura-positioning unit now?" she asked, desperate for a sign that her parents might be all right.

Dar drummed her fingers on the joystick. "First, we need a hiding place. Wandering the hover highways of Googleopolis forever isn't the best strategy. Let's set down somewhere safe. Any suggestions?"

"How 'bout that park we went to the last time we were here?" Elsie suggested, making an effort despite her thoughts being centered on the APU and her parents.

"Uh," Larry said, "It's after dark. Where I come from, the police get pretty excited about kids loitering at a park in the middle of the night."

"Yeah," agreed Vlas, "I think they take the same interest in our time. We don't want to bring ourselves to the attention of a bunch of cyborg officers."

"Would it be okay if we sat up?" Elsie couldn't feel her legs anymore.

"I guess," Dar said.

They took turns easing back into their seats so that no one took notice of all the kids suddenly popping their heads up in the HV. Elsie contemplated the Googleopolis lights from the transparency of the HV window.

"I got living-on-the-streets experience, but I need your help regarding the thirty-first century," Larry said. "First, are there any places that are open twenty-four-seven?"

The car was silent. Finally, Lelita said, "We never leave the academy. We don't really know what's open."

After a few more seconds, Borneo said, "I've got my hand-held holoputer. We could do a search."

"Thanks, man, that's helpful." Larry scratched his head. "Elsie, Everest, you've lived outside of the academy. You must know what's open later in the evening. Like in our time, grocery stores are open."

"Grocery stores?" Elsie asked.

"Yeah, like where you buy food."

"Like a restaurant?"

"No, like where there are aisles of tomatoes and cereal and meat and stuff."

"We buy food online," Elsie responded.

"Say, what? What if you want something right away?"

"Well, there are restaurants, but we have a space problem so there aren't a lot of stores. Mostly, everyone shops online and then there are distribution warehouses that deliver."

"Okay, what about entertainment? Anything open all night? Someplace for people to have fun together?"

Elsie looked blankly at Everest. "Not really. We do most of that virtually."

Larry sighed. "Jeez, when do you actually see someone?"

"Well, we do have parks, and I've already said we have restaurants."

"And?"

"Oh!" Elsie cried. "Sports centers are open pretty late. Places where you can organize a fight or find first-class exercise machines, or play a game of skyball."

"Okay, now we're cooking. Are they open twenty-four hours a day?"

Elsie and Everest exchanged glances. "Maybe some of them."

"But they won't let a bunch of twelve-year-olds hang out there," Dar slipped in.

"Yeah," Elsie said, "that could be a problem."

"The thirty-first century sure isn't easy for the homeless."

"We don't have homeless people," Elsie retorted. "The fact that your time period did is barbaric."

"Yeah, yeah, I get that. Since I was one of them, I ain't disagreeing. Aren't there any other hangout spots?"

"Did I mention we have a space problem?" Elsie asked. "About sixty percent of our agriculture is grown off-world. We have something like twenty billion people on earth. The earth can only hold so many of us, and off-world options all have downsides—unless you manage to emigrate to one of the Xlexuri planets—but you need more than just a fortune to get that visa. So space is a precious commodity."

"Jeez, girl, don't get all high-horse. What about bridges?"

"What about them?" Elsie asked.

"Well, do you have nice big bridges that people can hide underneath?"

"Uh, we have some bridges, but they're pretty narrow. I wouldn't say that people can hide under them."

"No cars in the thirty-first century, Larry," Dar said. "We only need walking bridges."

"Yeah, yeah." He frowned. "Okay, I guess we're going to have to break into a building again. But which one? Can anyone tell me what's in all these buildings right now?"

"A lot of them house people," Elsie said.

Borneo had pulled out his tiny holoputer, and it was now floating in front of him as he silently communicated with it. His look of intense concentration kept the rest of the kids from asking him what he was looking for. He would tell them when he was ready.

Dar took random turns with the HV—left then right then left then left, her speed moderate. She kept pace with the other hover vehicles, drumming her fingers on the joystick, her mouth pursed as she thought about options.

"How 'bout churches?" Larry asked. "In bad weather, I've hunkered down in a few houses of God."

"Mostly, people worship virtually nowadays," Elsie said. "But I think there are a still a few churches out there—especially the few that survived the Vlemutz wars."

"So we've got sports centers, religious centers. What about business offices?"

"Again, a lot of business is handled virtually. People mostly holocommute. They work from home and use holoputers to meet."

"Man, this world sure is anti-social," Larry said. "Don't you ever want to meet face to face?"

"Sure," Elsie said, "and we do, it's just that it's not always necessary."

"Googleopolis is the center for virtual entertainment device gaming technology," said Everest. "But that's something that can be developed via holoputers. No one needs to be in the same room to manufacture games. Now wine making—that still needs a manufacturing plant and a warehouse. But there's no winemaking in Googleopolis."

"Schools are still in person," Elsie said. "We can do a lot virtually, but most cities believe that person-to-person interactions are an important part of the development process."

"Here's a list of schools," Borneo said, popping out of his intense session with his inky-dinky holoputer. "I also tracked down all of the fitness centers, churches and restaurants in a ten kilometer radius."

Larry chucked Borneo on the shoulder. "You are the man."

Borneo populated the air below the windows with multiple holocopies of the lists, along with a series of aerial views of each building.

Distracted by the list, Dar bumped into the HV in front of her and their vehicle wobbled. The family swiveled around to glare at Dar, and she waved apologetically. Placated, they waved back.

"A school makes the most sense," Dar said. "We're the right age so if we have to, we can try to blend in during the day. SHADARA, show us the closest school to our current location."

"It's this one," Borneo said, pointing to the top of the list—a school named Bright Minds Academy.

'Okay, thanks, Borneo," Dar said. "SHADARA, take us to Bright Minds Academy."

The HV veered off to the right and joined all of the other jellach vehicles heading toward the city's center.

Elsie absently stroked Pooker's fur. "Larry, I think you should test your powers again. It's been over fifteen minutes."

"Yeah, you're right. I'm still seeing about the same distance." He took on a look of intense concentration and pretty soon blew hot air into the car again. "Still got the Superman in me."

"Hey, I think I see it," Vlas said excitedly, pointing down to a J28 compound. The school consisted of one tall building in the shape of an open book that was the color of a translucent blue sky. The building was surrounded by play areas and gardens.

"Okay, let's join the academy," Dar said. She told SHADARA to drop gently to the ground.

As they started to descend, all of the advertisements went haywire, and a siren racketed across the sky. All lights whether on buildings or signs went bright yellow and started to blink wildly.

"What the heck?" Larry asked.

"It's the emergency system," Everest yelled over the high-pitched siren.

"Wonder what's up?" Elsie asked.

After a few more seconds of bright yellow lights and sirens, all of the advertisements displayed a series of holophotos—holophotos that were frighteningly familiar—Dar, Everest, Elsie, Vlas, Lelita, Larry and Borneo, even Pooker. For Dar, they showed her with cap and without, and with hair down as well as pulled back.

Large print words stated boldly: *Clones on the lam. Extremely dangerous—kidnapped children, killed scientist, stolen car. Do not approach. Clones armed with flasers. Any information leading to the whereabouts of these criminals, urgently contact Director Lester-Hauffer at the Academy of Superior Learning.*

The flashing sign gave the director's access code.

Elsie's heart sped up and her hands went clammy. What a mess. The sirens made her think of cyborg police. What would happen if they were caught?

CHAPTER 20
On the Run

Larry said a few choice words that Everest knew were illegal in the thirty-first century.

All of the kids besides Dar dived to the HV's floor, but it was already too late.

"We're so busted," Larry said. "Both the HV in front and the one in back recognized us. I think there might be a third vehicle too. All of them are contacting the director. We gotta get out of here."

Everest didn't need Larry's super-hearing to know that.

"The only good thing," the boy added, "is that everyone seems to be afraid of us, so they're all scattering. At least no one's trying to tail us."

Dar ordered the vehicle back up to commuter height and took as many turns as she could to confuse whoever might come looking for them.

"Larry, I could use a co-pilot," she said, "and you've got the best vision right now. The rest of you stay down."

Larry eased around Vlas into the chair next to Dar.

"Deng, we're going to have to pick another academy," Dar said. It was so loud with all the sirens blaring that she had to yell. "Bright Minds is way too close. Let's pick one outside of Googleopolis. Worst case, we'll dive into the past for a little while, but let's hold off till we have no other choice. If the Baskers are alive, they're in the here and now. If we keep hiding in the past, we'll never find them." She finally thought to say, "SHADARA: soundproof!" The interior of the HV went silent. The air seemed heavier.

"That may work for the rest of you," Larry said, "but I'm still stuck with a jumble of sirens and shouts and babble. This Superman thing has a downside."

"Poor, poor Larry," Dar said in a zetta pitiful voice.

Larry laughed. "Knock it off."

Everyone except Dar scanned the new information Borneo displayed for them.

"What about this one?" Everest asked, pointing. His heart still pounded at a ridiculous clip, and he hated seeing holophotos of them splashed all over the sides of buildings, the ground, even on hoverbuses. It was freaky. "The place is called Wisdom First, and it looks as if it's about two kilometers outside of Googleopolis."

Dar told SHADARA to take them there. "When we arrive we need to find a safe place for this vehicle. It's our safety net."

"There's a parking garage at Wisdom First," Borneo said. "But there might be a security guard."

"There's bound to be some sort of security," Elsie said.

Everest was so tired of this. He felt closed in and claustrophobic. He could relate to the bobcat who was growling deep in her throat. Even the soundproofing didn't seem to help. It just made him more claustrophobic like he was in a bubble. Though he couldn't hear the siren anymore, he felt as if it was piercing his brain. He wished he could lie down in his own room and just sleep, or at least chill for a very long time. By himself.

A particularly nasty holophoto of him staring blankly with his mouth wide-open showed up on an advertising billboard.

Vlas chuckled.

Everest groaned. He wished being on the floor of the vehicle would make it impossible to see the images, but the funny angle just made them worse. The only way he could escape the visuals was by closing his eyes.

A holophoto of Vlas appeared, but in his case, it was a great picture. And then there was another one of Dar in her cap so that folks could recognize her without seeing her striking facial features and her rich golden hair. Borneo's holophoto turned him into a big white beacon in the sky. There weren't a lot of albinos wandering the streets of Northern California. How were they going to blend into a school with Borneo and Dar in tow?

"Uh, Dar," Larry said, "we need disguises—especially for you and Borneo. We can't land anywhere till you two look different. Maybe we should go back a few days in time so we can pull together camouflage without everyone and their brother recognizing us while we shop."

"Unfortunately, everything gets delivered," Dar said. It would be almost impossible to find something and have it delivered to a safe spot."

"If we're in the past, we could have them deliver it to the academy, and we could wait for it to show up."

"We now know that pretty much everyone is a criminal at the clone academy. That means it's not safe in any time period— the past or the present."

"Well, something's got to be done," Larry insisted. "You are one recognizable clone, missy. And Borneo here is an even worse case."

'Missy?" Dar glared but couldn't hold the expression and quickly broke into laughter.

They all nervously joined her. It was as if they needed to laugh at something.

"Do you think they are advertising our disappearance in all the cities, or have they already tracked us to Googleopolis?" Elsie asked after the laughter died down.

"I suspect we're being broadcast all over the Bay Area," Dar said. "Who knows? Maybe we've made national and international news. Our bad guys seem pretty well-connected and are clearly confident that their story will be believed over ours."

"But it doesn't make any sense," Elsie said. "Our parents are the ones who are missing, and we know we haven't been kidnapped by rogue clones. If we turn ourselves in, we can explain what happened. Why are the vlems so sure that no one will believe us?"

Dar looked over her shoulder thoughtfully. "Good question. I'm guessing that either a) they are planning to flaser us before we get a chance to spill our side of the story, or b) their friends are in such high places that they know the truth will be ignored."

Everest wrestled with what Dar said. There had to be someone they could trust.

"We should go back to Adriatic Mink," he said slowly. "Go back in time again, maybe just a few minutes after we left the first time. He can help us disguise ourselves, and he can give us advice. He's more powerful than anyone. He can ensure that our side of the story is believed."

Dar's eyes went blank. "I don't think so."

"Why not?" Larry demanded. "He's the dude. We need his help."

"I don't trust him."

"Get out. He was the man earlier. You trusted him then. He don't need no superpowers to be a superhero. He's Batman. He's it, girl."

"He's powerful, true. And he's helped us out, I know. But I can't trust him anymore. I've tried a million ways to make this work in my head, but it's not workable."

"Make what work?" Elsie asked.

"Before I left, he pulled me aside."

Everest remembered that moment. It had seemed weird, and Dar hadn't wanted to talk about it.

"Get on with it, girl," Larry said, frustrated by Dar's long pause.

"Stop calling me 'girl,'" she spat. She tugged on her ponytail. "Deng, there's no other way to interpret this—only the bad way." She sighed and shook her head. "He asked me for a femto-booster. He told me to pocket one once we opened the pendants, and he warned me not to tell anyone, just to do it on the sly."

Larry let out a long, slow whistle. "He must have a reason."

"I can't think of a good one."

"But he had us in his grasp. Why not just take the pendant from us then and there?"

"Maybe he wants or needs us to find the Baskers. Maybe he's not exactly in cahoots with the director, maybe he's in an opposing faction. But how can I trust him now that we know he's after the femto-boosters too? It's not safe to go to him. There's no one more dangerous than Adriatic Mink if he's your enemy."

"Man that's bogus," Larry said.

A feeling of hopelessness sunk into the pit of Everest's stomach. He'd been so sure that Adriatic Mink would swoop in and save the day. Larry looked as if he was fighting back tears.

But Vlas was just his same old cheerful self. In fact, his eyes lit up. "Let's go back to Larry's time. They have stores we can buy from directly. We just need to track down some local currency." He flexed his fingers. "That shouldn't be so hard."

"You can't steal currency!" Elsie exclaimed.

"Desperate measures. We could figure out some way to pay them back. Or we could borrow the costumes then return them later." He grinned wickedly. "If we're still alive."

What was the matter with Vlas? Did he have a death wish? Or was he really that unconcerned about potential threats?

"Stop!" Lelita pressed her hands over her ears. "I don't want to hear anything else."

"You're forgetting that we can't go back in time to the twenty-first century," Dar said. "This vehicle wasn't created in that time period."

"True." Vlas shrugged then waved at Larry. "But he was."

"Larry?" Dar said, her eyes narrowing. "No way, no how. Not in a zillion light years."

"What are you talking about?" Elsie demanded.

"I'm not sure that would work," Borneo said, his expression zetta serious.

"But what if it did?" Vlas asked.

"It's not an option," Dar said. "I won't allow it."

"Won't allow what?" Larry asked.

Everyone stared at him. Everest wondered if he had misunderstood Vlas. It was zetta dangerous. Larry could be killed. They all could be. Had anyone even tried it before?

"Uh," Borneo said. He cleared his throat. "Vlas is suggesting that we use you as a time-travel machine since we don't have a car from the twenty-first century." He went bright pink.

A string of illegal words shot rapid fire from Larry's lips. "Is it possible?"

"It's a ridiculous idea," Dar said.

Larry's eyes narrowed. "Why?"

"I've researched time travel," Dar said. "Using a human as a time-travel machine has never been tested. There's been some speculation, a few research notes written, but no one's been crazy enough to try it."

"Have they tried it on animals?" Larry asked.

Lelita gasped. Everest fought to keep his cool.

"This isn't the twenty-first century, yocto-brain," Dar said, shaking her head. "Animal testing is against the law."

Larry looked around at all the horrified expressions. "Jeez, give me a frigging break. Why do you think anything would go wrong?"

"Well," Dar said, "first, there's the whole 'when were you created' debate. Was it when you were conceived or when you were born? If we get the timing wrong, we're off by nine months. Mostly, scientists think it's when you were born, but they don't have conclusive proof. Then there's a theory that the force, the pressure would be extreme. There's some question as to whether a person could be used as a time-travel machine without disintegrating. A vehicle offers considerable protection."

"We traveled in a convertible. It had no top, but we didn't blow up."

"The time-travel object absorbs most of the force."

"Hey, I'm still Superman," Larry said. "That's gotta help."

"Those powers might dissipate before we return."

"Then I'll use another femto-booster."

"We need those to save our parents," Elsie said.

"Girl, if we don't find disguises, we ain't gonna get the chance to save them. Anyway, we won't need me as the machine on the return flight. If we have the HV, it can time-travel us back. What else do we have to worry about?"

"We shouldn't take the hover vehicle," Everest said. "If someone sees us hovering in the sky, it could change the course of history."

"We can't leave it here," Larry said. "The creeps'll find it and there goes our Batmobile. So, we hide it real good in the twenty-first century until we're ready to return. No one's going to know the SHADARA user name. No one'll be able to make it go.

It'll just look like some crazy statue of a wild car from the future."

Dar sighed. "Larry, it's just not right to experiment with a human being. You're our responsibility. We brought you to this time period. If something happens to you, it's our fault."

"Hate to tell you this, your Darship, but your track record for keeping me safe ain't so good already. Besides I know this is dangerous, so it's my fault if something goes wrong. Heck, it's no one's fault, really. It's just the way the cookie crumbles."

"Huh?" Elsie had a confused expression on her face.

"Jeez, it's an expression. Things fall the way they fall."

"We digress," Dar said tersely.

"I don't understand why Larry has to be the time-travel machine," Everest said. "Didn't all of us go back in time? Shouldn't any of us work?"

Dar shrugged. "Time travel depends on objects that were created in that time period. Only Larry was actually created back then. There may be other possible solutions, but they're even more risky than what we are thinking about doing right now."

"Look," Vlas said, "not everyone needs to go. A few of us can go back in time, get some disguises, and return. I'm up for it. It was my idea anyway." He grinned.

"Just for the sake of argument," Dar said, "if we went on this hypothetical trip which of us would stay behind? I'm too recognizable so I should probably go back with you. Borneo too. Obviously, if we try this crazy scheme, Larry has to come with us." She looked at Elsie speculatively. "Sorry, Elsie, but there aren't a lot of domestic bobcats in the twenty-first century; I don't think Pooker should go back in time. Someone might decide to shoot her." Dar sighed. "Then again, she's going to get you caught in this timeframe too."

Elsie clutched at her cat. "You're just trying to scare me—as if I'm not scared enough. What if you never come back? How long do we wait before we decide you aren't coming back? There's no way I'm staying behind."

"Elsie, it makes sense," said Everest.

She rounded on him. "It makes sense, does it? I suppose you're thinking you'll go on this time-travel trip without me. And if you never return then I've lost every family member I've ever had. That just stinks."

"We're talking hypothetically here," Dar said.

"Yeah, right. Well, hypothetically, it doesn't make sense to leave Lelita and me behind. We'd be lost without the rest of you."

"No you wouldn't," said Dar.

"Yes, we would. We all know it. If we're going to do this, if we're going to try to go back in time using Larry as a time-travel machine, then we go as a team. We'll just have to hide Pooker in the twenty-first century so that she doesn't draw unwelcome attention."

"Jeez, Elsie, Pooker's going to put us all at risk." As far as Everest was concerned, that bobcat was the biggest pain.

"Uh, Dar," Larry whispered, "my super-sweet vision is telling me we don't have a lot of time to argue about this. I think our friends from the academy may have caught up to us. We better just do this time-travel thing."

Biting her lower lip, Dar maneuvered the HV to the far left and zipped into another block of vehicles. She bounced into one and then the side of a building, but she kept the hover vehicle rocketing along at high speed.

"I need a safe place to land, then a few minutes to reprogram the time-travel device. Since Larry's the one with superpowers, he should hold onto as many of us as possible, but we need to hang onto him as well. Larry, don't you dare let us spin into oblivion."

He grinned. "No prob."

"When and where were you born?"

"2:03 AM on October 12th, 1989 at Valley Med. My ma used to swear at me about her emergency c-section. That was a date and time I was never allowed to forget."

"Lucky for us. Borneo, check for this Valley Med Hospital and find out the distance between it and the mall we went to a month ago. I need latitude and longitude. Larry, what was the name of the mall again?"

"Vallco Mall," Larry said.

Borneo jacked back into his holoputer.

"So what do you all think?" Dar asked the group. "Are we doing this? It's zetta risky."

"It's a sure bet that we'll be caught otherwise. We need those disguises, and we're not going to find them here," said Vlas. "Beside, we'll be making history. How zeller is that?"

As usual, Vlas was in for anything. The boy had no fear. Everest wished he could be like Vlas.

"I say do it," Larry said. "I got a good feeling about this."

"I don't think it's such a good idea," Elsie responded. "You said yourself that using a human as a time-travel machine has never been tested."

Elsie would expect Everest to agree with her, but he wasn't sure what he wanted. Finally, he said, "It would be better to come up with disguises in this time period."

"How?" Dar asked. "It's not as if I want to use Larry as a human time-travel machine, but I'm out of ideas. We can't go to Mink's. We can't go to the clone academy or any other school. Everyone is alerted to who we are and why they should capture us." She tapped her fingers on the joy stick. "Borneo, is there a theatre nearby? Maybe we could try to break in and steal some makeup and wigs."

Borneo concentrated on his holoputer. "I see a couple of theatres, but the plays are still in progress. It's only 22:00. We would need to hide until everyone clears out."

"I doubt we'll have that luxury."

Bright lights beamed onto them from above so that all of the occupants of the HV were illuminated, including the very distinctive Borneo and Dar. Pooker growled.

They could see cyborg police shouting and waving their hands. Since they had soundproofed, Everest couldn't actually tell what they were saying, but he had a pretty good idea.

And Larry confirmed it. "They are ordering us to surrender. Immediately."

"Oh no," Lelita whispered. "What do we do now?"

Everest wondered the same thing.

Vlas said in a very low voice, "Dar let me take over."

She looked at him speculatively then quickly swapped seats.

"SHADARA, free fall," Vlas commanded.

The vehicle dived, twirling without rhyme or reason. They all screamed as the HV fell through the air. It bounced into a couple of vehicles but mostly just twirled around and around. The cybercops followed as best they could, but they weren't quite as crazy as Vlas was. Everest's face rippled as they plummeted to the earth. With only five meters to spare, Vlas whooshed back up and began to weave in and out of skyscrapers. The ones made out of J28 were forgiving when you hit them, but the steelorq packed a pretty good punch even against jellach.

"Okay, we better do this," Vlas said. "If anyone wants to get off this time-travel bus let me know now. Otherwise, we're all jumping into the abyss together."

Everyone remained silent. Everest had a hard time swallowing. He could actually feel his throat close. What if they died trying to go back in time? This felt like the worst decision in a long series of lousy decisions. But they had no other choice besides giving up.

"I'm taking silence as a vote for time travel." Vlas motioned to Dar. "How close are you to setting up the device?"

She didn't answer right away, and instead just kept on plugging in information. After a few seconds, she said, "I'm getting there. Borneo, I need the location now."

The boy rattled off latitude and longitude numbers for both the hospital and the mall parking lot.

"Make it a Saturday," Larry said. "Otherwise, adults will want us in school."

"Okay, I'm going to make it early morning as well— hopefully just a couple of days after you came to our time." From her pocket, she pulled out a little packet of purple pills and passed them to Lelita. "Hand these out. This ride could be bumpy."

"This is such a waste of time with our parents' lives hanging in the balance." Elsie moaned. "We need to be doing something for them."

"We'll return within minutes of leaving, so it will be as if we never left. No time wasted."

Elsie scrubbed at her face, and Everest wanted to do the same. It felt as if they'd been awake forever.

"I need us to try the aura-positioning unit first," she insisted.

"There is no time for that," said Dar.

"Yes, there is. I won't go otherwise."

Dar sighed. "Deng you're stubborn."

"Yes, I am. We need to know whether they're alive. And where they are."

Dar was already dragging the aura-positioning unit out of her oversized backpack.

She set it down. "Do you have anything with their aura on it?"

Elsie dug into her pocket and brought out two small steelorq cards. "Yes, we always carry these with their DNA on them, just in case. That should be able to provide their aura, right?"

"If they're in the database then this should work." She quickly scanned in the DNA from the little cards. After just a couple of minutes, she gave a crow of delight.

"They're alive!" She shook her head. "See?" She pointed at the screen of the APU. "Two blips, not far from here—somewhere in the Bay Area."

Elsie burst into tears. Everest swallowed hard, fighting back his own. He wasn't crying in front of Dar—no way, not in this millennium.

'Jeez, Elsie," Dar said. "Keep your aura on. This is good news, not a tragedy."

"I'm so happy." She sniffed. Lelita squeezed her hand.

"Well, don't get too excited. We have no idea what condition they're in."

"We know they're alive."

She grabbed Everest's hand, and he immediately tried to yank it free.

"They're alive!" she said again.

Dar cleared her throat. "Okay, Vlas, I think I'm ready. Just park her someplace safe and I'll set up for the jump backward before more cyborg officers show up."

"We may already be too late," Larry said. "I can see them approaching in the distance. I'm guessing you'll see them in about twenty seconds."

"Then twenty seconds is all the time we've got."

Vlas made a very quick and relatively clean landing on some street moss in a narrow alley. Dar took the time-travel device she had been programming and stuck it into Larry's pant pocket—it peeked out just enough for her to be able to press the final button. "Okay, everyone, group hug. Larry, touch as many of us as you can," she said with a grimace as she climbed mostly into the backseat. "You all need to hang onto Larry's shirt and not lose contact." With one hand, she clutched his shirt and with the other she grabbed one of the vehicle's chairs.

Everest wasn't much for the idea of a group hug, but he preferred that to disintegrating into little pieces. So he stuck one arm around Larry and his sister Elsie, and he let Larry clutch his wrist.

He had no trouble admitting—at least to himself—that he was terrified. Everyone grabbed a hold of everyone else. Elsie grasped Pooker's pico-trainer. Even with the soundproofing, Everest heard sirens approaching. If this didn't work, they were doomed.

"On the count of three." Dar took a deep breath. "One, two, three…"

CHAPTER 21
Back in the Twenty-First Century

Elsie screamed at the intensity of the initial jerk. It was different from any of the previous times. The force was outrageous, and she felt as if she flew and spun at the same time. She couldn't stop screaming, and yet she couldn't be sure she *was* screaming. She heard nothing, saw nothing. But she could feel pain and force and pressure, and she was sure her teeth chattered like crazy.

Would they survive? Or would they explode into a trillion pieces of dust? What had they been thinking, taking such an enormous risk? It would have been better to give themselves up to the cybercops.

A panicky feeling swept through her as she realized that she couldn't feel Pooker. She forced back the fear and held on where she remembered holding on. She tried to count, but the numbers were jumbled in her brain. She reminded herself that her parents were alive. Nothing else mattered.

Then the wild, out-of-control spinning ceased, and there was the familiar moment of utter nothingness. Elsie was relieved, and then she was terrified. She couldn't feel anyone else's presence. Was that different from before?

A bright flash exploded in her brain, and it was as if a big light switch turned back on again. Her heart was beating too fast, and she felt heavier than usual. She could hear Pooker's low growl and her own ragged breathing. Her sight flooded back along with a healthy dose of relief. A quick glance showed her everyone was still intact.

"Whoooo-hooooo!" Vlas yelled. "Deng, what a ride."

Lelita giggled. "It was wild."

148

"You think your ride was wild," Larry said, "mine was frigging unbelievable—a rock 'n roll rollercoaster." Larry laughed. "Look at me! I'm a Superman time-travel machine. Talk about zetta cool."

Pooker was wild-eyed. Elsie had a feeling she looked equally crazed. Borneo had a glazed, beyond-fear look. Her brother was keeping his expression blank.

"Lucky we had those little pills," Dar said as she looked around. "I'm betting most of you would have lost your stomachs without them."

They were in a large, empty parking garage. The dark gray sky had that eerie, slightly pink aura that happened near dawn, and the air was crisp. There were a lot less cars on the road and therefore, a lot less noise. They had misjudged things a bit because the HV was on the sidewalk in front of the doors rather than in the actual parking lot.

"SHADARA, rise a few meters and move to the far right corner," said Dar. The HV lifted and slowly wended its way through the garage to the darkened corner. When they arrived, Dar jumped out. With her hands on her hips, she started marching around the vehicle, muttering to herself. Elsie was impressed. She had a feeling she would collapse if she tried to stand up right now. Her whole body felt rubbery like jellach at its softest.

"Uh, Dar," Larry said. "I still have superhero hearing, and I think one of those words you mumbled is illegal in the thirty-first century." He grinned wickedly.

"Lucky for me, we aren't in the thirty-first century!" she retorted. "I'm trying to figure out where we can hide the HV. Come on out everyone. I need to see how small this is when it shrinks down to its most compact form."

"We need a car cover," Larry said.

"That would be handy, but I doubt we'll find one at this time in the morning."

As wobbly B12s slowly exited the HV, it began to shrink, eventually reaching about half its former size. Elsie had to pick up Pooker to get her out of the vehicle. The cat kept collapsing whenever she tried to walk on her own.

"Take everything out of the HV," Dar said as she removed her backpack from the floor of the passenger seat. Once everything was removed, she stepped back a couple of paces.

"SHADARA, please shrink more." The jellach vehicle made a sucking noise as it shrank further in size, becoming much more compact and also more solid-looking.

"SHADARA, shrink more." The HV lost another third of its size in an exercise that involved a lot of popping and sucking.

Dar circled around the vehicle, and Elsie had the distinct impression she was measuring it in her head.

"SHADARA, shrink more," she repeated. But there appeared to be no more pop in the now relatively tiny vehicle. It gave one half-hearted, little sucking noise, but there was no obvious change in size. It looked as if it could hold one person, but only if that person was zetta small.

Dar glanced over at Vlas. "It's probably too heavy to lift."

"Yeah, it's pretty dense. I could squeeze in and fly it somewhere."

"There's nowhere else for it to go," she replied. She crouched down in front of her backpack and rummaged inside. After a few seconds she pulled out a thin bundle and a ball of fine string.

As she started to unfold the thin bundle, Elsie saw that it was Vlatex II material. Dar gripped one corner and held out the rest of the material. "Vlas, take that corner. Elsie, Everest, take the other two. Let's cover this baby."

After it was covered, Dar and Vlas used the string to tie the cover down. When they were done, Dar stood with her arms crossed and contemplated the covered HV.

She turned to Larry. "What do you think?"

"I'm not sure how, but that material really makes it disappear. No one's going to notice it."

"It'll have to do," Dar said. "I wonder if we arrived when we thought we would, or whether we're nine months early?"

"Hey, I was a preemie, so it would have been more like seven and a half months," said Larry.

Dar pointed at him. "If we arrived early, then we're going to need to make sure you don't run into yourself."

"I don't think we have to worry just yet. Me, I'm a creature of the night. If I'm still there in the past, there ain't no way I'm getting up at the crack of dawn."

"Then I guess we'll concentrate on our other big issue first."

"And that would be?"

"Where in blazes are we going to hide this bobcat?"

They all stared at Pooker who was stretching, taking full advantage of finally being out of the cooped up HV. She looked as if she had recovered from the wild ride.

"Could we disguise her as a dog?" Larry asked.

"Yeah, right," Vlas snorted.

"Is there anything else she could be?" asked Dar.

"She's too big to be a cat," Larry said.

"Yeah, that's out." Dar tapped her finger against her lips. "This is a tough one."

"We're going to have to split up some anyway," Larry said. "Otherwise, we'll look like a frigging gang. We can take Pooker and Elsie and maybe Lelita and Borneo to Crazy Sue. She'll hide them while we round up some disguises. All of us will have to brainstorm ideas for what to do with Pooker when we go back to the thirty-first century. She's just not disguisable."

Elsie stared. "Crazy Sue? Why do I have a bad feeling about this?"

"Crazy Sue's okay. She squats under the highway overpass a few blocks from here. There's some brush there. She can hide you and Pooker till we get back."

"What if she turns us in?" Lelita asked.

"Girl, Crazy Sue wouldn't go anywhere near the police. If she balks at helping us, we'll just promise her some dough to keep you safe."

"Exactly how are we going to get dough?" Dar asked.

Elsie remembered that dough in Larry's world was money, not the makings of a loaf of bread.

Larry grinned. "I got some ideas."

He was up to something. Elsie didn't know what, but it was trouble.

"We can't steal," Dar said.

"I would never steal," Larry said righteously.

"That includes borrowing."

"Good, 'cause I'm planning on us *earning* our money. I'm glad you're so agreeable."

Dar's eyes narrowed. "How, exactly, do you plan to earn it?"

"Only one legit way for us to earn money fast, and that's as street performers. You've got a phenom voice. I've listened to those old Shadara audios."

"No—absolutely not," she said tightly. "I don't have the singing voice that Shadara had."

"Course you do," Larry said. "Jeez, it's for a good cause. My voice is okay, but yours will bring in the big bucks."

"No way," she said again.

"No one will ever know in the thirty-first century. It'll be our little secret."

"I—don't—sing," she said in no uncertain terms.

"Guess I can do the singing, but a pretty thing like you with a great set of chops would rake in a lot more dough."

"I'm not a pretty thing, and that's just too bad. Exactly where do you plan to do this entertaining?"

"It'll depend a lot on what today's date is. We can always head downtown, but there might be something closer. If it really is Saturday, and if it's the right Saturday, then we might be able to go to the local flea market. Do you have any idea what the date is?"

"You weren't the most reliable time-travel machine," Dar said. "But I'm hopeful that we arrived on the Saturday after we met you."

He pursed his lips. "Well if anyone sees a newspaper dispenser let me know. We can check out the cover and confirm the date. It sure would be sweet if we landed on the first Saturday of the month."

Elsie asked, "What's a newspaper dispenser?"

Larry made a face. "Do you know what a newspaper is?"

"Uh, should I?" she asked.

Dar was shaking her head and biting her lower lip. "I sure hope we didn't land on the first Saturday of the month because that would mean we arrived before you left. That would not be good."

Larry shrugged. "It would be cool to see myself. It would be like a living, breathing mirror!"

"Yeah, and you'd probably blow up or something," Vlas said with a grin. "Wouldn't that be zeller?"

"Uh," Borneo said. "I don't think he would blow up. He might suffer some sort of brain dysfunction, but spontaneous combustion doesn't actually happen. No cases have ever been proven."

They all looked at him then burst into laughter. His ears went pink.

Lelita immediately sobered. "We're not laughing at you," she said quickly.

"Of course we aren't," Dar said. She punched Borneo in the shoulder. "You are one hundred percent right. No one's going to blow up by seeing themselves in the past."

"Anyway, we better get going," Larry said. "Crazy Sue'll know today's date."

Elsie rubbed Pooker between her ears. Larry was being zetta decisive and in charge. Was that because he felt comfortable in his time period or because he had superpowers? Maybe it was a little bit of both. She didn't like the idea of hiding away all day, especially with someone named Crazy Sue, but she also got it that Pooker was in danger here in the twenty-first century. If someone saw her and thought she was a wild animal, they would take steps to eliminate her.

"It's awfully early for a visit," Elsie said. "Will Crazy Sue be mad?"

"She ain't mad, she's just crazy." Larry laughed like he was a real allen. "Sorry," he said, wiping his nose with his sleeve. "Seriously, she might be a little irritated because she's not a morning person, but she's decent. She won't stay mad for long. She likes me." He poked himself in the chest with his thumb.

"Can she keep a secret?" Elsie asked.

"Don't matter if she can or can't. No one believes anything she says. They just think she's crazy as a loon. And she's known for her tall tales. She takes pride in them." He waved to the kids. "Let's go. Can we drape a little of that invisibility cloak over the cat?"

153

"The Vlatex II?" asked Dar. "Sure."

"If we keep her in the middle of our pack, maybe no one will see her."

They left the parking lot and turned right at the street. A few cars cruised past, but it was quiet at this time of the morning. They were walking slightly up hill toward what looked like an intersection in the traffic. Elsie couldn't quite figure out how it worked.

"That's the overpass for Highway 280," Larry said, pointing, "Crazy Sue squats underneath that overpass. She's got primo space—been there for years. No one bothers her 'cause she's got the eye. One dude tried to take her space a few years back, and the next day he got stung by an entire swarm of wasps. The day after that, he got hit by a bus. You do not mess with Crazy Sue."

"But neither of those incidents could have anything to do with her," Elsie said.

"Tell that to the judge, girl," Larry said. "Before that, a wacko lady called Two-Can Isabel tried to steal Crazy Sue's shopping cart. The next day Isabel was found dead as a doornail, struck down by a massive heart attack. That Crazy Sue, she got the eye."

Dar rolled her own eyes and exchanged looks with Vlas. Elsie couldn't help but think that Larry's twenty-first-century thinking was zetta primitive, but she wasn't going to embarrass him by rolling her eyes too. She glared at both Dar and Vlas.

"Ooh, looks as if the ute-baby over here is trying to give me the eye," Vlas said, choking on his laughter.

"We'll see who's laughing after you meet Crazy Sue," Larry said seriously.

They passed a ramp that seemed to dump into a large thoroughfare. Even at this time of the morning, lots of cars raced by. Beyond that, a bridge jutted out over the highway. Larry leaned over the side to look for Crazy Sue. "I'll just jump down and see what's up."

"We forgot to check on your powers," Elsie said. "What if they're gone?"

"It's cool. I got the vision and hearing still, and I'm feeling zetta strong. I brought y'all to the twenty-first century, didn't I?"

He looked over his shoulder at the rest of the B12s. "Don't try this at home." His grin was zetta wild as he jumped off into thin air.

Lelita gasped and stepped backward, but the rest of them crowded the ledge to try to find him. He stayed close to the edge and away from the cars. When he landed with a dull thud, he waved and disappeared from view. Now he was in the land of Crazy Sue.

CHAPTER 22
A Visit with Crazy Sue

Everest wasn't exactly comfortable with leaving Elsie at the mercy of someone named Crazy Sue. What would their parents think? Course he wouldn't mind getting in trouble as long as he could actually see them again. Everything was so topsy-turvy that it was hard to know what made sense anymore. He tried to imagine what his parents were going through right now. It was such a relief to know they were alive and on Earth, but were they being tortured to reveal the secrets of the femto-boosters?

He still had a hard time getting his head around his parents having invented such amazing technology. It didn't seem possible that anyone could have invented femto-boosters, let alone his parents. He'd always known they were cerebrum-heavy, but flasers, this went beyond being zetta smart. This was genius. How come he and Elsie weren't brilliant like that?

A deep rumbling voice shouted from below. Everest didn't understand all the words, but it was obvious that the owner of the voice was irritated. There was the indistinct sound of distant conversation then Larry became visible again. "Can y'all scramble down or do you need help?"

"We can make it there on our own," Dar said and proceeded down the hill with speed and dexterity.

Lelita needed the most help, and Everest held her hand on the final portion of the would-be path. Borneo stumbled a bit but managed the hill without serious injury. Elsie did fine, though she wasn't quite as fast as Dar or Vlas. And Pooker went down nimbly, like the cat that she was.

The side of the hill was a sea of long, bristly, weedy grass and wildflowers. At highway level, cars whizzed by at a much faster speed than Everest remembered from their last visit. They almost sped along like hover vehicles, only on the ground rather than in the air. All he remembered from their last visit was a lot of cars having been stopped in traffic, but here the vehicles flowed smoothly.

"Well, lookee what the boy dragged in," Crazy Sue said in a low rumble, staring with deep-set eyes. She was partially hidden by the brush that covered the side of the road, but after a few seconds, she stepped out. Behind her, there was just the hint of a grayish-tan tent along with a hodgepodge of cooking utensils and wares.

Crazy Sue was a heavy-set woman, her skin a mass of brown leather wrinkles. Everest thought she was darkened by the sun rather than genetics. Her natural skin tone was probably much lighter than his. Her hair was gray, the steel color of a sea lion. Stringy and dirty, it hung in messy waves down her back. She wore more than one outfit. At least that was how it seemed to Everest. A sack of a dress hung shapelessly over ratty jeans that were like the ones Everest wore during the timed field trip. Underneath the shapeless dress, she wore one or maybe even two t-shirts.

Her fingernails were dirty and split. She wore thin brown sandals repaired in a couple of spots with duct tape, and her toes were filthy and misshapen. Numerous silver earrings worked their way up both her ears, none matching.

Everest felt repelled. She was more alien than any human or non-human he'd ever met—so unkempt and wild-eyed. The only person who came close was that grimy man who'd asked him for a dollar on their field trip. He felt shaky just looking at her.

Crazy Sue flinched when she saw Pooker. "Holy moly, Larry, I thought it'd be more like a kitty-cat. You sure that thing is safe?"

Elsie nodded. "She's very domesticated, and she's also wearing the latest pico-trainer. She wouldn't hurt a mouse."

"Humph, if you say so." The woman jabbed a dirty fingernail toward Larry, but kept her eyes on Dar, savvy enough to discern the leader of the group. "He says you is from the future, an' y'all need Crazy Sue's help."

Everest's jaw dropped as he stared at Larry. He'd told her? What was he thinking?

"Jeez, Larry, tell the world why don't you," Dar said irritably, putting into words Everest's thoughts.

Larry shrugged. "No one lies to Crazy Sue. It's like an unwritten law."

"In case you've forgotten, our period has a written law that says we don't tell the natives about time travel."

Larry grinned. "Sorry, sister. I don't think anyone ever specifically told me about that rule. Besides, Crazy Sue rules trump all others."

"That's ridiculous," Dar said. "You've jeopardized the future as we know it."

"Crazy Sue can keep a secret," he responded.

The woman trained her scary eyes on Dar. "Larry knows better than to lie to me. So, tell me straight, are you kids from the future?"

After a stare-off that went on for at least a minute, Dar dipped her head. "Yes."

Crazy Sue tilted her head and looked up at Dar from under her eyelids. It gave her a wild look that matched her name. "Yer a pretty one, ain'tcha? But you hide it unner that cap, like yer some boy."

Dar didn't respond. She just looked right back at the woman, her expression dead serious.

"Heh, heh, heh, yer a funny one too." She pointed. "I like you. They grow 'em tall in the future. Y'all tower over my boy, here." She jabbed another dirty finger at Larry then she jabbed at Lelita. "'Cept you. Well, one mystery solved, thank the good Lord. Wasn't I scared to death when I heard my Larry'd gone missin'? Almost two months. Makes my heart glad to see you back."

"Two months!" Dar said. "But we took him in April."

"Yeah, and this here is June, ain't it?" Crazy Sue said.

"June?" Dar yelled. "That's impossible."

Larry shrugged. "Must have to do with me being a preemie." He turned to Crazy Sue. "What day in June?"

"June 1ˢᵗ."

"Tell me it's a Saturday," he said.

"Well, of course it is," said Crazy Sue.

"Yes!" Larry pumped his fist. "First Saturday of the month. How sweet is that?"

"Why's that, baby-boy?"

He grinned. "Flea market."

Crazy Sue laughed. "Whatever floats your boat; I'm just glad to have you back."

"I'm not staying. I'm going back to the future."

Her eyes widened then turned into slits as she stared from under her eyelids. Everest thought her stare might be the most uncomfortable one he'd ever encountered. Her mouth pinched, showing deeply etched lines. Finally, she raised one gnarled finger and pointed at Larry. "You do what makes you happy. You only got one life; you gotta make it a good one." She shook her head. "Can't say I won't miss ya, but I've missed plenty before you, and I'll miss plenty more after yer gone." She punched him affectionately in the shoulder. "Just don't get yerself hurt."

Larry laughed. "You know I can take care of myself."

She threw her head back and let out a deep belly laugh. "Yeah, I know, but that don't mean I won't worry about you." She scratched her temple. "Yer just a scrawny kid, for all you bein' the smartest I ever did meet."

Larry flexed his muscles. "Hey, I got superpowers now."

Elsie gasped and something like a growl came from deep in Dar's throat.

"Cool it, Larry," Dar said in a low voice.

"This is Crazy Sue. I told you, she's no snitch."

'Honey, the day you become a superhero is the day I eat my tent."

"No, really," he said. "Look, I'll jump up to the top of the overpass."

Everest grabbed his arm. "Are you crazy? Someone might see you."

"No one's going to see me." He threw off Everest's hold.

Everest shook his head. He couldn't believe Larry was being such a ridiculous showoff.

Larry," Dar said. "Stop it now. This is no time to play around."

Larry paused. "Come on, it's no big deal." He sighed when they all kept glaring at him. "Okay, I won't jump, but I'll pick up Crazy Sue instead. No one will see, and she'll stop worrying about me."

"Hurry up, then," Dar said irritably.

"Don't you be pickin' me up," Crazy Sue said, backing away. "I'm a big woman and yer a scrawny kid. One or both of us'll get hurt."

Larry laughed. "No really, I got special powers." He walked up to her and put his arms around her waist. He lifted. Crazy Sue's heel raised an imperceptible amount from the ground. Larry grunted and let go. "What gives?"

"Your powers must be waning," Dar said.

Larry looked around wildly. "I can still see far away."

"Maybe excessive strength is the first thing to go. How long has it been?" Dar glanced at the rest of the kids.

"It's been three hours and fifty-two minutes give or take a couple of minutes," Borneo said.

"Larry," Crazy Sue interrupted, "you and yer friends sure're a riot and a half. You just love to pull my chain an' now you have a gang to help you. You had me goin'." Her laughter was a deep rolling sound. "Superpowers." She shook her head and waggled her finger at him. "You is a piece of work. But joking time's over. You got to get down to serious business, Superboy. Which means yer off to the flea market to round up some dough?"

"Yeah, gotta sing for our supper. Don't suppose you'd like to lend us your guitar?"

She laughed from deep in her belly again. "Larry, you is the finest young boy I ever did meet, and you is wicked, wicked smart, but you can't play no guitar. Didn't I try to teach you myself?"

"Hey, I could learn. I just need time to practice."

"Yeah, about a thousand years."

Larry shrugged and grinned. "That can be arranged, but I don't need to play." He pointed at Dar. "She can."

Dar rounded on Elsie. "How dare you tell him?"

Everest had no idea what Dar was talking about and was completely floored when Elsie turned alien and burst into tears. Jeez, she was such a suzo-shrimp sometimes.

Elsie shook her head wildly, dashing at her tears with the back of her hand. "No, Dar, no, I didn't; I didn't tell. I never would have."

"Man, Dar," Larry said. "What's the big deal? I already told you I checked out some of Shadara's performances. And I followed you to your little kiddy daycare a couple of weeks ago. Saw your little performance there. You can't snow me with the whole 'I can't sing' thing." He made a face and wiggled his fingers in the air. "I know perfectly well you can."

Dar whipped back to Larry and shoved him hard. "You spied on me? What's the matter with you?"

Jeez, Dar was overreacting. It wasn't like it was a secret that *Shadara* could sing. It would be zetta weird if Dar *couldn't* sing.

"Uh, girl," Crazy Sue interjected. "Me, I like a woman with spunk, but yer goin' to draw attention to us, an' I like my privacy. If you can't control yerself, yer goin' to have to leave my squat, and leave it right fast."

Dar dropped her hands to her sides and slowly took a step back. "I apologize for my behavior. I don't need the guitar. I won't play it."

"Dar, you got to get over this stage fright," Larry said with a wicked grin. "It's so not you."

The sound she made was like a snarl.

Larry's grin grew wider. "If you play that guitar and sing the way you and I both know you can sing, we'll make more money, and we'll make it faster. That means we get our disguises sooner, we get back to the thirty-first century sooner, and we save the ute-babies' parents sooner."

"What's a ute-baby?" Crazy Sue asked.

"It doesn't matter." Larry waved it away. "What matters is that Dar is acting like a *real* baby; she needs to stop throwing her little hissy-fits about using her God-given talents and get on with it." He turned on her. "Are you going to let that Shadara-woman define who you *can't* be as much as who you *can* be? Does it really matter if she was the world's greatest singer? Does that really mean you have to stop yourself from singing at all? So what if she was the diva to end all divas? Because Elsie and Everest's parents are scientists does that mean they can't be? Even if they really love science, really love the idea of inventing crazy stuff, do you *really* think they should switch to managing virtual currency instead? 'Cause if that's what you think, you're a loony-tunes, for sure."

Vlas crossed his arms and looked at Dar thoughtfully. "He's got a point. It's not really your style to run away from things. What's the harm in singing and strumming a song or two if it means getting the job done?"

"You don't understand," Dar said.

"I guess I understand better than anyone," Vlas said, "since I've been hiding my talents too. Maybe we need to rethink things, though. Why shouldn't we be able to use our natural abilities?"

Lelita stepped forward. "I could try to sing."

Dar sighed, shaking her head. "Thanks, Lelita, but I'll do it. Jeez, what a bunch of nags. Just for the record, the reason I don't sing is because I don't like to perform. The little ones like it, but that's different; that's not a performance. If I don't like doing something, I shouldn't have to do it. In this case, I agree that our plan requires me to sing, but I don't have to like it." She turned to Crazy Sue. "I would appreciate the use of your guitar. I promise to protect it and bring it back to you."

"Well," Crazy Sue nodded approvingly, "can't say any better than that." She clapped her hands. "The flea market starts up at 8:00 AM, but I wouldn't get there any earlier than 8:30. Even at 9:00 there are still vendors setting up. It's been awhile since I visited that big old yard sale. You got anything to eat? We could have ourselves some breakfast if you'd like."

"Yeah, we brought some protein bars," Larry said, rolling his eyes.

"And Blackholes," Lelita said, shyly holding one out.

"Black holes? Girl whatcha talking about?"

"Calorie-free chocolate," she said.

"Calorie-free? Are you pullin' a funny on Crazy Sue?" The older woman rubbed her hands together with glee. "Bring it on."

"We have some dried fruit too," Elsie said.

"Not sure I should be eating prunes while I'm squattin'." Crazy Sue gave her belly laugh again.

"Dried seaweed?" Everest asked.

Crazy Sue waggled her finger at him. "Now yer just pullin' my chain again. Don't be doing that to old Crazy Sue." She snorted. "Seaweed!"

She motioned them to where the overhang plus the tall brush kept the tent at least partially hidden. While they sat and snacked on the various items they had brought from Mink's she made them instant coffee on a small burner.

"Do you live here all year round?" Elsie asked.

"Mostly, yeah, this is my squat. Once or twice a year, the police try to harass me into another location—like a shelter or somefink, but that's not for Crazy Sue. I'm a free spirit. If'n they kick me out, then after a while, I kick myself back in. 'Sides, I'm a better choice than any new squatter. Better the one you know, eh? They know I don't cause no trouble. Never been a drinker. Don't distract the drivers cuz I hide real good. They say, 'that Crazy Sue, she's harmless.' An' they're right. I mind me my own business; keeps to myself."

Despite the way she looked and the way she talked, Everest liked Crazy Sue. She was a character and not like anyone in the thirty-first century, but he had the sense she could be trusted. He was no longer afraid to leave Elsie here while he went with Dar, Larry and Vlas to find some disguises. Well, maybe he was a little afraid. What if the police chose today to come by and check on Crazy Sue? He wished they didn't have to split up. But Pooker was a problem. They just couldn't bring her around town. Someone would notice that she was no little house cat.

"Elsie, will you be able to keep Pooker hidden?" he asked. "It will defeat the purpose if we leave you here and then Pooker makes herself known to the cars zipping by."

"I'm pretty sure she'll be okay," Elsie said, glancing thoughtfully at her bobcat. "I'll keep her calm."

"Try to get her to go farther back into the shade."

"I think she'll do that naturally."

Crazy Sue clapped her hands. "Okay, time for those of you headin' to the flea market to start walking. It's gonna take some time, unless you got money for the bus."

"Nah, we're walking," Larry said. "We'll be back as fast as we can."

"Yeah, yeah, no one's goin' to hold their breath. Just be safe, an' bring me back somefink pretty." Her grin showed a couple of missing teeth.

"Sure, Crazy, I got something in mind."

"You always do," she said and waved them away.

CHAPTER 23

Dar Draws a Crowd

By the time they arrived at De Anza Community College where the flea market was being held, they had to have walked and jogged at least three kilometers. Crazy Sue's guitar was slung across Dar's back.

"Hey, Larry," she said, "how's your sight?"

"No more superpowers—just normal vision." He sighed. "It sure was fun being all powerful. Feel sort of weak now. Probably just the contrast, but I swear I need another one of those pills just to be able to do normal things like walk or lift something." He eyed the pendant. "Maybe I should have one more femto-booster."

Everest stopped walking and stared. Were femto-boosters addictive? Larry's reaction was a little creepy. "Maybe you should give me the pendant for safe keeping."

Larry drew back, tightening his hold on the locket and drawing it close to his belly. "It's me who's kept it safe from the beginning. First Elsie loses hers then you give away yours. What makes you think you should be the one to watch out for it?"

Dar looked at Larry speculatively. "I think you could use a break from guarding that thing."

He swung around and glared. "What do you mean?"

"Those femto-boosters may have some unexpected side-effects, such as being highly addictive, for one." She held out her hand. "Why don't you give me the locket? You have my word I'll just protect it. No femto-boosters for me. You know you can trust me. Besides, after your boosted fight with super-vlem, the bad guys will attack you first. They'll assume you have the locket."

"It's my pendant," Everest said irritably. Okay, so technically it was his sister's, but flasers, Larry, and for that matter, Dar, had zero rights to the femto-boosters.

"Yeah, I get that," Dar said. "I'm just suggesting that I can be a neutral party."

Larry tangled his fingers into his tight curls. "Yeah, yeah, that's cool. I don't want to feel like this. My mom was a total burnout. No way am I ending up like that. Take it." He handed the pendant to Dar who slipped it around her neck. "And keep it away from me." He paced back and forth. "Jeez, I could use some water."

Dar squeezed his shoulder. "We'll get you some."

Everest had the irrational urge to hit someone. Larry should have given the pendant back to him. Once again, he and Elsie were being treated like outsiders. He imagined himself dragging the locket off Dar's neck.

"Sorry, man." Larry held out his hand. "It would have been fairer to give the pendant back to you or Elsie, but that really is a bad idea—almost as bad as me keeping the darned thing. That's the first place any creeper will look. We need to be able to buy time if the bad guys catch us."

Everest slowly unclenched his hands. He got where Larry was coming from. After a shaky breath, he reached out his right hand and the boy slapped it. Then Larry clasped and shook it before ending with a knuckle punch.

The boy shook his head and said one of those bad twenty-first-century words. "Didn't expect such a strong reaction to the pill." He looked at Dar and the pendant hanging around her neck. "I still want another one, but the feeling isn't as desperate as it was a few minutes ago."

"I guess that tells us one thing for sure," Dar said. "We need to rotate the use of the femto-boosters. If someone uses one, they don't use another unless it's an emergency."

Larry shook his head. "You don't have to act like I'll freak out or something if I take another femto-booster. All of us may need to use one at some point."

"I know," Dar said. "If we need everyone to be superheroes then of course you'll be femto-boosted. I'm just suggesting we use a bit of caution. There's no history on these babies. We're using them blind. Who knows what Everest's parents knew that they haven't documented? Who knows what they haven't figured out yet?"

She asked her dot-clock for the time. When it wriggled and stretched and popped into a display of 8:35am, she straightened her shoulders. "Okay, time to get down to business." She looked at Larry. "How do you go about performing for money in the twenty-first century?"

"We need to find a good spot surrounded by awesome vendors so people are hanging around. We gotta stay away from the food court 'cause it is way too close to the information booth where the guys in charge hang out."

Everest took in the already mobbed scene. This was the last place he would ever go of his own free will. He couldn't stand crowds. He kept reminding himself that they were trying to save his parents. Everywhere he looked there were tents with merchandise and signs advertising wares and food. With all of the thirty-first-century markets being virtual, he'd seen nothing like this before.

Dar gave a low, appreciative whistle. "Lelita would have loved it here. Look at all the shopping potential." She turned to Larry. "Are you sure they won't get mad if we perform?"

"We-ell, I wouldn't say I'm sure. But I've performed here before and got me a little bit of money before I was kicked out. That's the worst thing they'll do." He blazed them all with his most winning smile. "I'm so sorry, officer," he said to a fictitious and invisible police officer in a pleasing lilt. "I didn't realize you had rules about performing here. We'll leave right away, sir." He bowed to the B12s. "We're lucky that we're kids. We can totally get away with it. They don't actually care if we perform; they just care about us getting money for it." He looked around. "This corner is probably the farthest from the info booth. Once we track down some empty stalls, we'll be in business." They found exactly what they were looking for in the middle of aisle 'S.'

Dar reluctantly swiveled the guitar off her back and strummed it. There was a look of pain on her face like she was about to be tortured.

"Uh, Dar," Larry said, "can you try to look like you're enjoying this? I'd swear you just ate a bag of lemons."

She grimaced even more. "I'm doing the best I can."

"How 'bout taking that hat off and fluffing your hair?" Larry tilted his head. "You're hot when you want to be."

She lunged and grabbed him by his collar, twisting it tightly and jerking him forward so that their noses almost touched. "I don't ever want to be hot, and the next person who says I am will find out what it feels like to be braided into a twenty-first-century pretzel. Jeez, I'm twelve years old. If I don't want to be hot, I shouldn't have to be."

"I doubt beating me up'll be good for business, but you never know," Larry managed in a strangled voice. Despite his raspy delivery, he didn't act afraid or even irritated.

Dar dropped her hold, stepped back, and wiped her hands together as if to remove a layer of dirt.

"I really hate this," she said.

"No kidding?" asked Larry. "I hadn't noticed."

Dar made a face. "I don't even know any twenty-first-century songs."

"No worries; just sing what you know. We'll say these are original pieces. Mostly people won't ask."

Dar sighed again. "Deng, I hate this."

"You're repeating yourself." Larry didn't even try to hide his amusement. "Come on, this is a walk in the park."

"Yeah, yeah, yeah." She shook her head then did a few practice bars on the guitar.

She began to softly sing a song that Everest had never heard before. It sounded like a lullaby. It was a simple song and she was barely audible. Yet Everest felt uncomfortably spellbound. He had the unaccountable and zetta disgusting desire to cry. Flasers, talk about alien.

Almost immediately, the people closest to them stopped speaking and shopping. They turned their heads, straining to hear.

Dar's voice grew stronger as she progressed, telling the tale of a small girl who waited for her mother to come home from a trip to another galaxy. Though she sang without amplification, she had no problem projecting her voice so that it carried to her growing audience.

When Everest realized what she was singing about, he nervously looked around, but no one seemed to notice the actual words, only the delivery, the soaring notes, the lower warm tones. Dar's range was amazing.

By the end of her song, a crowd had formed, and a number of people had dropped coins and rectangular pieces of paper into a shallow box that Larry had scrounged for just that purpose. Dar distanced herself from the applause, refusing to look at the audience, to smile or interact in any way. Immediately, she moved on to another song that was not familiar to Everest.

It was low and sad, the story of lost love in the chaos of the Vlemutz war. Again, Everest worried about the subject matter and what it might reveal to the listeners, but once again, they all just stared dumbfounded. She could have sung about anything.

"Man, that girl has chops," Larry said, sidling up to Everest.

"Huh?" He assumed Larry meant Dar could sing, but he'd never heard it expressed that way.

"She can sing! Jeez, I ain't never heard anything like it. And she's practically glowing now that she's forgotten to be uncomfortable. Are you sure she's human?"

"Shut down, Larry," Vlas said, standing to the boy's right. "Of course she's human. What kind of yocto-brained question is that? Dar would kick your keister to the Xlexuri Galaxy if she ever heard you."

"Hey, I'm just saying that things have evolved a lot in a thousand years if singers sound and look like that."

By now, the audience was beginning to get in the way of those who were trying to check out the nearby stalls. There had to be fifty people crowded around Dar. Many of the women were openly weeping and there were plenty of men rubbing their eyes. One heavy-set guy wearing a green shirt with bright purple exotic flowers all over it had tears streaming down his face. He slowly made his way over to Dar then dropped a bill into the box and walked away, turning his head multiple times to continue watching her.

Larry let out a very low whistle. Even that small sound had many irritated audience members using their eyes to throw daggers at him. He tried to look contrite.

"That guy just gave us a twenty-dollar bill," he whispered to Everest. "Now that's zeller."

When Dar's song came to an end, spontaneous applause, whistles, and cheers erupted from the audience.

Larry shook his head. "She could make a fortune in this time period."

"She could make a fortune in any period," Vlas said, "but she won't do it."

Keeping her head down, Dar immediately began to strum again. A steady stream of onlookers dropped dollar bills into the tip box. Most of the members of the audience couldn't bring themselves to move on.

In the next song, her voice took on the quality of a flute. She sang in a higher key and the words were harder to make out, but once again she mesmerized. More people arrived, and there was shuffling and jostling to make room.

"Oh, oh," Larry whispered. "Coppers." He motioned toward a man and woman standing back from the crowd dressed in crisp black uniforms.

"Get ready to make a run for it."

CHAPTER 24
Crazy Sue's Glimpse into the Future

Elsie couldn't help feeling grumpy at being left behind. She got it that Pooker was a liability, but she would have liked to go to the flea market too. Instead, she was stuck with Crazy Sue who was currently looking at her in that really alien way she had of squinting and staring up from under her eyelids. It made Elsie want to squirm big time.

Lelita let out a long sigh. "It would have been zeller to go shopping. What's a flea market like?"

"Flea markets used to be monster garage sales," Crazy Sue said. "But they've gone all fancy-like now—all boutiquey—smelly soaps an' candles an' gewgaws."

"What's a monster garage sale?" Lelita asked. "Do you have monsters in the twenty-first century?"

Crazy Sue snorted. "Girl, there are plenty of monsters in any time period, but I meant monster as in large or big."

Lelita's pretty brown skin went a dark shade of pink. "Oh."

"I still don't get it," Elsie said. "Why a large garage sale?"

Crazy Sue shook her head. "You kids from the future sure don't know nofink. People sell used stuff from their homes and call it a garage sale cuz they're basically cleaning out their messy garages."

"So a flea market is a bunch of people selling used things?" asked Elsie.

"Yeah, originally, but like I said, now they've added all sorts of new gewgaws and gadgets too."

"Gewgaws?"

"Already told you—soaps an' candles an' wooden boxes an' hats an' jewelry an' stuff. Hell, Larry and I got a friend who sells these fancy puppets there that cost a fortune. He carves them by hand out of wood. He sells used stuff too cuz that's what people expect to see at a flea market, but he's making a name for himself with his puppets."

"He must be a great artist to be using wood," Elsie said.

Only the best of the best were given permission to carve wood in the thirty-first century.

Lelita sighed. "The flea market sounds zeller."

"Zeller?" Crazy Sue snorted again. "What's that?"

"Uh." Lelita looked at Elsie.

"We use 'zeller' instead of the word 'cool' in our time period," Elsie said.

Larry used the word "cool" a lot so she new what it meant even though it wasn't a common term in the thirty-first century.

"Zeller." Crazy Sue rolled the word over her tongue. "I like it. It's zeller."

Elsie exchanged glances with Lelita and Borneo. Had they changed history? Would Crazy Sue start using the word in normal conversation? It sure was complicated interacting with twenty-first-century natives. At least with Larry, they had been able to keep him in the thirty-first century.

Elsie had to fight off a fit of the giggles thinking about bringing Crazy Sue to the thirty-first century.

She swallowed a few times then said, "I don't think you should use that word."

Crazy Sue rolled her eyes. "Honey, if'n yer worried I'll start some movement around the word 'zeller,' you can set yer mind at ease. No one listens to old Crazy Sue." She leaned forward, her shoulders hunched, her eyes heavy-lidded, her head cocked to the side. "Tell me about the future," she whispered with her forefinger up to her mouth as if she were shushing someone. "I can keep a secret."

Elsie's jaw dropped. "We can't tell you about the future. That would be a disaster. Besides, it's against the law."

Crazy Sue nodded her head slowly, soberly. "Against the law," she whispered then she offered them a wild grin. "Ain't you breaking the law coming back in time like this? Tellin' me a little about the future ain't nothin' more than a minor transgression." She wiggled her fingers. "An itsy-bitsy little infraction. Heck, I already know that bobcats are domesticated. How did that happen, anyways?"

"Even in your time period, people have pet bobcats," Elsie said, unable to help herself. She glanced over at the forest of weeds where Pooker had sprawled. Mostly she was camouflaged, but her ears were visible.

Crazy Sue's eyes went round. "Really?"

"Sure," Elsie said. "Just not as many. And it's not as if we have that many bobcat pets in our time period. Just enough to keep the species on earth. Most have been farmed out to wildlife preserves on other planets as the only way to keep them from going extinct. There just isn't enough wild land left on earth to provide them with a natural habitat."

Borneo cleared his throat. "In 2840 the United Nations of Earth passed the 'Natural Born Animals Act' also known as the 'NOAH Act.' It states that all known species should have at least ten representatives on Earth. If an animal can remain wild on Earth without going extinct, that's great; otherwise, foster families or care facilities are found and subsidized to ensure that the animals are provided with all they require to remain healthy and strong."

"The title of the act is a bit misleading," Lelita added shyly. "Some of the animals have been cloned in order to ensure that they don't go extinct."

"Cloned? Well don't that beat all?"

Elsie exchanged a nervous glance with Lelita and Borneo.

"So how come y'all sound like college professors? Hoity-toity-like?"

"Uh," Elsie mumbled, "we learn languages in the womb, so we have an extensive vocabulary."

"Get out! Like when your momma is still carryin' you?"

"Yes," she reluctantly replied.

Crazy Sue let out a string of words that were some of the bad ones that Larry liked to use. "Tell me more." She leaned in even closer.

Borneo cleared his throat again. "No one is homeless in our time period."

Crazy Sue's eyes narrowed to slits. "Do you kill off the homeless? Jail 'em?"

"Flasers!" Elsie cried. "Of course not."

"We make sure everyone has homes," Lelita added. "Food and clothing too. No one goes hungry or without shelter."

"And everyone who wants a job has a job," Borneo said.

"Humph," Crazy Sue responded. "Don't trust no government-run programs. Probably they just get rid of anyone like me who won't conform. I seen them sci-fi movies about the future."

"Our government isn't evil," Elsie said. "It's very important to Earth's leaders that everyone has a place to call their own. That's one of the reasons Earth has been voted second best planet in the Milky Way Galaxy to raise a family."

"Yeah, yeah, yeah, that's what they all say."

"Well," Lelita said, "people are also offered the opportunity to go to any other livable planet in the galaxy with their relocation cost paid for by the government."

"Now, we're gettin' to the truth of the matter. Them so-called leaders ship off us undesirables to other planets where we all die of starvation or are eaten by giant alien frogs."

Lelita shook her head vigorously. "No, really, no one would ever do that—honest."

Borneo bit his lower lip and stared off into space. "Well, I guess there's no way for us to actually know what happens to people once they relocate off planet. They never come back, so how do we know?"

Crazy Sue pointed her gnarled finger. "That's what I'm talking about, boy."

Lelita folded her arms and frowned. "Jeez, Borneo, how can you even suggest such a thing?"

"Well, *we're* not treated the way people should be," he said, going pink at the ears. "Just because we're clones, we get put in a boarding school for our entire childhood, and then we're expected to do something productive in our adult years to pay society back for someone having funded our creation. We're like indentured servants."

Elsie and Lelita stared at him open-mouthed.

174

"Whoa, boy, ain't you the closet radical?" Crazy Sue snorted and grinned wildly. She gave her full-bellied laugh.

He shook his head and sunk weakly to the ground, crossing his legs and doubling over with his head almost resting in his lap. "I have no idea where that came from," he said, his voice muffled. "I'm grateful that someone decided to create me."

Crazy Sue laughed again. "I like you bein' a rebel."

Elsie crouched down next to him. She had the scary notion that Borneo was right. Clones *were* treated badly despite Earth's high ranking. She patted him awkwardly on his shoulder. "Don't feel bad. It's the rest of us who should feel rotten because of how clones are treated."

Borneo raised his head. "Yeah, but you're the one whose parents are missing. I shouldn't be spouting off like that when there are more important issues at hand."

Elsie sighed. "I keep thinking I'll wake up, and this will all be a bad dream." She bit her lip, unsure if she should say her next thought. "And now I feel guilty for even having parents to worry about. I can't imagine what it's like for you, Lelita, and the others not to have family. I'm sorry."

Borneo shrugged. "I don't mind being a clone."

"Whoa, whoa, whoa," Crazy Sue exclaimed. "Y'all keep talking about being clones. Are you freakin' serious?"

Lelita froze, and Elsie remembered how frightened she was of anyone in this period learning about their clone status.

"Uh," Elsie said, "we'd appreciate it if you'd forget you ever heard that."

Crazy Sue shook her head. "No can do, girl. If y'all are clones, I gotta know."

Elsie said, "I'm not a clone."

"You promise?"

"Of course," she said. "Everest and I are twins. There's no way we could be clones."

Crazy Sue tilted her head again and zeroed in on Elsie with her disturbing stare. Finally, she jabbed her gnarled thumb at Lelita and Borneo. "What about them?"

Elsie, Lelita and Borneo all exchanged nervous glances.

"Ha!" Crazy Sue shouted. "Admit it, they're clones. Borneo already said so, anyway. Super sci-fi clones. Whoo-whee, ain't that a kick in the pants?"

"Uh," Borneo said, "it would be dangerous for you to tell anyone about us. People in the twenty-first century don't like clones."

"You kiddin'? We love clones!" She twisted her neck and looked down at him. "Mebbe we don't love 'em as real human beings, but as figments of our imagination, they're the bomb."

It struck Elsie that Crazy Sue had the weirdest way of talking. Sometimes she was backward in her vocabulary, and then other times, she sounded almost sophisticated. She was hard to figure. Elsie would have loved to hear her story. She wondered if Larry knew it and if he would share it with them. Or maybe they could ask Crazy Sue, herself.

Borneo cleared his throat. "We're not figments of anyone's imagination, so I guess that means people here won't like us. Please don't turn us in."

"Please," Lelita pleaded, her eyes huge with terror.

"Honey," Crazy Sue responded to Lelita, "yer secret is safe with me. I'm an outcast—remember? I don't cause trouble for other outcasts, an' they don't cause trouble for me." She nodded her head with purpose. "That's my philosophy." Then she grinned. "But you gotta tell me more about bein' a clone. How do they decide who gets cloned? What's the process? Why do you live in a boarding school instead of gettin' adopted?"

After a long pause, Lelita spoke hesitantly. "Someone has to be willing to fund the cloning process. Typically, the powers-that-be clone someone with special talents, but mostly there just needs to be a sponsor who has enough money to pay for the process and the royalties afterward. The sponsor needs enough clout to get the United Nations of Earth to approve the cloning activity. Often the sponsor is someone who knew the original. Sometimes, it is the original himself or herself who pays for the cloning. Very rarely, the government decides to sponsor a clone—but that's only when the original was a zetta unique genius."

"It's awfully expensive," Borneo added. "Only the wealthiest of the wealthy can afford the initial costs and the royalties afterward."

"So who sponsored you?" Crazy Sue asked.

Elsie had wondered the same thing.

"Actually, the government sponsored me," Borneo said. "My original was a famous scientist."

Crazy Sue waved her gnarled finger at Lelita. "And you?"

"Uh," Lelita said nervously. "I was sponsored privately. I don't know who my sponsor is. I don't really know why I was sponsored. No one has ever said."

"Hmm. A secret. Seems to me, you should be told. Maybe you should ask."

Lelita pursed her lips. "I guess I could, but I've always been afraid to ask."

Elsie slung her arm around Lelita. "You don't have to do anything that makes you uncomfortable."

The girl leaned into Elsie. "I am curious. Maybe I should ask. I just don't know how I'd ever work up enough courage to do that."

"Girl," Crazy Sue said, "courage to ask ain't hard to come by; it's the courage to listen to the answer that's hard."

Lelita slumped down to the ground next to Borneo. "No kidding."

CHAPTER 25
Being Sarah Drew

As Dar finished her song, the coppers, as Larry had called them, worked their way through the crowd until they reached her. Despite being regular human beings instead of cyborgs, they still bore a marked resemblance to police officers in the thirty-first century.

The female cleared her throat. "Hello," she said, "I'm Officer Gonzales and this is Officer Vanderhoff."

Dar finally made eye contact then glanced over to where Larry, Vlas and Everest stood nearby.

When she offered the officers her killer smile, Everest felt as if he'd been punched in his gut.

The male officer sucked in his breath.

"That was lovely," said the female officer. "But we don't allow street performers at the flea market."

"I'm so sorry; I didn't know." Dar spoke calmly and Everest had a feeling she was doing her best to channel an innocent twelve-year-old girl from the twenty-first century.

"Yes, we're sure you didn't intend to break any rules. You have quite an extraordinary talent, and I suspect we'll be hearing about you in the future. But for now, I'll have to ask you to cease and desist."

Someone from the audience booed. Another boo followed. Pretty soon everyone was booing.

'Let the girl perform," someone yelled.

"She's not hurting anyone," came another shout.

The male officer turned around with his hands out. "I'm sorry, but we can't. If she really wanted to perform she should have purchased booth space."

Dar widened her eyes. "I'm so sorry for breaking the rules. Am I in big trouble?"

Everest rolled his eyes.

"Of course not," Officer Gonzales responded gently. "I'm sure you meant well, and everyone enjoyed your performance."

Dar nodded her head and moved Crazy Sue's guitar to her back. "May I go now, please?"

"Yes," Officer Gonzales said. "You do have a lovely voice."

"Yeah," said Officer Vanderhoff. "Amazing. You're going to go places, kid. What's your name?"

"Sarah Drew," she lied glibly.

Everest choked, but fortunately, all eyes remained on Dar.

"Okay," Officer Vanderhoff told the crowd, "the show's over. Time to get back to shopping. Let's hear a big round of applause for Sarah Drew. I'm sure she'll be famous someday." He smiled at her.

She smiled back. Everest thought he might puke.

While Dar packed up, a steady stream of fans strolled up to her tip box and threw down change and bills, all of them complimenting her as they walked by.

The officers hovered in the vicinity but didn't intervene with the tip line.

"Like taking candy from a baby," Larry whispered, his eyes gleaming, though he held back from rubbing his hands with glee since the police officers were watching. "Too bad she doesn't like to sing. Tempting to take advantage of it."

Everest shook his head as if to clear it. "It's alien having her sing. I don't like it."

"Yeah, my head's still spinning," Larry said. "She's crazy good."

As the crowd dispersed, the B12s checked out the box.

"Is there enough?" Dar asked quietly. The police officers were now at least thirty yards away, but they were still making their presence felt.

"I think so," Larry said as he started to tally their take. "There are at least six twenties, and plenty of fives and ones. I'm guessing you raised over two hundred dollars with three songs. Now that's efficient." He shoved the wad of money and loose change into his pocket which sagged with the weight. The coins jingled as he moved.

"Three songs too many," Dar said.

"I don't buy it," Larry said. "No one can sing like that and not want to do more. You're fooling yourself if you think you aren't glad to have such an amazing talent."

"*Whatever*, Mr. Psychologist," she said irritably. "Can we go now? Where are we getting the costumes?"

"Well, Sarah Drew," Larry began.

Vlas snorted at the reference to Dar's made-up name. All three boys doubled over in laughter. Dar made a sound in the back of her throat that was a lot like a growl, and the look on her face almost made her ugly. Not ugly, Everest had to admit, but definitely scary.

He choked back his laughter, and there was an uncomfortable silence.

Larry said, "I'm hoping our luck will hold out. I have a bud who used to let me and my ma sleep in his theatre on rainy nights. He had a thing for my ma. That was a long time ago, but we've stayed in touch. Crazy Sue knows him too. Besides owning a theatre, he works the flea market—sells old theatre programs and used books. He makes these crazy puppets too. If he's here, he's our dude."

He studied Dar. "You and Borneo will need something pretty drastic to hide your hair and skin color, but we all need disguises. We can buy sunglasses to cover Borneo's eyes, and we'll use wigs so we don't have to dye our hair. There's this theatrical putty stuff we can use to change noses, cheeks, chins..."

Dar jammed her cap more firmly on her head. "Flasers, what a pain. A wig is just alien, but dye doesn't work on my hair. Believe me, I've tried."

Larry cocked his head and pursed his lips. "Too bad no one wears glasses in your time period. That always helps disguise people. At least during the day you can wear sunglasses like Borneo."

Dar grimaced. "Let's go find your friend. What's his name?"

"Bobby—Bobby Presley." Larry sort of growled the name and struck some kind of weird pose with his hands and legs all

180

contorted. "He loves sharing a name with the great one. He even gets gigs as an Elvis impersonator."

Everest stared blankly. What in flasers was Larry talking about?

Larry's eyes narrowed. "Elvis Presley? The King?"

"The king?" Everest asked. "When was he king?"

Dar groaned. "Elvis Presley was the equivalent of Shadara a couple of decades before Larry's time," she said. "He was a singer back in the twentieth century—'the king of rock and roll.'"

"Man, I've never met anyone who didn't know who Elvis Presley was," Larry said, shaking his head. "That's just sad. Come on, let's go find Bobby. He's usually over by the pin guy. While we're there, I'll pick up a few pins for Crazy Sue."

A hive of shoppers swarmed the various tents, but the pavement was wide between the rows of kiosks so there was plenty of room to maneuver through the crowd.

Even so, Everest's chest tightened, and he had to fight the urge to run as fast and as far away as he could.

Vlas avidly took it all in. "Flasers, Lelita would love this place."

"Yeah, so would Elsie," Everest said. "I'd rather have my teeth regenerated than come here on purpose to shop."

Vlas laughed. "No kidding."

Larry took off at a fast pace, weaving around strollers. He looked over his shoulder, "Get a move on. We ain't got all day."

Vlas snorted and whispered under his breath, "Just a millennium."

Everest surprised himself by laughing again. What was the matter with him? How could he be so miserable over his parents one minute and then the next have almost forgotten their circumstances.

It was so alien to know that they weren't actually alive in this time period. Deng, they wouldn't be born for almost a thousand years. Talk about zetta bizarre. If he thought too much about all of this, he'd go bonkers and be shipped off to that Dementurnum planet with all the other crazies.

They passed a stall with an assortment of brightly-colored flags that for some reason reminded Everest of the light murals from their time. Next they passed a kiosk that was a hodge-podge of old items. One table held a collection of beat-up wooden boxes decorated with faded images. It was hard to imagine what those would cost in the thirty-first century. They were priceless. He breathed in deeply. Even the smell of cut wood was a treat.

Right before they reached the end of the aisle, Larry stopped abruptly and dived into a stall on the left that had shawls and scarves in every color and combination of colors imaginable. He grabbed two of the multi-colored scarves and one black shawl with a silver pattern.

"Crazy Sue'll love these," he muttered, "and I promised to bring her back something pretty. These are dirt cheap. I can still buy her a few pins for her collection."

After Larry completed his purchase, they took a sharp right at the end of the row. Larry ignored multiple aisles till he took another sharp right and started to swivel his head back and forth in search of Bobby's stall. He stopped abruptly and broke into a big grin.

"Heyyyy, Bobby!"

A man looked up from behind a strange wooden creation that looked like an overlarge head bearing a grotesque nose, beady eyes and a scary grimace. The creature wore a midnight blue wizard's robe embroidered with silver moons, stars and swirls.

Bobby's eyes widened and he flinched as if he'd seen a ghost, and Everest realized that he had. No one had seen Larry for two months. Who knew what the word was on the street?

"Son of a gun! Larry Knight, as I live and breathe…" Bobby let go of the puppet, and it sagged to full height—about a meter tall. He navigated out of the crowded stall. Snagging Larry into a full bear hug, he said in a muffled voice, "I thought you were dead. Where in blazes have you been?"

Bobby was aging, but he was trim and fit. His hair was so black Everest wondered if it could possibly be real. It was poufed up high in the front and slicked back on the sides. A few strands of hair hung down over his black eyes. He sported sideburns. There had to be some major gunk in his hair because it was zetta shiny. He wore a white t-shirt and black pants made out of the same material that Everest had worn in blue only a month before for their field trip. Bobby was a handsome man though strange in appearance. Strange even for this period.

"Uh, it's a long story," Larry said in a muffled voice. He squirmed out of the hug, and reached up to punch Bobby in the shoulder. "But I'm cool. Only I need a favor."

"Shoot," Bobby said with a relaxed smile.

"I need your help with some costumes me and my friends are pulling together."

"Costumes?" Bobby asked thoughtfully. "You putting on a play?"

"Uh, not exactly." Larry shrugged. "It's complicated."

Bobby ran a hand over his slicked-back hair. Now he frowned in earnest. "How complicated? You've been missing for months, and now you're asking me for costumes? Being eccentric doesn't make me stupid, Larry." He grabbed the boy by his shoulders and leaned forward to look him in the eye. "How much trouble are you in?"

Everest swallowed hard and exchanged nervous glances with Vlas. Dar stood off to the side with her arms crossed. She didn't take her eyes off Larry.

The boy shook his head adamantly. "Don't get crazy, man. I ain't in trouble. Just need some costumes, that's all. Just makeup, maybe a few wigs, some of that nose putty. What's the big deal?" His expression was pure innocence. "It's not like I'm asking you to hand it over for free. I got dough." He dragged out and held up the wad of paper money that Dar had just earned from her performance.

Bobby pushed away in disgust. "I'm not taking your money, Larry. I just want your trust. You owe me that. After all these years, after everything I've done for you."

A shopper jostled past Everest, and he took a step forward to avoid more passersby. Someone tried to interrupt Bobby and Larry's exchange to make a puppet purchase, but Bobby waved the person away, refusing to engage even when the man spoke belligerently.

Finally, Bobby swung around. "I'm busy," he said sharply. "You'll have to come back."

"Like hell!" The man stormed away.

"Jeez, Bobby," Larry said. "You can't just go off on your customers."

"I can do whatever I want," he replied. "That's why I run my own business; so I don't have to deal with anyone's crap." He dragged Larry a bit further from the kiosk. "That includes your crap."

"Tell him, Larry," Dar said quietly.

CHAPTER 26
Bobby's Disguises

Everest couldn't believe what Dar had said. Even Larry looked shocked. This sure was a turnabout for her.

"What about the whole 'disturbing the natives' problemo?" Larry asked.

Dar shrugged. "Rules were made to be broken."

"Jeez, you sure do like to change your tune. You went sideways on me when I told Crazy Sue."

"Yes, well, now that you've set a precedent, we'll just keep working under the assumption that your rather colorful friends can be trusted."

"Stop talking like an old lady," Larry grumbled.

He looked to the right then the left as if to gauge how much privacy they had. Then he grabbed Bobby and dragged him off to the side. Tugging on his sleeve, he motioned for him to bend close. He stood on his tiptoes and began to whisper into Bobby's ear. He spoke for a number of minutes. Bobby's eyes widened until they looked ready to pop, and he sort of gasped in his throat.

"Are you kidding me?" he asked.

Larry shook his head. "Telling you straight, man."

"If this is true then I am one hundred percent convinced that Elvis is still alive," Bobby responded, "because nothing can be more bizarre than your story."

Larry grinned. "Yeah, pretty zeller, huh?"

"Zeller?"

"Don't ask," Dar said. "It's just thirty-first-century slang. Now are you going to help us? We really need those disgu— costumes."

"Don't try to bamboozle me, little lady," Bobby said, watching her intently. "Obviously, you're looking for disguises, and yes, I'm going to help you. But I gotta find someone to take over the booth for awhile." He skirted around his tent and into the one next door. After a few minutes, he came out with an older woman who was slightly overweight, and had white hair, worn blue eyes, and a pretty smile. "This is Faith. Faith, some friends. I need to grab them something from my van. Shouldn't take more than twenty minutes. Thanks for taking care of my booth in the meanwhile."

"No worries, Bobby. I got you covered."

"You're my babe and a half, Faith."

She turned a pretty shade of pink, suddenly looking a decade younger. "Aren't you the charmer?"

With a little flourish of his hand, he turned away from his booth and strode toward the parking lot. Everest had to move quickly to stay up with the man.

"Wait a sec, Bobby," Larry said. "I gotta grab a couple of pins for Crazy Sue."

He darted into a simple, white-tented booth that sported an American Flag and an eagle. In the tent were cases of pins and also towers of sunglasses. An older man with a leathery face, that looked as if it had fought with the sun and lost battles but not the war, stood behind the front table. He wore a military cap. He smiled at Larry and exchanged a few words as if they knew each other.

In less than a minute, Larry collected three pins in exchange for a bill and a handful of coins. He dashed back and shot right past them in the direction of the parking lot as if he hadn't made a detour at all. They quickly followed.

"Ain't Bobby's puppets amazing?" Larry asked as they moved at a fast clip. "He makes the best ones in all of the United States."

"Zetta zeller," Vlas agreed.

"Yeah, cool," Everest said, trying out the archaic word.

"Zetta zeller," Bobby said, chuckling. "I like it. I've always been a sucker for a good 'z' word." As he walked he studied the group of B12s. "Do you all need disguises?"

186

"Well, some of us more than others. Vlas there," Larry pointed to indicate who he was talking about since he hadn't introduced the kids, "doesn't need much. Maybe he could just change his hair a bit." Then he shoved his thumb in Dar's direction. "She's gonna be a case. With the way her skin glows sometimes, people notice her."

Bobby assessed her. "I can see that. Are you actually human? That sheen isn't exactly normal—at least for this time period. I guess in a thousand years skin tone may have changed. Maybe it's some reaction to global warming."

"Of course I'm human," she said bitingly. "FYI, you'd look pretty alien in our time period." She rounded on Larry. "You might want to inform your friend that I have a zunner, and I'm not afraid to use it on twenty-first-century yocto-brains. In fact, it would be a pleasure."

Bobby laughed. "No need to get riled. It was an innocent question."

Everest was impressed by his laid back reaction to Dar's threat. Then again, Bobby couldn't actually know what a zunner was since it hadn't been invented yet.

"There's nothing unusual about my skin," Dar said.

"Well, it does sort of sparkle sometimes," said Vlas.

It was obvious that Dar barely held herself back from going after Vlas. She flasered the boy with her eyes. Only Vlas could get away with saying what he'd just said. But it was true that Dar's skin did sort of glow at times. Everest noticed the change when she was singing. It was zetta alien, as if a sunergy rod lit her from within.

Dar's irritability didn't seem to faze Bobby.

"It's going to be hard to hide all of that hair," he said. "Any chance you could cut it off?"

"Cut it off?" Her voice was as cold as Pluto.

Even in its standard ponytail, Dar's hair looked zetta thick. Everest didn't think he would be able to touch the tips of his fingers with his thumb if he grabbed it.

"It's a reasonable question," Larry said. "You don't really care about how you look, so why not cut it off so you can more easily hide what's left under a wig?"

"Why don't we just shave your head?" she replied.

"If that's what it takes. Heck, I got no ego. I thought you didn't either. Didn't realize you have this vanity thing going for your hair." He wiggled his fingers in the air.

"I don't have a vanity thing going," Dar said through gritted teeth. "Do you know what my hair would do if we cut it short? We *would* have to shave my head, and I'd never be able to grow it back. Short, it'll stick straight out. There isn't a gel in this century or any other that could tame it. At least now, I can throw it into a ponytail and be done with it."

"Girl hair is so alien," Larry responded.

"Deal with it," she said.

"Okay, children," Bobby said. "We'll try a skull cap with a larger wig to hide the bump." He turned to Larry. "Is that it?"

"Uh, no, we have something tougher. One of the boys in our group is albino."

"Albino?"

"Yup—pure white." He snapped his fingers. "Oh, and I almost forgot. We got a bobcat we need to disguise."

"You're kidding, right?"

"Uh, no, but that's all."

"The albino I can deal with, but I can't just disguise a bobcat. You want me to turn it into a dog?"

"Can you?" asked Everest.

"No," Bobby responded, "I was being facetious."

"We're going to have to find someplace to hide that denged bobcat because there is no way to disguise it," Dar said. "We'll have to figure that out later."

They walked along a path toward a large parking lot that was a sea of twenty-first-century cars. Under other circumstances, Everest would have jumped at the chance to check out each zeller ride independently.

"My bus is on the far side," Bobby said.

They followed him across, Everest and Vlas swiveling their heads back and forth to see all the cars.

"Everest-Vlas—time to wake up and put on some light speed. This isn't a field trip."

Dar was maybe twenty meters ahead of them, standing with her hands on her hips, looking zetta exasperated.

Everest exchanged a sheepish grin with Vlas and started jogging to catch up. Dar pivoted around and strode forward. Bobby and Larry were a little ahead of her. She quickly caught them, and Everest and Vlas made up the distance too. They were a unit when they arrived at an automobile that was so ancient-looking it could easily have starred in the academy's museum.

Vlas let out a low whistle. "Whoa…"

The vehicle was a large, slightly-rounded rectangle, its windows covered by dingy material that may have been dark blue in a past life. A dirty-white container on wheels was attached to the back of the bus via a hitch. At one time, the automobile may have been light blue. Everest detected a hint of peeling paint in that color, but now most of the vehicle was covered in rust.

"Hey, she's holding up pretty good." Larry stepped back to take a long look at the bus.

"Yeah, I had to rebuild the engine a year ago, but she's hanging in there. Fortunately, I don't have to take her on a lot of road trips nowadays. Last year, more than half of my sales were via the Internet. Who would have thunk?"

Vlas sidled up to Larry. "What's attached to the bus?"

"That?" Larry pointed at the white box on wheels. "It's a trailer. Bobby keeps his merchandise there, and he stores other stuff like his makeup and wigs there too." He started helping Bobby open the trailer door. "How're the puppets doing and the rest of the junk you sell?"

Bobby shrugged. "I get by. That and the Elvis gigs keep me off the streets."

"Yeah? Still a market for Elvis?"

"He'll always be the king. I just did a birthday party last weekend. Made two-fifty. Not bad for two hours of work. Takes me a lot longer to make the puppets, and I can only charge a hundred for them."

He walked up the ramp and disappeared into the recesses of the trailer. His voice muffled, he yelled out, "Any preference on hair color for the wigs?"

"Something drab for Dar," Larry said as he followed Bobby into the trailer. "Anything brown?"

"Sure. She'll need curls to obscure that wad of hair she'll be stuffing into a skull cap."

"Yeah," Larry agreed.

Bobby returned to the front of the trailer. "Hey, Dar, try this on." He held out a wig cap and a curly mess of brown hair.

Dar looked at the items with distaste.

Larry sidled up next to Bobby. "I think Dar's been hiding an ego," he said, taking in her expression. "She doesn't want to hide all that golden beauty."

"Go dive into a black hole." She snatched the items out of Bobby's hands. With a yank she had her ball cap off and quickly started to stuff her hair into the wig cap. Thick tufts of hair kept fighting their way out.

"Do a French-braid first," Bobby said.

She looked at him blankly.

"Hmm," he said.

With small steps, he ran down the ramp and swirled his finger to indicate that Dar should turn around. She did but kept watch over her shoulder. She looked anxious—a zetta strange expression for her Darship.

"This will only take a second." Bobby grabbed her hair, and Dar flinched, startled by his touch. "I promise I won't bite," he said. "I'm just going to French braid your hair. It's the best way to get all of it smoothly into the cap and then under a wig."

Everest watched in amazement as Bobby took strands of Dar's thick hair and weaved them together. He was fast and efficient and her hair was completely weaved in less than two minutes.

"How do you do that?" Everest finally asked.

Bobby turned his head and smiled. "Lots of practice. When you run your own theatre, you learn to do a little of everything. I'm a great hair stylist. What can I say? It's a gift."

Once the golden rope was woven together, he twirled it around and around and then tucked it under the wig cap. The hair still bulged, but there was nothing anyone could do about that, short of shaving her head. Bobby positioned the wig then played with it, adjusting the sides. Dar shook her head and the wig remained firm. Once he was satisfied that her new hair was going to work, he went back inside the trailer to find some more items.

"Cool," Larry said. "She doesn't look so Shadara-like now. But what about her skin? We can't afford for it to go all sparkly at the wrong time."

Again, Bobby's voice came out muffled. "I'm getting the makeup. It'll darken her skin tone, and it has a matte finish so she shouldn't glow."

"Excellent."

"I look like a complete suzo-shrimp," Dar said edgily.

Larry tilted his head. "Nah, you look studious, older, like a librarian, or a teacher. I think it'll work as long as we can get rid of your skin's light-show."

"I don't glow!" Dar insisted.

Bobby came out with a duffle bag filled to the brim. "Okay, I have four more wigs in the bag—pretty much cleaned me out. And I've got makeup in multiple tints, also some containers of putty. I threw in a bunch of sponges, some sunglasses and various colored, non-prescription contact lenses. What am I missing?"

Larry took the bag and rifled through it. "This is awesome, Bobby. You are the king." Putting the duffle down, he pulled out their bundle of money and shoved it toward the man.

Bobby's two arms came up as if a cyborg officer of law had told him to freeze. "Nuh-uh, no way. I don't need or want your money. I just want you to be safe, Larry."

Larry proffered the money again. "No, you gotta take it. We can't do anything else with it. I'd rather you had the dough than it just go to waste."

Bobby dropped his arms and took Larry by the shoulders. "Don't go back to the thirty-first century with these kids. It's too dangerous. I'm happy for them to have the disguises free of charge as long as they leave you here with me. You can bunk at my place till you have your rhythm. And if you keep that money, you'll have enough to get by for quite a while. Whatever's going on in the thirty-first century, it's not your business. You don't need to be involved. For your mom's sake, you gotta listen to me. She always wanted more for you than she had."

"Thanks, Bobby. I appreciate it; I really do. But there's nothing for me in this century. I want to stay in 3002. It's exciting. And I have friends. They're even my own age. Plus, they need my help."

Was Larry about to cry? His eyes looked pretty shiny. Everest decided it was a trick of the light. The boy didn't get all emotional.

"Larry," Dar said curtly, "Bobby's right. You should stay here. We can handle this fine by ourselves."

Larry rounded on her. "You think I'd just leave you to the Panktars and Director Lester-Hauffer and James? What kind of coward do you take me for?" He turned back to Bobby. "I appreciate the offer, but I ain't turning tail and running. That's not my style. Plus, I like it in the thirty-first century."

"You're crazier than I thought," Dar said.

"Takes a crazy to know one," he replied with a grin. "Now let's get this show on the road."

With a heartfelt sigh, Bobby bent down and retrieved the duffle. "I'll give you a quick lesson in theatre makeup and putty."

It was Vlas who ended up being the most skilled at applying everything. He managed to increase Larry's nose to double its normal size and still make it look like a nose. When Bobby deemed them competent with the tools of the trade, he gave Larry another bear hug, shook hands with each B12 and waved them off.

He'd finally accepted about half of the money, telling Larry that they might need some cash during the rest of their stay in the twenty-first century. When he found out that the other kids were with Crazy Sue, he told Larry to give her what was left over.

"Break a leg," he yelled as he walked back to the Flea Market.

"Huh?" Everest asked. "What in flasers does that mean?"

"He doesn't want you to break a leg," Larry said. "It's something they say in the theatre. Like, 'Give 'em heck,' or 'Go get 'em.' It's for good luck."

"Okay," Vlas said, "that's officially alien."

"Everything about the theatre is alien," Larry agreed. "In any period! That's why it's zeller too, and we've just joined the theatre. We're a live-action, street-performing theatre troupe heading out for our first ever gig. We gotta be pros 'cause our audience ain't the forgiving type. Time to pick up the rest of the cast and hit the road to the future." He slung the duffel bag over his shoulder and set off back toward the overpass. "It's showtime, folks!"

CHAPTER 27
Pooker's Adventure

Crazy Sue taught Elsie, Lelita and Borneo how to play a game called Crazy Eight which seemed appropriate given her nickname. Lelita was the best at the game. Either that or she was just plain lucky. Elsie figured the girl won at least two-thirds of the hands. After they'd played for awhile, Elsie and Lelita dozed, but it was uncomfortable because there weren't any extra chairs, and the ground was hard and itchy. The morning progressed slowly.

When Lelita wasn't sleeping, she was whining about not being allowed to go shopping at the flea market. And Borneo couldn't stop anxiously watching the highway as if a car was going to flip over and land on top of them.

For the most part, Crazy Sue left them to their own devices while she puttered around with her pots and pans and miscellaneous bags, muttering and singing to herself.

After napping for awhile, Elsie went over to where she had settled Pooker in the tall grass, but Pooker wasn't there. She swiveled around in a big circle. No Pooker. She slowly circled around in the other direction. Still no Pooker. Her heartbeat sped up just a little.

"Pooker," she hissed and then whistled. She waded through the scratchy weeds further up the hill. "Pooker," she said a little louder. She whistled a little louder.

"Elsie," Lelita called, not quite yelling but speaking at a higher volume than normal.

She looked over her shoulder.

Lelita stood a little ways down. "Is everything okay?"

"Sure," Elsie said, forcing a smile.

"Really?" Lelita looked worried. Borneo joined her.

"Of course." Elsie widened her smile. "Pooker's just being a suzo-shrimp. Nothing to worry about."

"Where is she?" Lelita asked.

"Um," Elsie said, "she's just over there." She pointed vaguely. "I'm getting her right now."

"Okay," Lelita said. "Crazy Sue thinks we should stay in the shade of the overpass."

"Sure," Elsie said. "I'll be back in just a sec."

She kept moving uphill and hissed again, "Pooker!"

Anger mixed with fear so that her belly knotted up into a tangle and her heartbeat pounded loudly in her chest. Where was that deng cat? She made it to the ridge where Larry had jumped down earlier this morning, and still there was no sign of Pooker. Cars whizzed by—many more than there had been at dawn. Elsie scoured the area and gasped. About one hundred meters away, in the direction they had come this morning but on the other side of the road, Elsie saw the stupid bobcat.

"Flasers," she whispered.

Keeping her eyes on Pooker, she yelled, "Lelita, Borneo, I'll be right back."

She took off at a full sprint toward the yocto-brained bobcat. When she saw a small break in traffic she raced across the street. A car honked and she jumped at the shrill noise, but she arrived safely on the other side of the road. Up ahead, Pooker loped away from her.

"Deng," she mumbled under her breath.

She ran as fast as she could. Fortunately, the bobcat wasn't moving that quickly.

"Pooker," she yelled.

The denged Pico-trainer was supposed to keep her bobcat from doing these things.

Possibly startled by her yelling, Pooker veered into the traffic and crossed over to the island in the middle.

Elsie gasped and took the street on a diagonal, desperate to make up ground. A car screeched to a stop nearby, then a number of high-pitched honks pierced her eardrums. She barely registered the chaos around her. She had to get to Pooker. Somehow, she arrived at the island a few feet from the bobcat.

"Pooker," she said sternly but quietly, "come to me."

The bobcat padded over as if she had never run away.

"Flasers, you are one yocto-brained cat," she whispered, grabbing the thin pico-trainer device.

She studied it, trying to figure out what could have gone wrong. Had time travel affected it?

A siren sounded in the distance, growing louder as it approached. The noise was shrill and irritating. She lifted her head and saw flashing lights moving closer. She bit her lower lip. Surely it didn't have anything to do with her or Pooker? Unless someone had alerted the authorities that a wild animal was on the loose?

The police officers were coming from the general vicinity of the highway. She had to hide at light speed. She headed for the parking lot where they had parked their hover vehicle.

Her hand on Pooker's neck, she whispered, "Come!"

As soon as there was a break in the flow of cars, she ran out into the street with Pooker at her side. Landing on the sidewalk, she ran for the parking garage and ducked inside just as the police zoomed by on the far side of the street. The street's island made it impossible for the police cars to reach her without making a U-turn at the next light—an unexpected benefit of transportation rolling instead of flying. She still didn't have much time.

"Pooker, you are in so much trouble," she whispered.

She was pretty sure that the police saw her enter the parking garage. How could they not? She was the only one with a wild bobcat in tow. Fortunately, the garage was empty of people. She ran as fast as she could for their jellach HV. When she saw some people exit the mall, she immediately slowed to a fast walk and tried to look casual, doing her best to hide most of Pooker from view on her right side. Maybe they would mistake the bobcat for a dog.

What if the police found their vehicle? What then? The future would be in jeopardy. Because of her. All because she hadn't kept watch over Pooker. If only a black hole could swallow her up. She'd had only one responsibility while the others were at the flea market—to take care of Pooker. Instead, she'd talked and played cards and napped. Everest was going to flaser her.

When she got to the HV, Elsie stared at it hard. It was really tiny right now. No way would it fit both her and Pooker. And the sirens seemed to be splitting the air with their decibels. The officers of law were way too close.

She fought the knots that kept the Vlatex II cover secure. Because she was anxious, it felt as if it took more time than it should have. She choked back a sob as she finally pulled up a corner of the cover. The cop cars hadn't turned into the garage yet.

"SHADARA, expand for two small people," she said. With a slight popping sound, the HV grew just enough. The vlatex cover stretched but held.

"SHADARA, open," she said and the door on the driver's side erased. Pooker would be claustrophobic in the small space. Without the pico-trainer working properly, it could be dangerous, despite Pooker's affection for Elsie. Elsie really hoped the pico-trainer was back on track.

"Come on Pooker."

She scrambled into the HV and grabbed the bobcat by the pico-trainer to drag her in as well. Once they were inside, she maneuvered around so that she faced the driver's erased door. Reaching out, she grabbed the Vlatex II flap and shoved it down over the HV. Now it was dark.

"SHADARA, close." Even *she* felt the tight quarters, and she wasn't usually bothered by small spaces.

Pooker growled, low and threatening.

"Shush," Elsie whispered.

A police car screeched into the parking garage. Through the Vlatex II she saw the flashing lights.

Scrunching down further, she hugged Pooker close, giving and seeking comfort all at the same time. In her head, she said over and over again: *Please don't find us, please don't find us, please don't find us.*

Another sirened vehicle arrived. Now there were four officers of law within spitting distance. She bit her lip and kept repeating her mantra in her head.

The officers murmured amongst themselves, their words indistinct. What if they saw the little vehicle in the far corner of the lot and wondered why it was there?

Pooker made another low growl and bumped her head against Elsie. She swallowed hard against the threatening tears. Then she swallowed again. If only she could see more than just lights. The last time she and Pooker had hid, she'd been able to see a lot more and hear more as well. This time, all she could do was wait. She had no way of knowing when it might be safe. As minutes ticked by, she lost all feeling in one of her legs.

A car started up and moved off. Then another one did. She couldn't see blinking lights anymore. Did that mean the police had left the garage, or was it a trick? Were they lying in wait for her?

How long would she have to wait before she and Pooker could try to return to Crazy Sue's squat?

Elsie debated what to do for a long time, paralyzed by fear. After awhile, she heard footsteps in the distance. At first, they just seemed remote and slightly menacing. Then they grew ever louder and scarier. Her heart acted as if it was going to explode out of her chest. Its beat deafened her. The footsteps were right next to the HV when they came to a halt, and everything went quiet. Everything, that is, except her heartbeat, which pounded so loudly she wouldn't have been surprise if it could be heard in the thirty-first century.

Someone whipped off the Vlatex II material, and Elsie screamed.

CHAPTER 28
Back to the Future

Everest had never felt more relieved in his life to see Elsie hiding in the HV. When he'd arrived back at Crazy Sue's, Lelita and Borneo were losing their auras over Elsie having taken off after Pooker. They had watched the police cars give chase, and they hadn't known what to do.

Dar had barked out orders for them to calm down. Then she had commanded Larry to hand over the rest of their currency to Crazy Sue. With quick thank yous and goodbyes, they had rushed off after Elsie. Dar was convinced that Elsie and Pooker would be with the hover vehicle. Amazingly, she'd been right. If he hadn't been so relieved to see his sister, Everest might have been zetta irritated that Dar was right again.

After Dar dissolved the door, Everest said, "Jeez, Elsie, could you power down? Every police officer in the Bay Area must have heard you scream."

She rubbed her hands over her face. "It's not my fault that Dar decided to wear a freakazoid costume. I didn't recognize her."

"Yeah, right," Everest responded. He wasn't going to admit how shocked he'd been by Dar's new hairdo, especially since he'd actually watched her transform. "Can't you keep track of that denged bobcat for even a few hours? She could have ruined everything."

From what Lelita and Borneo had said, disaster had been zetta close.

"I handled it, didn't I?" Elsie scrambled out of the jellach vehicle with Pooker following. "There must be something wrong with her pico-trainer."

"Really?" Vlas asked, his eyes lighting up. "I bet I can fix that."

"She's never gone off like that," Elsie said.

"She's nothing but trouble," Everest grumbled.

Elsie punched him. "Stop being such a vlem."

"Could you two stop your bickering?" Dar asked. "Elsie, we have to find a safe place to leave Pooker when we get back to our time. Do you have any suggestions?"

"What about Zulu?" Everest asked.

"Zulu? But won't we put her in danger?"

"Maybe," Everest said, "but we can't keep carting Pooker around. She's going to get us caught."

Elsie ran her hand through her hair. "Yeah, you're right."

"Okay, so we'll bring her to this Zulu girl," Dar said. "Where does she live?"

"She lives near us in Redwood City."

"Pretty sure we need the actual address for the hover vehicle to find her home," said Dar. "For now, we'll concentrate on getting back to our time and losing the bad guys. Then we can head north." She turned to Vlas. "When we get back, you're in charge of losing the cybercops. Then we'll let the HV know where we're going."

Vlas pursed his lips. "Those disguises would improve our chance of not being found."

"Yeah, but I think we've outstayed our welcome here. Too many twenty-first-century cops on the look-out for that denged bobcat. Once we get to Elsie's friend, we can work on our appearances. At least I'm mostly disguised now."

"There's no time to waste," Elsie said. "Who knows what they're doing to our parents?"

"Yeah, yeah," Dar said, "I get it, but we need a plan before we go after them. For now, let's get Pooker safely to Zulu's. We'll cloak the cat with Vlatex II till then."

Everest's stomach churned as he contemplated going back to their time where not only would they have to face cybercops but also some pretty terrifying bad guys like the Panktars and Superman James. Not that anything would keep him from going back to track down his parents. He just couldn't turn off the fear.

"This shouldn't be as herky-jerky since we're using the HV as our time-travel machine," Dar said.

"You complaining about my flying?" Larry asked.

Dar laughed. "Nah, but we got lucky. Thank the Light for your superhuman power. I'm pretty sure we'd have been galaxy dust without it." She'd pulled out the time-travel device from her Vlatex II backpack and was busily reprogramming it for the return trip.

"Don't forget that we were off by two months when we came back to this time period," Elsie said.

Dar snorted and rolled her eyes, not even bothering to answer. Everest had a feeling she didn't forget much. He swallowed a sigh of relief that they wouldn't be using a human time-travel machine for the journey home. Their ride with Larry had been a lot scarier than any of their previous attempts.

Dar handed Vlas the packet of purple pills, and he passed them around.

"As soon as we get there, we need to do another aura positioning," Elsie said after she swallowed her motion-sickness pill.

Everest wished she'd stop stating the obvious.

"Try to remember that we'll be coming back within seconds of when we left," Dar said. "Your parents should be exactly where we left them."

"I wish I could have said goodbye to Crazy Sue."

"We said goodbye for you," Dar responded curtly as she finished up her calculations.

"Did you bring Crazy Sue anything from the flea market?" Elsie asked.

"I really need to concentrate," Dar snapped.

"Yeah," Larry said, "I got her some pretty stuff, and we gave her cold hard cash too. She'll get a lot more use out of that than any flea market gewgaw."

"Help me get the Vlatex II off," Dar said, clearly irritated by the exchange. They all took portions of the material to drag it off. Dar shoved the bundle willy-nilly into her backpack.

With a quick check to ensure that no one watched, Dar spoke softly. "SHADARA, expand."

The vehicle popped and grew.

"Okay, folks, pile in," Dar said.

She sat in the front passenger seat, letting Vlas take the controls since he would need to do the fancy flying once they were back in their time. Elsie had to force Pooker back into the vehicle.

Everest dropped his duffel bag of makeup to the floor.

Surprisingly, Lelita had found a seat next to him. Normally, she stayed close to Elsie or Dar.

"What did you get at the flea market?" she asked.

"Not much," he said.

"Can I see it anyway, please?" She smiled sweetly.

Everest realized that in her own way she could be just as persistent as Dar and Elsie.

"There isn't time, Lelita," Dar said shortly. "Everyone strap in."

They scrambled to put on their straps before Dar sent them home.

As Dar had predicted the travel forward was a lot smoother than the travel back. Everest still lost all feeling, and he still felt the strange spinning sensation, but it was smooth and controlled. He felt pressure but not the ripping apart that he had felt with Larry as their anchor.

And the landing was as smooth as the Borealis basin on Mars. After a few heartbeats of utter nothingness, his heart suddenly pounded like crazy and sensation returned to his legs. As expected, it was dark—still nighttime—but the Googleopolis sky was mega lit. It was also eerily silent.

"SHADARA, soundproof off," Vlas said, and noise came back with a vengeance.

Everest felt like a suzo-shrimp for forgetting about the soundproofing. He'd assumed the heavy silence had to do with the time travel.

"Okay, Vlas, get us out of here," Dar commanded.

"SHADARA, straight up," Vlas said and the jellach vehicle rose fast, barely missing another object that was in a free fall. Whatever it was, it skimmed their HV and they heard it land with a thunk on the ground. Everest's body went limp. He wanted to say something, but he was so weak he couldn't even open his mouth. He tried to lift his head, but it felt as if it weighed about a thousand kilograms.

"Elsie," he barely managed to whisper. He wanted to reach out to her but couldn't. What was going on?

"Stay—calm," Dar managed, her voice straining to project. "We—arrived—too—early. We're—here—in—duplicate."

Ah jeez, he thought. The flying object that had fallen next to them *was* them. They were practically on top of themselves.

"How—long?" Vlas managed to tear out the words.

"I—don't—know," Dar dragged out.

Everest wished he could lift his head so he could check whether Elsie was okay. He tried to look to his side, but it was no use. He might as well be fully passed out. He just had to hope she was fine. He fought to swim out of the lethargy as if he were trying to burst out from the bottom of a pool of water.

Then everything popped and he could move again. He gasped, hearing similar gasps next to him.

"Okay," Dar said. "That was interesting." Her voice was muffled. She had her head down and was taking deep breaths.

"Alien," Vlas said.

"I don't understand," Elsie gasped. "We've done that before, been double in a time period before. Why did we lose all our energy this time?"

"Maybe it's because we were so close to our other selves," Borneo said. "I think we actually touched hover vehicles as we rose. We were like magnets, fighting each other's energy. But the other selves had more because their piece had already happened."

"Vlas, you better get us out of here," Dar said. "Remember, Larry saw the cyborg officers in the distance when we left. They must be close."

"Yeah." He took a deep breath. "Jeez, we're still going up."

Everest looked out the window. They were much higher than the highest HV.

"SHADARA, regular commuter height, please." Vlas's instruction caused the HV to reverse itself into a freefall. "SHADARA, slower, please." The jellach hover vehicle adjusted and eased back into mainstream traffic.

They had a quick glimpse of the cyborg officers of law parked below on the street moss, searching the alley, but then SHADARA moved forward and they lost the visual.

"They must have seen us disappear," Elsie said.

"Yeah," Dar said. "That's not good. Now they know we're doing time travel." She shook her head. "I guess it doesn't matter. They probably already knew we were, and there's no way for them to figure out where we've been going." She worried her lower lip. "Maybe trying to figure it out will keep them busy. That would be a good thing."

She grinned. "Vlas, mix it up a bit. Let's take the slow route to Redwood City."

CHAPTER 29
A Reunion with Zulu

"We need to use the APU," Elsie insisted.

It might not be logical, but she needed new proof that her parents still existed. It didn't matter that by hitting themselves coming back they knew they hadn't lost any time. She needed the connection.

Dar attempted to push her ball cap further down on her head before realizing that she wore a wig rather than her hat. Her hand clenched into a fist for a heartbeat then slowly eased open. The girl stared at her hand as if it were an alien from Xlexuri galaxy.

Finally, she responded. "Okay, we might as well. We'll save the coordinates, and Borneo can work out where they are being held." She rifled through her backpack and pulled out the aura-positioning unit. "Give me the cards you used to identify your parents last time."

Elsie already had them out. She handed them over.

Dar scanned the DNA and quickly found their auras on the Galactic Knowledge Bank. Once again they identified the two auras as being somewhere in the Bay Area. Dar sent the coordinates to Borneo's illegal holoputer.

"Do your magic, Borneo."

From his absent expression it was pretty clear he was already working on it.

As they flew, they saw broadcasts of their images on large screens. But they still had privacy mode on their HV, and the only people visible were Vlas and Dar with her wig. No one gave them a second glance. The only thing that was a little weird was that it looked as if the HV could have shrunk but hadn't. Still, that wasn't so unusual. They could have been transporting large objects. Also, since everyone was on the floor except Vlas and Dar, Elsie worried that someone might see them from below and become suspicious. She wrapped her arms around her knees and tried to make herself smaller.

"We need Zulu's address or her full name," Dar said as they approached Redwood City.

Elsie rattled off the address from memory. She had practically lived at Zulu's before they had moved to the academy.

"Okay," Dar said. "We can't just rush in. Their house could be under surveillance. Hopefully, rather than station a cybercop there, they just asked Zulu's family to be on the lookout and to turn us in if we showed up."

"Oh no," Elsie said. "Do you think they did that?"

"They'd be yocto-brains if they didn't."

Elsie felt as if Dar was calling her a yocto-brain since it never crossed her mind that someone would approach Zulu and her family. Or worse, spy on the family in case Elsie tried to make contact. Would Zulu turn them in? Under normal circumstances that would be impossible, but if Zulu thought that Dar and the others were holding Everest and her hostage, she might.

How were they going to sneak into Zulu's? The security system for Zulu's house was pretty typical for this area, but they had paid extra money so that her room avatar could act as added security by sensing that someone new had entered the room. Zulu could identify that person as being a friend, but she had to do so immediately and right now, Zulu could be asleep. It was a school night and nearly 23:00.

"Can we try to contact Zulu? She might be jacked in. I could try to holocomm with her using Borneo's IH."

"Odds are good they're monitoring her comms."

Elsie explained what she could remember of Zulu's home security.

Dar drummed her fingers against the jellach dash. "I think you're going to have to go in by yourself. It's least likely to cause a ruckus. Weren't you already identified as welcome?"

"Yeah, but that might have been revoked."

"This is not a good idea," Everest said. "What if someone's watching the house waiting for Elsie?"

"Then we've lost one but not all of us," Dar said with a shrug. "She's the only one we can send in there."

Elsie wiped her suddenly clammy palms against Pooker.

"We need a better plan," Everest said.

"Okay, smart guy, tell me what to do."

Elsie had a feeling she should interrupt and just say she would go inside solo, but the whole idea scared the living bejabbers out of her.

Everest didn't respond right away. Elsie could almost hear him thinking. Dar had swiveled around and was glaring at him. Since she sat on the front seat and he crouched on the floor behind her, she looked a lot more intimidating than he did, even though he glared right back.

"Well?" Dar said.

"Shut down," he said. "I'm thinking."

"We don't have all night."

"We have time," he said grumpily. "We haven't even checked for whether someone is watching the house."

Dar folded her arms and rolled her eyes.

Elsie stared down through the clear bottom of the HV. They were here. She recognized the limonino tree in Zulu's front yard. Vlas slowly took them past the house.

It felt beyond good to see Zulu's home. It was like a second home to her. She loved the garden of purple and white flowers that grew on the rooftop and balconies of the three story unit. The walls of the home were covered in street moss. Though it wasn't visible, she knew there was also a basement that went down two levels.

"If I could get some sort of message to her."

"Do you have a special code?"

Elsie shook her head. "Not exactly. But we have some things I could say to let her know it's really me."

"What about PicoBoy?" Everest asked. "Could we send him in? Have him bring a message from Elsie?"

Vlas and Dar exchanged looks.

"Yeah," Dar said. "That might work." She gave Everest a thumbs-up. "Zeller idea."

Elsie couldn't remember Dar ever telling Everest he'd had a passable idea let alone a zeller one. He looked uncomfortable and pleased at the same time—sort of alien.

They passed by Zulu's house again.

"Anyone see anything unusual?" Dar asked.

"No," said Elsie, "but I can't actually see what's going on. You and Vlas have the best chance of seeing anything out of the ordinary right now."

"Okay, let's park for awhile," Dar suggested.

Vlas settled the HV on the green street moss a few houses away with the jellach vehicle facing the front of Zulu's home.

Everyone eased up onto the seats to watch the street. It was zetta quiet. No activity. No vehicles besides theirs had people sitting inside observing the street.

Since it was closing in on 23:00 and it was a school night, most families were already tucked in bed. Though Zulu probably had gone to bed by now, she could be awake. She wouldn't have gone to bed that long ago. Usually, she h-comm'd with her friends for awhile.

Vlas had pulled out PicoBoy and was programming him for his visit.

"Start writing your message," Dar told Elsie. She held out a dropper bottle. "Everyone needs nighteyes too."

Elsie felt a bit panicky. What should she say? As a stalling tactic, she grabbed the dropper before any of the other B12s could and squeezed a couple of drops into each eye. She pulled a jellach journal out of her pocket.

"Wait," she said. "Borneo, have you figured out where my parents are?"

"Well," he said, "I'd like to verify my conclusions, but I'm betting they're on Pelican Island."

"Pelican Island?" Elsie and Everest both said in one breath.

"Yeah, you know, in the San Francisco Bay."

"We know where it is, but why? Isn't it empty except for pelicans?"

"Yeah, it's supposed to be. But there are rundown buildings there from eons ago."

"But it's barely a couple of rocks," Elsie said.

Borneo gave them a helpless shrug. "I think it's bigger than it seems, and it's definitely bigger under the water. I'm pretty sure it was much larger a millennium ago, but it got eroded by earthquakes and time."

Elsie told herself to stop being so skeptical. Borneo was zetta cerebrum-heavy. If he pointed to Pelican Island as where her parents were, then that's where they were.

"Who owns it?" she asked.

Dar cleared her throat. "Elsie, write your denged message. We can't go after your parents till we hide Pooker somewhere. There will be time later for all your questions." She pointed down at Elsie's journal. "Write."

Elsie made a face and started writing.

Dear Squish-squash, she entered. That was her nickname for Zulu since she had an orange tint to her skin, and pumpkins were orange and from the squash family.

Don't believe everything you hear. I'm alive and with good people. Anyone who says otherwise is bad—especially my uncle. Remember how I always said he smelled like rotten vegetables? That's because he's rotten to the core.

I need your help, SS. I'm scared because of all the bad guys who are after us. More scared than when we got stuck up on top of your roof and had to climb down using the plants on the side of your house.

Please, don't tell anyone I've contacted you. Zetta promise and seal it with Blackholes. If you squeal, I'll tell everyone you like JT. No, worse, I'll tell everyone you like TD. You know they'll believe me. Then you'll never stand a chance with JT.

Turn off your security and open your window, okay? Wave Glagdog out the window when it's safe for me to come in.

Love ya,

Double-trouble

Talk about embarrassing. They all would know Zulu's nickname for her. Could she download it onto PicoBoy without anyone reading it?

"Vlas," she said. "I need to transfer this without you seeing it. Can I do that?"

Dar snorted. "It's not like we want to see your pathetic little communications with each other. Stop being a ute-baby."

"Actually," Vlas said, "she really should read the message out loud. That way PicoBoy can repeat it using her voice, and the message will have more cred."

"Read it out loud?!" Elsie screeched.

"Jeez, Elsie," said Everest, "I'm pretty sure the cybercops heard you across town. Can't you just do what Vlas says without losing your aura?"

"This zetta stinks," she grumbled, wishing she could wipe Dar's smirk right off her face.

After a few minutes, Vlas held up PicoBoy. "Okay speak slowly and clearly." His grin was ridiculous.

Elsie read the message she'd worked so hard on. After she spoke, PicoBoy repeated it back.

"Squish-squash?" Larry asked.

She glared and refused to answer.

"Glagdog?" asked Everest.

"Her childhood stuffed animal. And if you ever breathe a word that you know about him, I'll have to hurt you."

"Guess we all know what Double-trouble refers to," Dar said.

"If you call me that, you'll be Shadara till the end of the universe."

"I'm terrified." Dar grinned from ear to ear.

Her curly brown hair really modified her look, but it didn't change the wicked delight in her expression when she thought Elsie was coming off as a total suzo-shrimp.

"Don't think I won't do it." Elsie said, wishing she had a better comeback line.

"Hate to interrupt when you're both having so much fun," Vlas said, "but could you tell me which room PicoBoy should go to?"

Elsie leaned forward over Vlas's driver's seat. "See that window on the second floor—the one with blue curtains and a few stars on the glass? That's hers. She's about my height, maybe a few centimeters shorter. She has skin with a tinge of orange and her hair is reddish orange and crazy curly. She's half Glagchian which is why she has that orangish skin tone and the curly hair. Her eyes are a light shade of turquoise. Her mom isn't Glagchian so Zulu's the only girl in the house with that orange hue. She has a brother, but he looks more Earthling than Glagchian."

"Got that PicoBoy?" Vlas asked. The little picobot chirped. "Okay, time to rock and roll. Go find Zulu," he told the bug-sized, man-made creature.

It jumped into the air and flew out of the HV toward the house.

They saw the flying robo-bug for a few seconds before it disappeared into the gloom. Elsie thought she saw PicoBoy land on the windowsill, but it was probably her imagination. Even with the HVs and lit advertisements, it was still dark down where the houses were. Lighting was a targeted art in the thirty-first century. Just because there were lights in the sky didn't mean they glared into peoples' homes. She was too far away, and PicoBoy was a little too tiny for her nighteyes to be of any real use.

However, she did see a dull nightlight turn on in Zulu's room. It wasn't bright, but it was noticeable.

"Oh, oh, if someone's watching, they'll see that," Elsie said.

"We've been here for awhile," said Dar. "As far as I can tell, no one is spying on the house. If anything, they might be monitoring it from afar instead. I'd bet good VC that they *are* monitoring *your* house. We just have to hope they don't have enough money to watch every friend you and Everest have in this world. That would be zetta expensive. And these guys are into making VC, not dishing it out."

Just then, a silhouette appeared in Zulu's room and a heartbeat later, the window opened. Something was stuck out and waved frantically. Then it was settled on the windowsill.

"That's Glagdog," Elsie whispered, her heart speeding up.

"Are you sure?" asked Lelita nervously. "It could be a trap."

Elsie looked over her shoulder at the girl and smiled. She wished they hadn't dragged Lelita into such danger, but she had to admit it was nice to have someone here who was more afraid than even she was.

"Yeah, it's Glagdog. See how there's one floppy and one straight ear? And you can sort of see the tongue hanging down." She touched the door and asked it to open. "Guess that's my signal. To quote Vlas, 'time to rock and roll.'"

"How are you going to get up to the window?" Dar asked.

"I've done it before. That limonino tree is pretty easy to climb. Then I just have to reach over to the window from the limb on the right." After Elsie exited the HV, she leaned back in. "As soon as I get inside, I'm going to remove Glagdog from the windowsill. If it's safe and it makes sense for you to join me through Zulu's bedroom, I'll put Glagdog back where you can see him."

"How are we supposed to bring Pooker into the house?" Dar asked.

"I guess we'll have to sneak her in from the bottom floor."

"Then there's no reason for us to go in through Zulu's bedroom. We'll wait till you can get us in on the ground."

"Okay, look for me on the front porch." Elsie squared her shoulders, took a deep breath and headed for Zulu's room.

CHAPTER 30
A Safe Place for Pooker

With a quick look to the left and the right, Elsie climbed the limonino tree. Its extreme sour smell both overwhelmed and comforted her. She felt as if she'd lived a hundred years since she'd last seen Zulu. Jeez, it had only been a month.

The bark of a limonino was so smooth it didn't feel like wood at all but more like polished stone or marblon even. It was strangely cool to the touch. The leaves were glossy and so fragrant you felt as if you could eat them. But they were poisonous. Only the fruit was edible—though she had heard that in Bandogiar there were doctors prescribing limonino root for a new and rare disease that exhibited symptoms similar to the long extinct cold.

When Elsie reached the limb that stretched to the window, she carefully crawled out, her hands holding tight. She'd fallen out of the tree once when she was nine years old and broken her arm. Her mom had laid down the law about no more tree-climbing, and she hadn't been allowed to visit Zulu for two full weeks. They'd been miserable. Zulu's parents had threatened to cut down the limonino, but they both had begged them not to. Later, Elsie realized it had been an idle threat since killing trees was zetta illegal.

Thank the Light! Without the limonino tree it would have been hard to sneak in. She would have had to scale the wall of the house— no easy feat. Though she probably could have used the spider gear.

When she reached the window, Zulu was waiting, her expression anxious. Within seconds the girl had dragged her inside.

"Flasers, Elsie," she cried and gave her a monster hug.

"Power down, Squish-squash," Elsie said in a whisper.

Zulu flinched. "Okay, okay," she whispered. "You're right. Cyborg officers came to our house earlier today. They said bad clones

213

had kidnapped you. We're supposed to call them if we hear from you." Her large turquoise eyes were even wider than usual, making her look younger than twelve. With her heightened emotions, she was practically emanating orange. "I thought you were dead." Her voice broke and her eyes swam with tears.

"Zulu, don't cry. I'm fine, but I do need your help. You have to calm down and listen." Elsie drew her over to the jellach bed and settled them both on the edge. It automatically firmed up, sensing they were looking for a place to sit rather than to sleep.

"First, what's the deal with your avatar?" Elsie sort of expected the Glagchian warrior to pop out from behind a piece of furniture.

Zulu's parents had thought it mildly amusing to program Hachori, the famous Glagchian female warrior, as Zulu's avatar. After all, they often said, the avatar's most important job was to protect Zulu.

"I told Hachori I needed privacy," Zulu whispered. "For my twelfth birthday, my parents reprogrammed her so that I could ask for thirty minutes of privacy twice a day. Part of growing up, they said."

A couple of weeks ago, Elsie had been heartbroken when her uncle had refused to take her to Zulu's birthday party. So much had happened since that she'd actually forgotten that Zulu had recently turned twelve.

After having spent a month without parents, Elsie couldn't help but think that Zulu's were being excessively overprotective. She could just imagine what Dar would say about only having sixty minutes a day without supervision.

"We're zetta lucky that I never used my second thirty minutes today. After the cyborg police left, I was so scared; I didn't want to be by myself." Zulu grabbed Elsie's hand. "How did you escape? We need to tell people you're safe."

"No, Zulu." Elsie shook her head vigorously. "The cybercops can't help me. The real bad guys have them under their thumbs. The clones didn't kidnap me. I ran away from the academy and took them with me. They had nothing to do with this mess. It's all my doing." She shook her head again. "No, that's not right. It's not my doing. It's my uncle's and a bunch of other bad guys."

"Huh? You aren't making sense."

214

Elsie leaned close and squeezed Zulu's hands. "Listen to me. My parents are the ones who are kidnapped. They invented something that a lot of people want—bad people who would kill to get what they want. Everest and I need to save our parents. The clones—my friends—are helping me. I know it's almost impossible to believe, but it's true. And I can't trust anyone. The cyborg police seem to be working with the bad guys. But I trust you, and I desperately need your help. I don't know what I'll do if you turn me in."

Zulu worried her lower lip. Her face looked as if it might explode from orange. Elsie had never seen her skin so excessively bright. Her eyes were impossibly large and the turquoise had deepened. Her face always showed her emotions. Elsie could read a galaxy of confusion and worry.

"Flasers, of course I'll help you," Zulu said, "but we only have, like, twenty minutes before my avatar returns. I don't think Hachori's going to understand. She'll alert the authorities before you can blink."

"Then we'd better move at light speed. I need you to hide Pooker. There's no way to disguise her, and people know I have a bobcat. The rest of us can change our look, but she can't. I need her somewhere safe where she won't get me caught."

Zulu nodded, but she looked uneasy. "Okay, let me think." She jumped up. "Auntie Zu. Auntie Zu will take her."

"Auntie Zu? She must be like a hundred and thirty, and last time I visited she seemed a little goofy." Zulu's ancient aunt lived in a smaller unit next door. Elsie visited her occasionally. The woman was sweet but zetta daffy.

"Well, maybe a little but she'd do anything for me. And she's full Glagchian so she automatically doesn't trust Earth's cyborg police force. She can keep a secret. Go get Pooker and meet me at Auntie Zu's front porch."

"What about the security systems?"

"I've already shut down ours, and I have full access to Auntie Zu's house. I take care of her almost every day. Fortunately, her avatars haven't been alerted to your kidnapping. No one bothers with Auntie Zu. I'll offer to be her companion for the rest of the week. That way, I can take care of Pooker and no one will find out."

"At least Pooker has been there before so she shouldn't be too upset. But won't your mom go over there?"

"You know how much Auntie Zu and mom get on each other's nerves. Dad's off planet on business for a few days. I can tell mom that I'll take care of Auntie Zu until he gets back. She'll be ecstatic. She's working on a big project." Zulu pulled Elsie up from the bed. "Come on, let's go."

They ran into the corridor straight into a flock of pico-brownies.

"Are your brownies set up for security?"

Zulu rolled her eyes. "Jeez, Elsie, have you forgotten? We live in the burbs. We don't need pico-brownies beefed up with the latest security features. Nothing happens here."

Elsie grinned as she jogged next to Zulu. "Your parents have Hachori watching over you twenty-four-seven. Why wouldn't they have security pico-brownies?"

"Well, that's different. I'm their only child. They're freakazoids when it comes to my safety. But they aren't actually worried someone's going to break into our home. We live in Bores-ville, USA."

"You would not believe how bizarre life has been since we left the burbs," Elsie said. "I'd give anything for life to be boring again."

Zulu snorted. "I'd give anything for an adventure." Then she frowned. "I'm sorry. I'm a total vlem for saying that when your parents have been kidnapped." She started down the stairs, taking them two at a time.

"Don't be silly, Squish-squash," Elsie said as she followed her down. "Besides, earlier today we thought our parents were dead. Things are actually looking up. At least we know the worst hasn't happened."

"It's so hard to believe. Your parents kidnapped! Things like that just don't happen."

They reached the foyer.

"Exit, please," Zulu said.

The door smoothly rearranged itself and disappeared.

"You remember Auntie Zu's place?" She pointed to the right. "I'll open up and wake her. Bring Pooker inside."

"Can I bring the others?"

"I guess." She hesitated on the porch. "I've never met a clone before."

"They're the same as us," Elsie said irritably.

She'd been the same as Zulu a month ago. It was alien now to see how she must have seemed to Dar and the others.

"Jeez, Elsie, I didn't mean anything weird," Zulu said. "I'm half Glagchian for goodness sake. It's not like everyone's met one of me before. Anyway, we're down to fifteen minutes. So rocket!" She shooed Elsie away and raced across to her auntie's house. It mostly mimicked Zulu's, only on a smaller scale with one less floor and a slighter build.

Elsie rushed over to the jellach vehicle and banged on the window which immediately disappeared. Vlas had to duck to avoid her fist as it went through the erased space.

"Jeez, Elsie, we saw you coming."

"We need to bring Pooker to Zulu's aunt's house next door," Elsie said breathlessly. "We have fifteen minutes before Zulu's got to be back in her bedroom. Her avatar wakes up then and will for sure set off all sorts of alarms if Zulu isn't in bed with her lights out."

"Okay, light speed, everyone," Dar said.

Elsie grabbed Pooker and dragged her out of the HV. "Come on," she said.

The bobcat trotted docilely next to her, seeming to have forgotten that she had ever decided to disappear earlier today. Elsie hoped that no one was looking out their windows right now what with seven kids and one bobcat loping across the street moss.

The door to Auntie Zu's was still erased when they arrived at the threshold. They entered slowly. The foyer seemed to have more plants than the outside did with tall ferns, fantasy orchids and succulents. Elsie had always loved Auntie Zu's home. Glagchians were known for turning their living quarters into garden paradises.

Pooker went straight to the plants and sniffed them. For once, she didn't look irritated or frightened, just curious. Did she remember Auntie Zu's house?

Dar requested that the door return to its solid state.

Zulu stood at the top of the stairs holding the arm of a very elderly female.

Not that it was obvious that she was ancient. She looked amazing. Her skin was unlined, her hair still a beautiful shade of orange, her figure trim, and she held her head high. But the Glagchian culture used fashion to indicate a person's status in society. An older woman wore her normally curly hair perfectly straight and long to indicate that though she had been worn down by the seas of time, she still survived with her own unique beauty. A wreath of leaves encircled her head—a crown to honor her wisdom.

"Elsie?" Her voice quavered with age.

Elsie rushed forward and took Auntie Zu's hand as she reached the lowest stair. "Yes, Auntie Zu, it's me."

"Zulu says you're in trouble."

"Yes, I need your help."

"Why aren't you asking your parents for help?"

Elsie glanced at Zulu who shrugged her shoulders. "Well, my parents sort of need *my* help right now."

"Ah, yes," she nodded, "a wild story about your parents having been kidnapped."

"Yes, will you help me?"

"Of course. What do you need?"

Relief rushed through Elsie. Thank the Light! Auntie Zu was lucid tonight.

Zulu squeezed the woman's arm. "Auntie Zu, I told you. Elsie needs you to take care of Pooker for her."

"Pooker?"

"Yes," Zulu said. "You know, her pet bobcat."

"What's a bobcat?"

Zulu sighed. "Sort of like a derndyl only bigger and less cuddly. You've met Pooker before."

"A derndyl is the Glagchian equivalent of a cat," Dar whispered to Larry.

"A derndyl!" Auntie Zu exclaimed. "I had one when I was young. Her name was Seli. She was purple and brown." Her eyes went moist. "She slept with me." She turned to Zulu. "I miss Seli."

"Of course you do, Auntie. You'll like Pooker. In fact, you already like her."

"Who's Pooker?"

This time Zulu couldn't hide her exasperation. She sighed deeply and spoke more slowly. "Elsie's bobcat. The one you're going to take care of for her."

"Oh." She turned back to Elsie. "You have a bobcat? I had a derndyl when I was young." She smiled sweetly. "Her name was Seli. She was purple and brown. I used to sleep with her at night."

Elsie looked at Zulu nervously. So much for being lucid. Was this woman capable of taking care of Pooker?

"It's okay," Zulu said. "I'll check on her often during the day."

"Check on whom, dear?" Auntie Zu asked.

Zulu kissed her cheek. "Check on you, Auntie."

"Aren't you sweet? Now, where's that bobcat?" Suddenly her eyes gleamed and she looked twenty years younger.

Elsie gave a sigh of relief. "Pooker," she called.

The bobcat padded over.

"Oh, isn't she sweet. Just like Seli. Only not purple, but she's got a lot of brown, and she's bigger than Seli, and her ears are different, and she's got those funny tufts of fur." She furrowed her brow. "But she's very similar." She made kissing noises and put out her hand.

Pooker contemplated her for a few seconds then moved closer, sniffing her fingers. Surprisingly, she licked Auntie Zu's hand. She wasn't generally demonstrative with strangers, and she had only met Auntie Zu a few times.

The woman's face lit up. "Isn't she sweet?"

"Okay, Auntie Zu," Zulu said. "I have to leave. Do not tell anyone about Pooker. Promise me. I'll be here first thing in the morning to get you breakfast and to take care of the bobcat."

"That'll be lovely, dear," said Auntie Zu.

Zulu turned back to the B12s. "You should get out of here. Don't worry, Pooker will be fine."

"You've only got five minutes to get back to your room," Elsie said.

"Yeah, I'll just settle Auntie Zu and be back in my room at light speed." Zulu waved Elsie and the others out of the house. "Rocket!" Then she ran to where Elsie was and hugged her hard. "Take care, Double-trouble. I'm not keeping Pooker forever. You come back safe or I'll be zetta angry."

Elsie laughed and cried at the same time. Zulu was more sister than friend.

"Hate to break up this touching moment, but Zulu's right. We need to get out of here before someone spots us." Dar grabbed Elsie's arm and yanked her away. "Thanks, Zulu."

The girl wiped tears off her cheeks. "Good luck."

She turned away and took her Aunt's arm. They slowly worked their way back up the stairs.

Elsie worried that Zulu wouldn't make it back to her room in time, but it wasn't going to be any faster if they stayed. They'd just slow Zulu down further. She stopped resisting Dar and pivoted around. They jogged silently back to the hover vehicle.

When they reached it, Elsie turned back. "Maybe we should have asked to stay at Auntie Zu's for the night. It would have given us a place to put on our disguises."

"No," Dar said. "It would be best for them if we got some distance between us and this burb. We'll find another place to hang till we've got a plan for your parents. I think we can put on most of the disguises while we're en route."

Elsie looked at Dar, seeking reassurance. "Do we have a chance?"

"Of course we have a chance. They're alive, aren't they? We had zero chance with them dead. Now anything's possible."

CHAPTER 31
Home Sweet Home

"What else have you learned about Pelican Island?" Everest asked Borneo.

It was a little after 23:30 and they were flying with the dwindling traffic. They had traveled from Redwood City to San Francisco to cover their tracks. Now Vlas wended his way back and forth throughout the city. Lelita had applied makeup, contacts, and a wig to Borneo, giving him black hair, brown eyes and brown skin.

Larry snickered when it was done, but Everest had to admit that Lelita was good at this. Maybe as good as Vlas.

Elsie leaned over. "It's a great disguise, Borneo."

"I feel silly," he said mournfully.

"No one will recognize you," Lelita said.

"Yeah." That cheered him up. "I guess that'll be pretty zeller."

Dar swiveled her seat around. "We like the old Borneo best," she said forcefully, "but this will keep you safe."

He smiled gratefully.

"Okay, Everest, time to become a blond," she said.

"No way! She can go blond." He pointed at his sister.

Elsie rolled her eyes. "We both have to do costumes, and there are only so many wigs left. There's a blond wig that looks like it'll work for a boy and a black wig for a girl. I'm going to use the black wig, unless you want long hair, in which case I can go with the boy's blond look."

"I'm going to look like such a suzo-shrimp," he moaned.

"What's new?" Dar asked.

Larry snickered again.

Everest did his best to act as if he hadn't heard Dar. He'd practically handed her that line so he deserved it.

He sighed and dropped down to the floor so that Lelita could apply the wig and some nose putty. He squirmed a bit because the putty tickled.

"Pelican Island?" he asked again.

"Uh," Borneo said, "it was some sort of preserve for birds until, not that long ago, someone claimed they had rights to it."

"Rights?" asked Elsie.

"Yeah, under the Vlemutz Wars Reparation Act."

"Huh? That was a really long time ago. It doesn't seem as if anyone could prove anything."

"Yeah, I guess it was pretty big news about five years ago. Believe it or not, this guy had documented proof that his ancestors owned the island at the time that the Vlemutz did their damage."

"Who is he?"

"His name is John C. Brown, but there's not a lot about him in the public portion of the Galactic Knowledge Bank. Not even an image."

"Really?" Dar asked.

Everest could just hear her brain cells noodling on that one.

"Yeah, you might want to work on him a bit. I can't seem to get anywhere."

"What's the island look like?" Elsie asked.

"It's not much more than a big rock most of which is now under sea level. In the old days a lot more of it was above the water. Way back, they actually called it 'The Rock.' It also went by Alcatraz at one time—a messed up version of pelican in Spanish. From what I can tell, Mr. Brown was the person who officially changed the name to Pelican Island. During the years when it was a bird preserve it was identified by a number."

"I know Alcatraz," Larry said. "It was one bad prison in its day—for the scariest dudes."

"A prison?" Lelita asked.

"Yeah, for the baddest of the bad."

"Have you been there?" Dar asked.

Everest snorted. It sounded as if she was asking Larry if he'd gone to prison.

Larry grinned. "Sure, I went there on a field trip right before my ma died. After that I didn't go on any more field trips." He said one of the illegal bad words. "That was one wild place. Ghosts a plenty. It was majorly creepy."

"Do you remember any more details?"

"Sure, I remember stuff, your Darship, but it's been over a thousand years. I'm pretty sure it doesn't look the same as when I was there. In fact, I know it doesn't since Borneo here says it's mostly under water. Your fancy Galactic Knowledge Bank must have a lot more to say about it in the thirty-first century."

"Can we go there now?" Elsie asked. "How far away is it?"

Lelita had finished Everest's disguise and was now adding a bump to Elsie's nose.

"Maybe we should have a plan first?" Dar asked.

"Uh, we have another problem to deal with before that," Vlas inserted. "All this flying around means we need a sunergy fix zetta bad."

"Oh-oh, how far can we go?" Dar asked.

"Another thirty minutes? If we're really lucky, maybe an hour, but then we're done till the morning."

"Ideas anyone?"

"How 'bout a vacant house?" Larry suggested.

"I doubt anyone has left out a sunergy generator on the front doorstep," Dar said.

"Earlier tonight we considered going to another school academy," Lelita said as she stroked on makeup over Elsie's nose putty. "Maybe we should try one up here. We could do a search for schools in San Francisco."

"Risky, but a possibility. Other ideas?"

"We could try our house," Everest suggested.

"We already ruled that out," Dar said. "It's bound to be swarming with cyborg officers."

"Not if we go backward a couple of weeks." He rubbed at his itchy hairline. "We have a regular sunergy generator and a portable one too. And our home holoputer may have research papers from our parents."

"We could check the family vault for any papers or more pendants," Elsie said excitedly.

"Exactly how are we supposed to get back to that time?" Dar asked.

"Use one of us. We know it works now."

"It worked with someone who had superpowers," Dar said. "We don't know if it can work with normal kids."

"It's only two weeks," Elsie said excitedly. "Or we could go back one week. That's not very much time, so it shouldn't pack much of a punch. I think it could work."

Everest could see his sister was caught up with the idea, but he wondered if it would be the right decision. It could be very dangerous. They really didn't know how safe this type of time travel was. He had a feeling she just wanted to go home, more for comfort than anything. He wasn't sure they would find a lot there.

Borneo cleared his throat. "I think maybe I could pull together some sort of model based on our previous time travel to determine the safety probability."

They all turned to stare.

Everest didn't know if he should be reassured or not by the idea of a safety probability. "I'm beginning to agree with Dar. Maybe this isn't the best idea. Maybe Borneo should be looking up local academies."

"Everest!" Elsie shrieked.

"Well, if something goes wrong we won't be able to save our parents."

"Okay, okay." Elsie looked a little teary-eyed.

"Jeez, Elsie, stop being such a blubber," he said.

"Give her a break," Dar said.

Everest stared. Dar was defending Elsie?

"Dudes, Adriatic's bat mobile is from this time period," Larry said, interrupting the sudden silence. "Why can't we just use it as our time-travel device?"

Dar grinned. "Okay, now I feel like a total yocto-brain. I must be zetta more messed up by the time travel than I thought. You're right, Larry, that'll work—no problem."

Elsie cleared her throat. "Dar, a month ago you told me that people weren't supposed to time travel without at least a few hours in between. We've been doing quite a bit of back and forth. Is that an issue?"

"So far we've done okay," Dar said, "but maybe that's why we're not as sharp as we usually are. None of us have had sleep in like a gazillion years either." She shook her head. "We'll just hope that it helps that two of the trips aren't that far back in time."

"Borneo," Vlas said, ignoring Elsie's question, "give me your holoputer. I'll make the calculations."

It didn't take long to reprogram the time-travel device. Dar refused to hand out the purple motion sickness pills because she was running out. Fortunately, the actual trip back two weeks was so smooth that Everest almost didn't believe they had traveled back in time. If he had blinked he would have missed the mounting pressure, the loss of feeling, and the chattering teeth.

They arrived in their sleepy little neighborhood in the middle of the night. They lived less than a kilometer away from Zulu on a street that was built very similarly to hers, with rows of independent townhouses, three stories up and two stories down. They were constructed with green roofs and green walls and each had a small courtyard garden in the front and back. The rest of the ground between the homes and on the street was covered with street moss for parking and flying over. The streets were lined with trees that grew to exactly the height of the family homes.

They landed a few houses down and across the street.

Everest swallowed hard. It wasn't easy looking at their home. His stomach churned with too much emotion.

"Do we need to break in?" Vlas asked, looking way too happy at the prospect.

Elsie rolled her eyes. "Don't be silly. The house will recognize us."

"It's pretty," Lelita said. "I like all the purple flowers on the walls."

"Me too." Elsie smiled. "Mom let me pick them out."

"Uh, can we talk about more important things than flowers?" Everest asked. *Jeez*, was all he could think.

"Does everything look normal to you?" Dar asked.

Both Everest and Elsie nodded. "Yeah," Elsie added.

"No extra hover vehicles on the street?"

Everest took a second look. Most of their neighbors had two HVs each. A few had three because of older kids. All of the vehicles were shrunk down to their smallest size except for a neighbor's a few doors down. He was too lazy to ever command his HVs to shrink that far.

"I don't see any extra HVs," Elsie said, as usual the first to respond.

Dar looked at Everest for confirmation.

"Yeah, it looks pretty normal," he said.

Dar absently flicked her finger at the door, a repetitive motion that caused the jellach to indent then pop back out. "Okay, I think just a few of us should go in first. If someone looks out the window, two or three people entering will be a lot less noticeable than seven."

"Yeah, in the twenty-first century, people would call us a gang," said Larry.

"I'm pretty sure we qualify as a gang in this time period too," Dar said. "We just lack a dangerous reputation for another two weeks." She grinned. "I'll go in with Elsie and Everest." She rummaged in her backpack and pulled out a large earpatch vial, one they had taken from Mink's weapon room. "Earpatches all around."

She turned to Elsie and Everest with the vial. "Are your nighteyes still working?"

"Yeah," Everest mumbled.

Dar always made him feel like a total yocto-brain when they were on a mission. If he'd been in charge, he would have just gone inside the house without any prep. Was all of this really necessary? It was best to play it safe. He needed to try to think the way Dar thought—as if everyone was an enemy and every situation dangerous. But even after everything that had happened, it was such an alien way to think.

When they exited the hover vehicle, he realized Dar *had* influenced him after all. He found himself checking every shadow and flinching at the slightest noise. Jeez, it would be a full two weeks before their parents would go missing. Why would bad guys be lurking now?

Elsie moved closer to him on his right, and that made him feel even more nervous. Why did they have to live in constant terror? Would life ever return to normal?

When they reached the door, Elsie touched it. "It's Elsie and Everest," she said, "requesting entry."

The door immediately erased.

"Your home is zetta trusting," Dar commented.

"There's never been a crime in this area. We've never even known someone who's had to deal with a crime of any sort. Besides, the door reads our vitals." Elsie stepped into the foyer which was white marblon.

Everest and Dar followed.

"Lights, please," Elsie said.

The hallway lit up, and a man dressed in a sober gray suit wearing white gloves shimmered into view.

"Elsie and Everest," he said, "this is an unexpected pleasure. I see you've brought a guest."

"Jeeves!" they both exclaimed.

Everest was so glad to see their family avatar. Their parents were avid readers of novels from all millennia, so all the avatars in the house were interpretations from books. The character Jeeves was a recent find. His series had been lost for hundreds of years until an underground library had been discovered with an extensive treasure trove of books from before the Vlemutz Wars.

Because the door sensed that there were no others waiting outside, it solidified. With Jeeves standing so prim and proper, the room felt normal and safe. Everest took it all in—the narrow staircase up to the bedrooms and down to the entertainment and storage areas, the chipped marblon to the right of the door where he had dropped a school science project when he was nine, the purple light mural on the left wall that Elsie had begged their parents to buy.

An almost overwhelming feeling of homesickness hit him. He missed his bedroom, his skyball setup in the entertainment room, his games, his jellach bed, his kitchen. He missed his dad's so-so cooking and the stash of Blackholes in the family room cupboard.

"Jeeves, this is our friend, Dar. Have you heard from our parents?" Elsie asked.

"Elsie!" Everest was horrified. What was she thinking?

"No, Miss. They have not been in touch since they left a couple of weeks ago."

"Have you heard from anyone else?"

"Your uncle has been in contact."

"Our uncle?" Elsie asked loudly.

"Yes, Miss. He was here for a few hours a couple of days ago."

"What did he do?" she asked urgently.

"I'm afraid I do not know. He asked for privacy."

"Jeez, Jeeves," Everest said. "Why would you give him privacy?"

"Your parents gave him full clearance. I complied with their wishes." Jeeves sniffed loudly, clearly insulted by Everest implying that he'd done something wrong. "If my actions displease you, you may, of course, take it up with your parents when they come home."

"No, no," Elsie said, glaring at Everest who scowled back. "You've done nothing wrong. We were just surprised that our uncle came here. He didn't mention it to us."

"I admit I was taken aback, myself," Jeeves said, "but it is not my place to contradict your parents' instructions."

"Of course, you did exactly the right thing," Elsie said. "I assume the house is empty right now?"

"Yes indeed."

"Zeller. We have a few friends waiting outside."

"Shall I request that the door be erased again?"

"No, thank you, Jeeves. That will be all for now. We'll let you know if we need you."

"As you wish," he said and melted into nothingness.

"Vlas, Lelita, Borneo," Dar said. "You all can join us."

"We'll be there faster than a black hole can eat a flyby comet," Vlas said.

Elsie told the door to dissolve, and in less than a minute, the rest of the kids had joined them.

"I'm zetta tired," Lelita said, yawning widely. "Can we please go to sleep?"

"I think we should check out the house first," Dar said. "If it feels safe, people should definitely rest. All that time travel at once isn't healthy. Who knows how many hours we've actually been up?"

"Yeah, Mom, thanks for pointing that out," Larry said.

Dar pushed him into Vlas, but she grinned.

"I'm totally exhausted," said Elsie. "I feel as if I've run a dozen Mormor miles."

All of a sudden it hit Everest too. He could sleep for a millennium. He stumbled a bit as he walked to the stairs.

Dar was a few steps behind. "A couple of us should stay awake and on guard in case something unexpected happens. We're not the only people who know how to time travel, and even without time travel there could be people searching your home now in this time period. They could be looking for something while your parents are away."

"I don't think I can stay awake," Elsie said. She blinked, trying to keep her eyes open.

"That's okay," Dar said. "I'm not tired."

"How in the universe could you not be tired?" Elsie asked.

"I've always been able to go for a long time without sleep."

"I can stay awake," Larry said. "I'm pretty buzzed from all that superhero business. I'll probably start getting tired in a few hours, but not yet."

"Okay, we'll take the first shift while the rest of you sleep. In a few hours, we'll wake up Vlas so that Larry gets some rest."

"What about you?" Elsie asked.

"I told you," she said, "I don't need sleep. I'll be good till at least tomorrow night."

"That's zetta alien," Elsie said.

Dar shrugged. "It's just the way I am."

Everest had a vague sense of déjà vu. Hadn't Shadara once famously commented that she could go for days without sleep? He sort of remembered reading that there had been lots of speculation that she used drugs to keep herself awake, but maybe it had been simple genetics.

"But you sleep at the academy," Elsie persisted.

"Yeah, sometimes. Often, I just meditate. I probably average about two to three hours a night." Dar looked over her shoulder. "Vlas, take Borneo and Everest downstairs to check for bad guys. I'll take Elsie and Lelita up. And Elsie, Everest, before you go to bed, I need you to log me into your home holoputer. I'll do some research while I'm up." She started to climb the stairs, and then paused. "If you see anything, anything at all, that doesn't feel right, let me know. Once we've checked out the house, I'll collect the earpatches and send everyone but Larry to bed."

CHAPTER 32
Respite

To Elsie, each step up the staircase was like dragging herself through a Sleztar bog. When she finally slogged her way up to the landing, her bedroom door was a far off beacon. She stumbled down the hallway, ignoring the staircase that led to the third floor as well as the door to her brother's room. In her ear, she heard a steady stream of babble coming mostly from Vlas and Larry. Everest was silent. She tried to tune out the noise as she requested entry to her own chamber. Then she whispered, "Earpatch, mute," and their chatter disappeared altogether.

A diffused glow brought her bedroom into focus as soon as they entered.

Lelita gasped with delight, making Elsie smile. It *was* a zeller room with the walls awash in iridescent opal tones that moved from light to dark and then light again. For Pooker's sake, she had an oversized jellach bed that was an ever-changing blend of jewel tones. Elsie loved this place.

Nothing seemed unusual or out of place—besides the chamber being spotlessly clean. That was alien. But her parents had insisted that she tidy it before leaving for the academy, and it looked as if pico-brownies had been diligent in her absence. Even now, a flurry of brownies scrubbed with industry in the far corner. Individually, each brownie was too small to see, but they had collected to dust her little jellach journal case.

"Anything out of the ordinary?" Dar asked.

Elsie looked around one more time to make sure. "No, it's the same as when I left." She called out, "Mary?"

A young woman with black hair and a starched soft gray uniform shimmered to life. With her hands folded at her waist, she contemplated the girls, her lips pursed. As usual, Elsie's avatar had a no-nonsense expression on her face.

"Elsie, dear," she said with an oh-so-proper British accent. "I thought you were at the academy."

"Yes, I'm just here on a short visit." Her words felt as if they were caught in the back of her throat. By the Light, she was tired. "These are friends of mine, Lelita and Dar."

"Nice to meet you, Mary," Lelita said politely.

Dar nodded her greeting.

"The pleasure is mine," Mary said briskly.

Dar raised her eyebrows. Leaning over, she whispered to Elsie, "Your parents programmed Mary Poppins as your avatar?"

"They like ancient literature," Elsie said, feeling defensive.

"Jeez, you're twelve and you still have a nanny!"

Elsie was too tired to respond. She glared at Dar through half-closed eyes. She liked her avatar.

Dar smirked. "Okay, let's check the rest of the house."

Everest's room was a much starker, less colorful living space in comparison—at least, that was Elsie's opinion.

Again, Dar asked if anything was out of place. And again, Elsie couldn't find anything, except that it, too, was sparkling clean which was a first for Everest's room.

They moved up to the next floor where Elsie's parents' room was. The stairs dumped into the spacious chamber, and another staircase to the side went up to the roof garden. Her parents liked a streamlined environment. Their jellach bed was simple with a clean white appearance. The only other furniture was a corner sitting area made out of white nanofiber and two Zentor vood desk units. An entire wall was covered with vood shelving that overflowed with jellach journals. The other wall displayed a white mural that changed shades of white and displayed various white shapes. It was lit from within so that the white glowed and hinted of pink, yellow and orange.

"This is so beautiful," Lelita said. "I can't imagine having a home like this, someplace all your own."

Knowing that Lelita had never had a place to call home, Elsie felt almost embarrassed that this was hers. "Yeah," she said, "we've been lucky." *But not now*, she thought.

Dar said, "Vlas, how are things down below? Anything unusual?"

Elsie quickly whispered, "Earpatches, un-mute."

Just in time, she heard Vlas's response. "Everest doesn't see anything alien downstairs."

Dar said to Vlas, "Is there anyplace down there for sleeping?"

Elsie responded, "There's a couch that turns into a jellach bed."

Vlas said basically the same thing in her ear.

Dar rolled her eyes. "Jeez, Elsie, I don't need to hear the information in surround sound."

"Well, jeez, Dar," Elsie returned irritably, "I'm tired, and I want to go to sleep. Do you want to know about other beds in the house or don't you?"

"You sure get cranky when you're sleep deprived," Dar said, her eyebrows raised. "Please, do tell."

Elsie gave a long, drawn-out sigh. "I've got a portable jellach bed in my room and so does Everest. Lelita can sleep in my room, Vlas can take the couch, and later Larry can either sleep in Everest's extra bed or he can switch with Vlas."

"Okay," Dar said. "Where's your family holoputer?"

"There's no family holoputer. We each have our own. I'm sure my parents took theirs. We took ours to the academy—not that we've been allowed to use them. But my parents do have a backup unit. It's probably in one of their desks." She crossed over to her dad's work space. There was a pretty image of her mom floating in a large, man-made crystal a few centimeters above the desk. She leaned down to look at it. It hurt to see her mom. She was so young looking, so pretty. What were they doing to her?

She took a deep breath and opened one of the vood drawers. She rifled through but couldn't find a holoputer. Neither did she find anything in the other drawers. She crossed over to her mother's desk and had more luck with the top drawer where she found an older holoputer. She handed it over to Dar.

She muted her earpatches again then said, "I'm pretty sure the password is Pooker00, but if they had to change it, they probably would have done a sort of Basker anagram like Krabes with some number. Or they've sometimes done anagrams of Pooker like Kooper. There might be something that requires voice recognition for one of the family." She yawned, unable to stop herself. "Maybe I should try to stay up."

"Nah, I can handle it," Dar said. "But just to be safe, say your name and your birth date." Dar held her palm out and revealed a black dot.

"What's that?"

"It's a recording device. That way I have your voice if I need it."

Elsie slowly said her name and then her birth date.

Dar grinned. "Okay, you and Lelita take your naps." She cracked her knuckles. "Time for me to have some fun."

"You won't mess up anything on my parents' holoputer, will you?"

"Who me?" Dar asked, wide-eyed.

Elsie suddenly felt like the biggest yocto-brain, giving away her parents' passwords and secrets.

Dar must have read something in her expression. "Jeez, Elsie, keep your aura on. I'm not going to do anything bad to your parents' accounts."

Now Elsie felt dreadful—after everything Dar had done for her. "I'm sorr—"

"Shut down!" Dar held up her hand. "Take your nap. You're tired. A lot has happened. It's no big deal."

Elsie felt as if she should apologize again, but one look at Dar's zetta intimidating expression and she just couldn't work up the energy. Instead, she pulled out her muted earpatches and handed them to Dar. Lelita did likewise. Dar returned them to the large vial and turned away.

Stumbling like a malfunctioning robot, Elsie made her way down the stairs to her room. Lelita followed.

"Extra bed, please," she mumbled as she fell onto her jellach mattress. Mary reappeared, now in starched blue and white, to usher a bed out of the closet.

"Thanks, Mary," Elsie managed to say.

The woman bustled around, pointing at lights to dim them. "You look ever so tired, Elsie. You go right to sleep."

"Yeah." Elsie sighed as the jellach conformed around her to provide a gentle massage. It felt like a dream. With everything they'd done, all the going back and forth in time, they had to have been closing in on a good twenty-four hours straight without sleep.

"Elsie," Lelita whispered, "it's so zeller not to be afraid for once. I was terrified when those Panktars kidnapped me. But I feel safe here."

Elsie tried to concentrate on Lelita's words. She'd been so focused on her own problems she'd somehow forgotten what Lelita and Borneo had gone through. Her parents' disappearance was all she'd thought about. And Lelita was an innocent. She shouldn't have had to deal with brutal Panktars.

It took a huge amount of effort, but she lifted her head to look at the girl. With her big eyes and softly rounded face, Lelita could have passed for much younger than twelve. At their age, they weren't supposed to be fighting bad guys. They were supposed to be playing games and eating no-cal chocolate.

At worst, they should have been fighting with each other, not with true vlems.

"I'm so sorry," she said.

"Why?" Lelita asked.

"You should be back at the academy having fun and going to school, doing normal things. It's my fault that you were kidnapped and nearly killed, my fault you're on the run."

"No," Lelita said. "The vlems who kidnapped your parents are the ones at fault. I don't blame you. Not one bit. But I *am* scared and tired, and I wish those horrible monsters would go away or be kidnapped themselves."

Elsie rolled onto her side. "Lelita, you're a good friend."

The girl smiled shyly. "You are too."

Elsie smiled back then rested her head on the jellach. "I'm going to fall asleep." Her eyes were already closing and her words were slurred.

"Yeah, me too," Lelita whispered.

That was the last thing Elsie heard.

235

CHAPTER 33
No Safe Haven

A minor earthquake woke Everest out of a deep sleep. The jellach bed shook and something landed on his shoulder, pinning him to the bed. He had to escape, but he couldn't seem to move.

"Wha—"

"Rise and shine," Vlas said cheerfully.

Everest stared at him through bleary eyes. "It can't possibly be morning yet."

Vlas looked wickedly happy about waking him up.

"Yup, Dar wants us to get moving," he said.

Everest looked over at the other bed and saw Larry sleeping soundly, curled up with his hand loosely fisted beneath his chin. "When did you swap with Larry?"

"He woke me up a couple of hours ago. We'll wait as long as possible to wake him—at least till after you take your shower. I already took mine, and man was it zeller. Given the trickle we get at the academy, I'd figured water coming out of a pipe at full force was just a figment of someone's imagination."

Everest grinned. "Yeah, I never appreciated it till we were stuck at the academy. If only I'd known, I'd have taken more showers when I'd had the chance." For the longest time, his parents had had to take away privileges to get him to even take a shower. Now it felt like a luxury.

"Dar says to put your disguise back on after you clean up," Vlas said. "If you need help with the makeup and putty just let me know."

Everest rolled out of the jellach bed and headed for the bathroom. Ten minutes later, he felt a lot more awake. He'd even managed a change of clothes, having pulled on some old exercise

236

gear that he'd left behind when they'd moved to the academy. Now he was starving. He wished they had fresh food in the house, but they were going to be stuck with shelf-food for the duration.

He forced himself to reapply the lighter makeup, then the blond wig and the larger nose. Vlas had left some putty on the counter. His new nose looked broken, but at least he didn't look like himself. He didn't think he looked like he was wearing a costume either. That was all that mattered.

He wandered downstairs and found Dar sitting at the kitchen table jacked into the holoputer, a faraway look in her eyes. Her lips were moving, but he couldn't make out the words.

Vlas was exploring meal choices in the kitchen. Even with no fresh or frozen supplies there was plenty of food.

Lelita came down next. She wore one of Elsie's smaller outfits from a couple of years back. Luckily, their parents were always too busy to go through their closets. Otherwise, the old stuff would have been given away years ago.

Lelita was smiling and refreshed and greeted everyone cheerfully. She wore minimal disguise since she was least likely to draw attention and be noticed. She had given herself bangs which immediately modified her looks and made her seem even younger. She also had lightened her skin color and changed her nose ever so slightly. Finally, she'd used a set of colored lenses to change the color of her eyes to a greenish-blue.

Elsie followed in her darker wig and makeup. She still looked tired but not super grumpy. Everest figured she'd had a pretty good night's sleep.

"Did Dar find anything?" she asked.

Now that was a yocto-brained question since Dar was still busy with the holoputer. Everest started to say so, but Elsie must have read his mind because she shot him a dirty look and held up her hand to silence him.

She thumbed her hand at Dar and asked Vlas, "How long has she been jacked in?"

Vlas shrugged. "Not sure. When Larry woke me up for my shift she was already in there. I interrupted her and got some assignments, but she's been back with the holoputer ever since, except for once when she told me to wake up Everest."

"What did she have you do?"

"She had me research femto-technology," he said.

"What did you find?" Elsie asked.

"Well, I watched your mom give a lecture on ethics and femto research."

Everest leaned forward. "Really?"

"Yeah," Vlas said, "it was at the Googleopolis University. She was hysterical. She kept the students laughing and interested. Your mom's wicked zeller."

Everest swallowed. "I've never seen her speak like that. Did you learn anything?"

"Well, she wasn't into abusing the technology, that's for sure. She had a list of rules that she thought should be followed. And she thought government should regulate the technology before any products were released to market."

"Sounds like mom," Elsie said. "She's into rules."

"Yeah, but that was the only part of her lecture that even came close to being boring, and even it wasn't so bad because she was so funny. She gave examples of ways that the technology could be used. Mostly she talked about a more efficient way of fighting back all the germs that were mutating. She talked about Shlemel's Law where mutations were happening exponentially every ten years, and she said that current technology just couldn't keep up. But she thought we could create killer anti-germs out of femto-technology. She made it sound like a war on the scale of the Vlemutz ones. It was pretty exciting. Made me want to study femto-technology and work with her someday." He grinned. "She really fired up the students."

Everest felt an alien sense of pride. He wanted to hear his mom's speech. He wanted to help her. "I wonder why they were working on the femto-boosters. It's not exactly the same thing as creating anti-germs, is it?"

"Maybe it's more commercial. Maybe she was trying to raise money for her other research."

"But wouldn't people invest a lot of money to keep diseases from coming back?" Elsie asked.

Vlas tilted his head and contemplated her question. "Maybe, but some of the questions at the end of her lecture made it sound as if not everyone agreed with Shlemel's Law. Some people think that current techniques are adequate to keep disease at bay. It seemed as if some people thought she was over-sensationalizing the problem. It's hard to get money for controversial research.

"After I watched your mom, I looked into the investors in femto-technology for pharmaceutical purposes, and there weren't that many. There were a lot of articles debating whether disease will ever be an issue again. The scientific community at large seems to think that we've got that under control with regular pico-technology. Even your dad and mom have slightly different views. Your mom is much more adamant that Shlemel's Law is real, and your dad is more conservative. He agrees that there's a possibility we'll hit a point in time when current methods aren't enough to fight off disease, but he's not a hundred percent convinced that it's a given."

"I still don't get why they're making superhumans. It doesn't seem to fit their philosophy."

"Well, it's a pretty extreme example of the power of femto-technology."

"But Mom and Dad have always been seriously negative about anything that could be used against society."

"Maybe they thought it would be regulated and only used for good, like for people living off-world who have to deal with harsher climates," Vlas said. "Your dad spoke recently about Earth's overpopulation problem."

"He did?" Elsie asked.

"Yeah, he was a pretty good speaker too. Not quite as funny as your mom, but interesting. He talked about incenting people to settle on less-populated planets."

"How?"

"Well…by providing jobs, quality of life, adventure."

"But everyone has quality of life here," said Elsie.

Vlas shrugged. "I'm just telling you what he said. He said that Glagcha has a great incentive program for citizens who wish to explore the universe. He suggested that Earth could do better. You know, 'Gotcha Glagcha' stuff."

"I wish we could just ask them."

"Yeah, it's hard to piece together what they were thinking. They clearly had a plan, but it's not easy to figure out what it was." Vlas pursed his lips. "Did they ever talk about emigrating off world?"

"No!" Both Elsie and Everest responded.

Elsie shook her head adamantly and added, "They never would have considered it."

"If you say so." Vlas shrugged. "It just seems as if they were really caught up with this idea that Earth needed to solve some serious problems—overcrowding, the threat of a pandemic because of zetta-resistant germs." He leaned over and shoved Dar in the shoulder. "Hey, Dar, take a break. We need an update."

Everest was impressed by Vlas's lack of fear where Dar was concerned. He'd never have the guts to be that assertive.

Dar jolted out of her holoputer session, glaring at Vlas. "Thanks a lot," she said irritably.

"You bet," he said, grinning. "Tell us what you've found out."

"Where's Larry," she asked.

"He's still asleep."

"Well, wake him up," she said.

"He's only had a little over two hours," said Vlas.

She raised her eyebrows. "And your point is?"

He laughed. "No point. I'll wake him."

"Good." She stood up and stretched.

Everest preferred Dar's brown wig and brown makeup. She was duller than usual which was less distracting. But she also looked older than usual, and that was just plain irritating since even before the disguise she had looked a couple of years older than the rest of them.

"I need something to eat." She went into the kitchen and came out with a package of brown rice and beans and a spoon. The food automatically heated up when opened.

Larry and Vlas came down the stairs, Larry grumbling about his lack of sleep and Vlas entertaining himself by giving Larry a hard time.

"Can I eat in your lounge area?" Dar pointed to the couch and chairs next to the kitchen table.

"Yeah, sure," Elsie said.

They all slouched on the furniture. Everest leaned forward, waiting for Dar to fill them in on what she'd learned while they'd slept. He still couldn't believe that she was awake and didn't even seem to need sleep yet. It was so alien. Could it be that she really did have some off-world blood? If so, what blood could that be? He'd never heard of an alien race that didn't sleep. Then again, she looked pretty alien with the way her skin sparkled. Still, there had never even been a hint that Shadara was of mixed blood. The media would have gone nuts over that piece of gossip.

"So what did you find?" Elsie asked

"Your parents' holoputer was pretty clean. Initially, I couldn't find any research on it, but then I went to the deleted files. There was an area of supposedly permanently deleted items that I was able to recover. I found a draft of a research note on femto-technology, specifically the notion of femto-boosters. It was co-written by your parents a few years ago."

"What did it say?" Elsie asked.

"It speculates about the sort of boosts that might be possible. When they wrote the article, there was no hard evidence—everything they spoke of was theoretical. They talked about physical strength a lot, speculating that the research could lead to a replacement for cyborg technology with regards to officers of law. They thought that people's metabolism could be sped up or slowed down to help them deal with certain environments and situations. Slowing down the metabolism might help someone stave off starvation, for instance. Speeding it up could help someone accomplish something that required a huge boost of energy. The paper started to talk about ways for a femto-booster to increase certain senses like sound and smell, but it ended abruptly at that point. It was just a draft. Probably written on a day off and then transferred to a work holoputer and completed there."

"Did you find anything else written about femto-boosters?" Everest asked. Why couldn't his parents have left behind a femto-booster "How To" document? That would have been handy.

"No." Dar chewed and swallowed a spoonful of rice and beans. "But I spent a lot of time last night researching John C. Brown. Get this! He's tagged by the authorities for having smuggled Barbie dolls into the thirty-first century."

"Barbie dolls?" Elsie asked.

"Twenty-first-century, *plastic* dolls." She raised her eyebrows.

Elsie gasped. "Could he be Mr. Snickers?"

"Maybe."

"But why would he have anything to do with our parents?"

Dar shrugged. "He's a pretty mysterious sort of guy. But if he's Mr. Snickers then he's in cahoots with your uncle and good old Gerard. Which makes a lot of sense since Gerard and Brown, at least, are both convicted for smuggling plastic items from the twenty-first century. That's a zetta huge coincidence. The recent Barbie incident was Mr. Brown's first tagging. Up till then, no criminal accusations had ever stuck. Now he's not allowed off-planet, and he's on probation for time travel. Eventually, they have to give him back his privileges...unless, he messes up a second time." She leaned forward. "I also found out some interesting details about his ownership of Pelican Island."

"And?" Elsie asked.

"About five years ago, he shows up with this ancient paper document—over four hundred years old, right? It's falling apart, but it's still pretty well preserved. He claims he found it in an airtight vault that his family had always thought was empty. The doc was very official and it clearly stated that his family had sole ownership of this island called 'the Rock' or 'Alcatraz.' Supposedly, the Vlemutz ripped it right out of his family's hands. Once the document was found, he got back the property as sole heir."

"Other families got their property back, right?"

"Yeah, but there's no other record of the island having been privately owned. All of the documented history says the government owned it. Native Americans did occupy it briefly, but they couldn't hold onto it. It eventually reverted back to the government. For a long time it was a tourist destination then it went into disrepair. Unfortunately, not much is written about Alcatraz in the century leading up to the Vlemutz Wars, so it's difficult to dispute Mr. Brown's claim."

"Do you think it's legit?" Elsie asked.

"Mr. Brown is known for using time travel to his advantage," Dar said. "What if he went back in time? Got someone to create a document that looks pretty official. Paid a local administrator to put a seal of approval on it. Then he stores it underground till he's ready to make the claim—just like the Hasty Hawley toys were stored so they would age properly. It's the same method! Another point in favor of him being Mr. Snickers."

"Yeah," Elsie said, "but how do you prove it?"

"We don't have to prove it," Everest said curtly. "Let's just assume that he did it. Why go after our parents?"

"Well," Dar said, "he's got another little passion."

"Huh?"

"He's been collecting information about extending life past what humans currently see as our limit."

"Flasers, how did you find that out?" Elsie asked.

"I found some auction transactions where he purchased documents on the subject. I'm guessing he's a collector, because he spent a lot of VC to obtain those documents."

"Why would they cost so much?"

"These documents aren't available on Earth. He got them at various intergalactic auctions. That's why there were records. The United Nations of Earth has a lot of regulations about intergalactic commerce. Mostly to keep someone from buying a weapon of mass destruction from another planet."

"Oh," Elsie said.

"I could only access the titles and abstracts." Dar glanced over at Vlas, her lips twitching. "One was about using the combination of cloning with a process for switching auras as a form of everlasting life."

Lelita gasped.

"Don't worry, sweetie. That theory's been around for awhile, but it is zetta illegal on Earth."

"It's horrible," she cried.

Elsie leaned over and hugged her shoulders. "No one would ever really do that."

"Sorry, I shouldn't have mentioned it," Dar said, "but Vlas and I like to collect the most yocto-brained uses of cloning that we can find. Someday, we'll publish an article on the topic." She drummed her fingers on her knee. "Anyway, I think this Mr. Brown may be interested in femto-technology because he wants to live forever or at least a zetta long time."

"Creepy," Elsie said.

"No kidding. But didn't he get lucky that his associate, Captain Reeses, just happens to have the premier scientists in this area of research as his sister and brother-in-law?"

It all fit, Everest thought. Mr. Brown had to be Mr. Snickers.

Elsie sighed. "Borneo couldn't find an image of Mr. Brown. Did you have any more luck? Were you able to find out anything else about his background?"

"It was nearly impossible to find a digital image of him, which was zetta amazing given that he's been tagged by the cybercops. His aura's not even on record. He must have erased both of those recently." She rubbed her hands together. "But I looked up his known business associates and found one image of him from a distance. Someone had tagged him in the photo! Bet that will really irk him when he finds out, since he obviously went to some effort to erase his image from the GKB. I did some work to zoom in and re-image the photo for better clarity. He's handsome, but it looks like he put zetta VC into his appearance. He's average height and slightly bigger than average around the middle. I'm guessing he enjoys more caloric-rich food than most people. The details were a bit hard to make out. His hair is light and thick enough that it's probably enhanced. His features look pretty much perfect, but I'm not sure we would notice him in a crowd. He's sort of forgettable." She flexed her fingers. "As far as his background, there's really nothing available. It's hard to tell he even exists."

"But they wouldn't give him the island with such a murky past," Elsie said.

"Yeah, I know. He must have ensured he had a solid, upstanding history at the time, but when it was no longer necessary he wiped it from the GKB. That's really hard to do, by the way. What I don't get is why he would have erased his records. Let's face it, the cybercops have archives and I doubt he's been able to erase those. Too bad we can't gain access to the cyborg officer of law records, but we're not exactly speaking to them right now."

"I guess we're not going to find any easy answers here." Elsie shook her head. "But I'm glad we came back. It's good to be home, even if just for a short while. Can we stay here while we make plans to rescue our parents?"

"I don't know," Dar said. "I have this bad vibe. Why hasn't anyone checked your parents' home via time travel? It's a pretty obvious thing to do. They're looking for us, and they know we've been using time travel. Why not look for us here?"

"It's not as if there's any reason for us to go here at this particular time," Elsie said.

"Why do you say that?" Dar asked.

"Yeah," Larry said. "Everyone goes home. It's like a rule of frigging nature."

Vlas nodded his head. "I would have looked for us here. It makes a lot of sense. You can't go back when your parents were here because you would have been here too. We all know how hard it is to be in the same place twice. We were pretty much trashed. So you would have to come back sometime during the last month. If I were the authorities, I'd stake out the place. So why haven't they?"

"Jeeves," Dar called.

The butler avatar immediately shimmered into view, his now black suit immaculate and pressed though slightly fuzzy around the edges. "Yes, miss?"

"Besides Elsie and Everest's uncle, has anyone else visited since the Baskers left?"

"No."

"Are you quite sure?" Dar pressed.

"Of course, I'm sure. I have a perfect memory."

"Okay, I know this is a silly request. Of course, your memory is perfect, but I would very much appreciate it if you could do a quick review of the last two weeks. Just check that nothing unusual has happened during that time." She smiled sweetly, and even with her extraordinary looks hidden under dull makeup and brown hair, her smile still was persuasive.

Pursing his lips, the avatar dipped his head and complied. It took only a few seconds, but his briefly blank stare made it obvious that he was in another space. When he refocused on the B12s, his demeanor hinted at unease, a very unusual state for an avatar.

"What is it?" Dar asked.

"I don't understand," he said.

"Just tell us. Maybe we can help."

"There's a small window of time that I can't seem to recall."

"How small?"

"Thirty-two minutes and fifty-two seconds."

"When is this gap?"

"Two days ago. At precisely 11:28 am."

"Okay. When did Fredrick Lester-Hauffer visit?"

"That same day, but he arrived earlier. At 8:00 am. He left at 11:04 am."

They all looked at each other. Everest's heart suddenly beat faster. This was not good.

"Jeeves," Dar said, "you may go."

The avatar blinked away.

"I think it's time for us to leave," Dar added slowly.

"Yeah," Larry said, "this stinks like a bogdog from Sleztar."

Usually Larry using a thirty-first-century phrase made Everest laugh, but this time all he could think was that it did stink. It stunk all the way to the next galaxy.

Elsie started walking briskly to the door. "Let's get out of here."

"No!" Dar said. "Hold on. Someone could be waiting for us." She turned to Vlas. "PicoBoy—now!"

Vlas pulled out his picobot. "PicoBoy, go outside. Report back immediately on what you find."

Dar started passing out earpatches. She also pulled some zunners from her Vlatex II pack. "Vlas you take one. I'll take the other. Does anyone have theirs, or did they leave them in the hover vehicle?"

Elsie groaned. "I'm such a yocto-brain."

Everest felt like a yocto-brain too, but he refrained from speaking.

"No, I should have said something last night. We all get credit for being yocto-brains this time." Dar handed out some stinkers and foggers. "This is all I've got."

PicoBoy returned, chirping at Vlas excitedly. Vlas studied his display, his expression bleak. He quickly had PicoBoy project a visual on the wall.

Cyborg officers of law surrounded the perimeter of the house. There had to be at least a couple dozen.

"Oh no," Lelita cried, clutching her chest. She seemed to be having trouble breathing.

Dar shoved her down onto the couch and pushed her head between her legs. "Do not faint on us, Lelita. We need you to be calm. We're going to get out of this.

"We're going to be killed," Lelita gasped.

Everest had to agree with her.

"Stop it," Dar commanded. "We've been in worse situations. We'll make it through."

Was she completely insane? Everest thought. How could they make it through that many cyborg officers of law? They should just give themselves up.

Dar grabbed him by the arm. "Don't lose your aura. I need you all not to give up. Just give me a second to think."

Like that was going to help.

Cyborg cops—they were doomed.

CHAPTER 34
Caught

Elsie fought hard to stave off the tsunami wave of fear that slammed her and tried to transform her into pulverized driftwood. She both feared cyborg officers of law and secretly wished she could grow up to be one. If Dar thought for even one moment that they could escape a posse of cybercops, she should be sent to the planet, Dementurnum, to hang with all the other lunatics. No way, no how.

"Okay," Dar said, "we're going to create a diversion and make a break—"

"Are you nuts?" Elsie realized she was actually screeching and took a deep breath. "No one escapes from even one cyborg officer let alone an army of them."

"I'll take a femto-booster," Dar said, "and fight off the cybercops till all of you escape."

Everest shook his head. "Even if you manage to pull ten of them into a fight, there'll still be more than that waiting for us."

Dar's nose flared. She clenched her fists. "We don't go down without a fight."

"I think we do," Elsie said.

Dar grimaced. "Ute-babies. Vlas, *you're* with me."

Vlas grinned. "Yeah, I've got a thing for these no-win situations. Besides, if we're captured, it's us clones who will get the worst of the punishment. They'll swizzle everything till it's one hundred percent our fault."

Lelita took a hesitant step forward. "What can I do?" she asked, her voice breaking.

Dar's grimace instantly turned into a broad smile. "I can always count on you."

"M-m-me too," Borneo managed quietly.

248

"You're all crazy." Elsie grabbed Lelita by the arm. "Dar's wrong, and so is Vlas. There's no way they'll be harder on you. Everest and I brought you into this. We'll tell them and take the consequences."

"It is way beyond a simple joyride by a bunch of kids now," Dar said. "For all we know we're being accused of murder. No adults are going to listen to you. You're twelve years old."

"ELSIE AND EVEREST BASKER," boomed a deep voice from outside.

Elsie couldn't tell if it was a man or a woman. The house actually shook from the decibels.

"COME OUT SLOWLY, YOUR HANDS FREE AND VISIBLE, PALMS FACING OUT. ALL PERSONNEL IN THE HOUSE FOLLOW THE TWINS. I REPEAT, HANDS FREE AND VISIBLE."

Dar looked at Vlas. "Have PicoBoy tell them we aren't coming."

Elsie was already walking to the door. She looked over her shoulder. "Speak for yourself. We're going. It's over."

"So that's it?" Dar spit out. "What about your beloved parents? You're just going to let them rot?"

"I'm going to tell the officers of law everything—like we should have done at the start—and I'm going to hope they'll be able to find my parents."

"Uh, girlfriend," Larry finally said, "coppers aren't usually on the side of the runaway. I doubt they'll give you a lot of time to tell your side of the story."

"ELSIE AND EVEREST, WE RESPECTFULLY ASK THAT YOU AND YOUR CLONE FRIENDS COME OUT IMMEDIATELY. DAR, VLAS, BORNEO, LARRY, LELITA, EXIT THE BUILDING NOW. HANDS UP AND EMPTY. WE WILL NOT ASK AGAIN."

Elsie took another slow breath and reached out to touch the door, to speak the words that would erase it and make her visible to the cybercops.

"No," Dar said, her hand clamping down on Elsie's. "You can think we're nuts, or just plain yocto-brained, but no one's going anywhere. If they want us, they'll have to come and get us. Meanwhile, let's get working on an escape plan."

Elsie fought Dar's hold. "What do you think you're doing?" Cyborg police officers didn't dink around. Who knew what kind of torture they could inflict if they really wanted to? She struggled against Dar's hold, and they fought back and forth in a funky retro tug-of-war.

"Hey," Everest said, "stop that."

He reached for their hands, and they both slapped him away.

There was a slight popping noise. At least a dozen cyborg police appeared in their house.

Elsie shrieked and only felt slightly less humiliated when she realized that Everest yelled too. A lot of people yelled, maybe even Vlas and Dar. The noise was out of this galaxy.

The cyborg officers of law pointed rectangular objects directly at the kids. Elsie heard a strange tone, low and ominous. A blast kicked her off her feet and flung her across the room.

Everything went black.

Elsie's eyes were glued shut. Even with a fuddled brain, she knew that she wasn't at home. It didn't smell like home, something about the old-fashioned herbs and flowers her mother liked to strew throughout the house. Wherever they were now had the strong absence of odor, almost overpowering in its lack. She tried hard to open her eyes, but they wouldn't budge. A wave of nausea pitched and heaved and rolled through her. What had the cyborg officers done to them?

Someone touched her hand then weakly clutched it.

"Elsie?" Lelita whispered. "I don't feel so good, and I can't open my eyes." Her speech was slurred.

From the other side she heard Dar mumble. "S'okay. Don't try to open them. Give it a few minutes."

Thank the Light Dar had responded, because Elsie couldn't make her mouth move. She did her best to squeeze Lelita's hand comfortingly, but her finger muscles didn't seem to work either. She hoped she wouldn't get sick.

Larry spewed out an incomprehensible tirade of words, some the bad ones they weren't supposed to say, others just garbled from whatever had happened to them.

She heard someone retching, maybe Vlas.

Her heart pounded so loudly in her ears she was surprised she could actually hear anything else. Building pressure in her chest made her wish she could press her hand to it, but she still couldn't lift her hand.

She tried to open her eyes again, and this time she managed to pry one open. A cyborg officer of law stood at attention in front of her, legs splayed, fists jammed into her waist, elbows out. Half of her was brilliantly silver and zetta more powerful than the other half. The cybercop stared straight ahead, the human portion of her face equally as serious as the machine half.

Elsie fought hard to open her other eye. The effort hurt. Finally, she managed to squint with both eyes, but that just made the cyborg officer blurry and sort of double. With only one eye open she had reasonably clear vision but the effort brought more pain. She closed her eyes and breathed deeply.

"Officer Lilituck?" she heard Dar say.

Surprise helped her pry her eyes open again.

It *was* Lilituck who stood before them. Elsie's muddled brain tried to work out whether this was significant, but she couldn't seem to think. She was struck by the fact that Officer Lilituck was the only cybercop in the barren room. Elsie tilted her head back and forth to ensure she wasn't imagining things. A wave of dizziness made her head spin, but she did verify that no one else was in the room except her friends and Lilituck.

Why?

The officer had almost imperceptibly come to life when Dar spoke her name. Remaining perfectly still except for her lips, the female cyborg said, "Hello Shadara."

Dar dragged herself up to a sitting position and said, "Call me Dar." Her voice was ragged and gritty.

Elsie let go of Lelita's hand and tried to push herself up as well. Everest was struggling to do the same. Gasping, she lost control of her arms and collapsed back down in a heap. She tried again. Her body just didn't want to work. The room spun.

When the room finally came to a standstill, Elsie saw four barren walls, no windows, and no furniture. When she managed to sit up, she realized she was close to one of the white walls. She scooted back and leaned heavily against it, trying to regulate her shallow breathing.

"What's going on?" Dar asked the officer as she dragged herself to her feet. "Why have you brought us here? Where'd all your cyborg buddies go?"

"I shall debrief you as soon as all of you have fully regained consciousness," Officer Lilituck said calmly.

Only Borneo remained completely knocked out. The rest of the gang slowly struggled to their knees, then to sitting positions. Like Dar, Vlas had managed to stand, but he was bent over and gagging. Larry crawled over to Borneo and shook him by the shoulder.

He glared at the officer. "What did you do to us? Why's he still passed out?"

"We did nothing irreversible. Some bodies take more time to recover. We used a crude, old-fashioned infrasound device. Forty-four cycles per second. Borneo's genetics may make him more susceptible. While it's a relatively archaic weapon, it works well for us because cyborgs are impervious to these sounds, especially at this particular speed. Borneo should regain his faculties shortly. For a short time, you all may experience disorientation, loss of equilibrium, nausea, slurred speech, poor muscle coordination and perhaps some irritability. These symptoms may be worsened by the fact that we had to bring you forward in time as well." The cyborg paused momentarily then continued, "I'm sorry for your discomfort, but it was imperative that we bring you into protective custody immediately."

"Imperative?" Dar asked sharply. "Why?"

"Countless humanoids throughout this galaxy are searching for you. Most of those people are not ones you would like to meet at any time of the day or night. In fact, those who search for you don't much care whether you are dead or alive as long as they find what they seek."

"And that would be?" Dar asked.

Elsie's hand finally worked well enough to reach for her necklace, but then she remembered she didn't have it. Dar did.

Lilituck cocked the eyebrow on the human side of her face. "The prototype femto-boosters."

CHAPTER 35
An Unexpected Alliance

Everest had reason to be grateful that his reflexes were still slow due to the effects of the infrasound device. Otherwise, he wouldn't have been able to stop himself from looking at Dar, and he didn't want to give Lilituck any sign that the girl was the keeper of the femto-boosters.

If even the officers of law were scrambling for his parents' invention, what hope did they have that anyone would save them? It didn't look as if Adriatic Mink would. Their uncle certainly wouldn't. And their parents couldn't.

What a zetta mess.

"So you're offering us protective custody?" Now Dar was the one with an eyebrow cocked—in disbelief. She stood with her arms crossed and her shoulders back, projecting a much older image than her twelve years.

But Everest thought he saw tiny cracks forming as if a spring thaw was breaking away her older façade, leaving behind a young girl, terrified and desperate. He shook his head. He must be imagining things. Dar wasn't afraid of anything. He was the one who wanted to run and hide.

As Lilituck contemplated them, Everest checked out the stark room. Elsie had propped herself up against one of the walls. He wished he was near one himself. It would look pretty pathetic to crawl over to the wall just to lean against it. Instead, he forced himself to follow Dar's example and stand up. The exercise made him feel as if he slogged through waist-deep mud. When he finally was upright, he felt precarious, as if at any second he might collapse again. His head spun and his stomach was woozy. Dar couldn't possibly be as solid as she seemed to be right now.

That infrasound device had really blasted them.

Finally, Lilituck said, "I realize that it may be hard for you to believe, but I am committed to protecting you."

"Because?"

A cyborg smile always seemed a little lopsided because the human side was naturally much wider. Lilituck's was no exception. Somehow the flawed smile made her seem more human.

"Because you are children?" Lilituck suggested.

"Hah!" Dar said. "Try another one."

"How about because some of you are clones and therefore precious commodities?"

"That may be true, but it's not the whole answer."

"She wants something from us," Larry said, his arms crossed and his expression cynical.

Lilituck dipped her head. "That is not the whole truth either."

Everest noted that she didn't dispute Larry's claim. Like everyone else she was after the femto-boosters.

"It might help matters if you understand that femto-boosters are not compatible with a cyborg's physiology. We cannot take advantage of the technology. You need not worry that I will steal the femto-boosters for my own use."

"How do you know that femto-boosters aren't cyborg friendly?" Dar asked.

Yeah, thought Everest, *they had the only prototypes, didn't they*? He exchanged knowing glances with Elsie. This cyborg had to be lying.

Lilituck hesitated. Her machine hand clenched then eased back slightly. "What I'm about to reveal is highly confidential. I shouldn't be telling you, but I can see you won't trust me otherwise." Her uncertainty made her seem more human than machine. "One of my colleagues is currently undercover working for the man known as John C. Brown. Mr. Brown also uses the alias, Mr. Snickers."

Everest exchanged glances with the other kids. They'd been right!

Lilituck continued, "My colleague managed to steal a femto-booster from the lab and try it. However, he received no superpowers. If we could have taken advantage of the femto-boosters, we would have rescued your parents already. But someone who is femto-boosted is at least ten times as strong as a cyborg. We're no match." She sighed and gave her crooked smile again. "That is not an easy thing to admit."

"Okay, let's say that's true," Larry said. "That doesn't stop you from selling boosters on the black market. They gotta be worth some major VC."

"No doubt." Lilituck shrugged her massive shoulders. "But I'm sworn to uphold the law, to pursue justice and righteousness. I'm not easily swayed to selling illegal contraband."

"Ha!" Elsie cried. "If you cybercops are so conditioned to be honest and righteous then how'd your cyborg friend convince the bad guys that he had joined the dark side?"

"Have you ever heard us say publicly that we are only able to work on the side of justice?"

"No," Elsie admitted.

"It's not something we advertise, but it is what we are. If we revealed that we could only uphold the law, we wouldn't be able to work undercover."

"How convenient," Elsie said weakly though Everest was sure she meant her voice to be sharp. "You secretly can only be good guys. Course there's no way for us to prove what you've just said. There's no way for us to be sure that you even have an undercover cyborg with Mr. Brown. We just have to take your word for it. People keep asking us to trust them, but so far, no one has proven trustworthy."

"You are right. I'm asking you to take a pretty big leap of faith, and for all you know you'll be diving straight into a black hole. But everything I've said is true, and I'll also swear that I am committed to saving your parents. I've been following Mr. Brown's movements with avid interest for a long time. Over two months ago, I managed to collect enough evidence of wrong doing to justify tagging him so that we at least knew where he was at all times. Unfortunately, I couldn't obtain the proof required to put him in permanent custody. Once he removed himself to the island and took control of the femto-technology, he made it impossible for us to follow him. Now we know where he is, but we can't reach him."

Elsie closed her eyes and clenched her fists. Everest groaned. She was going to lose it again. He breathed a sigh of relief when she cleared her throat but did not burst into tears. At least she was keeping her aura on.

"What if we accept your story?" Vlas asked. His color was back and he no longer gagged. "What next?"

"We make plans to save Elsie and Everest's parents, we bring Mr. Brown and his cohorts into custody, and we shut down their makeshift femto-booster lab."

"Why would you work with us?" Dar asked.

"Yeah," added Larry, "we're just kids. What do you need us for?"

Everest found himself holding his breath as he waited for the response. He wanted to believe that Lilituck was on their side. But he'd been disappointed over and over again.

"I told you," Lilituck said. "Femto-boosters don't work on us. We need you to boost yourselves and go after Mr. Brown and company."

"Us?" Elsie and Everest spoke as one.

Everest looked at the others in disbelief.

"You're kidding, right?" Elsie added.

There was that cocked eyebrow again. "You want to save your parents, don't you?"

"Well, yeah," Elsie said. "But you have to admit this is hard to swallow. Why us?"

"We've already ruled out cyborg police because of the femto-boosters," Lilituck said. "Since it is imperative that femto-boosters remain a well-guarded secret, we want to avoid bringing anyone new into the picture. You're young, but we may be able to make that work to your advantage."

"I don't buy it," Dar said. "You must have non-cyborgs in the police force. Why use twelve-year-olds when you can use your own staff?"

"We don't have that many non-cyborgs in the police academy," Lilituck answered stiffly.

Dar pursed her lips. "And you want to keep it that way. Femto-boosters threaten your very existence. A cyborg can't take advantage of the technology to become even more super. In a femto-boosted police force cybercops are obsolete."

"You are oversimplifying," Lilituck argued, though the human side of her face had reddened slightly. "Perhaps it is not in cyborg interests for there to be widespread knowledge of femto-technology, but we also think it may be too dangerous for pure humans to use. And it is our sworn duty to protect humankind. My colleague who is acting as spy on Pelican Island has reported unusual behavior by those who are, or have been, femto-boosted. The boosters appear to be highly addictive, and they may have other adverse side-effects. People who have been using them regularly are experiencing heightened emotions and exhibiting erratic behavior."

"So, you're going to let a bunch of kids—mostly clones— use the technology? Aren't you afraid of the side-effects for us?" Dar spoke with a controlled fury. "Are clones now expendable?"

"Actually," Lilituck said, "we'll have some seriously unhappy sponsors if anything happens to you. If we could, we'd only send non-clones on this mission, but Elsie and Everest can't do this on their own. As a team, you are the most rational candidates."

"The most rational?" Dar laughed. "Do, please, entertain us with how you came to that conclusion."

The cyborg paced slowly across the room, flexing her metallic hand as she did so. "You already know about the femto-boosters. Therefore, you pose no additional security threat. One of you has already used a femto-booster so you have some knowledge of how to use the technology."

Everest exchanged a look with Dar. How did Lilituck know about Larry having been femto-boosted?

After a momentary pause, Lilituck continued. "Elsie and Everest care deeply about the outcome of this mission. It's their parents who are kidnapped. They have a vested interest both in finding their parents and in protecting them from harm."

Lilituck pivoted around and paced back the way she had come. "Your group has been surprisingly resourceful, even suited to a dangerous mission. On the downside, you are adolescents and therefore even more susceptible to the addictive qualities of the drug. But we can use that to our advantage. By making you aware of the risk, we believe you will be more cautious in its use."

All of Lilituck's statements were rational, but Everest wondered if she was stating the whole story.

"Tell us the rest," Dar said.

She had an uncanny and irritating way of mirroring Everest's thinking.

"There's something you aren't telling us and it's important," she added. "Tell us, or we won't help you."

"I'm betting Elsie and Everest *will* help me," Lilituck countered.

Dar shrugged. "Perhaps, but as you said, you need every last one of us. Elsie and Everest need us too. Together, we stand a chance."

Lilituck sighed. She paused as if in deep thought. Everest wondered if she was in fact accessing the Galactic Knowledge Bank. She had that jacked-in look.

Finally, she turned somber eyes on them. "I believe you will regret striking such a tough bargain."

"We cannot go into this without all the information," Dar said. "If our roles were reversed, you'd feel the same way."

"Very well. The cyborg police force is divided with regards to Mr. Brown's gang and the kidnapping of the Basker scientists. There are those of us who will do everything possible to ensure that the Baskers survive. Not only are they brilliant scientists, but they are also human beings worthy of our protection. However, others do not feel their survival is a necessary outcome."

Her statement brought Elsie to her feet with a gasp. Everest sucked in his breath.

Lilituck held up her hand. "Make no mistake, we want to rescue the Basker scientists *and* capture Mr. Brown and his cohorts. Our goal is to salvage the femto-booster research but keep it highly confidential." She stretched her neck both ways, and there was an audible pop from the machine side. "However, the other cyborg faction wants to destroy Pelican Island. Wipe out everyone and everything. In one fell swoop, we get rid of a dangerous gang and make it so that no one will be able to duplicate femto-boosters for a long time, because both the prototypes and the creators will be gone. No more abuse of time travel, no more forged documents regarding the Vlemutz Wars Reparation Act, and no more threat to the existence of cyborg officers of law. Just incinerate the place."

"No!" Elsie cried.

Everest swallowed hard. Blow up their parents?

"I'm against this," Lilituck said. "I've got approval to launch a rescue mission on Pelican Island, but here's the tricky part: I have only eight hours to accomplish this mission—more like seven hours now. After that, we go to Plan B: Operation Obliterate."

Deng, thought Everest, *seven hours before their parents were destroyed?*

That changed everything.

CHAPTER 36
Gathering Intelligence

Elsie fought down panic. Her parents were not going to be blown up. They had Officer Lilituck as an ally now. They would find a way to defeat Mr. Brown, Uncle Fredrick and any other vlems who came their way.

She took a deep breath. "What do we do?"

Lilituck pointed toward the wall and displayed a three-dimensional view of Pelican Island. As they already knew, it was little more than a large slab of rock that jutted out of the bay. A rectangular, two-story steelorq building sat on the slab. Stubby trees dotted the landscape. Birds floated overhead and some perched in clusters on the rock. She was pretty sure they were pelicans, but they could have been sea gulls. She thought she could make out rose bushes which for some reason surprised her.

"We know the buildings have two more floors below sea level," Lilituck stated. "It is our guess that your parents are being held below. We've been sending out probes and our readings show forty-two humanoids currently in residence on the rock."

"Forty bad guys," Elsie croaked.

Lilituck cocked her head, squeaking just slightly. "There could be other hostages besides your parents. However, we have not heard any reports so it's unlikely."

"But you have someone on the inside. Shouldn't you know all of this?"

"He hasn't been able to get any word to us for days—hence our reliance on probes."

"So we assume forty bad guys," Dar said. "Seven of us, forty of them... not bad odds if you're on the side that wants to rule the universe, but zetta weak for us."

"Including myself, I can get you ten additional cyborg officers of law."

"Just ten?" Larry asked. "There were more than double that when you took us."

"True, but not all are suitable for this mission."

"Ten might help," Dar said, "but I thought you were no match for the femto-boosted villains."

"We're not, but we can go in first with our infrasound technology and take out everyone who isn't boosted."

"Won't that affect our parents?" asked Everest.

Elsie had been about to ask the same thing and was surprised Everest beat her to it.

"Yes, but not fatally. You recovered quickly enough. It might actually keep them from being slaughtered in cross fire. Being passed-out isn't the worst form of defense."

"If you say so," Elsie said skeptically. "But what happens then? What about those who are femto-boosted?"

"At that point, the cyborgs will need to get out quickly before we're slaughtered. You'll take over the mission."

"How many do you estimate will be taken out by the infrasound?" asked Vlas.

"We're hoping to drop at least twenty. Maybe more. We think the infrasound will work on both humans and Panktars. It just depends on how much femto-booster inventory your parents have managed to generate and how widely dispersed it is. If there are a small number of femto-boosters and they still have a limited lifespan, then they won't have been used as indiscriminately. Mr. Brown would keep them for important missions and as protection against an invasion. Knowing Mr. Brown, he's not going to waste boosters on personnel who he sees as dispensable."

"Okay, so you take out the unboosted," Dar said. "We go after the boosted. Seven of us against upwards of twenty of them. Better odds but not great. Is there a way we can turn this rescue mission around so it's more in our favor?"

"If you have a better plan," Lilituck said stiffly, "then by all means share it with the rest of us."

"Fair enough," Dar responded. She shot the officer a wicked grin. "Give me a few minutes."

"I don't get it," Larry said. "You must have hundreds if not thousands of cyborg officers of law. Why can't you just overwhelm them? Why not just trample them to bits?"

Lilituck smiled slightly. "Good question. The officers I'm offering are the only ones who are in my camp *and* have high enough levels of security to be privileged with the information about the femto-boosters."

"You're kidding!"

"This technology could obsolete cybercops. That's not the type of intelligence we want to share widely amongst the ranks."

Dar stepped closer to the view of Pelican Island. "How do you plan to storm the island? Via hover vehicles? Or a transporter of some sort?"

"Transporter."

"Is it already hidden on the island?"

"No, we have something new—the same technology we used to enter the Basker residence and bring you to this place in the present. It's a hybrid of transporter and time travel technology, and it no longer requires a transporter device at the destination site."

"Zeller," Vlas breathed, his eyes lighting up.

"Okay, that's handy," Dar said. "How many devices do you have?"

"I can get my hands on five—each can transport up to five humanoids simultaneously."

"Including cyborgs?"

"Yes, of course."

"And I assume you can transport objects as well?"

"If they are no larger than the largest humanoid it should be safe."

"Okay," Dar said. "Vlas, how's PicoBoy holding up?"

"As zeller as ever," he responded.

PicoBoy peeked out from Vlas's pocket.

"Good," said Dar. "We'll transport PicoBoy first. He can send back more details on the setup and where the Baskers are being held."

Elsie wished she had thought of that. She was glad Dar had. If they had eyes on the inside that would significantly improve their odds.

PicoBoy chirped as Vlas gave him instructions.

"Interesting device," Lilituck said, her eyes lighting up, especially the cyborg eye which glowed. "You made it?" she asked Vlas.

Vlas shrugged. "Maybe."

Vlas was so weird the way he downplayed his accomplishments. Elsie would have been hard-pressed not to brag about being able to build something as complex as PicoBoy. As far as she knew, the man-made creature was unique. Clearly, Lilituck had never seen one like it.

"We've got to hurry," Elsie said. "We only have seven hours."

"I'm aware of the time." Vlas looked around. "I need something PicoBoy can transmit visual to."

"He can send it to me," Lilituck said.

"How do we get instructions back to him?" Vlas asked.

"I can transmit instructions. I'll need to download a program so that our communication is secure. You've set him up for downloads?"

"Yeah, no problem," Vlas said. He turned to PicoBoy and commanded, "Connect to Officer Lilituck."

With another chirp, the small creature launched over to the cyborg and seemed to sniff at her, mostly on the machine side. After a few seconds, it zoomed back to Vlas, now chirping excitedly.

Vlas looked to Lilituck who nodded.

"Nice device. We'll be able to communicate."

"Zeller," said Vlas. "So where in the building should we transport him?"

"I'd go for the floor right below sea level," Lilituck responded. "From the probes we've done it appears to be the least occupied."

Dar pursed her lips. "Okay, let's get moving. The sooner PicoBoy sends us back some good intelligence, the sooner we can get this mission kicked up to light speed." She looked around the sterile room. "Where's the transporter device?"

Lilituck pulled out a slim wafer from her uniform inner pocket and held it up to show the B12s. "Since I'm now connected to PicoBoy, I'll be able to send him there and pull him back without the device physically on him."

Vlas grinned. "Zetta zeller."

"If something happens to me during this mission, then you'll need to find him and physically bring him back with one of the transport devices. Understood?"

Vlas nodded seriously.

Elsie tried to block visions of all the things that could go wrong.

Vlas cleared his throat. "What about a jellach journal? Is there something I can use to log PicoBoy's journey?"

"I will log everything internally," Lilituck stated. "However, I have no objection to you keeping a log as well." From within her uniform jacket, she pulled out a slim jellach journal folded in quarters. "You may use this."

"Thanks," Vlas said as he settled PicoBoy on the wafer. "Okay, PicoBoy, you know what to do."

PicoBoy chirped as if to say "Yes."

"Remember," Vlas said, "no chirping on Pelican Island. Silence is the name of the game." It seemed as if the picobot had to physically hold itself back from chirping.

Elsie smiled despite her mounting tension.

Lilituck made some adjustments to her arm, treating it like a holoputer.

"Transport engage," she commanded.

In a blink, PicoBoy disappeared.

Lilituck scanned the room. Elsie couldn't help feeling a little shaken when their eyes met.

"We shouldn't have long to wait," the cyborg said.

Almost immediately, Lilituck's metal arm jerked and she raised it to point toward the wall. A new visual displayed; only this time, it moved like an old-fashioned, two-dimensional movie. The visual was in black and white. It was an insect's eye view of an empty room—a room with low ceilings, no windows and an erased door.

"Picked a good location for PicoBoy to land," said Dar.

"Yeah," Lilituck said, "sometimes luck happens."

After a quick view of a corridor, PicoBoy dived into the next room which was also humanoid-free. It had multiple rows of beds, mostly bunk beds. They were all jellach but older, simpler models than even the ones at the academy. There were hooks on the walls with a simple uniform hanging from most of them. The uniforms were lightweight jellach bodysuits, not that different from the kind the clone academy used for fights. Helmets were lined up on the floor against the wall.

PicoBoy flew back into the corridor and jolted to a stop when he saw a hulking man guarding the next door. The man stood at rigid attention. The door was solid and appeared to be locked. The visual went blank for a second, and then a new room appeared.

Elsie whipped around. "Deng, how'd he do that?"

"Yes, Vlas," said Lilituck, "how did PicoBoy manage that?"

Vlas grinned. "I fixed him up with a zetta tiny matter-mover."

"Sweet," Larry said.

"Impressive." Lilituck's expression was thoughtful as she stared at Vlas.

"Shh," Dar said. "Watch."

Elsie focused back on the visual and gasped. This was an armory, filled from floor to ceiling with weapons—flasers of all shapes and sizes as well as stun guns and some devices that Elsie didn't recognize. She thought they might be explosives of some sort. Just looking at the shelves of weaponry sent terror coursing through her bloodstream.

"That could come in handy," Dar said.

Elsie couldn't believe how calm she was.

"How do we get the coordinates for that room?" Dar asked.

"PicoBoy has communicated them to me," Lilituck stated. "In fact, your picobot already has sent us much richer detail than that which we obtained from our probes."

Lelita reached out and clutched Elsie's hand. Three humans who had to be soldiers for hire stood strategically around the chamber. They each held sleek flasers.

Vlas leaned over to Dar. "Not good."

She shrugged. "Not bad, either. We knew there would be weapons and guards and bad guys. These guards are set up for traditional combat, probably without any boosting. That means the cybercops should be able to take them out with infrasound. They won't be our problem." Dar turned to Lilituck. "Can you get us information on these weapons? We're not arms experts. It's not something they teach B12s at the academy."

Lilituck remained impassive. "I've already catalogued the weaponry PicoBoy has shown us."

"Zeller." Dar returned her gaze to the silent movie.

The next three rooms were empty, but the corridors had sentries stationed every twenty feet or so.

PicoBoy hit a staircase.

"Go down," Dar whispered.

As if the little creature heard her, he zoomed down the stairs, passing a cluster of pico-brownies on the right.

Vlas whispered to the room in general. "I told him to locate the Baskers first and then do a more thorough survey of the rest of the facility."

"Thanks," Elsie murmured.

As Lilituck had predicted the lowest floor was much more active than the one above it. There were people milling around in the corridors. PicoBoy took still shots of each human he passed.

"I'm checking these against the GKB," Lilituck said. "I shouldn't have any problem identifying the humans."

When PicoBoy reached the first door on this level, Lelita let out a small cry. A Panktar was stationed there. Elsie squeezed Lelita's hand in comfort.

Borneo chewed on his lower lip as he tightened and then released a fist over and over again. Because of his makeup his expression wasn't a tell-tale pink, but Elsie felt his tension even across the room.

"Can Panktars be boosted?" Elsie asked hesitantly.

Lelita's eyes grew wide and terror distorted her sweet features.

"I can only speculate," said Lilituck, "but I would hazard to guess that yes, they can be boosted. They are not a hybrid of humanoid and machine."

Lelita let out a choked sob. "We can't fight them. They're too strong even without a boost. With it, they'll be invincible."

"Maybe," Dar said, "and maybe not. We don't know how the femto-booster interacts with other types of humanoids. As far as we can tell, the Baskers only tested the femto-boosters on themselves. The current formula might not be strong enough for a Panktar's biology."

PicoBoy had worked his way down most of the corridor, entering rooms and sending visuals, especially of each person or alien he found. Almost every room on this floor was guarded by a Panktar but only three of the rooms had someone inside. Many of the smaller rooms seemed to be utilitarian sleeping chambers.

When he entered the last room, there was a collective gasp.

This chamber was a hub of activity: humans, Panktars, one cyborg—presumably the one working undercover—a large contingent of robots in one corner, and two scientists in the middle of the room who both wore white smocks. One of the scientists was male, the other was female, and both bore a striking resemblance to the Basker twins.

"Mom, Dad," Elsie reached out, inadvertently sticking her hand into the visual display, causing it to waver crazily.

Everest grabbed her by the shoulder and pulled her back. "They're there," he whispered as if he couldn't quite believe it.

"Your parents." Dar's voice was funny, almost tinny, in Elsie's ear.

"Yes," Elsie barely replied. She tasted something metallic in the back of her throat.

Her mom was bent over a quarkscope with her dad hovering nearby. They were having an animated discussion as her dad made entries into his jellach journal. Three Panktars stood nearby, flasers and stunners at the ready.

The man who called himself Dr. Jensa was in the room as well. Judging by the deference others were showing him, he was probably in charge. James Powers and Uncle Fredrick were nowhere in sight, but Elsie had a feeling they could show up at any moment.

Her mom lifted her head from the quarkscope and wearily wiped moisture off her forehead. She exchanged a glance with their dad that spoke volumes.

Elsie noticed that both of her parents wore strange metal chokers around their necks. Maybe they were full of femto-boosters like the pendants had been.

Wanting to burst into tears, she repeated in her head the family mantra: *The Baskers can handle anything, the Baskers can handle anything.*

Her dad raised his head and stared straight at PicoBoy. If Elsie hadn't known better she would have sworn he knew the creature was there. George Basker's eyes were bleak.

"Dad," Everest called.

Elsie felt her brother's extreme embarrassment when he realized he had called out to their dad even though they were not physically together in the same room. She wished she had the energy to tease him, but she wasn't up to it.

"Vlas, can we get sound?" she asked instead.

The boy shook his head. "Sorry, I've never been able to lay my hands on the necessary technology to pick up long distance sound waves."

Elsie rubbed her face with both hands and straightened her shoulders. She turned to Officer Lilituck. "What's with the metal collars? Do you think they're where the femto-boosters are stored?"

Lilituck's expression was grave. "They are custody collars. They're illegal on Earth, but a number of planets use them regularly on prisoners. The collars control them, making it impossible for them to escape."

"Can someone transport with one on?"

"No, the collar must be removed."

"How do you remove one?" asked Dar.

"Typically via a key."

"Standard issue key?"

"No," Lilituck said, "as far as I know each key is unique. Can't be duplicated."

"We have a universal unlocker," Vlas said.

"The technology has safeguards against the use of a universal unlocker. That's not advisable."

"Well then, we can use our object cloner," responded Dar. "We'll duplicate the key."

"It'll have to be an amazing object cloner."

Dar stared at Lilituck. "It is. But why do you say that? Is there something else we should know about the custody collar?"

"The collar will be alarmed. Possibly a silent alarm, but it's going to go off if anyone tries to mess with the collar."

"Great," Everest said.

The cybercop paused and her expression became bizarrely uncertain.

"What?" Elsie asked. There was something Lilituck wasn't saying.

The officer took a deep breath and rubbed her bald head with her human hand. "These collars are rigged with rudimentary flaser technology. If one is forcibly removed, the prisoner disintegrates. That's why Earth and Glagcha have both outlawed their use."

"Jeez," Everest gasped.

Elsie felt as if her head were floating on the ceiling while the room spun around her.

"Do not faint on us," Dar commanded, grabbing Elsie and shaking her. "No one's going to disintegrate. We just have to figure out how to remove the collars so that it looks as if they were removed legally. Maybe PicoBoy can scramble their frequencies—at least temporarily. Then we use the object cloner to actually unlock the choker. After that, all we have to do is take out the Panktars and those other military types. It's a day in the park. For fun, we'll stuff Dr. Jensa into a locker somewhere."

Vlas snorted and winked. "Ooh, let me."

"We'll have to draw straws for that one," Dar said, grinning back.

Elsie had the urge to wipe Dar's smile off her face. Her parents were rigged with explosive devices, and Dar and Vlas still acted as if they were having the time of their lives.

PicoBoy took a couple more laps around the laboratory to give them a comprehensive view of the place, but Elsie couldn't concentrate on anything besides her parents and those denged collars—those evil instruments of death. An anger welled up in her that went beyond anything she'd ever felt. She wanted to damage Dr. Jensa, James Powers, Mr. Brown and most especially her uncle. How could he do this to his own sister? He was a monster! An evil vlem! When she was femto-boosted, he would feel her wrath.

Everest grabbed her shoulder as if he could read her mind. "Elsie, we need to stay calm. I know how you feel; I do," he added when she tried to shake him off. "But it's not going to help. We need to think rationally. And I can tell you aren't. Believe me, I want to destroy them all too. But first, we save Mom and Dad."

She swiped at the tears streaming down her face. "Those horrible vlems deserve to die, and if I have any chance, any opportunity, I'm taking them out."

"You think that will make Mom and Dad happy? We're talking about our parents—the most peaceful people on the planet. They are not going to be happy if we turn into killing machines. Remember who we are. We're Baskers. Not vlems who will stop at nothing. We're the good guys. That's who Mom and Dad want us to be."

Elsie shook him off. "That's who we've always been. But look where that's gotten us. Maybe it's time to redefine what it means to be a Basker."

CHAPTER 37
A Daring Plan

Everest agreed with Elsie that those vlems deserved whatever punishment came to them, but their parents had never condoned violence. Did they feel differently now that they'd been kidnapped?

"We don't have time for a philosophical debate," Dar said crisply. "Let's stay focused on the best way to free your parents *and* stop the villains from stealing the femto-booster technology."

Everest could practically hear Elsie yelling in his brain, but she showed unexpected self-control and bit back the stream of words that had to be on the tip of her tongue.

With a shaky breath, he turned back to PicoBoy's display. He hoped he hadn't missed anything important. PicoBoy was still circling the laboratory. When the little creature paused near the robots in the far corner, Everest saw that the area was set up for clean manufacturing. The robots stared through a clear plate that floated above their work table and allowed them to zoom in on the miniscule work they did with their appendages.

"They're making the femto-boosters," Elsie said.

"No duh, ute-girl," Dar replied.

Elsie shot Dar a nasty look.

"They're making a lot of femto-boosters," Vlas said. "Zeller setup."

"Nice of your parents to help the enemy," Dar said.

Everest yanked Elsie back before she could do something really yocto-brained.

"Our parents are being forced to do this," he said. "You insinuate anything else and you'll need a femto-booster to survive our wrath."

"I'm so shaking in my skyboots," Dar said caustically.

"That'll be enough," Lilituck said. "Dar, you're out of line. All of you need to calm down. I realize you are children, but you cannot afford to act like ones right now."

Everest's cheeks burned. Lilituck was right. He had to keep his aura on.

"What's that?" he asked, pointing to a steelorq box to the left of the manufacturing area.

Dar pursed her lips. "Looks like storage. Maybe it's the holding area for the femto-boosters." She pointed to the device on which the steelorq box rested. "That looks like some sort of heater. There's a reason why they stored your femto-boosters in 1010511 lockets. The compound is naturally warm. Femto-boosters must need a certain level of heat to retain their effectiveness."

The rest of the level was anticlimactic after they saw their parents. PicoBoy moved on to the ground floor, two levels up, and found another contingent of Panktars. This floor was much more luxurious than the others. Each room was decked out in rich fabrics and colors and most amazing of all, real wood furniture. Here, each room was guarded by at least two Panktars. The final room was guarded by three.

"Mr. Brown must have a vast store of VC," Dar murmured.

"Smuggling has its rewards," Lilituck said dryly, "especially time-travel smuggling."

A slow burn started in the middle of Everest's stomach. His parents were the end to a means for Mr. Brown. The vlem could care less that they were humans with feelings and dreams. They were just tools.

The last chamber on sea level was the most luxurious. It appeared to be a sitting room with groupings of couches and chairs in an elegant nanofiber.

Dar leaned nearer as PicoBoy picked up a cluster of humans. "Closer, closer," she murmured.

Again as if he had heard her, PicoBoy zoomed in.

Dar sucked in her breath. "There, on the right," she pointed, "That's him—that's Mr. Brown."

The vlem sat on an ancient throne made of aged wood with gold filigree, very ornate and ostentatious.

"The man likes his thrones," Lilituck said. "Yes, that's Mr. Brown. I've met him before."

Everest stared hard, burning the vlem's image on his brain so that he would immediately recognize him on Pelican Island. If only the image were in color. Still he memorized the man's plumper than average figure. The extra kilos gave his face a baby-like quality with its softer, fuller cheeks, but it also gave him the appearance of having smaller than average eyes—squinty even. Or maybe that was just Everest's hatred coming through. If he tried to be objective, he could see why Dar had labeled him handsome. Mr. Brown had good features, but the overall effect creeped out Everest. He took a deep breath and continued his study. Brown's hair barely touched his shoulders. It waved a bit and was zetta thick. Everest agreed with Dar that it probably was enhanced. Brown's left ear was pierced twice and his right once.

"Ick, he just seems so ick," Elsie said then turned to Dar. "I don't know how you can say he's handsome."

"Well, I'm inclined to say 'ick' too, but I'm trying to be impartial," Dar responded. "He has decent features."

"He's so fake," Elsie said.

Everest had to agree. There was something about him that didn't seem real. He had a feeling the vlem was a lot older than he looked.

After a few more shots of the room and the people in it—the total count was five in the room and eleven on guard in the long corridor—PicoBoy zoomed up the final staircase to the top floor. It was empty—empty of furniture, empty of people, empty of Panktars—and eerily quiet.

"What's our countdown?" Dar asked. "How much time do we have?"

Lilituck consulted a display on her arm and said, "Six hours, forty-two minutes, thirty-seven seconds."

"What kind of weapons can you give us?" Dar asked.

"Flasers, stunners—what else would you like?"

"Do you have any zunners?" Dar asked.

"Just the ones you had when we took you. We're moving to zunners eventually, but no one in the force has received one yet. We were surprised to find you had two in your possession. Even one is a rare and expensive item."

"What about the ones in the hover vehicle?"

"No, I'm sorry. We didn't confiscate an HV."

"Dar," Lelita said in a very small, quavery voice, "I don't think I can use a flaser."

"If you want to stay back, we'll understand," Elsie said.

"No," Lelita shook her head emphatically. "No, you need all of us. I just don't know if I can flaser someone."

"You can have one of the zunners," Dar said.

"Thanks," Lelita said with relief.

Dar looked around. "Anyone who thinks they won't be able to use a flaser, speak now. We'll be going after people who have been femto-boosted which means we can't guarantee that flasers, zunners or stunners will actually work, but if the femto-booster wears off while we're there then we should be prepared."

After a small hesitation, Borneo raised his arm. "I'd rather use a zunner or a stunner."

Everest tried to imagine using a lethal weapon. Just a month ago, it had been unthinkable to even stun someone. When he'd stunned Larry he'd felt like the lowest life form. But these were true villains—evil vlems—though one of them was his uncle. Could he really flaser a relative? He flicked a finger in the air to gain Dar's attention. "Uh, I think I need both. I can imagine flasering Mr. Brown and James Powers or any of the Panktars in self-defense. I'm not sure I can flaser a stranger or even my denged uncle."

Dar nodded. "This isn't going to be easy for any of us. We've only got two zunners so we'll give those to Lelita and Borneo. Everyone else will get a flaser and a stunner—a couple of each if possible. These weapons will probably only work if the femto-boosters wear off, so mostly we'll rely on our hand-to-hand fighting abilities."

"How are we going to ensure that our parents don't get blown up before we save them?" Elsie asked.

Dar shrugged. "I don't think Mr. Brown wants to disintegrate your parents. If he loses the Baskers, then he loses his femto-booster source. We can use that to our advantage." She turned to Lilituck. "Will the infrasound trigger the choker?"

"I don't know."

"You don't know?" Elsie asked, her voice rising.

"I told you, these devices are illegal here. We have no experience with them. Master-mind criminals are a rarity on Earth, to say the least. Ever since we saw the devices around your parents' necks, I've been doing a search to determine if there are ways to disengage them."

"This is just great," she said through gritted teeth.

Everest sighed. "We only have six and a half hours, and then they're blown up anyway. The likelihood of them surviving all this is as bad as it gets. We're just going to have to take some chances."

"Take some chances?" Now she really was shouting.

"Jeez, Elsie, keep your aura on," Dar said curtly. "I can't think when you're screaming." She paced across the room. "We could hold off on the infrasound till the very last minute. If we're femto-boosted we might be able to take control of the room and remove the chokers before the cybercops do their damage."

Lilituck nodded. "Right now, besides your parents, there are eight people in the laboratory. There are also eight humanoids in the hallway on the same floor. We'll have to work quickly. Once the vlems realize Pelican Island has been breached, they will all race to the laboratory. Though we can't be femto-boosted, the cyborg officers of law can keep the villains occupied while you get to your parents. But it's risky. Someone in the room may have the authority to flaser your parents. We have no idea how valuable they still are to Mr. Brown. If he's already discovered the secret to their femto-boosters, they'll be expendable. Hopefully, your parents have managed to keep their formula safe despite their circumstances. It's their only bargaining chip."

"Gosh," Everest said, "I feel so much better."

There was no easy answer. There were so many paths that would bring his parents to destruction. But if they didn't use the infrasound technology, they would be dealing with a lot more bad guys—many of whom were Panktars—a serious threat whether boosted or not. All of the members of Mr. Brown's gang were bound to be packing plenty of flaser power too. The cybercops would be walking into a deathtrap on so many levels.

"I think we should chance the infrasound technology," he said. "The more Panktars we can put to sleep the better. And I think all of us should go in at the same time. The cybercops throw the infrasound at the non-boosted types—which will include our parents—but those of us who are boosted go in just as fast to disengage the chokers and bring down the boosted bad guys. The second we neutralize the chokers, we transport our parents out. After that, why not just go to Plan B? Just escape and incinerate the place?"

Lilituck cocked her head. "City officials would prefer to keep Pelican Island intact if at all possible."

"You guys are planning to destroy it."

"Yes, but we don't want to; If you can take out Mr. Brown, we'll salvage the island."

"You're asking an awful lot," Dar said. "The plan Everest just outlined is already a long shot. If we do manage to save his parents, the simplest thing would be to destroy the island."

"There's a 22.4 percent probability that there will be collateral damage," said Lilituck. "While our intention is to incinerate the place without causing a large explosion, our detonation could cause some of those explosives in the weapons room to go off. That could destroy nearby ships or hover vehicles, maybe even some of the coastline. There's pretty volatile stuff stored there."

"Jeez, well thanks for telling us that now," Dar said irritably. "Are we really under a six-hour deadline? Or are the cybercops going to chicken out because they don't want to deal with the consequences?"

"I'm not sure," Lilituck said. "Orders are to blow up the place in a little over six hours, but I think they are hoping for a better plan that will make it possible for them to rescind the order."

"What about a diversion?" Larry asked.

"Do you have something in mind?" Dar responded.

"A fire usually works. One of us could transport down and start a fire in one of the empty rooms on the same floor as the Baskers. Maybe add a tiny explosion. That person transports back pronto, but PicoBoy feeds us what happens next. If enough people come to see the action, that will make it easier to take out the ones left in the laboratory."

"Not bad," Vlas said.

"But someone who is femto-boosted can immediately stop the fire, right?" Everest asked.

Larry looked crestfallen. "Yeah, they'll be pretty quick to put it out. What if we spring a lot of diversions on them all at once?"

"A bunch of fires?" Elsie asked.

"Yeah, I guess," Larry said.

"Deng," Dar said, "Can't you ask your cybercop friends to give us just one night? A nighttime operation would give us a much better chance of success."

"I've already asked for an extension to the deadline," Lilituck said huffily. "I was told 'no.'"

"Did you already explain the logic behind a nighttime mission?" Dar asked.

"No," Lilituck admitted.

"Then take us to your leader," Dar said. "I can be pretty persuasive."

Lilituck and Dar stared at each other. Everest had the distinct impression that they were in a silent battle of wills.

Finally, the cybercop dipped her head. "It is sensible for the operation to happen at night. I'll make the request."

"No," Dar said firmly. "We'll make the request together."

"My associates won't negotiate with a child."

"Make them," Dar said. "You need us."

"I can't take all seven of you," Lilituck protested.

"Fine," she said, "take a smaller party—me, Everest and Elsie."

"Hey," Vlas said. "I should be there. PicoBoy is my invention. He's the one getting us all the deets."

Dar glanced at him then nodded. "Yes, Vlas too." She looked at Larry, Lelita and Borneo. "Are you okay with waiting here?"

Both Lelita and Borneo nodded their heads avidly and murmured, "Yes."

But Larry's eyes were belligerent. "You need me."

"Larry, be reasonable," Dar said in a low voice.

"I'm the only one *being* reasonable. I've dealt with lowlifes from the time I was born. Can you say the same? You need me. I got a built-in meter that knows when someone is trying to pull one over on me. I got skills."

Dar sighed then turned back to Lilituck. "Five of us. Take us now. We don't have much time."

Surprisingly, Lilituck rolled her eyes irritably. Her machine and human eyes were perfectly in synch, but it still looked strange. Then she froze, and her gaze drifted away from them. She remained immobile for so long that Everest wondered if she were in some sort of hibernation.

Finally, Lilituck's eyes regained their piercing nature. "You have till 4:00 tomorrow morning."

She had communicated with the rest of the cyborg officers of law from here? Everest hadn't realized they were so tightly linked.

"I thought you had to communicate verbally," Elsie said, mirroring Everest's thoughts.

"We've set up a secure link between us," Lilituck said.

Larry looked around the room suspiciously. "That was too easy, too quick." He glared at the cybercop. "They're spying on us, aren't they?" He stomped up to one of the walls and slapped his hand against it. "Where are they?"

"I don't know what you mean," Lilituck said stiffly.

"Come on," Larry said. "A bunch of cybercops are watching us like we're rats in a creepy lab experiment."

"We need their support," Lilituck said.

"Tell them to get their rear-ends in here or go dive into a black hole."

The cybercops had been watching them the whole time? Listening to their every word? Everest wasn't exactly sure why he felt betrayed, but he did.

"Look, both factions of cybercops are watching from separate observation points," Lilituck said. "I'd prefer to keep them separated from each other."

"Well, ain't they special?" Larry's eyes flashed.

"Keep your aura on," Dar said warningly, "We got what we wanted—a night op." She turned to Lilituck. "Thank you for obtaining their agreement." She turned to the wall and spoke to the hidden cyborgs. "Thank you to all of you who voted to support our plan. Now we need food, a more comfortable room— preferably one with chairs—and access to some holoputers."

"I'll see to that." Lilituck crossed over to the door and erased it with a touch of her hand. "I'll be back shortly."

With that, she stepped over the threshold and disappeared from sight as the door shifted back to solid.

CHAPTER 38
To the Rescue

Lilituck got word to PicoBoy to continue monitoring Pelican Island throughout the rest of the day and evening. The little man-made creature did a thorough search of the rocky outside, but besides a surprisingly small number of guards, only birds inhabited the rock itself.

They went over and over their plan, refining it each time. Twice Lilituck left the room and returned with fresh fruit, protein bars and other nutritious snacks. Everest forced himself to eat despite his lack of appetite.

Though Lilituck had insisted that they all be checked for infrasound side-effects, Everest knew it was just worry that caused him not to be hungry.

Later in the evening, Lilituck issued weapons along with belts to hold them—two flasers and two stunners each to Dar, Vlas, Elsie and Everest, one zunner and two stunners each to Lelita and Borneo. Lilituck gave lessons on flaser use and safety. She also handed out a variety of stinkers, foggers and other useful devices.

At one point they watched anxiously as Mr. Brown visited the Baskers in their laboratory. He acted quite jovial, rubbing his hands together, looking over their shoulders at their formulas, and slapping them on their backs with a show of camaraderie.

Everest flinched when his mom involuntarily jumped at the vlem's touch. He thought Elsie might turn on the waterworks again at the sight of their mom's expression of fear and loathing.

He wished he could hear what they said. Whatever it was, it wasn't good. Their dad looked as terrified as their mom, and both wore fury underneath their fear.

Around 19:00 the laboratory closed for the night. Two Panktars escorted the Baskers to a small bed chamber on the same level. Another Panktar arrived with two plates of food. Once the Baskers were inside, they were sealed in, and the two original Panktars stationed themselves outside as guards. After a slight blip in PicoBoy's transmission, it picked up again inside the chamber.

The Baskers sat on face-to-face utilitarian jellach beds eating as if their lives depended on it. They both had lost a lot of weight. Everest hated to see them like this—gaunt, helpless, anxious.

His dad finished eating first. No surprise since he was known for consuming his meals in a handful of gulps. But his mom finished shortly after. They both must have been starving.

They set their plates down near the door then sat together on one of the jellach beds. His mom reached for his dad's hand and held on as if it were a lifeline. They spoke, but he had no idea what they said.

He turned to Dar. "How soon should we go?"

"It would be best if they fell asleep. We don't want any screaming when you transport into the room. If they don't seem capable of sleep then we'll rethink our strategy."

"It feels like forever, waiting like this," Elsie said, "and there's so little time."

"Yeah, I know," Dar said, "but this is our best option."

Like robots, the kids ate the dinner that Lilituck provided for them, all the while avidly watching the PicoBoy show.

Since it no longer mattered that they hide themselves, they had all removed their disguises. Everest had been especially relieved to get rid of his blond wig.

After nearly an hour with the Baskers, PicoBoy made another round of the lowest floor and then zoomed up to ground level to see what Mr. Brown was up to. The man was eating chocolate, savoring every bite. He was the only one eating. He sat in his throne chair, enjoying the fact that he could do whatever he wanted while everyone else waited for him. James Powers lounged in a chair to the left of Mr. Brown, a scowl on his face. Everest's chest tightened with anger. It felt as if he were being eaten up from the inside by a wild all-consuming fire.

"Look." On her feet, Dar faced the visual with her legs slightly spread, her arms folded. "They're all there—Lester-Hauffer, Mr. Brown, Mr. Powers and Dr. Jensa. We'd have good odds even if we had to move now. But when they're all in bed, sleeping the sleep of the wicked, our odds will go up that much more."

She turned to Elsie and Everest. "This is going to work; we're going to save your parents."

Everest let out a shaky breath. That was all that mattered.

PicoBoy returned to their parents' chamber, and soon after the two fell asleep. They were barely visible as the shadows darkened and deepened, but Everest could see that they slept like the dead, clearly exhausted, neither moving even a fraction of a centimeter.

In the dark of the night, there was the tell-tale glitter of a flock of pico-brownies as they did their nightly cleanup.

"What are the odds they're rigged with security?" Vlas asked.

Dar pursed her lips as she watched. "Let's assume they are. What can we do to disable them before they rat on us?"

"If PicoBoy can figure out what frequency they're working at, he can send out a signal that shuts them down."

"Will they detect him mid-attempt?"

"Pico-brownies aren't zetta intelligent. They're pretty simple in their logic. If he works quickly, he should be able to catch the frequency and disengage them before they realize the threat."

"If that's the case, why would anyone pay for them to be part of their security package?" Elsie asked.

Vlas grinned. "What's simple for PicoBoy is not necessarily simple for anyone else. Let's just say his logic is a bit more sophisticated."

"We could use some devices like him in our force," Lilituck said.

"He's one of a kind," Vlas replied.

"For now," Lilituck acknowledged with a half smile. "Have you figured out if he can mess with the choker frequency as well?"

"No, can you relay both requests to him?"

"Yes, of course," Lilituck said crisply.

With her arms folded, Dar ignored the interplay between Lilituck and Vlas. Finally, she turned to the cybercop. "Ask PicoBoy to check the corridor."

In a few seconds PicoBoy was in the hallway. Though deep in shadows, numerous dots of light provided just enough illumination to clearly delineate two Panktars flanking the door of the Baskers' jail. Another Panktar slowly paced up and down the hallway. Sparkling masses of pico-brownies were out in force.

"Okay," Dar said. "It's femto-booster time."

She swiveled around to face the B12s who had created a loose semi-circle. "We have fourteen. That means each of us has two femto-boosters at our disposal. Hopefully, we'll only need one each to get the job done. We know that Larry's powers were waning after three hours and fifty-two minutes. It's midnight now. We don't want to be down there at four AM because that's incineration time, so let's get this mission accomplished well within three hours just to be safe." She paused, her eyes serious, her mouth a thin line. "The back-up femto-booster is just in case the effects wear off more quickly the more you use your superpowers. If you are caught, destroy the second femto-booster. The easiest way would be to ingest it. Whatever you do, don't let the vlems take it away from you."

"Yeah, yeah," Larry said. "We've run through this like a gazillion times."

"And we're running through it again," Dar said. "Only a suzo-shrimp goes into something this dangerous without reviewing the plan 'like a gazillion times.'" She mimicked Larry's voice.

Under other circumstances she might have managed to pull a chuckle out of Everest, but he'd never felt less like laughing. Vlas laughed though. Everything was a Pallaccii party to him.

"We have two missions," Dar continued, "one to save the Baskers, the other to take the vlems into custody. We can't afford for the bad guys to take the extra femto-boosters and run. If they do there's no end to the destruction they could wreak while conventional forces try to capture them. First, the Baskers. Vlas,

Everest, Elsie and I will go in, disable the chokers, and get the Baskers back here. We'll need to bring two transport devices to ensure we all get back safely. After that, the cyborgs will blast the place with infrasound, and we'll all go back in for cleanup."

Larry snorted. "I still don't get why I'm not going down with the first team. That's just plain prejudiced against twenty-first-century folk."

Everest glanced quickly at Lilituck. Jeez! What was Larry thinking telling the world he was from the past? It didn't look as if Lilituck had registered what he had said, though. She seemed to be busy watching and possibly communicating with PicoBoy.

"Shut down, Larry," Dar said through gritted teeth. "We're trying to minimize how long you need to be boosted because you're already showing signs of addiction."

"Once I take one, I'll have to deal with it anyway," Larry grumbled, but his face was red, giving Everest hope that he'd clued in to his mistake in referencing the twenty-first century.

"Maybe we'll get lucky and no one will actually have been boosted down there," Elsie said. "Then the infrasound will work on all of them, and you won't have to be boosted at all."

"Yeah, right," Larry responded with a grimace. "With all the femto-boosters those robots are manufacturing? They're using."

Dar shrugged. "Maybe, maybe not."

Larry snorted again.

"Jeez," Dar said. "The Baskers' bed chamber is zetta tiny. Four B12s are enough. If something goes wrong, it's important that someone with femto-booster experience be waiting in the wings to save the day." She looked around the room. "Any questions?"

"No," Elsie said.

The others shook their heads silently.

Everest took slow steady breaths, reminding himself that it would be his and Elsie's job to wake their parents without allowing them to make a sound. If anyone was boosted on that island, they'd hear even the smallest peep. He didn't want to imagine what would happen if boosted Panktars heard them. The palms of his hands were damp with perspiration. They needed time to remove those chokers.

"Ready?" Dar asked.

Everyone nodded.

"Okay," She said then stuck out her hand face down.

Each B12 in their turn placed their hand on top forming a tower. When they all had layered their hands, they counted, "One, two, three," then popped their hands off into the air.

The move reminded Everest of the many times they had done the same with their parents.

Everest moved over to Dar. They would be using one of the smaller transporters provided by Lilituck. The device was set to transport them directly to the little cell where their parents slept.

Vlas swaggered over, gleefully rubbing his hands together. "Can't wait to try one of those femto-boosters."

"Everest," Dar said. "When you go to muffle your dad's cries, remember that you will have at least ten times your strength. Try not to suffocate him or break his neck."

"Zetta thanks for that cheerful thought," Everest said. If that happened, he'd probably walk out and find the nearest Panktar to stomp all over him.

"Officer Lilituck, is PicoBoy ready to disable the pico-brownies?"

The cybercop stilled while she checked. "Yes, he is ready at my command."

"Then do it," Dar said. "The moment he tells you the pico-brownies are as dead as a black dwarf, we transport." To Elsie, Everest and Vlas, she said, "Time to swallow our femto-boosters."

Everest stared at the small, pink object—mere dust—in the palm of his hand. So tiny, yet so powerful. His breathing shallow and his heartbeat accelerated, he lifted his hand to his mouth and licked his palm so that the femto-booster was on his tongue. He saw Elsie do likewise. He couldn't taste the pill or feel it dissolve, but he knew he had ingested it. He would have sworn that he could see it racing through his veins, changing his chemistry, his biology, charging him with strange currents and inconceivable powers.

He met Elsie's wild eyes. She flexed her fingers then stared at them with wonder as if she'd peeled away the skin to the bone and cartilage below.

He felt intense heat, and yet at the same time, ice coursed through his veins. Everyone looked small to him, even Lilituck; he felt like a giant, and yet his size was the same as it had been a few seconds ago.

Dar spoke to Officer Lilituck, "What is PicoBoy's status?" Her words came in slow motion, and they were loud.

"PicoBoy has successfully disabled the brownies in the Baskers' chamber, and he has managed to scramble the two chokers as well—at least for the moment. You may proceed."

"Excellent," Dar said, rubbing her hands together.

Whoa, thought Everest.

Her voice resonated as if she were trying to make something heard two blocks away.

"Uh, Dar," he said, determined to whisper, but finding that it came out as a shout, "you need to lower your voice or they'll hear you everywhere on Pelican Island."

"You're a fine one to talk," she responded irritably. "You're shouting."

"I'm trying to whisper," he said. "What do we do?"

"As it happens," Lilituck interrupted, "you both are whispering, but you must remember that your hearing is amplified significantly. Everyone will sound louder to you, especially at close quarters. Just do your best to always think in a whisper. That should translate to a whisper on the outside too, regardless of how it sounds to you."

"Talk about alien," Vlas said, a maniacal grin on his face. "This is supernova, but I don't think we should talk at all. If someone is femto-boosted on that end, they'll hear us even at a whisper."

"Good point," Dar shouted. "Let's make this a silent operation."

"This is so alien," Elsie cried helplessly.

"Wait till you see how strong you are," Larry said, nearly splitting Everest's eardrums. "I guarantee you'll love your powers then."

"I'll have to take your word for it," Elsie said at a decibel that pounded right into Everest's skull.

Being femto-boosted already made him feel like a Zylorg with three heads and three splitting headaches.

"Transporting on five," Dar reverberated into Everest's head. "Everyone ensure you've got a good hold on me." She gasped. "Uh, Elsie, not quite that good. I'm pretty sure you'll crush my wrist if you tighten your grip just a fraction more."

Elsie blanched but loosened her fingers. "Oops, I'm sorry, Dar. This is hard to get used to."

"Be one with your superpowers," Larry said. "Jeez, like I said, you need me. You're a bunch of amateurs."

"We'll get the hang of it," Dar said. "Remember, no talking once we've transported. Only sign language." With four hands grabbing some portion of her left arm, Dar checked the transport device in her right hand briefly, and said, "Go."

Everest was flung into the void of being transported—that otherworldly sense of nothingness. Except this nothingness actually showered him with colors—vibrant, scary and overwhelming. He heard nothing, tasted nothing, touched nothing, but his senses were drenched in color. Was this change part of the hybrid nature of the transporter or was this because he was femto-boosted?

CHAPTER 39
The Baskers Reunited

Elsie came out of the transport into a chaos of color, noise and smell. Her senses were heightened beyond anything she'd ever imagined. It had to have something to do with being femto-boosted—unless the overload on her senses had to do with the new type of transport that incorporated time-travel technology.

She fought back a wave of nausea at the magnified odor of the food trays her parents had left by the door. This intensified sense of smell was not a desirable side-effect of the femto-boosters.

At a rap on her shoulder, she whipped around, but it was only Dar. The girl motioned to Elsie's mom. Elsie tiptoed to her mother, but it sounded to her as if each step was an elephant's stomp. If the Panktars *were* femto-boosted they had to be able to hear her. Hopefully, they would assume her parents were awake and pacing. She and Everest exchanged glances. With a shaky breath, she leaned over in unison with him and covered their mom's mouth as he covered their dad's. She gently shook her mom.

With a jerk, her mom came awake, fighting with all her strength. Elsie did her best to contain her without hurting her. She wanted to tell her to be calm, but she couldn't say a word. It took the longest ten seconds of Elsie's life for her mom to stop struggling and realize who held her captive. Her eyes widened and her mouth moved under Elsie's hand. Elsie shook her head urgently and placed her free finger on her lips to indicate silence.

She lifted her hand away from her mom's mouth and quickly signed, "We're here to save you." Luckily, a row of dim

288

nightlights gave just enough light for her mom to be able to see the silent communication.

"Thank the Light, you're alive," her mom signed.

Everest and their dad were wordlessly hugging.

Elsie felt her mom's arms go around her, and they hugged insanely. Though she swallowed back sobs, she couldn't stop silent tears from streaming down her face. Waves of love flowed between them. Having her mom's arms around her was indescribably comforting.

When someone tried to pull her away, she clung even tighter. Her mom gasped in pain, and she remembered her strength. She quickly pulled back. Surprise colored her mom's tear-stained face as she took in Dar. She started as if she'd seen a ghost. The girl tended to have that effect on people. With her disguise gone, she was back to being Shadara's twin.

Elsie's mom looked around the room and saw Everest and Vlas as well. At the sight of Everest she seemed ready to burst into tears again, but as she took in Vlas and Dar, she managed to fight back the waterworks. Elsie couldn't stop smiling through her own tears. She had to remind herself that they needed to hurry.

She quickly signed, "We need to remove your choker."

"No," her mom signed back, "that's too dangerous. You must leave now. The pico-brownies are transmitting everything in this room to Mr. Brown."

"We've disengaged them, and we've scrambled the chokers," Elsie signed. "We need to get those chokers off before the vlems realize and investigate."

"How?" Her mom looked incredulous.

Dar slipped in between them and signed urgently, "We don't have time for this. If you would please just stop talking now, we'll have you out of this choker in a couple of minutes."

The girl's irritation was a pulsing, living thing. Elsie's mom looked startled by Dar's words, but the girl ignored her and motioned to Vlas who immediately stepped forward, object cloner in hand.

Smiling cheekily and ignoring all the undercurrents, he raised the device to the choker where there was the tiniest of locks. Barely moving his lips, he whispered, "Unlock it." Unfortunately, they had no other way of using the object cloner except with a vocal command.

Despite his attempt to be quiet, the words reverberated as if he had screamed them. Everyone except Vlas watched the door. They could not keep it from erasing if the Panktars on the other side decided to investigate.

Meanwhile the object cloner stretched, then collapsed, then contorted into the tiniest of keys.

Elsie's mom motioned wildly, making explosions with her hands. She signed, "It's going to explode. Leave now."

"No, it's not going to explode," Elsie signed. "I told you, the chokers are scrambled. We know what we're doing, Mom."

Everest's fingers were flying as he tried to explain their plan to their dad.

Their dad shook his head wildly and lunged toward their mom. Dar caught him and held him back, her femto-boosted strength making it easy for her to stop a full-grown man in his tracks. He gasped in pain.

Elsie didn't know what to do. Their dad believed that their mom was about to disintegrate.

"She's going to be fine," she signed.

There was a slight click, and the choker released, leaving a crack of an opening. Vlas quickly twisted it off of Elsie's mom's neck. He handed the choker to Dar and moved over to Elsie's dad.

Her mom sobbed as she felt her empty neck.

Elsie signed, "We have to hurry."

As if the world at large sensed her urgency, a siren split the air, hitting their overly sensitive brains with a hurricane's fury. Elsie flattened her hands against her ears. This sound sensitivity was something her parents really had to fix in newer models of the femto-boosters.

Her dad backed away from Vlas as the boy urgently signed, "Stay still."

Elsie searched wildly for something to bar the door, but she knew that was useless. Nothing was going to stop a Panktar, especially if he was boosted.

Dar signed, "With me."

She ran to the door and went into a fighting stance, flasers in both hands. Elsie leapt to her side and pulled out her stunners, as did Everest. They would probably have to resort to hand-to-hand combat, but the stunners and flasers might slow down the vlems. They stood shoulder to shoulder in an attempt to protect their unboosted parents.

Their mom rushed to their dad and clutched his hand. He tried to pull away, clearly wanting to be the only one incinerated if the choker blew, but she wouldn't let go.

Vlas's voice reverberated as he told the object cloner to unlock the choker.

The door erased, and three large Panktars rushed in, single-file. Each wielded flasers but didn't immediately shoot. Elsie took that as a sign that they were under orders to keep her parents alive if at all possible.

Taking advantage of their hesitation, Dar shot her flasers, but it immediately became clear that the Panktars had been boosted. Instead of turning into a puddle of ashes, one went to his knees and the other two just paused briefly, one to crack his neck, and the other to crack his knuckles.

"Drop your weapons, or die," said the first Panktar, his voice as deep and gravelly as a bullfrog's.

"I don't think so." Instead, Dar flasered them again. But it was as if they were being attacked by an irritating fly rather than a dangerous weapon.

All three Panktars returned her fire, flasering Dar simultaneously. Elsie and Everest gasped. The force shot the girl back a few meters, but she remained standing and in one piece. She gave her stomach a curious look.

"That was interesting," she said.

"Femto-boosted," bellowed one of the Panktars and immediately directed his flasers on the other B12s.

A weird flash burned Elsie's left side, but she actually felt her body absorbing the deadly stream and neutralizing the foreign substance.

There was a snick and Vlas made a sound of victory. He flung the two chokers into the corner of the room.

"Come on," he yelled, and this time it really was a yell. Elsie thought her brain might explode from the sound.

Swirling around, Dar grabbed Elsie and her mom at the same time. Vlas did the same with Everest and his dad. Elsie felt another flaser stream burn into her back. In a heartbeat, they were transporting back to their base.

The last thing Elsie heard was the blaring siren and Panktars yelling for backup.

They landed in a heap where they'd left the others riveted to PicoBoy's show. Elsie's ears continued to ring from the din they'd just left.

"Jeez," Larry said, "could you possibly have caused a bigger ruckus?"

"Shut down, Larry," Everest said.

Who cared about the chaos they'd left behind? Elsie couldn't stop grinning. She'd never felt such extreme happiness before. Their parents were alive, and they had saved them! She couldn't stop hugging her mom.

Officer Lilituck spoke, "We need to get back there with the infrasound. John Brown must not escape with the femto-booster technology." Including Officer Lilituck, there were now ten cyborgs in the room.

"Mom, Dad, this is Officer Lilituck and her associates." Elsie gestured to Lilituck.

"Thank you for your help," her mom said. "You are right. We have to go back immediately. Mr. Brown and his cohorts are close to figuring out how to make the femto-boosters on their own. We can't let them get away with the samples or the manufacturing equipment."

Elsie's dad nodded, his expression befuddled as he took in the room full of cyborgs and children. "I don't understand how all of you have come to our aid, but it's imperative that we stop those horrible people. Obviously our children are boosted. Are there any more femto-boosters? Justine and I will need to be boosted as well."

Elsie shook her head. "You can't go back."

"We have to," her dad said, "but going down there without a boost would be suicide."

"No kidding," Dar said.

Elsie's mom glanced over at Dar, countless questions in her eyes. She turned to Elsie and Everest, her eyebrows raised.

"Sorry, this is Dar and that's Vlas." Elsie pointed as she introduced the clones. "That's Lelita and Borneo, and this is Larry. Everyone, these are my parents, Justine and George Basker."

Both her parents nodded and murmured 'hello.'

Her dad asked again, "Do you have any additional boosters, or are they all used up?"

"Elsie, Everest, give your parents your back-up boosters," Dar ordered curtly. She was watching PicoBoy's visual stream. "It looks as if our Mr. Brown could be making a run for it. We need light speed."

All of the bad guys had converged on the laboratory. The Panktars stood guard, and the vlems and their minions were inside. PicoBoy showed chaotic packing in progress.

"They could already be handing out additional femto-boosters," Dar said.

Elsie and Everest gave their parents the little femto-booster specks of dust. They quickly swallowed them.

"Do you know who is boosted and who is not?" Lilituck asked the couple.

"Most of the Panktars are boosted," Elsie's dad said. "Most of the humans are not, with the notable exception of Powers, Dr. Jensa, my brother-in-law, and of course, Mr. Brown. The man is very proprietary with his boosters. He seems to feel that the Panktars can adequately protect him. However, he has also forced an aggressive manufacturing schedule and may be planning to hand out more. He may be doing so as we speak."

"Did it ever occur to you to just say, 'no'?" Dar asked.

Elsie turned on her. "Mr. Brown would have killed them!"

Her mom's eyes were grave. "We didn't go along with Mr. Brown's demands to save our lives. If that was all we had to worry about, we would have welcomed our fate rather than give Brown such a powerful weapon. But what could we do? My own brother is involved—the person we left in charge of Elsie and Everest's well-being. Fredrick told us in no uncertain terms that he would not hesitate to kill them if we didn't comply with Mr. Brown's wishes. But you are right. This is our mess, and we have to fix it."

Dar contemplated Elsie's mom then nodded her head curtly. Elsie heard her mutter, "utes," under her breath. Given their boosted state, everyone heard Dar loud and clear.

Lilituck grabbed Dar by the shoulder. "This is no time for dissecting the past. We must return to the island before Mr. Brown escapes. Everyone in groups of four and five," she said. "Remember, the infrasound will happen first. If you find someone who appears to be unconscious from that, stun him just to be safe. My associates and I will transport those vlems to a secure holding place. Dar and Vlas will each have a transport device. We'll have three amongst the cyborgs. I'll have one, and my associates, Officer Sanchez and Officer Getchup, will also have transport devices." She motioned to two cyborgs, one male and the other female.

"Time for phase two," she said. "One, two, three…"

Before they disappeared into the molecular world of transportation, Elsie felt her mother's hand clasp hers.

CHAPTER 40
A Reckoning

They transported to the room that PicoBoy had used when he first arrived at Pelican Island. It had been empty then, and it still was—just a sterile room with a low slung ceiling. Despite the power coursing through his veins, Everest's palms felt damp as Vlas requested that the door erase. There could be guards outside.

But the opening revealed a corridor devoid of human life. The guards must have converged on the laboratory. Was the weapon chamber also unprotected? It didn't really matter since anyone not boosted would be disabled via infrasound, and anyone boosted would be impervious to mere weaponry.

A vibration rocketed through Everest, so intense he was surprised he didn't just explode into a thousand pieces. His body adjusted to the strange sensation in real time. The cyborg officers must have let loose with the infrasound. There was no denying that the extreme pressure hurt—his inner ear, his muscles, his organs, even the blood that churned through his veins all reacted to the low frequency sound—but it felt as if he stood outside the chamber of pain and watched it happen to someone else.

The cyborgs hustled into formation, three rows of three with Lilituck in front. "We'll find and incarcerate those who were taken down by the infrasound. However, if we are attacked by femto-boosted vlems, we'll have to abort." She contemplated them seriously. "Don't fail us. Bring Mr. Brown into custody or destroy him and his minions. Do not let them off this island."

Together the cybercops set off at a fast and perfectly synchronized jog, weapons at the ready.

"How do we take them into custody?" Dar asked Everest's parents. "What can we do to neutralize the technology? Where's the weakness?"

Everest's parents exchanged worried glances.

His dad signed, "Anyone femto-boosted can hear us speak. They would have heard Officer Lilituck too. They have to know we are here."

Lelita gasped.

It was the first sound she'd made up to this point. Everest had noticed that despite having superhuman powers, she and Borneo had been doing their best to pretend they weren't there.

Everest had a feeling his expression mirrored Dar's—one of acute embarrassment. It was one thing for the cyborgs to forget that they should be signing, but Dar had forgotten too! He was just lucky that his parents had reminded them before he spoke with equal foolishness. The vlems must have remembered because the only significant noise on Pelican Island was the now distant, but still loud, pounding of the cybercops' boots as they ran in unison.

Everest's mom waved her arms to gain their attention. With her fingers she told them, "We sabotaged the most recent boosters—everything in the last two weeks. A bad femto-booster has the same general attributes as a healthy one. But if someone boosted overuses their superpowers, the femto-booster will implode. Unfortunately, we couldn't test the virus so we may find it doesn't work."

"How did you insert a virus with the robots doing the actual manufacturing?" Elsie signed.

Jeez, Everest thought, *even now Elsie couldn't refrain from asking questions.*

His sister must have realized this wasn't the time for a question and answer session, because her cheeks reddened and she quickly signed, "Forget it."

Dar rolled her eyes then signed to Vlas who was watching the corridor. "Do we know where PicoBoy is?"

"No," Vlas signed back with a worried frown.

Dar turned to the Baskers. "If I understand you correctly, we need to make these guys mad enough that they pull out all the stops when they're fighting us. The more they push, the better chance we have of an infected booster self-destructing. And what? Blowing them up?"

"Yes, that would be the likely outcome," Everest's dad signed. "But it's all untested theory."

"So we fight to make them really angry or frustrated," Dar signed to the team. "We taunt and irritate them; we're the ticks buried deep into their keisters."

"Eww!" Lelita said.

Everest turned to his parents and signed, "Is there any way to tell if someone has one of the infected boosters?"

"We can test them before they've been ingested to identify which they are," his mom signed back, "but once they're inside a humanoid, there's no way to distinguish them until they self-destruct. Only the most recent ones have the infection. We've been manufacturing femto-boosters for Mr. Brown for over a month now, but we only figured out how to insert viruses in the last two weeks. Same timing as when we figured out how to increase the lifespan of the femto-boosters. Anything created before that is virus-free but also wears off after only a few hours."

"Okay," Dar signed, "let's hope the virus works. When we storm the laboratory, I want George and Justine to gather up all the femto-boosters and any research or equipment that could be used to duplicate them later. Vlas, give them the object cloner and the universal unlocker. Between the two devices, you should have access to any safe or locked drawer in the room. The rest of us will irritate the heck out of the vlems so that some of them destroy themselves, or at least, they are distracted long enough for George and Justine to get their job done. We no longer have the element of surprise. They know we're here, and they know we have transport technology. Since we don't hear anyone speaking, we have to assume they have instituted a rule of silence. They'll be ready for us in the laboratory, so we go in weapons blazing. The stunners and flasers won't work, but they'll be an irritant. Let's make 'em mad."

Larry looked as if he was going to bust a gut. It had to be hard for him, since he couldn't sign.

Everest clasped his shoulder sympathetically and motioned using his fingers like flasers trying to get across the point that they should flaser anything and everyone in sight. He wished they could explain the virus to Larry.

Elsie surprised Everest by giving Larry a small jellach journal with an explanation of sorts. It said, "Irritate the bad guys, make them mad, newer femto-boosters have viruses and may self-destruct."

After a slight pause, Larry nodded, his eyes wide, and gave her the thumbs-up sign.

So did Everest. Writing it down for Larry was a zetta level-headed idea. Now Larry knew that some of the femto-boosted creeps could implode.

"On the sign of three, we're transporting straight into the laboratory," Dar signed. She turned to Vlas, showed him her transporter, and signed, "Here are the coordinates. I worked them up when PicoBoy originally showed us the chamber. I had a feeling we might need them."

"Zeller," he signed back. He plugged in the same coordinates then motioned for Elsie, Everest and their parents to come with him. Dar took the rest of the B12s.

She held up one finger, then two, then three.

The transport itself took mere seconds. They landed in a kaleidoscope of wild colors and noises. Everest shot his stunner at anything and everything that moved. Since all he was trying to do was make them mad, he had decided the stunner would be enough. At least eight human bodies were already on the ground due to the infrasound attack. No Panktars were on the ground.

But there *was* a wall of Panktars and one cyborg—hopefully the spy—lined up between them and Mr. Brown.

"How foolish," Mr. Brown said, ignoring the bursts from their weaponry.

The noise was deafening. Everyone seemed to be screaming, but they could have been whispering for all he knew. His head exploded with the full force of a Zylorg headache.

"You don't want to be here." Mr. Brown was nearly jovial. "Your pitiful army of children cannot beat my boosted Panktars.

You know that, as do I. Make light speed out of here before you are destroyed. Warp speed, my friends."

"I don't think so," Dar shouted back.

"We'd rather die than let you get away with the booster technology," Everest's dad yelled.

Pushing back fear and doing his best not to think at all, Everest sprang forward. He heard Larry's warrior cry as he, too, pounced. Everest grappled with a Panktar. Its green skin was mottled with rock-like bumps. In some ways, that made it easier to wrestle. He gripped hard onto two nodules and held on.

The hulk punched him in the stomach, sending Everest across the room. He felt his body both accept and deflect the pain. He reminded himself that a boosted Panktar would be significantly stronger than a boosted human—especially a kid his age. He needed to improve his odds. Jumping straight up into the air, he twirled and landed on the Panktar's back. His job was to irritate, and that was exactly what he would do. With his arms in a tight choker hold around the Panktar's almost non-existent neck, he held on for dear life.

As the Panktar bucked and fought to escape, Everest searched for the others.

His parents had raced for the far corner where a large steelorq box sat. They immediately went to work on it with the object cloner. Two Panktars barreled after them and engaged them in battle.

From the corner of his eye, he saw that Elsie also had a strangle hold on one of the Panktars from behind, but she was being zetta banged up. The Panktar had been clever enough to back up against a wall and was slamming into it, and her, over and over again. Though her body would recover quickly, it had to hurt.

Everest grunted as the Panktar beneath him caught him with a flailing fist on first one leg and then the other. He fought back the pain and stayed glued, even tightening his hold. The monster suddenly made a gurgling noise as if he had trouble breathing.

Dar and another Panktar were exchanging punches that literally threw them across the room. Larry was using his speed to dive in, attack with two stunners, and then dive out. Lelita bravely fought a human guard. Borneo had followed Larry's lead and was attacking with his stunners.

But it was Vlas who truly embraced their superpowers. He turned himself into a human tornado and spun through the ranks of the Panktars who guarded Mr. Brown, Lester-Hauffer, Powers and Dr. Jensa while they emptied a large locker. His force knocked the Panktars to the ground. They quickly recovered, but it was a zeller attempt at being zetta irritating. The Panktars opened flaser fire on Vlas who continued to spin. His momentum turned him into such a whirl and flash of color it was hard to distinguish him as human.

Everest's Panktar jumped up and rammed both of them into the low ceiling. It didn't take much more than normal Panktar strength since the monster was only inches shorter than ceiling height. But he had to bend over so that Everest's head connected. Lights exploded in Everest's brain, but he managed to hang on and the pain quickly dissipated. The Panktar let loose with a battle cry that was loud enough to shake the walls of the building.

Good, Everest thought, *he was making the vlem mad.*

One of the Panktars picked himself up and threw himself at Vlas's whirling mass. Suddenly, the green monster shot fire out of his mouth.

Everest heard gasps.

"No fire," yelled Mr. Brown. "Too dangerous. Protect the femto-boosters!"

The Panktar in question immediately swallowed back the rest of the fire. With a bellow, he leapt at Vlas.

An explosion shook the room, and where the Panktar should have been, only fine dust settled.

The entire room stilled, even the whirling Vlas.

The virus worked.

A mixture of horror and relief coursed through Everest. Judging from the expressions his parents wore, they shared his conflicted feelings.

The bad guys stared in disbelief. Everest could almost hear their thoughts. They had to be wondering what had happened. Had the Panktar exploded because he had swallowed his own fire? Or had the B12s done something to incinerate him?

In that pause, Larry managed a clean flaser shot at James Powers. The force shot the man backward, but within seconds he seemed impervious to the flaser beam. Smiling evilly, he turned his attention on the boy who had escaped his clutches once before. His grin made it clear that he had no intention of letting that happen again.

Everest still hung onto his Panktar's neck, and they reengaged combat so fiercely that he had a hard time keeping track of Larry.

He did see Powers lift his arms and spring across the room with supersonic speed to tackle the boy. The two slid across the floor. Then Everest really had to focus, because his Panktar banged him against the ceiling again.

As he blew burning-hot air on the Panktar's neck, he caught a glimpse of Larry following Vlas's lead and going into a crazed spin. Larry bumped into Powers and then righted himself. He spun a tight circle around the man to box him in. Powers reached out to stop the whirling, but Larry's force batted his arm back. The man screamed with anger and blew a hot gale at the spinning boy that shot Larry back even as he continued to spin. Larry bowled into Elsie and the Panktar she fought, knocking them across the room.

James Powers sucked in his breath and emitted a new stream of hot wind. There was a loud click, and then he collapsed. They all watched him disintegrate into a puddle of fine ash.

Larry whooped, pausing in his spin to pump his arm into the air. Everest didn't know what he felt. He was glad that Powers could no longer be a threat, but jeez, what a horrible way to go.

Again, all the bad guys froze and just stared at James Powers' remains.

"What is this?" screamed Lester-Hauffer.

Everest saw real fear in his uncle's eyes, but Mr. Brown showed no visible reaction.

Two vlems down, but so many to go. At least the virus was working. And Larry had brought about the destruction of James Powers, the murderer of the real Dr. Yee. The man had been a monster, the worst sort of Vlemutz. He deserved to die, and yet, it was still hard to stomach the destruction of another human being, someone's son, perhaps someone's brother.

Everest struggled to pull himself together. This was war. If these villains escaped with the femto-boosters all of humanity would be at risk.

They had to keep fighting, keep taking out femto-boosted vlems, one by one.

But the bad guys now knew there was something very wrong indeed with their femto-boosters.

How would they respond?

CHAPTER 41
Touch and Go

"Panktars, to me," bellowed Mr. Brown.

Elsie hung on tight while the Panktar she attempted to choke used his or her legs to lumber across the room. The creature—Elsie decided it was a man—made deep gasping noises and used his humongous green fingers to pry at Elsie's arms.

Elsie imagined herself as an anchor. The more she thought of herself as dead weight the heavier she became. She could feel the Panktar becoming sluggish underneath her, but she knew her hold was precarious. There was no question that the Panktar had more strength. Elsie had just gotten lucky that she'd been able to jump onto the Panktar's back.

Suddenly, the Panktar's fingers seared her arms with a heat so intense that great welts formed. They almost immediately disappeared as Elsie's boosted body fought back. Still, everywhere the Panktar's hand touched, Elsie's skin was on fire. All she could think about was jumping off the creature's back so she could run from the pain, but that was not what a Basker did. Ever. She hung onto her death grip instead and let the pain flow over and into and around her until it finally ebbed away.

The Panktar continued to lumber across the room, but now he swayed back and forth banging Elsie from side to side in an attempt to buck her off. He continued to burn Elsie's arms, and she continued to fight through the pain so that the healing came before she could no longer bear it. With a strangled grunt, the Panktar pushed harder with his fingers and simultaneously shot into the air, banging Elsie into the ceiling.

Elsie heard ringing in her ears and felt her arms weaken. She imagined herself as solid steelorq, her two arms welded together into one invincible beam. Over and over again, she whispered that she was solid steelorq, interspersing this thought with the idea that Baskers never quit. The Panktar leapt into the air again, banging them both against the ceiling. This time, she lost her grip for a heartbeat. Before the Panktar realized what had happened, she managed to lunge and clasp both upper arms so that her choker-hold was back.

The Panktar tried one more time to burn Elsie's arms and bang her head in unison. But the third time was the humanoid's downfall. He collapsed and then, much to Elsie's horror, disintegrated into a pile of olive-colored ash. Face first in the Panktar's remains, Elsie flung herself away, rolling across the floor with no thought to where she was in relationship to any of the other people in the room.

She heard Mr. Brown's sharp intake of breath.

Elsie frantically rubbed at her body and face to remove the Panktar's remains. She'd never been responsible for someone's death before. It was horrible. She kept swiping at her face, terrified she had swallowed some of the dust.

"What's wrong with the femto-boosters?" Mr. Brown screamed at Elsie's parents.

"They are infected," her mom said defiantly. "If you try to use your powers you will die."

Elsie was becoming accustomed to the amplified voices. It didn't bother her as much, and she could distinguish between talking and screaming.

"I'll kill you," Mr. Brown said.

In his extreme anger, he forgot that the secret of the femto-boosters would die with them.

"I don't think so," Elsie's dad said. "We're femto-boosted now, and we're using the early untainted models. That gives us the advantage."

"You couldn't have infected all of them," Mr. Brown said. "You're bluffing."

Elsie still brushed obsessively at invisible traces of ash as her mom shrugged and asked, "Do you feel lucky?"

Mr. Brown waved two of his Panktars toward the Baskers. "Destroy them," he said in no uncertain terms.

The Panktars were green and huge and strong and zetta boosted, but their eyes held an expression Elsie had never expected to see on a Panktar—fear.

Her dad quickly egged on the Panktars' terror. "The only way you'll survive is by not using your superpowers. If you use them, you're as good as dead. If you don't use them, eventually the powers will dissipate, and the virus will be gone."

"Don't listen to them," Mr. Brown commanded. "They can't have infected all of the femto-boosters."

The Panktars exchanged looks, each breathing heavily through his ugly trio of lumps that acted as a nose. They lumbered away from Mr. Brown to sit heavily on the floor, their arms crossed. In a voice as deep as the center of the earth, one of them said, "The only way we'll know if we're infected is by being destroyed. We don't like that." He looked at Dar. "You tell your cybercops that we surrender."

"I'll let them know," said the undercover cyborg officer as he stepped away from Mr. Brown.

Mr. Brown's eyes narrowed. "Traitor," he hissed.

He raised his flaser and blasted the cybercop.

An expression of surprise shot across the human side of the cyborg's face as that half disintegrated into a puddle of powdery ash. The metal elements crashed to the ground with a brutal clang, melted and mangled but not quite dust.

Elsie cried out. Her brother shouted too, and Lelita burst into tears. A strong chemical odor hung in the air.

Mr. Brown shrugged. "We all know a cyborg cannot be femto-boosted. He was stupid to reveal to the world that he was a spy. He deserved to be flasered."

"You are an evil man," Elsie's mom said bitterly.

"Evil, good—such antiquated terms. I prefer to think of myself as merely a modern business person with today's virtual currency sensibility. My motives are simple and without malice. I make money. If anyone or anything gets in my way, it is in the spirit of commerce and competition that I remove the obstacle."

From the corner of her eye, Elsie saw Dar motion to all of them to start to approach Mr. Brown, Director Lester-Hauffer and Dr. Jensa. Slowly, they inched forward in a loose semi-circle.

305

Director Lester-Hauffer stepped toward Elsie's parents. "My dear sister and brother-in-law, why must we be at odds? This is all a terrible misunderstanding. We are family. Let us behave as such. I've been so worried about my nephew and niece, but now we can bring them back to the school and protect them from further harm."

"Do you think we're complete yocto-brains?" Elsie's mom asked. "You helped kidnap us."

"My dear Justine," he said, his arms extended, "this is a horrendous misunderstanding. I was taken in." He motioned to Mr. Brown. "Led to believe it would be safer for you to do your testing on earth. I was told your children were consorting with dangerous criminals. It was my duty to do everything in my power to return them to the bosom of my academy—a safe haven."

Larry snorted. "Dude, what fantasy world are you from?"

"Fredrick," Elsie's mom said, "nothing you say can excuse your heinous behavior. Please just shut down."

"In fact," said Mr. Brown, "let me help you shut down. Not only have you betrayed your family, but now you seek to betray me." Only a few meters away, he raised his flaser again and shot a deadly stream at Lester-Hauffer. Elsie watched as her uncle jerked back, but the femto-booster technology saved him from immediate annihilation. He doubled over in pain as Mr. Brown continued to aim a steady flaser stream at him, but he didn't disintegrate.

Dar exchanged her stunner for a flaser and shot her own blast at Mr. Brown. The man barely registered the attack though a small grimace sliced across his face.

"He's trying to overwhelm the femto-booster in Lester-Hauffer so it implodes," she told the others. She continued to flaser Mr. Brown.

The man laughed, though his face contorted. "I'll stop if you do," he said.

Lester-Hauffer jerked at each new flaser burst.

"On three," Dar responded. She counted slowly then stopped flasering Mr. Brown at the third count.

Elsie was shocked when the villain did likewise.

Lester-Hauffer collapsed into a weeping heap.

Elsie hadn't expected Mr. Brown to stop flasering her uncle. With some trepidation, she'd actually exchanged her stunner for her own flaser so that she could shoot the man if necessary to help overload his femto-booster. The weapon felt warm. She had to remind herself that everyone in the room could counteract the effects of the flaser. Here, it was just an annoyance, not an instrument of death.

Was the power waning from Uncle Fredrick's femto-booster? He seemed to have been hit harder by the flaser than Mr. Brown had been. Yet, he hadn't disintegrated either. Maybe he had one of the older pills that didn't carry the virus but had a shorter lifespan.

With all of Mr. Brown's minions afraid to fight, Justine and George quickly opened the steelorq box and started taking inventory of the femto-boosters. Dar and Mr. Brown stood in a face-off with Elsie and Everest at Dar's side. Vlas and Larry positioned themselves to watch over the Panktars, their flasers ready to force an overload if any of the Panktars tried to fight.

Lelita and Borneo bravely ran over to the Baskers to help them with the femto-boosters. Elsie's mom was jacked into a holoputer. Elsie's boosted eye-sight made it possible for her to see the inventory list her mom consulted as she compared it to the contents of the steelorq box.

Mr. Brown watched Elsie's parents with a small smile playing at his lips. Elsie didn't understand his expression. What was he thinking? What was he up to?

Silently, Dr. Jensa watched Mr. Brown. It was hard to say whether the man was looking for signs of an attempted escape or looking for a way to save himself at Mr. Brown's expense.

After what felt like hours but must have been less than fifteen minutes, Elsie's mom paused her comparisons and calculations. "There are femto-boosters missing."

Dar asked, "Are you sure?"

"Yes."

Dar turned to Mr. Brown. "Where are they?"

"I have no idea," he said, rubbing his flaser with his thumb. His other hand was casually inserted into the pocket of his vlatex slacks. "An accounting error, perhaps?"

"No," Elsie's mom said. "There are two dozen missing— early versions."

That meant they were pure femto-boosters, albeit with a shorter lifespan. Elsie bit her lower lip and exchanged glances with her brother. Anyone with those femto-boosters could wreak havoc.

From her pant pocket, Dar pulled out the small container of truth pills. "Let's get honest," she said.

Mr. Brown's lips twitched into an evil grin, and he slowly took his hand out of his pocket.

Elsie sucked in her breath. He held an identical device to the transporters they had used to get to Pelican Island.

With a cocky wave of his hand, he shimmered then disappeared.

CHAPTER 42
Chasing Mr. Brown

"Vlas, Everest, Elsie, with me," Dar said as she pushed the truth pills back into her pocket. "The rest of you stay here."

Everest's heart boomed in his ears as he ran to Dar. Mr. Brown had escaped with femto-boosters.

Dar quickly made some calculations.

Everest caught his parents' distressed expressions and swallowed hard against an unwelcome urge to cry.

The transport was over almost too quickly to feel the exaggerated motion. Everest's super-vision immediately adjusted to the dark. They were in the chamber on ground level where Mr. Brown had reigned with his ancient throne.

They arrived just in time to see him shimmer and disappear again.

Dar said a word that Everest recognized as one that Larry liked to use but shouldn't. His surprise must have registered on his face, because she frowned at him before calling out, "Lilituck, we need you. We're in the throne room."

The femto-boosted yell might have burst Everest's eardrums if he hadn't been femto-boosted himself. Everyone on the island and possibly half of San Francisco must have heard her.

In a few minutes, Lilituck and six other cyborgs arrived at high speed. *Were the three missing cyborg officers dust?* Everest's stomach churned at the thought.

"What happened?" Elsie asked, her eyes wide.

"We lost a few," Lilituck said in a clipped tone.

Everest couldn't get the picture out of his mind of the undercover cyborg officer who had been flasered.

"Mr. Brown has transported off the island," Dar said. "Do you have coordinates for his primary residence?"

"You let him escape?" Lilituck asked, her human eyebrow shooting up.

"We didn't just let him walk off," Dar said.

"He had a mini transporter hidden in his pocket," Elsie added.

Officer Lilituck frowned. "He is tagged. We can track him. Give me a few minutes to ascertain where he is."

"We don't have time," Dar said. "I'm convinced that he's gone home. Give me the coordinates now. You can confirm his whereabouts after. If I'm wrong, send the rest of our gang after him."

Lilituck sniffed in irritation but remained otherwise silent except to provide Dar with the coordinates she looked for.

Dar motioned to the others. "Let's go." She turned back to Lilituck for a heartbeat. "The rest of the vlems have surrendered in the laboratory."

The cybercop nodded curtly.

Everest took a deep breath in anticipation of the strange time-travel-transport hybrid that would take them to Mr. Brown's lair. Then he was sucked into a maelstrom of color. Despite the overwhelming feeling of nothingness, his body vibrated as if major earthquakes had taken over.

Though the room they landed in was dark, Everest's femto-boosted eyesight gave it an aura of light. It was more decadent than he could have imagined. Even Adriatic Mink's palace looked subdued compared to this place. He saw wood everywhere—real carved wood on the walls, the floors, and the furniture. Each richly-polished wooden wall displayed antique tapestries. The one in front of him told an intricate story of a unicorn and a young lady dressed in ancient garb. The unicorn dipped his horn into a golden cup that the girl held. The room's throne was even more intricately carved than the one on Pelican Island. Its arms were shaped into lions' legs, ending in impressive paws and the upholstery was a rich royal blue.

A hand waving in front of him snapped him to attention.

With her eyebrows lifted and her mouth frowning, a very irritable Dar signed, "Earth to Everest!"

"I'm all ears," he signed back.

"All fingers," Vlas signed with a grin.

"Yeah," Everest was surprised to find himself grinning. "Is he here?" he asked with his hands.

Dar signed, "He has to be. There's nowhere else for him to go."

"He could have traveled back in time," Elsie signed.

"I'm guessing he needed to come back here first," Dar returned. "He's on the premises somewhere. For how long is anyone's guess." She looked around the room. "It would be most efficient for us to split up, but I think we should stay together. Being infected by the virus could make him even more desperate and dangerous."

"I agree," Elsie fingered urgently.

Everest failed miserably in imagining what Mr. Brown might do next. Despite his hope that they had the upper hand, he couldn't help but be nervous. The man knew more than they ever would about being despicable and devious.

A strange noise came from the far side of the building—not exactly the sound of a person moving around, but possibly that of someone rifling through items.

"Time to kick Mr. Brown to Xlexuri galaxy," Vlas signed. He pulled out his flasers.

Dar took the lead, as usual, and Everest followed with Elsie at his heels. Vlas brought up the rear. They took off at a dead run. Since Mr. Brown was femto-boosted, he would be able to hear the tiniest of sounds. Therefore, it didn't matter if they were stealthy or not. They just had to reach him before he finished whatever task had brought him here.

Beyond the chamber was a landing with two circular staircases, one leading up and the other down. Since the noise seemed to come from below, they raced in that direction. Dim lights flashed a multitude of colors as they flew down the stairs. At most, Everest touched one stair the entire way down. These superpowers were unreal. As they circled around and down the staircase, they found themselves surrounded by a swarm of pico-brownies.

Everest barely had a chance to wonder if they had security features before the techno-creatures attacked like a hive of furious wasps. His arms burned from the stinging. Even having been femto-boosted, it still took a second for him to counteract each sharp thrust. An electric humming too quiet for a normal human ear to hear emanated from the little faux-creatures. It was as if the brownies buzzed like bees. If Mr. Brown hadn't already known they were there, the brownies would have alerted him to their presence.

"Ow!" Vlas gasped.

Everest almost yelled too as he slapped at the pesky pico-brownies. But he really didn't want to act like a ute-baby in front of Dar.

Dar picked up speed so that she blurred around the edges as she zoomed down the rest of the stairs. Copying her, Everest felt a rush in the pit of his stomach. They could have been hawks flying down the stairs, only they sounded more like elephants. These femto-boosters desperately needed volume control.

Humming followed them. The pico-brownies were in close pursuit. They weren't life-threatening, but deng, they were irritating.

At the bottom of the stairs the B12s paused, and the world exploded. They all cried out as they shot backward. Everest slammed into the staircase railing and heard it crack in half. His body compensated in real-time for his various injuries so that each slash of pain disappeared almost immediately.

Dar pushed herself back to her feet. She stretched, checking her neck, back, and arms for injuries.

"He's trying to slow us down," Elsie yelled.

Dar rolled her eyes. "Brilliant."

Another small explosion on the far side shook the room, but they were ready for it. This time, Everest barely felt the vibration.

"Don't touch the floor," Dar said.

She leapt, pushing away from the ceiling and pumping her legs so that she ran in the air to the far door. Elsie and Everest awkwardly followed. Everest almost banged his head on the ceiling but caught himself in time.

Another small explosion demolished most of the room. Everest had a hard time understanding how Mr. Brown could destroy so many priceless artifacts. The bombs were barely hurting the B12s, but they were turning amazing works of art to rubble.

Still the bombs *were* slowing them down. Maybe that was all Mr. Brown wanted. Once he got away with the pure femto-boosters, the world would be his.

Dar shot through the door, and the others followed in single file. The room was empty, so they quickly flew into the next chamber.

There, Mr. Brown faced them, his back to an open safe. In each hand, he wielded a flaser.

Immediately, he opened fire. Everest felt his body's molecules attempt to disintegrate. At the last minute, they firmed up again. The internal changes caused a strange and constant vibration. It was so weird being superhuman.

He aimed his own flaser at Mr. Brown and shot a steady stream. Because the room was dark, lights flashed around them as they flasered back and forth. Strangely, the room also appeared to be fully lit, probably due to his boosted vision.

Everest sprung at Mr. Brown, desperate to stop him from transporting away again. He slammed into the man, and they landed hard with the vlem taking the brunt of the crash. Mr. Brown grunted as he crunched into the wood floor. But he was boosted too so he would recover quickly.

His whole life, Everest had been trained not to hit an opponent in the face, but anger raged like an out-of-control fire throughout his boosted body. He found himself pummeling Mr. Brown, his fists flying and landing without rules or remorse. The vlem would have killed his parents. He would have killed any of them without a single thought.

Mr. Brown didn't fight back except to attempt to deflect the punches. Despite his claim that the Baskers couldn't have infected all the femto-boosters, he clearly was worried about overusing his powers.

Elsie landed on Everest's back and pushed, flattening Everest who then flattened Mr. Brown. Taking a deep breath, Everest calmed his mind and made himself into a dead weight. Elsie's additional force immobilized Mr. Brown.

With his peripheral vision he saw Dar reach the safe and search it with her hand.

"It's empty," she called. "He must have the femto-boosters on him."

Everest swung his attention back to Mr. Brown. The man jerked hard, but the combined weight of the Basker twins kept him within their power.

Dar quickly added, "You're going to have to ease off very slowly so we can search him. Vlas, see Mr. Brown's clenched hand?"

All of them stared at the fist as if it were on fire.

Vlas shot down and he and Dar reached Mr. Brown in tandem. They worked together to peel the man's fist open.

On his palm was the transport device which Dar quickly pocketed.

With two hands, Everest gripped one of Mr. Brown's wrists, and Vlas hung onto the other. They carefully lifted him to his feet so that he faced Dar and Elsie.

If Mr. Brown's expression could have killed, it would have. Fortunately, it appeared that femto-boosted eyes could see extremely far distances, but they couldn't be used as weapons.

"Where do you think the femto-boosters are?" Elsie asked the other B12s.

Dar eyed Mr. Brown coldly. "How'd you like to do the right thing and just tell us?"

Mr. Brown choked on laughter. "What an allen you are."

Dar's eyes narrowed, and she seemed about to speak, but Vlas beat her to it. "Look," he said, pointing at Mr. Brown's neck.

Everest gasped. The missing pendant! Holding onto Mr. Brown's wrist with one hand, he grabbed the pendant with the other.

"Be careful," Dar said. "You don't want to break it."

"Yeah," he said, "but I can afford to break the chain." He snapped it off Mr. Brown's neck and shoved the warm locket into his pocket.

"I wonder if that's filled with the original prototypes," Dar said, "or if he's added to them with the ones that have a longer lifespan?"

"Yeah, maybe I've put some infected ones in," Mr. Brown said.

Dar shrugged. "Guess it doesn't matter since we're handing the locket over to the cybercops." She stood up.

"Shadara, here, is lying to you," Mr. Brown said in a matter-of-fact tone.

"What are you talking about?" Elsie asked.

"That safe wasn't empty."

Everest looked at Dar.

The girl returned his gaze blankly. "Maybe he has a hidden compartment? I didn't find anything."

"There was a tube of femto-boosters in there," Mr. Brown screamed. "She's lying to you."

"What's the matter with you?" Dar asked, obviously puzzled. "It's over. We beat you. You're not going to break us apart now with ridiculous lies."

"Our senses are heightened," Vlas added, "it would be impossible for her to sneak something out from under our noses."

"Suit yourselves," Mr. Brown sneered. "It's nothing to me if you choose to ignore Shadara's lies."

"Between the two of you," Elsie said, "we'll put our VC on Dar as being the most trustworthy."

CHAPTER 43
Bad, Bad Mr. Brown

"Tell us where the other femto-boosters are," Dar said.

"You know better than I," Mr. Brown said.

"Don't play games. The cybercops will rip this place apart."

"They won't find anything," he replied. "However, if they search *everyone* here, they will significantly improve their odds of finding the missing boosters." He laughed.

Everest suppressed a violent urge to kick him. He was such a liar, such a Vlemutz.

Elsie touched Dar's shoulder. "He's just toying with us."

Dar nodded. "Yeah."

"Should we continue to search the property?" Vlas asked.

"He's got to have those other femto-boosters stashed somewhere," Dar said. "But let's give the cybercops the dubious pleasure of searching for them. They have more experience. We'll transport to Officer Lilituck's base."

An explosion ripped through the house, causing all of them to cover their boosted ears.

"That was close," Vlas said.

"Yeah," Dar said. "Do you smell the fumes?"

"Yeah," Elsie said. "Is it because of our super-senses?"

Dar swiveled back to Mr. Brown who wore a serene expression. "What have you done?"

Mr. Brown shrugged. "I'm not one for sharing. If I can't have this property, then no one's going to have it. Especially not a bunch of nosy little clone brats and clone wannabees. The place is rigged to blow—any second now."

"But what about you?" Elsie asked.

His lips twisted. "I *had* planned to transport away. Perhaps you all would be so kind as to get me out of here?"

There was a part of Everest that would have liked to have left him there to fend for himself. But he couldn't just leave him there to die. Besides, with their luck, the man would escape, and then he'd be loose and possibly packing more femto-boosters.

Another explosion wrenched the air, even closer now. The building shook. They saw flames lick across the floor of the room next door.

"B12s, to me," Dar said.

Everest and Vlas pulled Mr. Brown over to Dar. Everest took her wrist with one hand while keeping a firm grip on Mr. Brown with the other. Vlas did likewise and Elsie grabbed Dar's shoulder as the girl reprogrammed the transport device.

They heard yet another explosion.

As they transported away, they felt an intense heat, smelled an acrid smoke and saw the room shower down around them in thousands of pieces as if it had transformed into a massive hail storm.

They landed in a heap in the sterile room Lilituck had transported them to after their encounter with infrasound.

Lilituck and a number of other cyborgs were there.

So were their parents. Everest still held onto Mr. Brown, but Elsie ran over to them and collapsed into their mom's arms. He wanted to go to them too, but he couldn't let go of the vlem. Lelita, Borneo and Larry hovered to one side, but he didn't see his uncle or Dr. Jensa. Nor did he see any of the Panktars. They must have already been jailed.

Officer Lilituck strode over and planted herself with her legs spread, her arms crossed, and her face stern. "Mr. Brown, you are under arrest."

He nodded philosophically, a tiny smile playing at his lips. "I'm yours to command."

"You will go quietly with me?" Lilituck asked.

"Of course," Mr. Brown said simply.

"Larry and Everest, please come with us just in case our guest decides to use his boosted strength."

"Sure, yeah," Everest said.

Grinning, Larry walked over. "My pleasure, Officer."

"I'm coming too," Dar said. She glared at Mr. Brown who smiled pleasantly in return.

They moved with Lilituck who had Mr. Brown in tow. Four cyborg police officers stepped into formation behind them. They left the chamber, and at the end of the hall, they turned the corner. At the end of another long hall, they reached stairs which Lilituck led them down.

At the bottom, Everest realized he was in a stronghold. The walls were solid marblon, and there were at least twelve cells on each side of a long passage. Each cell was marblon, except for a square window made out of some see-through substance. As they passed one of the chambers, Everest saw his uncle lying curled up on an old jellach cot, his face turned to the back wall. He almost felt sorry for the man until he remembered that he had tried to engineer his own sister's death. *Vlem.*

At the end of the row, Lilituck placed her metal hand on the marblon door. "Open," she said. The door erased. Inside was an empty cell with only a cot and a small urinal.

"Larry, Everest," Officer Lilituck said, stepping back from her charge, "please stand guard while my officers search Mr. Brown."

"I think not," the man said. "I live by the motto, 'Always have a back-up plan.'"

Dar and Everest both lunged, but Mr. Brown had already shimmered away.

"Where'd he go?" Everest asked then felt like a yocto-brain for blurting out such a ridiculous question.

Dar slammed her fist into her other palm and paced like a lion in front of the empty cell. "Deng, we should have anticipated another transporter. It was all too easy."

Lilituck was busy consulting something on her robotic arm. "He's gone back to Pelican Island. Wait, he's already left again—" She looked up, and for the first time ever, Everest saw fear in a cybercop's eyes.

"He's at the academy," she said.

"The clone academy?" Everest asked.

"Yes," Officer Lilituck said.

"We gotta get there," said Larry.

"Yes," Lilituck agreed.

They pivoted around and ran for the others.

When they saw Vlas, he pointed excitedly at his shoulder where PicoBoy jumped up and down. "The cybercops found him and brought him back!"

Dar quickly explained the situation. They grabbed additional flasers and stunners and transported to the academy. Dar had provided coordinates so that they arrived in front of Pooker's cage of dancing lights. With the bobcat gone, the lights were out.

Because both the transport and the femto-booster had heightened his senses, Everest was swamped with the very strong combination of rosewillow and limonino. He even smelled the underlying bouquet of bobcat.

Next to him, Borneo sneezed.

Though it was still the middle of the night, lights blazed throughout the main towers. Mr. Brown had lost no time in making his presence known. With his extreme hearing, Everest easily made out screams and shouts. He also heard soft crying and even sniffling. He exchanged glances with his sister and parents. They looked as worried as he felt.

"Is that you, Shadara?" Mr. Brown's booming voice filled the garden.

In reflex, they all looked around for him, but the voice came from the house.

"Yes," Dar called out, projecting her voice so that it was equally as loud.

"Excellent. And I expect the Baskers are with you?"

"Yes."

"Good. Justine and George, we need a little heart to heart. I believe you have some femto-booster knowledge to impart. You better come in weapons-free and without any idea of putting up a fight. Otherwise, one of the B7s gets hurt, and then another, and then another. Did I mention that all of the seven-year-olds are with me? Sweet little tykes."

Immediately, Everest's parents started handing over their weapons to Officer Lilituck.

"Mom, Dad, you can't go in there," Everest said.

They didn't even pause.

"You have to listen to Everest," Elsie added urgently.

Mr. Brown's loud voice whipped through the sky. "If you want to be responsible for the disintegration of a seven-year-old clone, please do take your children's advice."

Flasers, Everest had forgotten that Mr. Brown could hear them.

Dar waved under his nose, then signed, "Shut down!"

Like he hadn't figured that one out?

Vlas ran up to Everest's dad. He held out PicoBoy and signed rapidly. "Take PicoBoy, he'll transmit what the situation is. We need to know what we're up against."

PicoBoy attached himself to George's shoulder.

As they ran toward the complex, Vlas turned to the rest and signed. "Those of us who are boosted should already be able to hear what's said, but we're close enough for PicoBoy to amplify everything. That means Lilituck and the other cybercops will be able to hear too. Mr. Brown won't be able to tell because he's already hearing everything amplified."

Everest watched his parents disappear inside the building. Almost immediately, a small display of the enormous entrance hall shimmered in front of them. Deng, PicoBoy was good.

In unison, Elsie and Everest sucked in their breath. There were a number of bodies strewn across the floor. He recognized the two instructors who must have been on duty tonight as well as a few of the older students. Huddled in one corner were about twenty small students—the seven-year-olds. Some were crying. Most held hands. Everest only vaguely recognized a few of them. Since the age groups generally kept to themselves, there'd been no reason for him to get to know the younger students.

"Hello George, Justine," said Mr. Brown—his voice both tinny and booming due to the combination of PicoBoy's amateur projection and their heightened senses. He stood with his back to one wall. One hand pointed a weapon at the small children while his other aimed at the instructors and older students lying on the ground.

It had to be a good sign that there were bodies. Everest didn't see any puddles of flaser dust.

Dar signed, "Left hand holding a stunner, right a flaser."

"What do you want from us?" Everest's mom asked.

"I want an antidote for the virus you've added to the femto-boosters."

"We don't have one."

"I don't believe you."

Everest's dad ran a hand through his hair. "We discussed various possibilities, but it was impossible to test any of them without giving away the fact that we were infecting the boosters."

"What were you going to do if someone just happened to implode while we were all on the island together?"

"We hoped one humanoid blowing up would just be a weird anomaly—that no one would get suspicious until multiple people disintegrated."

Mr. Brown's hand tightened on his flaser. He looked furious. Everest worried about what he would do next.

Slowly, the vlem relaxed his facial muscles and grip. "Here's the deal. I could have twelve hours before this femto-booster wears off, and while I'm boosted, I need to stay reasonably calm so I don't get obliterated. I need the tag that Lilituck implanted in me to be removed. That's it. If the cybercops immediately remove my tag no one else gets hurt. If they don't, then I start flasering people—to begin with, maybe one of the little seven-year-olds or maybe an instructor. After that, every three minutes I'll flaser another person. However, once my tag is removed, I'll transport out of here—no harm, no foul."

Dar signed to Lilituck. "Go in to remove the tag but stall as long as you can. Distract him if possible."

Everest's dad was talking again. "What's to stop us from just going head-to-head with you? Our powers against yours? We're not going to blow up, but you sure could."

"Ever heard of desperate measures?" Mr. Brown asked. "Right now my only choices are life-time imprisonment or running. I choose to run, but it does me no good if I can't get rid of that blasted tag. If you want to jump me, go right ahead, but that's when I start flasering every unboosted human in sight. You make the call."

"Jeez," Everest whispered then felt like a complete yocto-brain for speaking out loud. His cheeks heated up. The last thing he wanted was for Mr. Brown—or anyone for that matter—to know his thoughts. Fortunately, Mr. Brown didn't seem to notice his whisper.

"You might subdue me," Mr. Brown continued, "but not without serious casualties—many of whom will be zetta young and, as they are clones, outrageously expensive to replace." There was a long pause while they stared at each other, then Mr. Brown added with more projection, "Officer Lilituck, can you hear me? I realize you aren't boosted like the rest of us. You're just a weak little cybercop. In case you haven't heard, I need you to come inside and remove my tag. If you do it nicely, no one gets hurt. If you cause trouble, then you go poof and so do a lot of sweet little clones. If you haven't yet heard what happened to your cybercop friend who decided to play spy, I'm sure Dar can fill you in. It wasn't pretty." There was a pause before he continued. "Oh, and Dar, you better come too and bring those femto-boosters you stole. It's not nice to steal, you know, and I need those."

Dar's expression was both irritated and confused. In a loud voice, she said, "How many times do I have to say that the safe was empty?"

"Either you give me the boosters or one of the clone kiddies dies," he replied. "Guess we'll just have to hope some boosters magically show up in your pocket. Oh and bring the necklace that Everest stole from me."

"It's not a necklace," Everest muttered.

He jammed his hand in his pocket and dragged out the pendant. He scowled as he gave it to Dar.

Dar signed to Officer Lilituck and the rest of the B12s. "I'll play along, stall for time, and keep his attention on me while Officer Lilituck gets word to the Basker parents that we're saving the kids. Vlas, you make sure everyone on this end is ready to transport on my signal."

"Zetta can go wrong," Lilituck signed back.

"It already has gone wrong." Dar's fingers flew. "Now we have to improvise. When we're ready, I'll try to sign, 'go now.' If

322

not, Vlas just go in when you think we've distracted him enough for decent odds."

Lilituck held up her hand then signed. "Transport in when I lay my hand on Mr. Brown's shoulder. At that moment, as I'm removing the tag, even femto-boosted, he should feel blinding pain and be seriously distracted." She turned to Officer Sanchez who stood at attention behind her and signed, "Display PicoBoy's transmissions while I'm inside." The other cyborg nodded his head and raised his cyber-arm to make the connection with Lilituck.

Their link in place, Officer Lilituck turned on her heel and strode toward the main building. Dar handed her transporter to Vlas, and caught up with the officer in two femto-boosted bounds. They walked up the entrance steps and disappeared into the building.

Soon, thanks to PicoBoy and now Officer Sanchez, Everest saw Lilituck and Dar in the great entrance hall face to face with Mr. Brown.

"I can remove the tag, but it's going to take a few minutes," the officer said curtly. "First, I need to know from the Baskers that you have not harmed them or the B7s in any way. Also, I want your assurance that those unconscious on the floor are merely stunned."

"Dar," Mr. Brown stretched out his hand, ignoring Lilituck's command, "the femto-boosters, if you please."

"Not until you let the little ones go," she said.

"We both know that if I flaser one," he responded, "you'll turn over those femto-boosters zetta quick."

Dar positioned herself in front of Mr. Brown so that his view was partially blocked. "No femto-boosters if even one of those children is hurt. I'll take my chances and attack you instead."

Meanwhile, Lilituck ignored the flaser Mr. Brown trained on her and veered away toward the Basker parents. When she reached them she crossed her arms in front of her and asked, "Has Mr. Brown hurt you in any way?" Her back was to Mr. Brown, but PicoBoy had a clear view. Everest saw Lilituck's subtle signing to his parents as she explained the plan. Almost imperceptibly they nodded once then twice.

"We're fine," his dad said.

"But worried about the younger students," his mom added.

"Of course you are," Officer Lilituck said. She glanced over at the children who huddled together in the corner.

As Lilituck pivoted and marched over to Mr. Brown, Everest watched his parents ease closer to the children. His mom flexed her fingers as if she were gearing up.

Everest turned to the others. With his hands, he said, "Vlas, Borneo, Lelita, get the B7s out." He pointed at Larry and then at the other kids, trying to make him understand that he should go with them. Larry looked beyond frustrated. Everest mouthed, 'help them," then he continued to sign. "Elsie and I will stay behind with our parents to fight Mr. Brown. We'll do our best to protect the instructors and the older kids."

Vlas looked as if he wanted to argue, then he nodded his head. He signed, "You better beat that vlem."

"If I can kick your keister," Everest signed back with a grin, "which we all know I can, I can take Mr. Brown."

Elsie stepped up next to him, straightening her shoulders. "*We* can take him," she signed.

They watched as Lilituck reached Mr. Brown then paused to make some calculations on her robotic arm.

In just seconds, they would all transport in. Everest worried about Lilituck. She wasn't boosted. And with twenty little kids to save there wasn't enough room to transport her back. She was at high risk for being flasered into oblivion. Had she been friends with the cybercops who'd been destroyed on Pelican Island? What had it felt like to see them disintegrate? He wished she could just pretend to remove the tag and instead destroy Mr. Brown, but there was no way to do that with him femto-boosted.

Lilituck pulled back Mr. Brown's sleeve to reveal his shoulder. The smooth skin showed no sign that a tag had been inserted. She placed her machine hand there.

"Now," Vlas signed.

The last thing they heard and saw as they disappeared into the void of transportation was Mr. Brown screaming with his eyes bulging, the harsh cry bulleting into their femto-boosted heads.

CHAPTER 44
Retaking the Clone Academy

Though she felt, heard, tasted and smelled nothing, Elsie braced herself for the chaos when she landed. She needed to come out of the transport ready for war. She couldn't afford to be disoriented by the kaleidoscope of colors that would flood her.

When she landed in the grand hall, she went straight into a tuck and roll to avoid being flasered. Her body would counteract such an attack, but she didn't want anything to distract her from being able to go after Mr. Brown.

Coming out of the roll, she surged across the room, resisting the urge to check whether the rest of the B12s were doing their job and transporting the young clones out of the hall. She had to trust them. It was her job to stop Mr. Brown.

He still roared with pain, his eyes now shut. It was hard to believe so little time had passed.

As soon as he realized what had happened, he would turn on Lilituck. Elsie knew this without a doubt. Assuming that the small ones were transported away, the cyborg, the two instructors and the older students were the ones who would be vulnerable. That was presupposing that those lying on the floor were still alive. Right now, they weren't moving at all.

Her heart pounding, she exploded through Dar and Lilituck and tackled Mr. Brown. Where had he tucked away his transporter? She had to stop him from using it again, or if somehow he managed to transport away, she had to stick to him like spider boots.

She saw Dar protect Lilituck with her body.

A loud flash streamed into Elsie, and she felt its impact even as she turned it into just a minor irritant.

She rolled with Mr. Brown, struggling for his weapons. Managing to wrestle the flaser away, she threw it across the room. Mr. Brown twisted and rolled to gain the advantage. He got his hands around her neck and pushed with every bit of his boosted strength. She couldn't breathe, but she gave into the feeling and discovered that breathing wasn't necessary. At least, not immediately. Her body adjusted by both calming and slowing down.

With a loud thud, Everest landed on Mr. Brown's back, causing the man's hands to dislodge from Elsie's throat. The twins grappled with the vlem.

Mr. Brown lunged to his feet, bringing Everest and Elsie with him. Avoiding the ceiling, he shot up as far as he could, and threw himself into a spin. Elsie held on for dear life. His attempt to dislodge them was not going to work.

It hurt to swallow, but only for the few seconds it took for Elsie's throat to recover from Mr. Brown's attempted strangulation. She used her stomach muscles to pull in her flailing legs and wrap them around Mr. Brown's torso. He was not getting away.

He roared again and yanked at her hands. Everest still had his arms wrapped about the man's chest, but he was being flapped around just as she had been a few seconds ago. The spinning made Elsie see the room as a colorful blur, but her eyesight was better than usual due to the boost. She thought the corner where the smaller children had huddled was now empty. Vlas and the others must have done their job. She couldn't see where Lilituck or Dar were. She tried to find her parents but to no avail. She hoped they all had reached safety.

While she thought she could deal with this spinning for a zetta long time, she needed to turn the fight around so she and Everest could actually win. Right now, they were just holding on for dear life—not exactly heroic. But she couldn't let go. Without his tag, Mr. Brown would be able to escape and there would be no way to follow.

More flashes ensued as Everest fought the man for his stunner. In a jumble together, they banged into one of the walls.

It cracked with the force of their combined strength. They hit another wall.

Elsie wished she knew more about being boosted. She took a deep breath and blew hard at Mr. Brown, trying to imagine fire, and suddenly her mouth *was* on fire. Her body was able to immediately deal with the excess heat so that she didn't feel pain or incinerate herself. She breathed flame like a dragon.

Now that was zeller!

She torched Mr. Brown who yelled and broke his spin. Everest gasped, and she hoped she hadn't done more than singe him. She had caught Mr. Brown off-guard and even managed to inflict some pain. But he quickly recovered and blew back with an icy burst that froze her fire mid-air.

Her face went numb, his rock to her scissors. She released his neck with one of her arms and punched him in the stomach with all of her considerable force. That stopped his stream of ice for about a millisecond.

No longer spinning crazily, she was able to see that the hall was almost deserted. Besides Everest and her, only her parents and Dar remained. They were all femto-boosted and therefore not easily harmed. When Mr. Brown slammed Everest and her into another wall she gasped in pain and realized that while it wasn't easy to harm them, it wasn't impossible either. Mr. Brown was a mad man, cornered with nowhere to turn. There was nothing he wouldn't do in a fight.

"You have no place to run," Elsie yelled. "Just turn yourself in."

"*Au contraire*," he returned. "Without that tag, I can go anywhere, anytime. Once I flick off a couple of incredibly irritating fleas, the universe is mine."

"You're not getting rid of us anytime soon," Everest said through gritted teeth. "You'll implode first."

"I don't think so," Mr. Brown said. "I'm feeling lucky. I think my booster is virus-free. Otherwise, I'd have blown up by now."

"There are five of us," Elsie said.

"Yes, but you have to keep hold of me the whole time. I'll shake you eventually, and then I'll be gone."

He slammed them into another wall, then twisted and managed to fling Everest across the room. Elsie gasped as her brother flew backward. Immediately, her mom leapt onto Mr. Brown's back so that now she and Elsie were between him and his freedom.

"Push with me, Elsie," her mom said.

They pushed down with all their combined strength, slowly forcing Mr. Brown to the ground. He fought to stay in the air, but their doubled-up strength was inexorable. When their feet touched the ground, her mom called to the others, and they rushed over to help. Despite his bravado only seconds before, Mr. Brown seemed to have given up all resistance.

Then he threw himself into a maniacal spin so that he blurred around the edges. Caught unawares, Elsie's hand slipped off the whirling dervish, as did her mom's. Like a wild spinning top, he scattered them as he shot across the room. When he banged into the far side, he came out of the spin, laughed crazily and popped into thin air.

"Deng," Everest said, his hands clenched.

Elsie took a shaky breath and wiped angrily at tears on her cheeks. "He got away." How could she have let that happen? She'd been so determined. Then she had let down her guard. What a yocto-brain!

Forgetting she was femto-boosted, Dar kicked the wall, making a serious crack. "Yeah, he got away."

"He doesn't have any femto-boosters," their dad said. "Maybe once his powers have dissipated, the cybercops can track him down."

"I don't know," Larry said. "He could still have some femto-boosters. There's that missing set, the one he accused Dar of having."

"We'll just have to hope the vial was destroyed when he blew up his mansion," Elsie's mom said.

"He's in a different place," Dar said. "Soon he'll be in a different time. Probably he's got a lot of contingencies worked out—different identities, VC stashed away."

"It's not so easy," their dad said. "He can't replace his aura."

Dar exchanged glances with Elsie and Everest.

Elsie knew they were all remembering how easy it had been to introduce Larry into this world. Mr. Brown would find a way, and then he would be out there, ready to do damage and to exact some serious payback.

If only he'd swallowed one of the virus-infected femto-boosters. That would have solved their problems.

Elsie couldn't bear the thought that now he was a free man and as dangerous as ever.

CHAPTER 45
A Fresh Start

"What is going on in there?" Elsie paced the corridor in front of Director Lester-Hauffer's former office.

Everest wished she would stop.

He was just as irritated as Elsie, but he wasn't pacing all over the place like a total freakazoid. As soon as Mr. Brown had disappeared, the grownups had decided to treat them like a bunch of yocto-brained children again. Jeez, couldn't their parents see how much they had grown up during their month apart? Still, there was nothing they could do about it, so he wished Elsie would shut down.

Within hours, the adults had retrieved both femto-booster pendants, collected Pooker from Zulu's aunt, and settled all the B12s back at the academy, feeding them, patting them on the head, and sending them to bed.

When Adriatic Mink arrived the next day, the adults locked themselves in Lester-Hauffer's old office for a private discussion to decide the fate of the clone students. No doubt the director would be joining Instructor Gerard for an extended stay on Bleckor, the infamous prison planet situated on the other side of the Milky Way.

"Deng, Elsie, keep your aura on," Everest said. He grabbed her arm as she strode past. "This is like the fiftieth time you've paced by me. Can't you just chill?"

"No, I cannot! We should have a say in what's going to happen to the academy. What if they decide to close it down?" She wished she still had remnant powers from the femto-booster, because she would have liked to have thrown her brother across the room—just for the fun of it.

Dar straightened up from where she'd been lounging against the wall. "If the academy goes, it goes. It's not as if we care that much. It's just a school—or a prison—depending on how you look at it."

"That's not true!" Elsie said heatedly. "You know you care. You care about the other B12s and the younger clones too—" She stopped abruptly.

Everest had the feeling that Dar just barely managed to stop herself from lunging for Elsie. He remembered being with Crazy Sue in the twenty-first century, and Dar losing her aura because she thought that Elsie had blabbed some secret of hers— something to do with her singing to the younger clones at the academy. Dar really didn't appreciate Elsie's conclusion that she cared about the little kids.

Having infuriated Dar, Elsie momentarily shut down. Everest almost breathed a sigh of relief, but he knew Elsie's silence would be fleeting.

"Don't worry so much," Larry said. "I don't care what century we're in. If there's one thing I know, it's that a bunch of adults will always ensure that a bunch of orphans are institutionalized. That's a given." He looked around at the B12s. "There ain't no chance in hell that we'll be on the streets."

"But what about us?" Elsie asked.

"You?" Dar said. "You ute-babies will go home with mummy and daddy to your cushy state-of-the-art jellach beds, and you'll forget you ever lived here."

"No we won't," Elsie said hotly. She took a shaky breath. "It's different now. I don't care what you say, we're friends."

"Jeez, Elsie," Dar said. "Let's not get carried away. For the last month, we've been fighting a common enemy. But all the bad guys are gone. We don't need to be a team anymore. It's been zeller, but it's time to move on. This isn't your life, and it never will be."

Everest wouldn't have been surprised if his sister had screamed. She clenched and unclenched her fists and flasered Dar with her eyes.

"Don't listen to Dar," Lelita said softly. "We won't ever forget you, and we *are* friends."

331

Elsie stopped her pacing and went to the girl. They wrapped their arms around each other in a big hug. "Thanks, Lelita, I won't ever forget you either."

"Shouldn't we save the mushy goodbye scene for later?" Vlas asked, his eyebrow cocked. "I haven't had enough time to practice getting all choked up, and my crying still needs zetta work."

Larry snorted.

Borneo fidgeted next to Larry. "We'll all miss you guys," he finally said to Elsie.

Vlas laughed and punched Borneo on the arm. "You got a crush or something?"

Borneo went bright pink and sort of shrunk into himself.

Everest had to swallow back a snort when he saw his sister's skin turn an even brighter pink.

"Shut down, Vlas," Dar said irritably.

Everest knew from past experience that Dar was very protective of Borneo. It had nothing to do with her wanting to save his sister from embarrassment.

At that moment the door erased, and Adriatic Mink stood on the other side, his blue eyes gleaming.

Everest felt uncomfortable in Mink's presence. He couldn't stop thinking about how the man had asked Dar to steal some femto-boosters for him.

"Ah," Mink said, "a B12 delegation." As usual he was dressed elegantly in black with sparkling diamonds buttoning his Vlatex shirt. His black jacket had no buttons.

Wearing zetta serious expressions, Everest's parents stood behind Mink. Also in the room were Instructor Tchakevska, Instructor Bebe, and Dr. Wei. Dr. Wei looked even more irritated than normal.

"What's been decided?" Elsie asked urgently.

"My dear," Adriatic Mink said, "that will be announced to the school at large. It would be inappropriate for us to divulge such details to a handful of students before the rest are given the privilege of hearing the news."

Elsie turned to their parents, who had stepped into the hall. "But what about us? What's going to happen to us?"

"You'll be with us, of course," their dad said. "All is well, Elsie."

"But we don't want to go home," she burst out.

Deng. Everest wished she'd stop being so dramatic. The other B12s were going to tease them unmercifully about being suzo-shrimp. He wasn't any happier than she was, but he wasn't going to lose his aura over it. Sure, they had just gotten used to this place, and now they were going to have to leave. Sure, life was unfair. He wasn't going to moan and groan about it and act like a ute-baby.

"Shall we adjourn to the great hall?" Adriatic Mink asked. "Instructor Tchakevska, would you kindly let all the students know that there will be a special assembly in the entrance hall as soon as we can round up everyone? B7s and older for the assembly. We needn't concern the littlest ones."

"Mom," Elsie said urgently, "we need to talk."

Their mom exchanged a nervous look with their dad. "Elsie, it would be best if we spoke after the assembly."

"This is ridiculous," Elsie mumbled, scuffing her foot against the smooth tevta floor.

Everest shoved her hard and glared.

"What?" she asked, all big-eyed and cross.

"Shut down," he said under his breath.

"Shall we?" Adriatic Mink asked as he ushered everyone toward the great entrance hall.

It took the better part of a half hour to get everyone assembled, and Everest had to watch Elsie try multiple times to pull something from their parents. They refused to give her even the slightest hint. Now she stood near the front where their parents and Mink were in a huddle. She crossed her arms and tapped her foot.

"Stop pouting," Everest whispered.

"I'm not pouting," Elsie whispered back.

"Yeah, right," Everest muttered. "You are being such a ute-baby."

She punched him on the shoulder.

He heard her take in a very deep breath and then another one. Maybe that would help her relax.

Mink had set himself up with a volume booster so that everyone in the room could hear him.

"Good afternoon, boys and girls, I'm Adriatic Mink, one of the benefactors of this academy. We have made some changes to the management of this school and would like to share them with you." He smiled slightly. "First, I suspect it is no surprise that Director Lester-Hauffer has decided to leave this fine establishment for an alternative opportunity to serve."

"Serve his time," Larry whispered, snickering. The kids around him laughed nervously.

No one except those involved had the full story, but Everest had heard all sorts of convoluted versions of what had happened. The B7s had been quick to spread the story of their kidnapping, and now the Basker parents appeared to have superhero status.

Lester-Hauffer had never been liked, and it was clear that students weren't going to start missing him now. Someone in the back began to clap slowly, and then everyone was clapping and whooping and cheering at the news.

Everest looked around at the cheering crowd of clones. They had no idea what their fate would be, but the students knew that this, at least, was good news.

Adriatic Mink raised one hand to quiet the room. Slowly they calmed. "With the approval of your most senior instructors, a new leadership team has been formed."

Judging from the sour look on his face, Everest didn't think Dr. Wei had approved the decision—whatever it was.

"After some gentle persuasion, Doctors George and Justine Basker have kindly agreed to be co-directors of the academy."

The B7s erupted with shouts of excitement and joy. Some of the other clones joined in.

Mom and Dad? Everest couldn't believe it.

They were staying! He felt a wave of relief, but then he realized that it might be worse. Now, instead of being the nephew and niece of the director, they would be the son and daughter. He nearly groaned out loud. He shot a look at Dar and found the girl watching him, almost as if she were curious about his reaction.

A slow smile settled on Dar's face. When she raised her eyebrows at Everest, he frowned back. That made Dar laugh, and Everest had the distinct impression she was laughing at him.

Deng, one of these days, he was going to kick her keister to Xlexuri.

He tried to reassure himself that at least the B7s were happy the Baskers would be in charge. But that didn't make their lives any better. Not if the B12s decided to label them the enemy.

He heard his father's voice and realized he was missing important information.

His father was indicating how pleased he was to come to the academy. "We admit we don't have experience as directors of an educational facility, but we have been *members* of educational facilities our entire lives. We'd like to build on that knowledge, and we'd be very appreciative of your feedback."

His mother added, "There are some basic things we'd like to change, but we'll leave most things as is until we've had a chance to do more rigorous study of what is going well and what is not." She paused before continuing. "However, everyone is agreed that we need to give you a broader knowledge of the world outside the academy, and to that end, we're going to open up the institution in a much more systematic way to non-clones. You should not be segregated. Others shouldn't look at you as different. You are special, because you are unique humans, not because you were cloned from someone long dead. We'll announce other changes along the way, but as part of our desire to give you a more normal existence, we'd like you all to come up with last names for yourselves. You don't need one right away. You can think about it. But in the next few weeks, we'll confirm a last name with each of you."

The room fell silent, eerily so after all the cheering. Everest looked around. The clones seemed stunned, as if the thought of last names had never entered their heads. Dr. Wei's face was like marblon, expressionless yet furious at the same time. Why did it bother him so much that the clones might be treated as regular people?

After a long pause, Lelita raised her hand. Her fingers shook. It was zetta against character for her to speak in a public forum.

Adriatic Mink said, "Yes, Lelita?"

"I—" she started then stopped. "I've always wondered what it would be like to be part of a family—one like Elsie and Everest's. I've read about it, but I've never seen a family in action. I—," she paused again, "I may never have a family—not a real one anyway, but I want to honor the emotion—the love—between mother and daughter, sister and brother, father and son. I already know what last name I want." Now her voice wavered as well.

"Excellent," Mink said. "We'll—"

"I want Basker,' she said, her voice now firm.

Mink's eyebrows rose, and he shot a glance at Everest's parents.

Everest caught their initial look of surprise, but then a different expression blossomed, one that made him think of holidays and gifts and joy. For a second he was angry with Lelita for trying to horn in on his family, but then he felt an alien feeling of happiness. When he looked at Elsie, she was smiling so hard he thought it might hurt. Lelita's request gave him the sensation of having been accepted for the first time since they'd arrived at this deng academy.

His mom smiled at Lelita. "My dear, that's lovely. Of course, we'd be delighted for you to choose Basker."

Lelita's answering smile was incandescent.

Borneo raised his hand. "M-m-me too."

The B7s jumped up, all of the younger kids that his parents had protected from harm. "Me too," one of them yelled. "I want to be a Basker." It became a chant. One that started with the little ones, then rippled through other grades, even students who didn't know who the Baskers were. Only the older students, the more jaded ones, remained silent.

Everest glanced at Elsie who was watching the room go crazy with a look of utter bemusement on her face.

His parents gave each other helpless looks. "Of course, whoever would like to be a Basker has our blessing," their mom said. Both of their parents attempted to quiet the children by raising and lowering their hands.

Everest swallowed hard, intent on not being labeled a suzo-shrimp crybaby. He broke eye-contact with Elsie. He had no doubt she would be crying soon.

Dar stood a few feet to his side. When he looked at her, she raised one eyebrow. Here was one clone who wouldn't be so easily swayed to the Basker fan club. Standing next to her, Vlas grinned but remained silent—always Dar's wingman.

Larry had remained silent too. When Everest caught his eye, the boy shrugged, his mouth a thin twist of a smile. "Nothing against yours, but I've already got a last name. I ain't proud of my parents, but they're the only ones I've ever had. Guess Knight will have to do for me."

"Seems as if we've got enough Baskers," Elsie said with a nervous giggle.

"You had enough when there were just two of you," Dar said. "This is ridiculous."

Leave it to Dar, Everest thought. But he would have been zetta disturbed if she had just rolled over and become a Basker too. He was relieved she remained true to herself.

The room still exploded around them with the hysteria of the moment. Elsie punched Everest in the shoulder. He had been worried she'd do something zetta yocto-brained like hug him, so the punch was just fine with him. He watched his parents field the emotional outpouring in the room, the desperate desire by these clones, young and old to have family. He saw hope in the kids' eyes, hope that this time they wouldn't feel as if they were in an institution, that somehow this place would feel like home.

He swallowed hard. Only one month ago, he'd thought his parents were the most cerebrum-heavy geeks in the galaxy, and he'd been furious with them for leaving them at the clone academy. Then he'd had to deal with them being missing and presumed dead. Now, he didn't even want to identify all the emotions churning through him. He decided to focus on his relief that they would be staying here.

Nothing could have prepared him for that outcome.

"Better get some fight practice in," Dar whispered in his left ear.

He turned his head.

Dar wore an evil grin. "Don't you remember? We've got a rematch to finish. Vlas and I can't wait to finally kick your Basker keisters to Xlexuri."

"Yeah?" Everest responded. "Guess you'll have to learn the fine art of patience, since no matter how often you fight us, you'll be the one with her keister floating amongst the stars."

"I can be plenty patient," Dar said, "but somehow I don't think I'll have to be."

EPILOGUE
Dar's Secret

Adriatic Mink had settled into what used to be Director Lester-Hauffer's chair. The Basker parents were busy moving into their personal quarters.

Dar checked out the room, unsettled by Mink's request to meet with her privately. They'd met together many times before, but their last private meeting had left a bitter taste in her mouth. She no longer trusted her sponsor. As she ran her hand over a series of miniature soldiers from the Vlemutz time period, she stared into his eyes, trying somehow to read him. But it was as if he wore a mask. His eyes revealed nothing. His lips were formed into a kind smile which Dar met suspiciously.

Mink rested his elbows on the chair's arms and templed his fingers. "Tell me how you feel about everything that happened."

"We bungled it. We let Mr. Brown get away, maybe with femto-boosters, and definitely with plenty of VC."

"An error, true," Mink's head dipped, "but not insurmountable. I've got a team working full-time to track him down."

"He's got a lot of years and places in which to hide," Dar said. "Our only advantage is that he may want something in this time period. I'm guessing he'll be back."

Mink pursed his lips. "Did you by chance find any stray femto-boosters?"

"No," Dar shook her head, "I'm afraid not. The safe was empty when I arrived."

"Funny, I was told Mr. Brown swore repeatedly that there was a vial of boosters still in that safe."

"I believe we've already determined that Mr. Brown isn't a credible source."

"He was quite adamant that you took the vial."

"Yes, and the rest of the B12s saw that I could not have done so." She looked Adriatic Mink dead in the eye. "The safe was empty."

Adriatic Mink kept eye contact. "Pity," he finally said.

"Yes," Dar agreed. "I'm sorry to disappoint you."

"On the contrary," Mink responded. "You could never disappoint me." He rose from the director's chair. "Is there anything you need before I leave?"

"I thought those new transporters the cybercops used were zetta zeller," she said.

"Ah, I thought you might." He held out his hand and there were two small devices sitting on it, even more compact than the ones owned by the officers of law. "I would have been disappointed if you had not asked." His lips twitched, hinting at a smile.

"Thank you, sir."

"Do not hesitate to ask if you need anything else. Meanwhile, study hard and try to stay out of trouble."

"Of course," Dar said.

She pivoted around and left the room. When she was in the corridor she shoved the two devices into the pocket of her vlatex jacket and took a shaky breath. She always had this weird feeling that Adriatic Mink had some sort of alien blood in him that caused him to be able to read people's minds. It was as if he'd stared straight into her soul. Had he known she was lying?

She dug into her left pocket and felt for a tiny vial made out of 1010511. It was no bigger than the nail of her pinky. She swallowed. Had Vlas seen her sleight of hand when she'd pocketed the vial? He hadn't said anything. She'd been lucky that Larry hadn't been there. He had too much experience with pick-pocketing not to catch her.

She didn't know what she was going to do with the vial. But she wasn't giving it to Adriatic Mink. She wasn't giving it to anyone.

Acknowledgements

Without a beautiful group of individuals, I never would have been brave enough to publish independently. I could fill twenty pages with thank yous...here are just a few:

Thank you, Whaley boys: Conner, Austin, Brett and Spencer. Thank you, Garlock girls: Caitlyn, Meghan and Erin. Thank you, Matthews girls: Carrie and Molly. You make me feel like a rock star!

Thank you, Katie Rupel and Katie Kusa. I'm not sure I would have published the first Basker Twins without the "Katie" seal of approval.

Thank you, Allen Walker, for your absolutely gorgeous book covers. You are an artist extraordinaire and a dear friend.

Deep thanks to my critique group for molding me into the writer I am today: Barbara, Deborah, Judy and Pat—I love and admire you.

Thank you, teachers (and dear friends): Annette, Pam, Nalini, and Lydia, for all the fun times I've had in your classrooms with my writers' workshops. Thank you for spreading the word about my workshops. Thank you, students, for your brilliant dragon stories!

Thank you, Don and Mike. Don for pushing me to finish, Mike for your meticulous copy editing, and both for your constant support. You are seriously awesome.

Thank you, Becky and Sandy, for being my jobshare partners over the years. You gave me the gift of writing time and always had my back. I learned so much from both of you. You are amazing women.

Thank you, Lisa and Drew. I've looked up to you my whole life for being wonderful writers. It means a lot to me that you like my books.

Thank you, Zohreh and Jared at the Roasted Coffee Bean, for being fantastic friends and great supporters of local artists.

Thank you, Bobby Bernshausen at Virtualbookworm.com, for your professionalism and for being such a pleasure to work with.

Thank you, my fabulous community of friends and family. Each and every one of you means the world to me. I wish I could name you all individually—know that you are loved.

Mom: your creativity, beautiful prose, and artistry inspire me always. Dad: growing up with a rocket scientist gave me my love for the future, for technology, and for gadgets!

Sarah, when as a twelve-year-old, you believed with all your heart that the Basker Twins would soon be made into a movie, you warmed my soul. When as a twenty-year-old, you told me it felt good to know you had such a talented mother, you cannot even imagine how I felt. Thank you.

And Dan, you are the best spouse ever. Thank you for always loving everything I write and always encouraging me to follow my dreams. You are my champion, and I love you.

- **1010511:** A rare alloy that is purplish-silver and warm to the touch.
- **Allen:** Slang for comedian; comes from a study that identified 'Allen' as the most common first and last name for successful humorists.
- **Aura Positioning Unit (APU):** A device that pinpoints the geographical location of people via their unique auras.
- **Aurascan:** The scanning of an aura for a variety of purposes, such as identification, security, culpability. An auralizer is a specific aurascan device that reveals a person's true thoughts and intentions.
- **B12:** The twelve-year-old learning program at the clone academy; all twelve-year-olds are "B12s". Likewise, A0 through A6 are newborns through six-year-olds, B7 through B12 comprise seven-year-olds through twelve-year-olds, and C13 through C18 classify thirteen-year-olds through eighteen-year-olds.
- **Bandogiar, Xlexuri Galaxy:** A planet heavily populated with trees such as the Limonino tree with the sourest fruit in the universe. It is outrageously expensive to import trees and wood from Bandogiar.
- **Bleckor:** An infamous prison planet situated on the other side of the Milky Way.
- **Clegl:** Short, bald, black and white striped humanoids who have eyes in the back of their heads, making them the preferred officials for sporting events.
- **Cooligrar:** A fox-like creature from the planet Elxsir; cooligrars can't stop biting and scratching each other and therefore are virtually extinct except for the few who live separate and lonely lives in zoos.
- **Dementurnum:** An asylum planet for the insane.

- **Derndyl:** The Glagcha equivalent of a domesticated cat, often with more dramatic coloring, such as purple.
- **Dupe:** Slang for clone; derived from the word 'duplicate.'
- **Femto-technology:** Cutting-edge technology based on femtometers which are significantly smaller than picometers and infinitely smaller than nanometers.
- **Flaser:** State of the art laser gun. It is also slang for glaring as if you have laser beams in your eyes. "Flasers" is a tame curse word as well.
- **Galactic Knowledge Bank (GKB):** The all-knowing database that attempts to keep track of every humanoid in the universe.
- **Glagcha:** The planet in the Milky Way that currently holds the title of best planet in the galaxy to raise a family. Earth placed second.
- **Googleopolis:** A metropolis in the San Francisco Bay Area. Its center once was the southern most fringe of San Jose, California.
- **Holoputer:** The equivalent of a computer in the 31st Century though much more sophisticated.
- **Hover vehicle:** The primary mode of transportation in the 31st Century made out of a substance called jellach which makes it extremely safe. HVs expand and collapse in size and bump into each other without damage.
- **JED:** An electronic diary made out of Jellach; the acronym comes from "**JE**llach **D**iary."
- **Jellach:** An extremely pliable and strong substance. It can expand and contract and even conform to a person's body. Jellach is used to make everything from diaries to beds to hover vehicles. J28, a variant of jellach, is less pliable, denser and virtually indestructible. J28 is a common building material for skyscrapers.
- **Jell-off pipe:** A device that shoots a liquid that destroys jellach.
- **Liligild:** A tiny flower with gold-tinged blossoms that has a particularly sweet fragrance. It is from a planet named Blumflor.
- **Matter-mover:** A device that rearranges atoms to make temporary openings in walls.

- **Meldoon cat:** On the planet Meldoon, cats have two heads. The phrase, "Does a cat on Meldoon have two heads?" indicates that something is self-evident. Also, if someone looks at you as if you are a Meldoon cat, it's as if you've grown a second head.
- **Mestor:** The planet in the Andromeda Galaxy where Elsie and Everest's parents went on their secret mission.
- **Mormor mile:** A grueling distance. The terrain on Mormor is such that one Mormor mile is exhausting even for someone in perfect physical shape.
- **Nanofiber:** A tightly woven fiber based on nano-technology that is commonly used to upholster furniture.
- **Object cloner:** A device that starts out as a gooey, dirty gray ball and clones itself into another object.
- **Panktar:** A mercenary humanoid from the Xlexuri galaxy. These creatures are tall, wide, muscular and green. Rather than a human nose, they display a cluster of three ugly lumps.
- **Pico-technology:** Technology based on picometers which are much smaller than nanometers. Many devices incorporate some form of pico-technology. Pico-brownies band together to clean surfaces, picobots are tiny robots, and pico-trainers control pets.
- **Skyball:** A popular game akin to basketball. When a shot is good, the hoop lights up and makes noise and the ball careens back to the successful shooter.
- **Skyboots:** Athletic boots designed for serious ankle support and extreme jumping (via pico-spring technology).
- **Slarmi joke:** Slang for a practical joke. Slarmians are known for their practical jokes.
- **Sleztar bog:** The most treacherous bog in the universe. Bogdogs are the only mammals who can survive in one for any length of time. It is impossible to remove the thick layer of sludge off a bogdog.
- **Spider gear:** Gloves and boots that allow a person to crawl up or down most vertical structures.
- **Steelorq:** A substance like but much stronger than steel.
- **Sunergy:** Earth's primary form of energy derived, as the name suggests, from the sun. When it replaced fossil fuels the planet's climate fluctuations stabilized.

- **Suzo-shrimp:** Slang for being a wimp.
- **Tenorian:** A highly intelligent race of humanoids who have no ears and therefore sign instead of speak. They have an acute sense of smell, are known for being telepathic, and often sign in proverbs.
- **Tevta:** A smooth-as-glass, lavender substance popular in construction before the first Vlemutz invasion.
- **Ute:** Slang for someone born via a uterus rather than via cloning. Variations include ute-baby, ute-boy, and ute-girl.
- **Vlatex:** A common clothing material. Vlatex II can act as a cloaking device by allowing a person to blend into shadows.
- **Vlemutz:** A vile humanoid species that tried to wipe out all earthlings via a series of wars now designated "the Vlemutz wars." Labeling someone a "vlem" is the worst possible slur in the 31st century.
- **Xlexuri Galaxy:** The galaxy that holds spots one through sixty-two in the inter-galactic survey as "best place to live." Earthlings get a bit irritated about how "perfect" Xlexuri claims to be.
- **Xlexuri whitestone:** Incredibly strong, bright, and out-of-this-world expensive white stones from the Xlexuri galaxy.
- **Zylorg:** A race of humanoids with multiple heads who are prone to monster headaches. When a third head is mentioned it is typically an exaggeration since most Zylorgs only grow a second head.
- **Yocto-brain:** Slang for a tiny-brained idiot; a yocto is the smallest unit of measurement.
- **Zeller:** Slang for awesome or cool.
- **Zentor vood:** A man-made, hard, glossy black substance that replaced wood as the standard material for making furniture.
- **Zetta:** Slang for "very." Zetta is a very large unit of measurement, even larger than giga or tera.
- **Zunner:** A new stun gun that shoots faster than flasers but stuns rather than kills. The top setting takes its victim out for over an hour.